QUANTUM WORLDS

and the Entangled Man

Mark R.A. Shegelski
and Joseph Halden

Fanned Tome Publishing

Published by Fanned Tome Publishing.
Vancouver, British Columbia, Canada.

Quantum Worlds and the Entangled Man -- 1st ed.
ISBN 978-0-9947286-1-6 (print)
ISBN 978-0-9947286-2-3 (electronic)

Cover design by James, GoOnWrite.com

PART ONE

CHAPTER ONE

Off the Streets

Allan Gerrold sat out of the rain against a graffiti-strewn wall next to Pigeon Park Savings on East Hastings Street in Vancouver. Above the graffiti just at the edge of view, the bank's logo of an indigenous-art-styled pigeon joined Allan in watching the bustling streets.

Hastings was a fuzzy boundary of sorts between the gentrified upper-class and street urchins like Allan. It hadn't been too long ago—six months—that Allan had lived on the other side of that gulf, so it seemed fitting to him that he dwell in the grey transition zone.

Brick facades and rain-spattered verandas leaned over bustling yuppies and business people. To them, the people of the street were just more graffiti. To the construction workers jack-hammering on the other side of the street, everyone was just another obstacle to getting work done.

Allan felt more lucid today than he had in months, and he wasn't sure if it was a blessing or not. The clearer his thoughts, the more he felt out of place, and his stomach turned with the rising pressure to lower his standards and conform.

He wasn't incapable of working. He just refused to be shoved out of his field by the ostracizing cretins of his old job. He'd applied for many positions in various tech start-ups related to some of his old quantum work, but no one would touch him. No one called for follow-up interviews, despite the fact that, if there were any justice in the world, they would have recognized his massive contributions to the entire tech ecosystem in the lower mainland.

He was better than they ever hoped to be. This wasn't arrogance; this was an objective statement of what he'd accomplished. Yet, when it came down to it, who had been evicted? Whose credit scores and solvency had drained into the sewer like the constant Vancouver rain?

Stop it, he thought, pressing fists against the sides of his head. He was dangerously close to losing himself to yet another stream of internal anger that had already taken too many of his days.

He'd applied to a new position just yesterday. He hoped the Hastings Employment Agency would get a call back for him, and that on his regular morning check in he'd be delighted to find his skills wanted and valued.

But he wouldn't go begging, no matter how much his body ached from too little sleep and makeshift beds.

Rubbing his hands together, he wondered if the fall weather was cooling enough that he'd need to seek a fire tonight. The rain certainly didn't help. Allan just hoped the bank employees wouldn't mind him squatting under their overhang a few hours longer.

He pressed harder into the wall, shivering. He never would have thought a human could become so cold-blooded. Not in the spiritual sense, but in the biological one. His warmth, his chills, his happiness, his sorrow were now linked to that of the city's.

Thankfully, at the hub of so much activity, he livened and his thoughts cleared. Maybe the construction also helped to drown out the force of his anger and the growl of his father's voice in the back of his mind. The endless complaints blurred into the white noise of the street.

There was a logic to construction. There was a strong

push against the flow of entropy, a rebalancing of sorts, making the world better again. Allan found it soothing, even if it was a bit messy in the in-between states.

As Allan's life and sense of time had stretched thin and long, he'd found himself able to appreciate the improvements the endless construction afforded Vancouver. When he'd had a job, he'd never been capable of appreciating this facet of the city. Now, it was the surest sign that things could get better.

The workers across from Allan abruptly stopped jack-hammering, pulling away to inspect their handiwork.

As the ringing in Allan's ears died down and the rain's thumping grew louder, the rising tremor of his father's voice threatened to overwhelm all his thoughts.

Allan's breaths quickened.

Desperately seeking a new focus, he scanned and stared at a scratched red bicycle locked to a lamp post just outside the bank.

The pedals turn the gear and then the chain, he told himself, following the connected machinery along one link at a time, forcing himself to try and map out how things were connected, what each nut and bolt did. Working out this logic was much like the construction—a sense of order, of making things right in a world of chaos.

His gaze traced the rising crests and troughs of each connected link of the bicycle chain. He felt compelled to move along the chain, and in his thoughts the chain enlarged until each link spanned the palm of his hand. He focused all of his attention on it until he saw nothing but the chain, and fog everywhere else.

Standing with a massive chain link held in his palm, Allan couldn't see where each end of the chain disappeared.

Allan felt an oppressive need to see where each end of the chain went, and to ensure the links were strong. Some of the pins holding them together were bent, protruding out and threatening to snap under strain.

He travelled along the chain, knowing there was

something important he had to do. Somewhere he needed to be, perhaps at the end of the chain, to do something no one else could.

Maybe it was the job he'd been waiting, hoping for.

Allan pulled himself forward, sliding his fingers along the links. The fog thickened until the ground lost all colour, leaving a faint light glowing in the distance.

The light shone on a face far away. Was someone at the end of the chain?

The face seemed distorted and blurry, and Allan could only barely make out two eyes and a mouth.

It seemed familiar, bearing an aura—or an eminence—that Allan recognized somehow.

The face disappeared as the light waned.

Allan squeezed the chain tighter, wanting to go faster, to reach the end—to reach whoever it was—before time ran out. He didn't know where the urgency came from, but it felt as real as the oil accumulating on his hands.

The chain thinned in his grip, shrinking.

No! Allan thought. *Let me follow a bit longer. Please!*

The chain shrunk to a thread cutting into his palm. The links were indistinguishable, yet still Allan clung.

Then the chain dissolved into the air like wisps of cotton. Allan groaned. He gaped at the empty void around, devoid of up or down, left or right.

He'd failed.

A honking horn made Allan gasp. He awoke with a start to see a car making a barely-legal left turn, sparking immeasurable rage from everyone around.

For a few moments Allan couldn't remember where he was or how he'd gotten there. He padded his gaunt, scruffy face and grabbed a tuft of his long, oily brown hair. They were still there, as were his worn-out cargo pants and flannel sweater.

Then he saw the scratched red bicycle at the lamp post.

Its chain was a miniaturized version of what he'd travelled along. He squinted and could see that yes, some of the pins were indeed poking out precariously, a sure sign that the chain was ready to snap.

A dark-haired woman in a business suit came out of the bank and pulled out her keys, unlocking the chain that secured the bicycle.

Allan had to warn her. He may have been filled nearly to the brim with anger and indignity over what the world had done to him, but this was something he could—he had to—make right.

Maybe she was the one he had to reach.

He pressed himself to his feet, his hips aching, and hobbled through the rain. "Excuse me," he said, his voice croaking from little use.

"I'm sorry, I can't spare any money," the woman said, looking at him out of the corner of her eye.

The words stung. So many assumptions. Allan was tempted to give up, but remembered how he'd once been on her side of the class system, and had probably viewed things in the same black-and-white way.

"I'm not after your money," Allan went on. "It's your bike chain—it looks like it's going to snap."

Allan bent down and pointed at her chain, tracing the problematic links with his finger. They felt just as he'd imagined they would.

The woman's eyebrows shot up. "Oh. Thank you. I'll have to be careful."

Allan nodded. "It's probably rideable, but I just thought you should know."

The woman blinked, shaking her head as though she couldn't wrap her head around where this conversation had gone. "Yes, of course."

"Have a good day," Allan said.

"You too, and thanks again."

Allan found his spot near the wall, and was pleased when the woman waved to him before pedalling slowly down the street.

He was wet again, but it had been worth it. Part of the world had been made right again. If only Allan could do this every day.

Allan felt well enough to go for a long walk, and by the early evening his feet were sore but he'd managed almost eight hours without feeling the oppression of his anger or his father's chastisement.

Unfortunately, as the sun set and the streets quieted, his internal monologue amplified to fill the void, and as it happened every night, he shrank powerless against the voices.

His father's came as clearly and easily to him as if the old man had followed Allan down into the deepest parts of the urban canyons. Stumbling into a back alley, Allan knew he must look mad to everyone around, arguing with a ghost, but to him, the argument with his father was as hot and real as it had ever been.

"When are you going to find a real job?" His father's buttoned shirt and neatly-pressed slacks made him a king among the street sloths. "You have to start paying rent, contributing to society. No son of mine is going to flip burgers for a living. You've got to make use of all that schooling, son. The Gerrold name is not being ruined on my watch. When I was your age we had to work for what we got—we didn't get handouts."

Allan wrinkled his nose and mouthed, "I've never taken a handout."

"The hell you haven't, boy."

Allan waved his father away and bowed his head, hoping he could keep his father from coming back. He didn't have time to explain himself; there was far too much thinking to do. Too many problems to solve to be bothered with the rants of an imbecile. Like how he was going to re-enter quantum tech with something that would shatter the industry.

His father's snapping finger and loud voice rousted Allan. "Look at me when I'm talking to you."

You're talking at me, Allan thought, pressing his fingers

to his temples. "I've never taken a handout."

"Everything you've ever had is a handout." His father sneered. "Your mother and I haven't worked our entire lives so you could be a useless vagrant."

"I have nothing now," Allan said, meeting his father's gaze for a few seconds. "Everything I had is gone. I have to start over, and I'll do it on my own terms." He'd rehearsed the words in his head a thousand times, and though they didn't sound quite right, his chest slackened. He let out a long breath.

His father snorted. "You won't make it. You'll need another handout."

"No," Allan said aloud, standing up and peeling from the film of the wall's grime. "No." He took a few steps away from his father, and for a moment the image floated along the ground, remaining equidistant from him. Allan closed his eyes and turned deeper into the alley. Fingertips brushed his shoulder but he shrugged them off. With a shiver, he plunged farther from the streets and into its underbelly.

He continued, exhausted. Each step managed to quiet his father's rants a bit more, until finally his words just buzzed at the periphery. Allan's feet felt raw and his calves ached but at least he was free.

Isolation crept in. Mumbled moans rendered the grey scene uniform. People held their heads between their knees, rocking themselves to songs only they could hear.

Allan found his own corner within sight of a barrel in case he caved in to the need for warmth. The shallow camaraderie of mutual survival might quiet the screaming in his head.

He closed his eyes and sank into the wall. Sirens echoed along the brick fissures and made a dissonant lullaby.

Allan awoke with a jolt. He stared into his father's bloodshot eyes. Two pairs of arms yanked him off his feet while his father stood with hands on his hips. Their eyes remained locked the entire time, a smile curling his father's lips. "Can't run," he said. "Won't have it. Won't have you throwing away your education."

Allan tried to fight back with atrophied limbs, but even clenching took too much energy. The only thing he could do was be as slippery and unwieldy as possible.

"Can't run. Won't run? Won't stop." His father's form floated, puss trickling from bulging eyes. "Ready for your handout? You're going to get it handed to you, oh yes sir, boy, you'll get a handout you'll never forget."

The clawing words dug deeper than the hands that threw Allan into a van. He half-hoped his father would disappear into the shadows as the doors slammed shut behind him, but the eyes and teeth glittered like unrelenting camera flashes piercing to the center of Allan's skull.

"Don't worry; it'll be a surprise, boy. The best work you'll ever do. You won't thank me because you're an ungrateful vagrant, but just know that everything is because of me. Because you need a hand, the helping hand, the clutch of society to hold your throat above the chasm, the best and the brightest to squeeze blood into that lazy grey lump of your skull. We'll get it out of you before you're done, boy. You bet your socks we will."

Allan whimpered, trying to turn away and shut his eyes, but the red-rimmed pupils stared back at him no matter which way he turned.

Had he done this to himself? Or was he just a sacrificial pawn in a much bigger picture?

I should be the check-mater, he thought.

"Rook to the end, knights and bishops assemble, Allan," his father crowed, teeth sharpening into fangs. "Check and mate, the gates open, the trumpets blare for your prize. The crowds will know the Gerrold name before I'm done, boy, and they will know your thankless face because of what your mother and I did for you. Spread your hands in equanimity and pretend like you've crawled out of the forge and made yourself who you are. But know that Daddy had to do it for you, Daddy had to bring you where you needed to be, where you should be. Cut the cables wiring your wasted cortex, and get ready for your handout."

The sound of the van's engine drowned beneath the torrent of his father's words. In an effort to escape, Allan bit his lip. The hot metallic flow trickled out his mouth as rapidly as his mind.

CHAPTER TWO

Growing Up

Sixteen-year-old Ben Artemit was a lonely boy. That loneliness, however, was nothing compared to his childhood monsters. Part of the reason for his isolation was that nobody would believe a teenager still saw monsters under the bed.

He sat on his counsellor Heather Smith's hard grey couch with his back straight and legs tensed, ready to bolt out of the room. He tried to tell himself that Heather, sitting across from him with frizzy red hair, glasses and wrinkles, was there to help.

That she wouldn't send him to the loony bin if he told the truth.

Heather crossed her legs and leaned forward with her tablet. She smiled at him, radiating warmth and acceptance in an unfamiliar and disarming way.

She tapped her tablet a few times, then set it down.

"Well, now that we've finished those formalities, we can start our journey together. I look forward to getting to know you, Ben. As we start, can you do me a favour?"

"What's that?" Ben asked, looking between Heather and the tablet to assess whether she was going to trick him into something.

"I'd like you to take a deep breath with me and hold it, then release slowly," she said.

Ben did as instructed. By the time he'd counted to seven he already felt the swirling cloud of thoughts and emotions calming.

She was helping.

Maybe he could trust her.

Maybe he shouldn't have waited so long to see someone.

"Thank you," Heather said, slowly letting out her breath. "If you find it helpful, I'd like to start our sessions with that."

Ben nodded. If that were all it took, he'd hold his breath at the bottom of a pool.

"Now, did you want to tell me a bit about what you're hoping to get out of our time together?"

"You don't know already?" Ben stared at his shoes. He shifted his feet back and forth, rubbing the carpet in neat lines as though that might bring the peace he sought.

"I have a bit of information," Heather said, "but I'd like to hear it straight from you, so I can better understand. The more honest you are, the better I can help you, but what's most important is that you know and feel that you're safe here. If you're ever not feeling safe, let me know, OK?"

Ben nodded and took another deep breath. If these sessions were to be of any use, he would have to tell her everything—absolutely everything. He'd spent far too long lying to people, pretending the monsters weren't there.

His parents were the only ones close enough to know the truth—that the monsters were very much real for him.

For *him*. And no one else.

"I feel as though you're frightened, Ben. Are you worried about talking to me? Remember, as long as you're not hurting yourself or others, this stays between us."

Ben closed his eyes, and nodded. "I know. It's just hard to talk about. But I have to."

He began.

* * *

The golden prairie canvas stretched to the horizon, the only real movement that of wheat and canola swaying with the wind. Ben, age seven, thought time had frozen, and had to make sure Mom and Dad hadn't been frozen by the spell of monotony in central Alberta, Canada.

Finally, the land seemed to crack open, bending and twisting until rocky hoodoos dotted the landscape. Dinosaur signs greeted them as Ben's father wove their SUV into the town of Drumheller. They followed the dinosaur-marked signs toward the Royal Tyrrell Museum.

Ben sighed. They'd finally made it. His parents smiled back at him.

Three animatronic triceratops turned their heads to watch the Artemit family's approach into the museum, a metal and glass building on an outcrop in the badlands. It looked like a castle that could observe everything, and that had been tracing history since dinosaurs left the Earth.

The triceratops let them pass unscathed. Ben waved in thanks.

Past the ticket kiosk, automatic doors unfolded a portal through time, revealing the tragedies of mudslides and floods that left families of dinosaurs trapped, their bones and legacy to be unearthed millions of years later. To Ben, real eyes stared at him through the skeletons as much as the animatronic ones had earlier. He smelled the tropical forest, tasted the dew, and as he came upon the T-rex embedded in rock, he could hear the creature's roar.

Behind a window a fresh skeleton was being cleaned by one of the museum's employees. Ben pressed his face against the glass. The specimen was a spiked ankylosaur skull, a battering ram that meant the dinosaur must have fought long and hard throughout its existence. Ben took comfort

13

in picturing it dormant, taking a well-earned respite from dangerous struggles.

His mother tugged him away. He stared up at towering galleries of clawed lizards. The rooms got dustier and dustier until he stepped up to a brilliantly coloured tunnel — the *real* time tunnel, bringing him and his parents back into the Precambrian era. He glanced up at his smiling mother and his yawning father to make sure he wouldn't make the journey without them.

Creatures big and small surrounded him, all attempts at life, most of which hadn't succeeded. One looked like a vacuum cleaner with seven eyes.

Ben gradually understood how there had once been a time when God had played in a sandbox, creating all sorts of things without really knowing which was the best path forward. Ben's mother explained it to him in these terms, likening the explosion of life to a pile of lego dumped into a basement playroom, intangible potential as experiments clicked into place.

Ben wanted to make some of them real. It wasn't fair they weren't allowed to play anymore. Even as Ben was about to finish grade two and move into more serious grade three studies, he couldn't imagine a world without play.

He was tugged through millenia of evolutionary progress until he emerged into a giant sandbox with dinosaurs all around. He stood next to an apatosaurus's leg bone, close enough to touch.

It had the texture of tree bark, but was varnished like his family's dining table. Ben felt like he and the dinosaur were shaking hands.

Several other children behind him bounced in apprehension to have their turn to see the massive femur. Ben nodded solemnly to the dinosaur before letting go.

Ben passed the rest of the journey through the Royal Tyrrell in contemplation. There was so much around him that could only exist in the imagination. The museum did the best job it could to recreate and do the great beasts justice, but they were clearly shackled, relics that stood as emblems rather than dynamic players in the great game of life.

His parents asked him several times if he was all right, and he assured them with nods and pursed lips.

He had a lot of thinking to do.

He walked out of the Tyrrell castle with a great burden on his shoulders, determined to figure out a way to bring the dinosaurs back. He vowed not to rest until he had.

Both tasks were harder than he thought. In their beige-carpeted motel room, Ben stared up at a ceiling with fossilized trails of cigarette smoke. His parents were asleep in the other room.

Scientists in dusty lab coats could work wonders at the Tyrrell, but it wasn't enough. There had to be more. Ben would read every book until he figured out what it was. He wondered if the library was open, and if not, whether he could sneak in. There was too much to do and the dinosaurs had already waited too long.

As he debated the merits of breaking into the library through the vents or the back door, Ben fell asleep.

In his dreams he chose the back door, and as the door shut behind him he heard a security guard cry out. There wasn't much time. He ran up the concrete staircase and burst into the gallery. A few of the dinosaurs were missing, and he looked around for a place to hide. None of them had come alive yet—he'd need more time to think, to figure things out while the security guard passed. Hopefully after a while the big man would assume the intruder was gone.

Ben heard footsteps from the bottom of the stairwell. He sprinted through a tunnel featuring aquatic dinosaurs, then zipped past an Albertosaur. He headed back into the trees, back in time before the dinosaurs.

A hushed voice made him skid to a stop.

"Pssst," came a slippery voice. It seemed to glide around Ben. Nearby, a tall reptile hunched on two feet in a dark passageway between exhibits. "He won't find you this way. Come with me."

Ben took one last look over his shoulder, then darted to follow the creature.

A dinosaur was alive.

As the dinosaur rested a cold-blooded hand on his shoulder, Ben's heart raced. Maybe all the dinosaurs needed was acknowledgement, someone to come back in the magic hours of darkness and reawaken them with an offer of freedom. If Ben could help one, he could surely help the rest. The kingdom of lizards would be restored to its rightful place.

He couldn't see the dinosaur now that it had moved deeper into the shadows, but he heard the creature's whistle-like breath, a barely-audible hiss going in and out. He had so many questions to ask, but swallowed his words as he saw the security guard round the corner ahead.

Ben was in complete darkness, the damp air worsening the sweat on his face. The dinosaur stopped breathing; so did Ben. The guard wouldn't—couldn't—find them. There was no reason for him to come back behind the exhibit, was there?

The guard turned, and Ben felt like someone had just pinned him against his locker at school. The guard's flashlight was so bright Ben felt like he was suddenly onstage.

Ben barely made out the guard raising his gun.

"No," Ben said, putting up his hands, "I—"

BANG.

Ben snapped awake in moist sheets. He clutched his chest, burning where the bullet would have gone. He took long, ragged breaths.

The hotel room was as black as his hiding space in the museum. Ben shivered. Light rain pattered the pavement outside.

His parents were sleeping in the other half of the motel room, with the bathroom separating them. They wouldn't appreciate being woken up to hear of Ben's dreamed escapades in the Tyrrell museum. They wouldn't understand—Dad *definitely* wouldn't.

Ben propped himself on his elbows and looked toward their bedroom, finally discerning details in the gloom. He then scanned the walls to make sure the security guard hadn't followed him into the real world.

That was when he saw it. When he saw *them*.

He initially thought there was only one tall, skinny figure, but lurking in the dark recesses was another. One was right beside the bed, leaning toward Ben with slitted eyes and long, thin limbs. Its skin was smooth and glistening; its mouth stretched wide across massive jaws. Three long, knobbed fingers moved onto Ben's chest.

"We made it," it said, the words grating out in a scratchy voice as though the creature had just cleared mucous out of its throat. The space inside its mouth was a hollow night sky.

If this was what Ben had seen in the dream, then he'd been tricked. These weren't the dinosaurs he needed to save.

The treachery sank like an anchor tying him to the bed. Their malice and cruelty had been hidden by the fog of dream, and now Ben saw them for what they were.

They were monsters.

The one lurking in the shadows stepped forward. Its hunger permeated the air, suffocating Ben. He gasped, realizing he had moments before it was too late.

"Time can't keep you from us, Artemit," the monster said, closing the distance.

They would capture him, make him do their bidding. They'd unleash nameless horrors on the world.

Lead weights hung at Ben's sides, and he couldn't move. So he did the only thing he could do.

He screamed. Using every microgram of breath, he pushed his voice out until his throat cracked into silence. The creature, now beside him, pushed a three-fingered hand over his mouth. It felt like the okra Mom sometimes cooked, but colder and slimier.

"What—oh my God," Mom said with a gasp. She stood in

her pyjamas, frozen at the side of the room. The eyes of both monsters turned toward her; her power shattered the magic holding Ben to the bed. He twisted out of the creature's grasp and ran to Mom, spitting the monster's taste from his lips.

"Get away—" Mom said, wrapping her arms around Ben as he reached her. She kept her eyes fixed on the creatures. "My God, what—"

His mother froze for a moment, as all time seemed to stop.

"What is it?" Dad said in a hoarse voice, stumbling into the room. He fumbled for the switch and ignited a blast of light.

The monsters were gone.

"They were going to take me," Ben said, tears rolling down his cheeks. He quaked, praying his mother's protection would keep the monsters at bay. "Don't let them, Mom. Don't let them."

Mom crouched down and brushed soft fingers across Ben's cheek. Her brow furrowed and she pulled Ben closer. "What do you mean, honey? What did you see?"

"You saw them," Ben said, frowning. Mom wouldn't lie about something like this. She wouldn't play a joke of pretending the monsters weren't real. Had she just forgotten?

"The monsters," Ben continued. "They wanted... everything. They wanted me."

Dad raised an eyebrow and sighed, turning away. He grumbled to himself as he left the room, and Ben heard his body thump back into bed.

Mom's face knit with compassion, and she pulled him closer. "It's OK, Ben. There are no monsters."

"But you saw them, Mom."

A flicker of worry passed over her face before she tugged him into a hug. "It's OK, Ben. I didn't see them because they aren't there."

The blood drained from Ben's face. His lips trembled. What was going on?

"Can you stay with me?"

"Of course." She brushed her fingers through his hair, then cupped his cheek.

Mom's warmth beside him did little to comfort Ben for the rest of the night. His eyes flitted about the room to ensure the monsters wouldn't return. He stayed silent and unmoving, more out of a desire to keep Mom safe and let her rest. If Mom couldn't see the monsters, or couldn't remember seeing the monsters, then Ben would have to protect them.

The monsters had partially succeeded in their goal, because Ben felt like he'd been taken away from his parents. The only thing more frightening than facing evil was facing it alone.

CHAPTER THREE

Buttons

A llan Gerrold didn't realize he'd been kidnapped until the van had driven several blocks, when the rocking motions banished his father's ghost. The rocking was an anti-lullaby that sharpened and awakened him.

Cold metal rings cuffed his hands.

Oh God.

He pitched toward the doors, only to feel the choking harness against his neck.

"Help!"

A hollow echo answered him, followed by the low rumble of the van's engine.

It would have been better if he could see his captor. The van was dark enough that he might as well be tumbling through outer space.

For the first time in as long as he could remember, he wanted his father's ghost to keep him company, even if it was to rebuke him.

Had his old company's competitors kidnapped him, hoping to make him reveal his secrets? Squeeze every last drop out of intel out of him, by any means?

He clenched his jaw. This was an ugly world. Corporate kidnapping wasn't out of the question.

The van doors opened like St. Peter's gates to the blinding daylight of day. Rough hands reached out of the white and dispelled any illusion that this was a blessing.

Allan glimpsed a parkade before someone pulled a cloth bag over his head. A bitter smell filled his nostrils. He jerked, then darkness took him.

Allan awoke with a yelp. They'd torn the bag off, tearing out a tuft of hair.

He got up on his knees in a white padded room. He caught a glimpse of a bulky man retreating through the metal door and slamming it shut.

The room smelt of disinfectant, stale sweat and a hint of horrible things someone had attempted to mask with sterility. Allan didn't want to imagine the history.

His cuffs were gone, but the room's quiet leeched oxygen from the air. Allan inhaled barely-controlled gasps, pressing fists to his temples.

He'd always done the right thing, followed the best recommendations. When the dentist told him to floss every day, he had his mother buy an industrial supply. When teachers had told him he needed to study three hours a night, he got a lock for his bedroom door so he wouldn't be interrupted. He kept fit and stopped eating fast food as soon as he hit university. He stole the keys to academic success from every mind he could probe, doing everything they recommended. Reading four to five physics papers a day, researching into the small hours every night until he could publish in the most reputable journals, well past the number required for professorship. By the time Allan got his Ph.D., he had read almost every book on academic success.

His father had dogged him the whole way, doubting and criticizing Allan for turning away from the family's agrarian traditions.

Allan had worked hard with the hope and expectation he could be the first human being to *do it right*, to fight off mortality with every bastion of knowledge known to humanity. The history of every individual had been marred with mistakes, accidents, flaws Allan attributed to laziness, lack of insight, or a combination of both.

By doing everything right, Allan wouldn't grow old as quickly as everyone else. He wouldn't succumb to illness, weakness of mind, or grow fat. He would make a difference and serve as an example so the rest of humanity could follow suit and rise to the highest achievable level.

There were a few people who'd warned Allan about his total lack of social life. That was before it stopped existing entirely. Allan had deemed it necessary and an optional fill-in he didn't have time for. He would consider adopting those extra niceties once he'd gotten where he needed to go. Some people had offered vague spiritual aphorisms about many paths to the mountaintop, but Allan assumed they were rationalizing their compromises.

Until everything had been thrown in his face.

None of the effort had mattered. Wall-street crooks would determine the fate of his dreams just as easily as they'd done to scores of others. Being an expert scientist didn't give him any more power over the fate of his ideas than a high school summer student.

He had ended up on the streets because of a crooked investment and intellectual property system.

Now he was imprisoned. Was this an asylum? It was all so wrong, after he had proven his dedication to mind and body.

Allan growled, his throat vibrating. His pitch rose with all his pent-up energy.

Then he was yelling as loud as he could. Blurred dots swam in his vision.

Hours went by. The lights never so much as changed hue. Would his captors ever turn off the lights?

Exhaustion finally took him.

* * *

Black steel-toed boots greeted him, blurring into larger-than-life focus.

A chiseled figure towered over him, wearing an open lab coat a few sizes too small. His arms were crossed over a tight black t-shirt, and he wore dark, neatly-pressed dress slacks.

Allan shoved away, teetering on the cushioned floor.

The man laughed, leaning back.

Allan couldn't decide if this guy was a high school bruiser or a mad scientist.

A woman stepped into view beside the bruiser-man, and she couldn't have been more out of place.

She wore a bright aqua blouse tucked into a black skirt. Her short bob haircut was dark as midnight with gray flecks like the first sign of stars through shifting cloud cover. She held a tablet across her chest, standing tall and regal next to the bruiser-man.

"Dr. Gerrold," she said in a dry, sterile voice, "you have been brought here for a very special purpose."

Allan stared at her but her eyes looked coldly through him, as though she didn't recognize she was speaking to a human. Was he just a datum to her, a statistic? Or did she consider herself so far above everyone else?

Allan shuddered.

The bruiser-man's eyes lit up like a pit-bull eyeing a steak.

"We are going to run a series of tests on you," the ice queen continued, "and they can be rendered significantly more expedient if you cooperate."

Allan pushed back until he compressed the cushions on the far wall. He made a croaking noise, realizing his throat had dried like a prune during his captivity.

The bruiser-man leaned in, the smell of garlic pouring out between yellowed teeth. "What was that? We don't understand grovel."

Allan cleared his throat and opened his mouth a few times, his jaw tensing. "I'm not... a lab rat."

The bruiser-man raised an eyebrow.

"Of course you aren't," the ice queen said without a hint of tenderness. "You are much more than that. Otherwise we could have taken anyone, Dr. Gerrold. But we chose you." Her voice remained flat, the only trace of emotion a slight curl in one corner of her mouth.

Was this some of the recognition, the reward Allan had sought? His mind reeled. Could he take this as proof of what he'd wanted his entire life?

No. There was no way they'd chosen him for a grand purpose. The end held something sinister. It must, otherwise they wouldn't have had to bag him, drug him and lock him up.

There was nevertheless something irresistible about the offer of validation, whether sinister or not. An offer of purpose to a man without it.

He scrunched up his face. "What kinds of tests?"

The ice queen tilted her head. "We are going to measure you, Dr. Gerrold, but it is our hope that with your abilities we can make you one of the most incredible human beings on the planet."

His mouth moved but he couldn't hear himself. Whether it was from shame or denial, he didn't know.

* * *

Allan stood barefoot on hardwood floor, gaping at a room that was larger than any apartment he'd ever seen. It might have even rivaled the size of his parents' house. He felt he was tainting the pristine space with his dirty and scarred feet. He thought he'd grown accustomed to his own filth, but this room made him feel like a dust mite.

There was a large four poster bed Allan had only ever seen in movies and museums, tall oak posts framing a massive mattress. Was there something bigger than a King-size?

The desk on the opposite side of the room was also big

enough to sleep on, and housed a large screen, keyboard and mouse. Books filled two floor-to-ceiling shelves nearby.

Allan's steps echoed in the cavernous washroom. The shower might as well have been communal, and Allan jumped when water splashed down on him from three sides. The glass pane fogged up within seconds. Allan closed his eyes and soaked his weary muscles.

By the time he finished his skin was raw and red, as if he'd shed his cocoon and metamorphosed. Although he was naked, the clothing of civilization seemed to hang upon his shoulders once again. Words like dignity and properness, which only his mother had ever used, danced at him from the back of his mind. Now that he'd showered, his stench faded behind the aroma of fresh linen.

The drawers were stocked full of new clothes, all his size. Allan wondered if he could have done a better job if he'd shopped for himself, the choices plain and simple but nice.

The books were mostly non-fiction. The computer had access to an immeasurably large library.

He supposed that was all right. It was a small price to pay for all the luxuries that surrounded him.

Still, it was a bad sign that the bruiser-man and the ice queen refused to introduce themselves to him. When he asked them who they were, all the ice queen had said was, "It's better for our upcoming work if we keep a high level of professional distance."

He didn't know where he was, and he didn't know who held him captive. Was it still a small price to pay for the luxuries in front of him?

He tried not to think about the larger price he might have to pay in other currencies.

* * *

Allan held the liability waiver by its edges, as though it

might burn his hands if he fully grasped it. The form listed a corporate ID number as the other party, which did nothing to identify where he was, or who these people were.

He carefully re-read the long list of possible problems that would be no one's responsibility but his own. Beside him, the ice queen stood almost at attention with her tablet tucked behind her back.

"What sort of implants?" Allan asked, failing once more to discern anything from her face.

"Basic biometrics and additional feedback loops," the ice queen said tonelessly.

Allan might have pressed her for more information, but the bruiser-man was back, filling his room's doorway with crossed arms and a lingering sneer. If he hadn't been there, Allan might have said the liability waiver was too all-encompassing for such simple implants, and that there must be a catch. Kiosks in malls could put in similar devices without even a quarter of the legality—why was she being so cautious?

"We don't have all day," the bruiser-man said.

The ice queen looked at the bruiser-man with disinterest, then back at Allan.

Now that Allan had more to lose, it was harder to say no. It hadn't taken long to adjust to the luxury and now Allan wanted to make sure it was here to stay. What harm could a few implants do to a man living in a one-room palace? It was better than living on the streets.

He thought he would have been stronger, prouder, but the truth was that he was absolutely desperate for the stability they'd given him.

Besides, they already had him. Maybe the waiver was an indication they acknowledged him as a person worthy of respect—something they hadn't done when they'd dragged him from the streets.

Allan signed the form and handed it back to the ice queen, glad not to have to touch it anymore.

* * *

After the surgery, Allan's head throbbed. He wanted to let the pressure pour out his ears. His skull didn't seem to fit anymore, and he couldn't lift his swollen watermelon of a brain off the pillow.

Allan opened his eyes to find the ice queen standing over him, as though she'd been a sentinel there all along. He jerked and his neck spasmed, sending a flash to the base of his skull.

He cried out, squeezing his eyes shut and waiting for the sharp pain to subside.

A cold, soft hand entwined around his.

It was the ice queen's. He wished he knew her name.

"Are you ready to test the biometrics, Dr. Gerrold?"

He groaned. "It feels like you've synched a belt around my brain."

"That's to be expected," she said, nodding. "But you've had two days—more than enough time to recover."

Allan blinked, wondering where the bruiser-man was this early. It felt like six in the morning, but with the dense blinds there was no natural sunlight to confirm or deny his biological clock. He sighed, settling into the dull ache at the back of his eyes. "All right. What next?"

"Come with me," she said, helping him up.

She led him down the white halls and through a few doors, up to a heavy metal door. She keyed in a code, then pulled it open.

Inside was a white chamber, padded from floor to ceiling.

The ice queen held the door and beckoned him to go in.

This was where he'd woken after they'd first taken him.

"Dr. Gerrold," she said, waving him in.

"Are you planning to lock me in here?"

"No, Dr. Gerrold. We need this space for some tests.

Please, go on in."

Her words comforted him, even if her expression did not. Maybe her intentions were good, and this was all in his head.

After stepping in, he sank to his ankles.

Oh no.

The ground cushioned every step, making him sway as though adrift in the ocean. He steadied himself against the wall.

The fabric was smooth—too smooth.

There were only a handful of reasons why that would be necessary, none of them good.

The fabric suddenly felt very, very cold.

Allan wondered if the cushions would swallow him whole if the need arose. *When* the need arose, he might want them to.

If I don't have to spend much time in here, he told himself, *I could manage.*

His room was, after all, a sanctuary.

The shutting door's metallic ring was swallowed by their surroundings. Every movement was damped and silenced.

"Do the tests have to be done in here?" Allan asked.

"Yes," the ice queen droned.

The fabric smelled like it had been washed and bleached a hundred times.

The ice queen pulled a small black remote from her pocket. It seemed an anachronism compared to the multifunctional devices in everyone's pocket. The ice queen's remote was featureless except for two buttons—one red, one green.

Could those buttons be so singularly important, so encompassing, that the device needn't do anything else?

This room was the very definition of neutrality, of absorption. The remote's existence clashed with tangible electricity.

"Now, Dr. Gerrold," she said, each syllable swallowed by the shushing walls, "please sit down."

Allan did as instructed, letting himself sink into the padding. It wrapped up and around his legs. The ice queen smiled at him as he lowered, thousands of tiny hands pressing his haunches in a way that said, *Don't worry.* The net effect was more like lying down on a bed of nails—no immediate physical discomfort, but the ever-present awareness that if anything went wrong the pain would be worse than anything in the world.

Allan's gaze darted between the ice queen's brown eyes and the seemingly archaic remote, wondering where and how the nails would be driven in. And *when.* Most importantly, *when.*

"This is hooked up to your biometrics," she said, pacing before him. She seemed all-too comfortable on the surface, as though it had no effect on her. As though the pads were under her direction to swallow Allan alone.

She paused, then approached him. She touched a hand to the back of his neck, right near the base of his skull. "Your biometrics," she repeatedly softly.

"When I press each button, you will experience one of two sensations." She got up and took a few paces, then pivoted toward him, her hand hovering above the remote. "You will know pain."

She extended her right forefinger and raised the black box in her left hand. For a moment, she did not move. Allan's hands came up in front of his face. The ice queen moved her finger slowly toward the red button, paused, and pressed it.

Allan's skin tingled, and he flinched, expecting the worst. The hairs on his arms seemed to vibrate with a dull hum, and he looked down, waiting for the worst. This was more than manageable—it was almost like a physiotherapist's IFC treatment.

Click. The ice queen pressed the button again. Allan felt his muscles quake beyond their resonant frequency, bucking and jolting in a struggle for equilibrium. His head spun, but he fixed his gaze on the ice queen, who still held her finger above the button like the spring on a mousetrap. There was a hint of a grimace on her placid face.

Click. She pressed the button again, and the pain intensified.

Tremors traveled up and down Allan's arms, then into his legs and groin. He moaned. Ringing filled his ears, and his tongue burnt.

Click. The ice queen looked at him sheepishly, as though it were a funny accident that she'd pressed the button and made everything even worse.

His vision blurred. His spine twitched. Every part of his skin burned like some invisible hand was squeezing him, heating him up like a boiled frog.

Click. Another button press, and more pain.

Allan fell back and writhed. He struggled to resolve the ice queen as more than a silhouette. He cried out for her to stop, and the only response he got was a view of her white teeth bared in a grin.

Allan covered his head. His body moved, twisted and rolled like an automaton, a chemical burst seeking a way through the reaction, an end that wouldn't come. Allan caught glimpses of himself, coming through as though he were looking at some other being, getting up and stumbling, running, falling, over and over again, trying to find some refuge from the torment.

He was only mentally aware of the room yielding, accepting, which worsened everything. The ride after was tumultuous.

It stopped. In an instant, there was no outside evidence that anything was wrong—that anything had ever been wrong. Allan heard and felt ringing in every corner of his body. Muscles twitched in expectation of the next wave of stimuli. Outside noise trickled in like water through a breaking dam. The volume of the world gradually increased to a dull buzz, never blocking out the ringing in his ears.

Laughter rose as though the padded room's dampeners had been switched off. The metallic tang of blood burned his dry throat. The smell of sweat choked his nostrils. A cold, wet shiver went through him.

Breaths heaved in and out of his aching chest, and he gradually recognized the laughter as the bruiser-man's. When had he come in? How long had Allan been gone? Did clocks still tick in Hell?

He dared not get up, turn to face them, lest they begin the torture anew. He lay frozen aside from the rise and fall of shuddering breaths.

The ice queen's voice broke the fleeting peace like a tsunami crashing into a skyscraper. "Now you will experience the opposite." She paused, and Allan could sense the static of her finger mere centimetres from the green button. "Pleasure."

Allan jerked his head to see the ice queen put out a finger, then bring the remote toward it. Her finger hovered over the green button until she leisurely pressed it inward.

Click.

Warmth oozed into his muscles. It took several seconds for his body to acknowledge it, waiting for some trick, some twist that lay around the corner. When none came, Allan sank deeper into the cushions.

Click.

He felt a calm breeze, heard birds chirping in the distance. Leaves rustled and the smell of spring flowers poured over him.

Click.

Allan moaned, reaching a hand up in the direction of the remote, then letting it drop again. This was good. This was really good, and there was nothing more to want.

Click. Click.

Allan closed his eyes as all worry left him and coolness spread through his veins like a Morphine IV. He'd been hit by a drunk driver once, and after they'd removed the metal from his leg he'd been given a Morphine drip that had almost stripped him of all will to get up again.

This was better.

Click. Click. Click.

Allan's head ignited with ecstasy, and he twisted back in a serpentine arch. Everything burned away to warmth, the radiance ebbing into every aching portion of his corpse. There was nothing that needed doing, nothing that could provide anything better than this. He moaned again, letting the little remaining tension pour out of him. The reward, the recognition, everything had been achieved. His father's yells of disapproval bounced off him. Nothing else mattered.

His manhood throbbed, and felt wrapped in warm, intense feeling. He moaned.

The purpose was here and now, something so satisfying and joyous Allan's being came aglow and ceased being aware of itself. There was nothing and there was everything. The rippling electric pleasure washed away all the in-between trivialities.

He climaxed, then the cycle began anew, while Allan groaned and writhed.

It grew harder to think, but with every recession of conscious thought came an increasingly powerful wave of acceptance. Everything Allan ever wanted soared the currents of his cloud-nine thoughts, adapting deliciously to his whim with perfect synchronicity.

When it all stopped, the wrenching sensation made him cry out. Every pain of reality came crashing back like a freight train, and he clawed his way to his knees. He could barely see —didn't want to see—and said in a whimpering voice, "Please. Again. Just once. Just one more time." His hands clawed for the button, until the bruiser-man shoved him back into a pile of his own blood and drool. His pants were wet.

"Press the button," Allan gasped.

The ice queen tilted her head down at Allan, raising the remote like a holy symbol. Her voice was low, laced with the real menace of that tiny remote. "This is how you will feel if you succeed in what we ask," she said.

Allan nodded, slowly coming back, accepting some fleeting need to be a part of this world once more. If only for a single purpose. He felt bags under his eyes as he stared at the remote, the walls tinting green for a moment.

"The pain is yours when you fail."

CHAPTER FOUR

Shrunken

"**S**o Ben, have you had any dreams lately?" Heather Smith asked.

Her question was a trap, an underhanded way to imply Ben Artemit's experiences weren't real. He had told her over and over that the monsters weren't dreams, that he was fully awake and aware every time he saw them. But she didn't believe him.

He'd confided in her, fooled by the warmth and acceptance she exuded. Over several frustrating sessions, however, he'd grown convinced there was no way to make her believe him. He'd started these sessions afraid, and was now just frustrated because they only seemed to make the nights worse.

Ben saw the monsters every night. His mother always saw them, but only for a moment. She never remembered afterward.

His father never saw them, period.

A twisted cycle had been set in motion, and the only thing that had emerged from it was an increase in his anxiety and more trips to the shrink.

"No, I haven't had any dreams," Ben said coolly. He tried to mimic Heather's neutral expression.

She sighed, making a note on her tablet. "Have you seen the monsters, Ben?"

Ben avoided her gaze, looking instead at some of the art lining her office walls. There wasn't much one could do with a cramped corridor room, but Heather had managed to fill it with some of the cheapest abstract art Ben had ever seen. All except one piece, a sun-coloured mesh of lines that reminded Ben of the dendrites he'd learned about in biology. Brain cell networks, neural tissue, the root of what had brought him to this horrible place.

There was something hauntingly calm about staring at a representation of the human brain, as if by painting it a person could plumb the mysteries between synapses. Every time Ben looked at it, he saw something new in the patterns.

He wished the sessions gave him something close to the same experience. His parents were paying a small fortune for him to be here, and Ben knew their insistence on his attendance came from a place of love. He always emerged from the sessions to find his mother waiting with hope on her face. How could he deny her that, after all she'd done for him?

But he'd made no progress.

Ben let out a sigh of his own. "All right," he said. "I did see them. As I do every night."

"Good, thank you. How did you see them?"

"With my eyes," Ben said with a smirk. "Aren't you supposed to be discouraging me from having these visions?"

Heather folded her hands on her lap. "Do you consider them visions, Ben?"

Ben narrowed his eyes. "You know the answer to that."

Heather blinked. "No, I don't believe I do. I don't believe we've ever discussed what you think the monsters might mean."

"We haven't discussed it because the only thing they mean is harm," Ben said.

"But have they ever hurt you?"

Ben suddenly found himself unwilling to keep calm and

collected for anyone else's sake. He'd had enough sessions trying to be the reasonable boy everyone expected.

"Yes!" he shouted, standing. "I don't trust what I see. I rarely get more than six hours of sleep. I don't trust anyone. That's the harm they've done me. Do you need me to go on? I think you've probably noted even more problems with me because of the monsters."

Heather looked down at her tablet, then away. "Ben," she said quietly, "have you ever considered that the monsters represent everything you dislike about the world?"

Ben rolled his eyes. He'd had enough discussion of representation and symbols to skip the rest of his English classes. "There are lots of things I don't like in this world. I don't like the dentist, I don't like waiting in lines, I don't like the dumb kids who disrupt classes and push me around. I don't like these sessions, to be honest.

"But the monsters are not even on the same plane of existence as any of these other things. If all I had to complain about were school bullies and dentist visits, I wouldn't be here."

"That's not what I mean, Ben." Heather frowned and took a deep breath. "What I mean is that you attribute a lot of inadequacies you perceive in yourself and the world around you to the monsters. Most of the things you hate about the world, and your unhappiness with yourself, you attribute to the effect the monsters have had on you. Is that not true?"

Ben stared at Heather. The moments were rare, but every once in a while a flicker of gold would filter through what she said. Whether or not the monsters were real, there may be truth to her words.

Ben struggled to make friends, and had marked himself as a lone wolf for as long as he could remember. No, not as long as he could remember: as long as he'd seen the monsters. They watched him, beckoned him, wanted something from him, and there was no sign that they would ever let up. Without even realizing it, he had put his life on hold waiting for the creatures to go away. He had postponed being the person he'd wanted to become while waiting for the terror to pass. All the things he disliked about his life stemmed from the monsters.

He'd *let* them do that to him.

A tear rolled down his cheek. "Maybe I've used them as an excuse," he said, his voice hoarse.

"I don't know if excuse is the right word," Heather said. "Your behaviour is a natural reaction. We can disagree about other things, but the fear you feel is very real. And you've lived with it for a long time." She paused. "I've never told you this before, but I think you're a very strong person."

Ben blinked. *Huh?*

"But you're also very hard on yourself," she continued. "You haven't used the monsters as an excuse. They are some of the most frightening things you've ever seen and out of that—in order to deal with them—you had to develop some coping strategies. There's nothing wrong with that. What I'm suggesting is that you might be able to change the way you see them in order to lessen their effect on the rest of your life."

Ben stared at Heather, squinting then refocusing to see if some outward change had manifested itself in her features. Was she the same woman he'd been seeing the past few months? Or was this whole exchange something else that would be forgotten by everyone but him?

Ben's vision blurred. He would love to be able to change the way he reacted to the monsters. Did Heather have the tools to do such a thing? It seemed too good to be true, a vague promise as substantial as cotton candy.

The air in the room grew thick. Ben wiped his brow.

He wondered about the hundreds of other patients who'd sat on this couch before him. Had their trials been of a similar nature? Had their demons been any less real than his own?

"How..."

Heather waited through the lengthy silence while Ben figured out where to begin. His voice was barely above a whisper. "How can I change all that?"

Heather smiled a car salesman grin. "Well, you've already started Ben. Let's just keep going."

* * *

In the weeks that followed, Ben went through a rigorous cognitive behavioural therapy program, with daily exercises that consisted first of writing his reactions and negative thoughts concerning the monsters, then transforming them with a positive or more logical response. Initially it was difficult to try and use logic and reason against such great forces, but gradually the words gained more power.

The notion that the mind could create such intricate illusions and self-sustaining feedback loops humbled him.

Ben was awed by the nature of reality, the power of thought.

He put in more effort at school, going above and beyond in classes he'd otherwise just breeze through on natural ability. The world seemed lighter, as though a fog had been lifted, the aftermath of the monsters' visits waning.

Bit by bit, the two monsters drew away. They appeared in his room less frequently, more relegated to the shadows than they had been. That empowered Ben all the more, and he actually started enjoying his sessions with Heather.

Her techniques worked wonders.

He believed more and more that he had created the monsters as an illusion or a coping mechanism. If he was noticing such changes in his outward perspective just by doing a few daily mental exercises, it wasn't hard to believe that he'd created his own versions of the boogie monsters.

At the age of seventeen, Ben Artemit stopped seeing his childhood monsters.

He prayed they wouldn't come back.

CHAPTER FIVE

Training

A llan was theirs. He would succeed, not to avoid the pain, but to experience the pleasure.

That night, he tossed and turned in bed, as though by putting his brain on a spin cycle he might recreate the bliss of the pleasure button. He'd already checked his bathroom's medicine cabinet to see if there were any drugs he could mix to induce the same effects.

His captors had probably expected this, because the over-the-counter drugs that had been there before were gone, along with everything else.

He lay in bed and stared at the ceiling, counting sheep, then mountain goats, then snow leopards, then forest nymphs until something in him hit the off switch.

The next morning, Allan woke up in the shower under a deluge of cold water. The bruiser-man stood outside the glass pane, looking unimpressed as Allan sputtered and whimpered.

In his hands the bruiser-man held the two-button remote.

"Please," Allan said, "the button."

The bruiser-man hovered a finger over the red button.

"No!" Allan cried. "The green one!"

The bruiser-man motioned to press the red button, then

switched to the green at the last second.

A surge sent Allan catapulting toward a summit of light, and he gasped in ecstasy. Just a bit further…

Everything stopped, the coldness returning in a crash.

"Finish up," the bruiser-man said. "You're going to put some clothes on, and then you're going to run until I say stop."

Allan did. He pushed his body to the point where he collapsed. The bruiser-man eased up on him for a few minutes to allow him to recover, then made him continue until he'd ran six kilometres.

On the way to the tiny dining room they called a cafeteria, Ben stumbled and bumped into walls. The bruiser-man just laughed, twirling the red-green remote.

Eating ought to have been pleasurable, but it was a chore now, a barrier to the necessities. Allan scarfed down tasteless chunks, his eyes hollowed, his hands twitching like a junkie.

Classes began after breakfast, slides and videos with interactive quizzes. The material moved along at a brisk pace, a large metallic band strapped to Allan's head to monitor and ensure alertness. Each correct answer sent a spike of pleasure through him, which kept his concentration so well they had to drag him away at the end of the day.

He breezed through science, answering questions before they were done being asked. Mathematics was like breathing. Mythology and history seemed irrelevant to Allan, but he took to them with veracity nonetheless because of the carrot at the end.

When he didn't show zeal toward a task, he got the stick.

He started talking to himself in other languages, cementing the information being shovelled into him. By the end of the first week he had begun to expect any question from any subject. The gears of continuous mental engagement had been set in motion.

The subjects intensified but Allan kept up. The sense of pleasure from learning was only a fraction as fulfilling as what the remote offered, in the same way a swimming pool simulated an ocean. Learning well led to the remote's reward, though, so Allan pushed harder.

On the rare occasions when he'd had enough pleasure, Allan tried to find out why they'd chosen him and what they intended to do with him. The pain button quickly conditioned those questions away.

Within two months, Allan was running marathons and reviewing upper level calculus and quantum mechanics. He'd made it to the end of twentieth century history and could converse simply in French, Spanish, Portuguese and Italian. He'd begun learning Mandarin and writing Chinese.

Time stopped being marked by days, hours or minutes. The only ticking was the countdown to a hit of pleasure.

Electronic orbitals spun webs of probabilities; Allan calculated them all. He could give a detailed background of all the places where destruction could have been unleashed in the Cold War, and every scrap of past leading up to it. He knew how to make rocket fuel. Geography, geology, biology, and astronomy all implanted themselves, maps of tectonics, continents and heavens reflected in his grey-matter.

At some point his learning changed focus from science to deeper folklore and myth. Horned demons, fanged beasts, and the circles of hell took up residence in his psychological landscape. He knew how to analyze their meanings and origins, which were drilled into him as rigorously as calculus integrals.

His physical conditioning transformed into martial arts, the hits of a punching bag sending jolts of pleasure coursing through him. The rhythm was never fast enough. He became an efficient knuckle-buster, his callouses so large each knuckle was no longer distinguishable from another.

He moved from martial arts to guns, until gunfire itself triggered a pleasure response. Each bullet burst brought a brief ecstasy.

With every test and reward, Allan found more place in a world that had until now demanded justification from him.

Every pleasure hit acknowledged his soul.

His days were so busy that deeper emotions had no outlet. Although his emotional source was being boiled away by base desires, there was still enough to trickle at night.

In the dark hours, his conscience caught up to him, bringing nightmares.

The worst were those where he looked in the mirror and saw a double-image of the man he wanted to be, next to the man he was becoming.

He was becoming a great weapon, a force of reckoning.

It occurred to him on some level that he might be able to use his newfound abilities to escape. But the thought of losing the only thing that gave his life meaning, the sensation that was the means and the end, was inconceivable. There was so little left of the original Allan Gerrold that he owed his newfound existence to that remote, to that deep and profound pleasure. To destroy that fountain, or the hand that provided it, was tantamount to suicide.

Yet the mirror still came to him, in dreams.

CHAPTER SIX

Conference

When Professor Ben Artemit and his grad student, Sally Burton, attended the 2138 Canadian Association of Physicists (CAP) Conference, the first thing Ben noticed was a last-minute change in his session's programming.

Kitt Bell was presenting after him.

Kitt Bell.

It was as though the conference organizers took pleasuring putting the two competing theories in square opposition to see how much blood would spill before a victor emerged.

In both his and Kitt Bell's theoretical works, time stretched and twisted in dizzying matrices and wave functions. The profound implications that arose like stones from a draining swamp were that time travel was possible, or that was virtually impossible, depending on which theory you believed. There wasn't yet a way to prove any of it, though the pressure was building like a malfunctioning boiler. From the descriptions in the conference program Ben confirmed his belief that there were equal numbers in two camps: that backward time travel was possible in the so-called many universes interpretation of quantum mechanics, or that time travel was virtually impossible, and could only occur under the strictest conditions in a single universe if no paradoxes were created.

"They're going to have to give us our own conference soon!" Sally Burton exclaimed as she rifled through the program. "There's just too much!"

Ben looked over at her and forced a smile at his student. "The field's certainly grown more than I realized."

Why couldn't they have put him next to someone else?

* * *

The words of the presenter before Ben were a drone of fish sounds accompanied by a litany of Greek symbols. Applause constricted his veins.

Sally poked him in the shoulder. "You're next!" she whispered. "You need to get ready!"

He was next, and he'd almost missed it, lost in thought.

He stood woodenly and walked toward the stage, fumbling before the stairs as he realized he had to wait for the questioning period.

The stage lights were so bright they lit up clouds of dust.

Ben soon found himself before a crowd of two hundred. He clutched the presentation remote with shaking hands. He fought the urge to click to the end.

He'd done this before, but never with the knowledge that his rival was out there in the audience.

As he stepped back into the familiar territory of his work, however, the hidden depths excited him and took over. With deft hand and tongue he enumerated the merits and profound implications of years of hard work.

Unlike the visions of the monsters, this time people would believe him.

The nature of reality wasn't as many supposed.

He finished, his tongue numb.

Applause spread like an earthquake. Questions came, some being easy ones he had heard of before, or had already spent much time thinking about, others being ones he's not thought of and had to handle right there and then.

A woman in the front row asked a question, and Ben tried and failed to squint past the spotlights to discern her features. She had a hint of irony in her voice. Ben tried not to frown as she asked a question he dreaded, one of the few that straddled the gulf between known and unknown, the faint flaws in his derivations that could make everything fall apart.

He answered her as best he could, his knees weakening.

To his surprise, she responded to his answer with grace, acknowledging the difficult nature of the question itself and the merit of Ben's work. It seemed she could see his pain as much as he felt it, and she'd backed off.

Few researchers had such a balance of intelligence and compassion.

As Ben stepped down from the stage, his eyes adjusted and he saw the woman who'd questioned him. She gathered her materials and moved from her chair toward the stage.

His breath caught. Short blonde curls circled a bright face. She had a white long-sleeved shirt beneath a light blue vest. Her long strides in dark blue slacks carried the same grace as her words had.

It took him much longer than it should have to realize the woman was Kitt Bell. His intellectual rival was more compassionate and intelligent than he'd ever imagined.

Holographic shapes lit the space beside her, words drowning in a series of flickers that Ben only noticed lighting up every feature of her animated face.

Her presentation ended before Ben realized he'd barely caught a word of it.

After Kitt Bell's talk and her responses to questions had been completed, physicists moved quickly out of the room, no doubt heading for another session of talks. Ben watched them go and was grateful for their departure. He turned to Kitt Bell and noticed she was taking her time to collect her belongings. Ben thought he saw her glance in his direction. He knew had a window here to act. To his own surprise, he did.

"Excuse me, Dr. Bell?"

"Dr. Artemit," she said with a nod.

His knowledge of her previous papers came to the rescue from some recess of his mind. "I am intrigued by your use of closed, time-like loops to explain metastability in dark matter clusters," he said. "Would you have time for coffee, to talk more about this, or—" he glanced down at his watch, "—perhaps dinner?"

Ben couldn't be sure if he only imagined her eyes twinkling.

"I've actually got a few more questions about the implications of your many-universes. So yes."

* * *

It was only much later, when they'd ordered wine in the Marriott's restaurant and they had several uninterrupted moments to discuss research that Ben's chest relaxed and his tongue loosened.

He would have never thought the day would have turned out like this.

"You believe, Ben, that it is possible to send meaningful information—perhaps physical matter—into the past?" Kitt Bell asked.

"Indeed I do."

"But you don't believe you can change the past?" she said.

"Correct. Because—"

"—Whatever you send to the past leaves our universe and goes to a different one."

"Which cannot affect *our* past," Ben finished. It was refreshing to discuss the philosophical implications of the research. Usually conferences were mired with the minutia of calculations and field equations, drying out the succulent and profound conclusions their work had on the nature of the universe.

Kitt sipped her drink, set it down, then sighed. "It seems that we'll be stuck with our theories until someone builds a system capable of achieving such high energy densities. Until someone gets the funding for it, I should say."

Ben pursed his lips, unable to resist the urge to share his pet discoveries with her. "Well, I've heard there might be a facility starting to build the lab needed for it." He scratched his cheek and looked around conspiratorially.

Kitt's eyes widened and she leaned forward. "Are you kidding? I haven't heard of anything."

Ben smiled, enjoying the few moments to tease her curiosity. "Private corporation. They're keeping a pretty tight lid on it."

Kitt's brow furrowed. "Who? And how do you know this?"

Ben shrugged. "My mother used to work for them. She still talks to some of her friends there."

"Who?!" Kitt's hands rose off the table.

"Quantix," Ben said, then took a sip of his drink.

Kitt sat back and shook her head. "I don't doubt it, but I don't think we'll ever get access. They don't let anyone in there. Hardly even Canada's own citizens."

Ben swallowed and let out a long breath. "I know. My Ph.D. supervisor recently told me that the guy who's in charge of it—Al Turen—is a real piece of work. 'Young upstart', he said, even though he's our age." He laughed, then caught himself. He swallowed, hoping he hadn't offended Kitt by being presumptuous about her age.

To his relief, she didn't bat an eye. "Do you know much about the setup?"

Ben found his tongue again, and told her all he knew. She uttered a few "Wows" in response, and he let slip that he'd already gotten one of his students writing a proposal for some early diagnostic characterization, should any of the development become available to outside researchers.

"Your student's doing this all on her own?" Kitt asked, her high eyebrows arched.

"Sally's quite brilliant," Ben said, nodding. "I think she might not stay in this research area, and I can tell she hates being constrained by my guidance. But for the moment, she's doing this for me, and I'm grateful."

"How do you interact with difficult students?" Kitt said, leaning forward and resting her cheek on one hand. "I sometimes want to bang my head against a wall."

Ben's brow furrowed. "I'm sorry," he said. "I guess I've been blessed by mostly good students." He bit his lip, wishing he had the words or experience to comfort her. An idea struck him, and he set his drink down. Raising his finger, he said, "I think I might have something that could help, though."

He bent down unzipped his black bag, pulling out a crisp white rectangle and a long black, skinny cylinder.

Kitt raised an eyebrow. "What do you have there?"

Ben put the white rectangle on the table, letting it bend and flatten gracefully. He rolled the cylinder between his fingers. "You must've seen these before."

Kitt shook her head. "I'd heard about them, but you're the first person I've met to actually carry them around."

"Pen and paper?" Ben felt his cheeks flush. "I didn't think it was that strange."

"People actually used those?" Kitt asked.

"To write and calculate," Ben said.

Kitt frowned. "I thought they stopped making them in the 2040s or something." Her gaze alternated between Ben's eyes, the pen, and the paper. "Are you an antique collector, or what?"

"Well, I enjoy history, but I don't have a curated collection at home, if that's what you mean. History does have a lot to teach us, though."

"You seem like you've got something specific in mind. Come on, out with it."

"Well," Ben said, "your university probably has a closed intranet, right? The same as mine, and even Quantix, where only authorized people can use it, in specific ways?"

"Of course," Kitt said. "I'm in a book club that even has one."

"Right. But it's really small, close-knit, and regulated, correct? Well, it wasn't always like that. There used to be a world-wide Internet."

Kitt squinted, as though trying to recall a distant memory. "I think my great-grandma spoke about that once, but I was pretty little, and didn't understand much of it. I never thought when she said Internet that it meant a world-wide network. That's... that's crazy. It would be like having a world without countries, and only one government for the planet."

"Well, it was sort of like that," Ben said. "People all over the world could go on the Internet and chat and write messages and post announcements and share anything. They could even search any topic and find information pretty much immediately."

"You're kidding!" Kitt said, leaning back and rubbing her chin. "I guess that makes sense. Neat! Why would they have stopped it, then? It sounds great."

"It was, and it wasn't. It got out of hand in a few key ways. First, as with anything, there was a fair amount of criminal activity on it. Horrible things. Torture. Then there were other crimes that couldn't be fought."

"I doubt that," Kitt said. "What kind of crime can't be fought?"

"The worst two kinds were the invasions of privacy, and fake news. It got to the point where anything you did on the Internet could be tracked, and it was always for really invasive purposes. Companies paid top-dollar for access to deep personal data on everyone using the Internet, which was, well, everyone. They could change the experience anyone had, and effectively make everyone see a different reality through the Internet."

"But surely people would notice, wouldn't they? That the things they were finding on the Internet were different from each other?"

"They noticed, but they formed camps, divisions, and each claimed that what they saw was true, and that the other was fake. It got to the point where no one could agree on an objective reality anymore."

"Woah."

"There were huge international interests that would sway entire populations with fake news, and with such giants behind it all, there was ultimately no way to tell what was fake and what was real."

Kitt looked down. "I never would have anticipated that... from a global Internet. I can see now how that would be almost impossible to police."

"Exactly. In the end, the only way out was to break it apart into the small, tightly-controlled intranets we have now. Of course, there are still pirate groups trying to rebuild the world-wide Internet, but the authorities clamp down on them pretty hard."

Kitt smirked. "It seems you're not just a physics professor, but a history one as well. I bet you have a ton of antiques at home. Do you need to hire a curator, or do you still do it yourself?"

Ben bit his lip. Maybe he'd gone on too long. "Oh, quiet. I just keep antiques that I can still use—history lessons we can still learn from."

Kitt raised her eyebrows. "So can you actually use those?" She pointed to the paper and pen.

Ben felt the heat return to his face. She was going to think him crazy if he didn't demonstrate tangible evidence soon. "You bet. I do some of my calculations with them."

Kitt's mouth worked for a few seconds, then she shook her head. "Why?"

"The symbols are made by *me*, not by some computer. They grow into richer and fuller forms. *I* make them grow." Ben straightened, the corners of his mouth lifting.

"And... when you're done?" she asked.

She cut Ben off before he could answer. Her eyes opened and closed slowly as though she imagined the motions. "You copy them into your computer, then buy more paper? Or can you reuse the paper?"

"I can remove the ink, and keep using the paper over and over."

Kitt put a finger on the paper, brushing her skin delicately across the surface. "Show me," she said.

Ben held his breath before speaking. "It's...probably easier if I sit beside you."

Kitt patted the seat next to her, and he moved around to join her. He slid the paper in front of them while Kitt pushed her wine glass to the side. He drew a line on the page, and an arrow pointing up the line. He wrote *2 p.m.* at the top and *1 p.m.* at the bottom. Then he drew a dashed arrow in a semicircle from *2 p.m.* to *1 p.m.*

"Wait," Kitt said. She reached for the pen, searching Ben's eyes for the answer to her unspoken request. He nodded.

She took it from his hand, her fingers grazing his own. She wrapped her fingers around the pen and closed her thumb around them. She tried to write with it, but the lines looked clumsy. She lifted the pen from the paper, tilted her head and laughed. She leaned and extended the pen reverently back to Ben.

Ben breathed in the apple scent of her hair, and felt a tremble threaten to take his fingers. He knit his eyebrows together.

"Please go on," she encouraged. "Do you do this with your students?"

Ben nodded, letting out a long breath. She'd guessed the purpose to this whole exercise, and hadn't thought him crazy for carrying around clunky anachronisms. "I do. I find it helps flesh out ideas, and allow contribution from both sides. I have a larger canvas in my office where I can draw and derive. I've always found it less distant than digital media."

"All right, Professor," Kitt said with a smirk, "show me your experiment on paper."

Ben bit his lip, feeling her intelligent eyes watching his every move. He fumbled for words, as though his thoughts had to pass through molasses before being spoken. "Suppose... we have a machine that can send a message to the past, from 2 p.m. to 1 p.m. We make the machine send a signal to itself, but at the earlier time. That's what I'm indicating here by this dashed curve. Let's have this machine hooked up to a computer. We tell the computer *not* to send a signal out at 2 p.m., if it *does* receive the signal at 1 p.m. We also instruct the computer to send out the message at 2 p.m., if it receives nothing at 1 p.m. Therefore, if a message arrives at 1 p.m., nothing is sent out at 2 p.m."

"Right," Kitt said. "The seemingly-paradoxical case. Turen's system will finally be able to carry out this experiment. That's where we disagree, Ben: where did the signal come from?"

"Exactly," Ben said, downing his drink. Social lubricant slid down his throat, and he let out a satisfied breath. "My answer is that it came from another universe. From one of the infinitely many universes in the many worlds interpretation of quantum mechanics.

"Here, let me draw what happens at 1 p.m." He drew a line running up the paper from the bottom, and then two forks, one going up to the left, the other to the right, so it looked like a capital Y. "At 1 p.m., there are two possibilities: either the signal is detected or it is not. That's when the universe splits into two. Going up to the left is the universe where the signal was detected,"—he drew a wiggle on the left line—"and up to the right is the universe where it is not. Then at 2 p.m. the universe on the right, having not received a signal, sends one into the past, and—"

"—and that signal goes back to 1 p.m. and is detected in the universe on the left. Nice!"

"So there is no paradox. The universe splits into two universes at 1 p.m. In one universe the signal is not detected at 1 p.m. and thus sends one out at 2 p.m."

Kitt nodded. "And in the other a signal is detected at 1 p.m. and no signal goes out at 2 p.m."

"Therefore, the signal sent out at 2 p.m. goes to the other universe, where it is detected at 1 p.m. And this splitting into two universes is the idea behind the many universes interpretation of quantum mechanics."

"You mean the multiverse," Kitt said.

"No!" Ben said, a bit louder than he'd intended. His cheeks flushed, and he slowly smiled. "I never call it that. Sounds to me like a bunch of verses, some type of poetry."

"I'm sad you don't think there's anything poetic in all this," Kitt said, looking into her glass.

"That's not it. You must know what I mean."

Kitt smirked, but was silent.

Ben thought of all the additional subtleties hidden in the example he'd drawn, but worried that Kitt had already humoured him up to this point. It didn't seem that way, but he'd only just met her. Reluctantly, he got up and moved back to his side of the table.

Kitt took a sip of her drink. "You're not the first to suggest this, Ben, but I have to admit the proofs in your articles are the most compelling I've seen."

"Thank you," Ben said, struggling with his own pride. He had a hard time speaking, and stuttered as he said, "Yours is as well, Dr. Bell."

Kitt flashed a smile. "Just Kitt." She paused, then returned her gaze to the paper. "So this really helps create a stronger link with your students? Sally obviously understands the more complex aspects of the experimental setup. You communicate this to each other as well?"

"Yes," Ben said. "It works quite nicely."

"What do your students think about the splitting of the universes? Do they agree with your *misguided* thinking?" She grinned sardonically.

Ben blushed. "They agree that the most likely theoretical explanation is that the instant the signal is received, the universe splits into two."

Kitt sighed. "One where the signal is received, another where it isn't."

"Our two universes, Kitt."

Kitt shook her head. "I think there might be another 'universe', Ben." She leaned back in her chair. "One that says none of this is possible."

Ben cocked an eyebrow. "The universe of your work, I'm guessing? That says it can't be done?"

"That's the one."

Ben saw her gaze harden beneath the hint of playfulness that had been masking it before. There was a need there, the same need he knew he'd developed in himself through years of hard work on a project that demanded the utmost mental devotion. It was as much an exercise of faith as going to Church. Her eyes burned with it, and Ben wondered if she'd become more attached to her work than he had.

Ben felt a sudden pang in his chest. He and Kitt seemed to be kindred spirits, but their diverging theories could drive a piton between them, cracking the foundation in a spreading web of fissures. He wondered how he could maintain a professional relationship—or any other kind—without their work ultimately serving as a demarcation.

Maybe Ben should steer clear of any experiment— pretend Al Turen's machine didn't exist, or that he would never let them in. But on some level that would cheat his curiosity, do the greatest disservice to his devotion to truth. He wanted to say he could deny Al Turen if the man walked into the restaurant at this instant, but knew he wouldn't.

Relax, Ben, he told himself. *You've only just met her.*

Ben tried, unsuccessfully, to steer the conversation away

from research discussion. He wasn't much good at small talk, though, the mundane nature of weather-speak drying up his spirits as though they were a puddle beneath a Saharan sun. Kitt gave him a few querying looks, and smoothly brought them back to more comfortable topics. Ben discovered another small comfort: that at least he and Kitt agreed on the fact that the observation could only be considered to have been made if a conscious observer saw or experienced the results. In any potential future test, it could not be done by machine. The experiments would require a blood-fed neural network to collapse the wave function of quantal probabilities into tangible evidence.

Kitt had begun the evening friendly and compassionate, which Ben guessed must have been her regular demeanor. As the evening had progressed, she had leaned in more closely, laughed a bit more easily, and let the muscles of her shoulders relax. Ben suppressed thoughts of work and found himself letting go, too.

After they said goodnight, Ben walked through the dimly-lit halls to his room. Never in his life had so much time passed in a social situation without utterly exhausting him. There was new warmth inside him as though Kitt had left a part of herself with him as a soul souvenir.

He didn't sleep much that night. He wondered when he would see Kitt again. They worked at universities on opposite coasts of the country. Would he only ever see her at conferences, assuming they both attended the same ones?

Worse, he was plagued by thoughts of a future experiment which could separate them even more, and extinguish what little fire they'd nurtured.

CHAPTER SEVEN

Entangled

The bruiser-man entered the concrete workroom carrying two transparent basins. Although he and Allan probably now had similar bulk, Allan was still chilled whenever the bruiser-man was around.

Allan sat in a hard chair at a large metal table in the centre of the room.

The bruiser-man set the basins down, one next to the other, at the far end of the table. A single white mouse scurried about in each of them.

The ice queen stepped in and stayed near the door with her tablet. She and Allan hadn't spoken to each other much recently, though Allan knew she took her turn with the remote even when she seemed to be there only for observational purposes.

His captors' questions could come at any time, and Allan scanned the mice while searching his mind for everything he knew about them.

Mus Musculus, small mammal of the order Rodentia, bred and kept for scientific research. Most laboratory strains are inbred. Their high homology with humans, their ease of maintenance and handling, and their high reproduction rate, make mice particularly suitable models for human-oriented research.

The white fur of these mice along with the red eyes are among the most widely used inbred laboratory strains in the world.

The bruiser-man chuckled, walking around and leaning on the side of the table adjacent to Allan. He cast a sidelong glance at the ice queen, then nodded toward the containers with the two mice. "Keep looking, Gerrold. Look closer if you have to. Tell us how these mice differ."

Allan pressed his face against the plastic container, viewing the creatures from all angles. He wasn't sure how much variation there was from one mouse to another. "Mice are mice, aren't they? These two look pretty similar to me." He wanted to say, *Plus I've never cared much about mice until now,* but knew that led on a path away from the pleasure fix.

"Find a difference," the bruiser-man said, leaning closer and sneering.

Allan furrowed his brow. "Can I pick them up?"

"Go right ahead."

Allan gingerly took the lid off one of the containers and cradled the mouse inside. As he did so, the other mouse reacted as though Allan had grabbed it, too. The one in his hands squirmed this way and that, so it took much longer than Allan would have liked to assess every spec of its body. The brilliant red eyes were uniform. The clean white fur was spotless, the tail a peachy pink. All five claws were accounted for on each paw.

It was the same case for the other mouse. Eventually Allan held a rodent in each hand, flipping them from one side to the other to compare.

No difference. Allan put one of the mice back in the container, watching it carefully.

He touched the nose of one mouse, and it twitched away from him. The other mouse in the other container reacted the same way despite Allan not touching it.

Allan fingered one of the mouse's paws; it jerked and twisted its arm out of reach. The other mouse made the same movements in its container.

Their motions were disturbingly similar, if not identical to one another, as though they were mirroring each other. It was too strange to be true, yet Allan could find nothing to distinguish one mouse from the other.

He admitted he might no longer be in a position to judge strange from not. Was he just blind to their differences because he was a different species?

Allan twitched, readying for the pain. He set the other mouse back in the empty container. He hated admitting failure. He closed his eyes. "There... is no difference between these mice."

The ice queen tapped her tablet, while the bruiser-man bent and picked a mouse up, holding it in the light.

"They are, in many ways, identical. This one is the original. The other one is the copy."

Allan swallowed. "How can you tell?" His mind burned for the answer, the knowledge that would guarantee him a carrot.

"Tracers. Otherwise we'd never know."

The bruiser-man grabbed the mouse's container and walked to the far corner of the room. A moment later, the lights in that half of the room shut off.

"Are they genetically inbred to be nearly identical? Are they clones?" Allan asked, mind racing.

"No. And no. Better." The bruiser-man fell silent.

Allan couldn't make out his expression in the dim corner.

"Explain, Gerrold. We've trained you to be better."

"What is the copy, if not a clone?" Allan asked.

The ice queen spoke for the first time. "Think of a level beyond cloning."

Allan opened his mouth, but the bruiser-man cut him off. "Watch what happens." He dropped the mouse—the original one—into the container, watched it scramble to right itself, then readied a flashlight to shine at the helpless creature.

"Watch what the copied mouse does when the light is turned on."

He clicked the light on. The copied mouse jumped back, cowering and covering its eyes in the exact same way the original mouse did.

The bruiser-man repeated the process three more times, whether for Allan's benefit or out of some sadistic pleasure was unclear. Each time, both mice recoiled at the same instant.

The bruiser-man then switched the mice, taking the copied one into the dark corner. He flashed it with the light, and again, both mice jerked in response to the sudden burst of light.

"They're coupled," Allan said, probing for the answer as he stood and paced between the two mouse containers. "You're feeding the inputs from one to the other... and you can change which one is the source."

The ice queen held up the remote, her finger hovering over the red button. Allan's gaze shot over, a sixth sense that could trigger from miles away. The ice queen waited an excruciating few seconds while Allan shrank. Then she pressed the button.

Allan screamed, his flesh lighting on fire, his eyeballs tugging at their sockets. A moment later, the pain stopped and he was panting on the floor.

"No," the ice queen said.

He steadied his breaths, regaining full awareness. Was that a hint of irony in her voice? Allan studied her as he got up. Her back was straight and she held her head high. Her eyes bore a hole through Allan, as though she could see where the remote had tried to sear into his heart.

"Think, Gerrold. You know the answer."

Allan's thoughts ran. Maybe the mice had been raised together, given the same inputs for so long, that they started to mimic each other's behaviour. No—experiments with twins had long ago proven such ideas to be nonsense. Whatever bound the two mice together was much more than that.

Maybe they had implants that transmitted or shared electrical signals between the two brains. It was possible, but seemed unlikely that either mouse could continue functioning if that were the case.

Maybe their fates were entwined in a deep way; perhaps their quantum states were somehow closely related to one another.

That would require manipulation of particles and quantum mechanics at a fundamental level.

If his captors had achieved something like that, then they would have terrifying power. Allan refused to admit that, because it would usher in a litany of other dark possibilities.

"They are coupled electrically," Allan said at last, closing his eyes and awaiting the next jolt of pain.

"They are not coupled, Dr. Gerrold," the ice queen said, folding her arms across her chest and taking slow steps toward him. "They are entangled."

She paused, as though she knew Allan's mind well enough to see as a series of lightbulbs ignited in his thoughts.

"They're entwined, caught or twisted together?" Allan asked.

"Far more than that," the ice queen replied. "They are quantum entangled." She paused, then added, "You know all about Quantum Molecules. Such a disappointment you couldn't figure this out."

Her words drove into his psyche. The notion had been lingering on the edge of thought, but he'd retreated from it.

"Do you remember what quantum entanglement means, Dr. Gerrold?"

Allan rubbed his temples. "When groups of particles interact so that the quantum state of each particle can't be described independently."

The ice queen nodded. "Good. And how do such entangled particles behave?"

"As one particle. They share a single quantum state." Allan didn't want to think about where this train of thought led.

"No, Gerrold. You're almost, but not quite correct. They do share a single quantum state, but they are not a single particle. The two-particle quantum entangled state cannot be thought of as one particle. It is a different entity. It cannot be thought of as two single-particle states. You cannot affect one without affecting the other, no matter how far away the two parts are, although we should not really say 'two parts' because there are not two. There is only *one*, but it is *one* two-particle state.

"Every particle in the two bodies is entwined such that whatever happens to one affects the other. In a very real sense, the two bodies are a single unit that can no longer be broken apart. They move together, smell together—"

"What do they see?" Allan interrupted. He ached for these mice, wondering if their existence was plagued by confusing sensory information.

"That's a good question, but something we've yet been unable to determine," the ice queen said, her tone suggesting they might soon have the answer.

Allan shivered. Maybe he shouldn't have asked. Did the mice see a blurred image where the views from two sets of eyes were superimposed? No, that wasn't important; he was skirting the real question plaguing him.

"Why are you interested in entanglement?"

The ice queen and the bruiser-man looked at one another. The bruiser-man folded his arms and smirked. The ice queen scanned her tablet.

Every second that went by, Allan's thoughts raced through all the possibilities.

Did they want entanglement so they could send one body out to do horrible things, blackmailing it to carry out evil while the other body was back in the lab under threat? That seemed possible, but there were other, simpler ways to blackmail someone. Was it so they could torture multiple patients simultaneously without the cost of more than one set of equipment? Again, it was possible, but it was a lot of trouble to go to in an effort to cut costs.

Would entanglement remove free will altogether, wherein the two bodies would explore mutually exclusive outcomes to every decision?

"Entanglement holds incredible potential," the ice queen said at last.

That's not an answer, Allan thought.

"There were differences between the two mice, you know," the ice queen continued. "Because you can't copy the quantum state of one system to another identical system. The differences are too hard to perceive though, so we use the tracers my colleague mentioned. We didn't want you to worry about this, but merely be informed.

"Dr. Gerrold, we didn't spend all this time preparing you only to torment you with extreme quantum states. You're much too important for that."

But not, Allan thought, *too important to be tortured by other means.*

"The procedure takes a degree of mental... ingenuity... to endure. The reason we showed you the mice is so you can prepare yourself for what's about to happen. You will be the most advanced human being on the planet once the procedure's done. You will be the most intelligent and capable multi-tasker, if anyone can truly claim to multi-task. Your greatness will be multiplied, replicated so the world can benefit twice over from your many talents.

"What we offer is an incredible gift," the ice queen continued, spreading her arms. "But it won't come easily."

There was too much to say, far too much to ask, and the notions all jockeyed for position at the tip of Allan's tongue.

"So what you need to—"

"What if I don't want it?" Allan asked. "What if I don't want the gift? Surely someone else wants it more than I do?"

"Well, Dr. Gerrold," the ice queen said in a syrupy-smooth voice, "if you really didn't want it, we'd have to reconsider your regular doses of...this." She tapped the remote with her index finger.

The ice queen looked at Allan with her head tilted, then motioned to her tablet. "I've sent you recommendations for how to mentally prepare yourself. I suggest you follow them.

"Get some rest tonight, Dr. Gerrold. Tomorrow is a big day."

* * *

Allan paced in one half of a room, separated by plexiglass from another body. The chest rose and fell as it breathed. Allan could almost hear its heart beating.

Every heartbeat felt as though it might be the last.

That body was the *other*.

He'd have to open a rift for this...thing within himself, lest he be torn to pieces.

The body sat naked on a hospital bed, clean white linen draping over the sides much like how Allan imagined his sanity was seeping out his ears. Thick plastic conduit housing countless cables ran between it and a similar bed on Allan's side of the plexiglass.

On the other side, the bruiser-man and the ice queen moved with casual familiarity and near-ritual about the space, wearing masks and white clean-room suits. They opened seamless cabinets in the walls, turning dials before re-sealing them.

Goose flesh twisted up Allan's spine as he caught sight of a log display on one of the monitors.

The bruiser-man and the ice queen had done this before. And they'd never shown or talked about any evidence of success.

This realization still wasn't as horrifying as gazing through a window at his own fragile mortality.

It was an out-of-body experience, staring at the minor

bumps and curves of his arms on another body, the blackheads on his face, the wrinkles and notches that shaped individuality from a universal figure into an identity.

That identity had been stripped and laid bare.

The bruiser-man and ice queen had instructed Allan to inspect the body with great care. Familiarity, they said, would encourage the mind to accept the process.

It was like asking someone to swallow boiling water.

Allan didn't ask them where or how they had created Frankenstein's version of himself.

He wondered if smelling it might help. There was a plastic tang in the air, and Allan couldn't tell if that was from all the tubing and protective coverings, or from this copied body. His instincts were wrong though, because he knew the body was organic.

A level beyond cloning.

Though the lines of his experience were reproduced with terrifying accuracy on the body, there was nevertheless an unblemished quality to it, a sense that the thing had never walked a step in its life, nor glimpsed a sunrise.

Thank God its eyes were closed.

If the creature had been even mildly sentient, Allan might have lost the fragile grip on reality he still had.

Looking at his other body made him hyper-aware of every movement and sensation in his own body, as if it all might suddenly forget how to function. Compared to that, it would be psychological rapture to stare into a set of his own, independently moving eyes.

Allan shot a glance at the metal door barring any escape.

He heard the ice queen's nails tapping on the remote.

Please no. Use the remote as much as you like, just don't make me do this.

"Lay down," the bruiser-man said, startling Allan. He stood right beside him, grabbing him by the shoulders.

Allan fought to free himself, but then two other men rushed in and forced him onto the bed. They took off his gown, until he was as naked as the body on the other side of the plexiglass.

Rings clamped, then tightened around Allan's hands and feet. A smooth cup supported the base of his skull. Soft but firm material emerged from the cup, slid around his head, and held it fixed. Several curved slabs moved toward and enclosed his head.

The two assistants retreated, while the bruiser-man remained watching Allan with arms crossed.

"Please try and relax, Dr. Gerrold," the ice queen said through a speaker. "This will be far less painful that way. In one minute, we are going to scan and determine the state of your brain. The quantum state, of course. A similar array of transmitters is now positioned around your other brain."

My other brain, Allan thought. He swallowed thickly, trying to suppress a tremor at the notion that the thing on the other table belonged to *him.*

"The information from the scan will be copied into your second body," the ice queen continued. "The state of the second brain will be a duplicate of yours."

The bruiser-man moved toward Allan. He lowered his grinning face close to Allan, who stared back at him through a gap between the slabs. "And then, Gerrold, you know what comes next, don't you?"

Allan said nothing, refusing to give voice to a reality that shouldn't be.

For once, the bruiser-man didn't need his booming voice, and whispered instead. "We will link the two brains together.

"There's also another matter about the procedure, Gerrold," he went on. "You might not be capable of surviving it."

The room darkened as though a box lid had been slammed shut. Allan's pulse quickened.

Maybe this was all just a trick. A psychological game, a torture equivalent to another button on the ice queen's remote.

At some point she would release the button and explain what Allan needed to do next to avoid the torture.

"I've done everything you've asked of me," he whimpered, flexing against the restraints. "Why are you doing this to me?"

In response, a low hum quaked through the slabs around his head. Thousands of long, sharp needles stabbed through into his head, and he screamed, only feeling a peripheral sense of how deep they were going. A few bright flashes ignited his vision.

His breathing felt more distant than he'd ever experienced. His consciousness receded. He dug deep to try and coax it back, assert his place in the world while remaining open to the thing that was being quantum mechanically welded to his soul.

He drew his attention to the thousand needles until acceptance washed over him like a cool breeze. There was nothing he could do to stop things, and the new reality would come with or without him. Futile wisps of effort surged against the notions, gradually diminishing as Allan massaged them. *Over and through*, he told himself. *Over and through.*

The pain rose, ringing his ears, burning his tongue, searing his retina. His body felt distant but the pain remained.

Everything Allan knew about himself cracked underfoot. He was falling into the void.

Everything stopped. Silence. A siren wail of lingering pain. A buzzing inside and around.

The sensory pads moved away. Allan was dimly aware of his own body again. Then three things happened.

Allan opened his eyes and saw the room around him.

He opened his other eyes and saw the room around the other him.

And, to his horror, Allan was in both bodies. The bright white lights shone through two pairs of eyes. The buzzing resonated through all four ears. He was simultaneously aware of the perceptions and thoughts in both brains and bodies. Yet he was a single entity, a single Allan, with one mind.

CHAPTER EIGHT

The Template I

T oday was the day. The experiment of Ben's and Kitt's lives would finally happen, two years after they'd met and wondered who was right.

Ben and Kitt had both developed their theories more fully during their professorships at universities on opposite coasts. They had met many times at conferences, however, and had enjoyed dinners and discussions enhancing each other's work. Eventually they'd begun planning their travel so they could spend more time together as friends. Ben found it hard to imagine how he'd ever thought of Kitt as his intellectual rival as they grew so close.

They'd managed to grow their budding friendship in spite of the mutual exclusivity of both their theories, mainly because there'd been no way to test their proposals. He and Kitt could treat each other's theories intellectually without having to try to hold them both under the light of reality.

After a massive, nation-wide shift in university structure and funding put all of their future research in jeopardy, both Ben and Kitt had taken buyout packages and landed positions at Quantix, one of the only private companies doing fundamental quantum research.

Quantix had the funding and vision to actualize the

laboratory setups needed to put both Ben's and Kitt's theories to test.

Today was that day.

A small part of Ben was excited to finally see if he was right, but mostly he was filled with dread over the inevitable clash with Kitt.

The Quantix cafeteria was barren, as Ben had come to expect at 5:30 in the morning, and he wiped his hand over his face like a wet rag. He headed toward the usual spot: the far corner with a wall on one side and a window on the other, so he could be in shade but still watch the glow of sunrise on all around.

He stopped and stared—someone was in his seat. He was so tired he didn't recognize her at first.

"Ben?" Kitt's voice was quiet and hoarse. Dark circles hung below her eyes.

Ben coughed several times before formulating words. "Morning, Kitt."

She gestured and he took a seat beside her.

"Best seat in the house," he said.

Kitt smiled, despite every other clue on her body indicating the opposite emotion.

Even when she's stressed to the brink, he thought.

She rubbed her forehead. "I couldn't sleep."

"I barely did."

Kitt's notebook on the table had a bunch of scribbled calculations, repetitions of the work Kitt had derived many times over. Ben felt a pang of guilt for wanting to escape, go bury his head like an ostrich until the day was over.

Kitt hadn't slept out of worry over the experiment's outcome. Ben thoughts centred on what it would be like with Kitt afterward; experiments be damned. His gut felt like it had been put in the cafeteria's dough mixer, rhythmic clenching in his core.

"Whatever happens," he said, sliding his hand toward her, "life will continue on."

Eyes closed and hands steepled in front of herself, Kitt nodded.

"Whatever is right, whatever is wrong, doesn't detract from the value of our research," Ben continued. "Your work, and mine, is why we're here today."

Kitt opened her eyes and gazed ahead, out the window at the rising warmth of the land, the coming experiments, or both.

"Thanks, Ben," she said. The words seemed like a faraway broadcast.

Ben frowned at his hands. He could hardly blame her. It was all much easier said than done. In fact, it was probably easier to do the experiment than it would be to deal with the results.

*　*　*

Dressed in a hairnet, booties, and one-piece cleanroom coveralls, Ben stared at the gleaming reflections off the large spherical Jupiter chamber. Other technicians milled about, doing far more useful things than he could at this point. They knew the equipment much better.

From what Ben understood, these techs were only allowed to observe as much of the experiment as necessary to repair things if and when experimentalists—or theorists like Ben—broke them.

Usually Ben was content to let the techs do their business, but this time he wanted to join them, grab a wrench —do whatever was required, then go into the back room until he was called upon again.

If his theory was right, Kitt would be shattered. If his theory was wrong, his own work would be destroyed, regardless of what he had tried to sell Kitt earlier.

"Time to clear out, Ben," Al Turen said, surprising him from behind as he clasped his shoulder. "You're lucky I got you in here, but don't overstay your welcome."

Al Turen, the lead experimental scientist who'd rallied the funding and built the necessary labs from the ground up, had a lot to be proud of, but Ben had never seen anyone flaunt it so brazenly. He'd deliberately gotten both Ben and Kitt involved, eager to see one of them fail.

Ben didn't turn to look at Turen. Instead he stole one last look at the antimatter stasis chamber—the time machine—with instrument barrels protruding at odd angles like needles from a pincushion. He wondered if they'd forgotten something, overlooked a possible metric that would prove indispensable to the completeness of their results. He'd probably annoyed all the technicians with his probing of their probes, asking for increasingly unreasonable performance specifications until they were ready to throw him in the chamber so he could watch with his own eyes. But there weren't enough instruments in the world to assuage the anxiety toward external validation.

Another squeeze on his shoulder, and Ben followed Turen out. A recording played the lockout warnings over speakers, warning that in another minute the experiment would start. After that, the entire room beyond the concrete walls would be bathed in radiation generated by the experiment, cooking everything within.

* * *

This wasn't the first time Ben had met Al Turen.

About six years ago, Ben had been visiting the University of California at San Diego, Turen's old university, for an annual conference by the American Physical Society. It was there he'd met Sally Burton, the woman who would later become Ben's student.

At the time, however, she'd worked for Turen, who didn't do theoretical work, although he knew enough to understand it.

Sally had confided in Ben that she'd done a calculation against Turen's wishes because she found the attraction too great to resist. She'd worked secretly, believing Turen would be so impressed he would allow the analysis for her dissertation. She was only fifteen.

The last morning of the conference, Sally had gone in and waited until her supervisor arrived. Ben, haggard after two days of stimulation, was combing the hallways in search of the meeting room, a bit down the hall from Turen's office.

"Professor Turen?" she said, in a small voice. Ben turned and saw Sally's popular rainbow hairdo, going from red at her forehead, through all the colours, ending with blue and indigo at the base of her neck.

"Sally?" Turen said.

Sally stepped into Turen's office, leaving the door open enough that Ben could see them both. He watched quietly, curious how her project would be received.

"What is it?" Turen asked.

"I solved the problem. Here, I wrote a summary for you."

Turen took her tablet, then grumbled and muttered.

"I told you not to work on this!" Turen yelled suddenly.

"But I have—"

"You've wasted your time! Do you want to get your Ph.D. or not? Keep this up and you're finished."

Turen tossed her work into the garbage.

"Out!" he screamed, standing and pointing to the doorway.

Sally moved away, but Turen closed in until their noses almost touched. They were both exactly five feet tall.

"Do the work I assigned you. Or quit."

She backed out of his office. He slammed the door shut.

Sally cried as she ran away from Turen's office and out of the building.

Three years later, she became Ben's student.

In the meantime, Al Turen had published the work she

QUANTUM WORLDS AND THE ENTANGLED MAN

had done. He hadn't included her name on the paper, hadn't even mentioned her in his acknowledgements.

From what Ben had heard, Turen had done much worse to other students.

It was therefore with trepidation that Ben had agreed to meet Turen about some possible experimental work for Quantix.

He tried not to think of how much could go wrong, even if all the experiments went right.

To Ben's shock and dismay, Kitt Bell was in Turen's office the day their experimental proposals had been accepted. Ben knew both he and Kitt had submitted experimental proposals to Turen, but they'd intentionally tried to keep them separate.

Turen clearly had other plans.

Turen smiled at them, wrinkles on his face overemphasized by the shadows in the room, a receding hairline making his head look bigger than it was. He watched them squirm for a full minute.

"Welcome," Turen had finally said, dragging out the word. "I've gone through each of your proposals, and decided your work should be combined. It's also necessary to clarify a few important aspects often overlooked when theoreticians make the important step into the real world."

For the first time, Ben wished that he and Kitt hadn't followed the same path to Quantix. As wonderful as it was to work in the same building as her, this experiment could destroy everything they had.

"The Jupiter chamber will be required for the amount of data you hope to transmit," Turen continued. "You're getting access to the best facility in the world—do you know how lucky you are?

"So far we've only done calibrations and diagnostics to get the technology proven and reliable. I wanted both of you here for the first experiments, because your proposals embody the two possible outcomes. Kitt, in the camp saying time travel isn't possible, and Ben that it is."

Turen outlined the details of the experimental setup, treating Ben and Kitt as though they were subordinates rather than his intellectual equals. The experiments would be done manually at first with all three of them present, then automated for statistical rigor.

Turen had gone to the trouble of wiring a large red light to the input, so that if a signal were detected the room would be swathed in red like a mad scientist's lab.

Ben had gotten the impression that Turen was a man of show, and that it was a big part of how and why he got so much funding for his experiments. Ben's body was tight by the end of the presentation, his tongue bitten in a dozen places.

"This is going to make history," Turen had finished.

* * *

At the end of the countdown, only Ben, Kitt and Turen were in the lab office adjoined to the Jupiter chamber area. There were several swivel-chairs scattered around a large table, but Turen was the only one seated, twisting back and forth. In front of him sat a laptop with diagnostics, and a large, red beacon.

The beacon would light up when the time machine received a stream of photons—an alarm to signal the destruction of either Kitt's work, or Ben's.

Turen had rushed to take off his cleanroom coveralls after coming out of the experimental area, while Kitt slowly dragged herself out of them.

Ben could barely think straight, and kept his on.

Turen had decided the initial setup by a coin toss. They would do the so-called "paradox experiment" first—the one where a signal was sent back in time only if no signal was received, and no signal sent if one was received.

Turen sat barring their path so they couldn't tamper with the setup. They couldn't read the fonts on his screen, but they could see the menacing red beacon ready to blind and obliterate.

Ben stood between Turen and Kitt, protecting her as much as possible from Turen's aggressive prods. Ben kept his back to her, not wanting to see the pain on her face anymore.

The experiment was underway. There was nothing to do now but wait.

Ben would trade anything, he realized, in order to have the fate of his life's work unbound from the person most dear to him. Either he'd lose his life's work, or she'd lose hers.

As a result, they might lose each other.

A bright red flash shattered the tension in the air.

A signal had been received. *A signal through time!*

Ben jerked back. Coolness spread through his veins like a saline IV. He exhaled in a slow tide.

The signal through time been detected *before* anything had been sent into the past. Ben's eyes widened and he leaned in past Turen, staring at the screen. All he could see were the results.

Ben wasn't aware of anyone else as he spoke. "We'll now see that no signal will be sent—not by us. This means the message will have come from another world. Another universe. In that other world, the three of us did not receive the stream of photons, and so they will send a signal—a stream of photons to the time machine—the stream we all just observed." He nodded to the beacon, never letting his eyes leave it.

Kitt's high-pitched voice sounded far away, as though she were trying to shout through a waterfall. "No!"

Ben turned to see Kitt covering her mouth.

Kitt turned so Turen couldn't see her face. Her eyes glistened but she blinked back the tears. Her whole body taut.

She lowered a shaking hand and said, "This can't be happening. It's not possible. It doesn't... make sense."

"It does, Kitt," Ben whispered.

The words spilled out of him too quickly for Ben to remember where he was, who he was, and who had just lost. He'd been too focused on *his* theory, *his* work. He forced himself to look at Kitt again.

She was taking deep, slow breaths. She cleared her throat and smoothed her shirt, gaze drifting from the walls to the floor.

Every subtle avoidance, every tick struck Ben ten times as hard. His stomach tried to do somersaults in sudden revulsion at what he'd just done. His breath caught. He stared at Kitt in search of forgiveness. He moved clumsily toward her, then raised his hand with the hope there was still a window through which he could comfort her.

But Turen began speaking, and Ben's window closed.

"Ten seconds until we see whether or not the signal will be sent," Turen said.

Ben froze, and turned to see Turen smirking, drumming his fingers on the table.

"It won't be sent," Ben whispered, his whole body tensing as the competing desires struggled within him.

Kitt was silent.

They all waited.

The instant arrived.

No signal was sent.

CHAPTER NINE

The Signal Cycle

I n spite of himself and what he'd just done, Ben smiled. "We received the signal," he heard himself say, "and no signal was sent. So it must have come from a group like us... doing the same work in their own world."

Turen nodded. His snake-oil grin grew.

Kitt refused to meet his gaze.

Turen placed his bulk in front of her, finger wobbling in her face. "That pretty much settles things, don't you agree, Kitt?"

The scene in front of Ben seemed pulled from a showpiece where nothing mattered as much as the punchline, which struck him as the lens through which Turen viewed the world.

It was too much.

Ben had helped Sally, Turen's old grad student, but that was as far as his limited sphere of influence had been able to extend. Turen was now a god in the experimental world, though, and to burn a bridge with him was to walk into obsolescence.

But this was Kitt, a woman who had worked harder for everything she'd gotten precisely because she hadn't trodden over the fallen. Everywhere she went she lifted people up, often at the cost of her own progress. Her road had been long and hard, not fast and aggressive like Turen's.

Ben wished it were possible for *both* him and Kitt to be right. That would remove the chief source of Turen's pleasure —torturing the loser. It would save both him and Kitt, and most importantly, their friendship.

He closed his eyes and balled his fists, imagining such a world. He wanted to be a part of it so much his bones vibrated.

Take me there, he thought. *Take me where this can happen.*

He opened his eyes but remained distant from his immediate surroundings. He didn't want Kitt to be hurt. He rejected everything that was happening. The front of his head throbbed from his focus for that other, hopelessly contradictory world.

Then everything changed.

Turen lost his grin. The electricity in the air dissipated; the tension faded.

Everything felt better, like it had all been decided, and that everything was OK.

The tears were gone from Kitt's face, and any hint of the earlier upset had vanished. She seemed more puzzled than anything else.

Kitt turned to Ben and said, in a soft voice, "I don't understand, Ben. Why do you say we received a signal? We didn't. We all saw there was no red flash. No signal arrived. That's why one was just sent out."

Ben blinked, wondering if lack of sleep had tipped him into delirium. His jaw tightened and he stared at Kitt. What was going on? She wasn't the type to cajole him, especially in a matter so important. Yet the beatific expression on her face held no hint of any of the disappointment that had run rivulets on her cheeks just moments ago.

Kitt's words described the opposite of what had actually happened—what Ben had seen with his own eyes. He ran his tongue between trembling lips, forcing the words out. "Kitt, we *did see* the signal arrive. Just now. That's why no signal was sent."

Ben turned to Turen in silent appeal, hoping he would explain or confirm Ben's sanity.

Turen sat with a deep frown and reddened cheeks. He held a fist close to his lips. The room was still, the whirring fans of pre-conditioned cleanroom air making Ben's eyes twitch.

Turen dropped his hand and exhaled as though he'd been holding his breath. He gazed hard at Ben, then barked, "What are you talking about, Artemit? You saw a red flash? I didn't see a flash! No signal was received. That's why the Jupiter Chamber sent one out." He took a deep breath. "No signal arrived. So a signal was sent."

Ben's vision blurred and the room grew wider, as though the walls were stretching or his mind were retreating. His throat constricted.

An all-too-familiar feeling trickled in like rain through a failing roof.

He was losing his mind.

When our sensors that interact with the world prove unreliable, he thought, *reprogramming and reconditioning are necessary.*

With his childhood monsters, Ben had had more than his share of reprogramming. It had taken years to build confidence that what he observed in the world was correct. That what he saw was the *right* thing.

Ben had wanted so badly to tear out his eyes and trade them for a new pair—or not have them at all. It wasn't fair to feel things, hear things, see things no one else could. If there was a way to murder sanity, it was through constant self-doubt.

In spite of the many years since Ben's last episode with the childhood monsters, he felt the reality he had tried to maintain was a false one.

He could no longer dismiss the things he'd seen as a child.

Although he and others had spent years convincing him otherwise, the truth had been simmering beneath the surface, waiting for him to wake up.

Maybe this experiment was the chance to finally recognize and acknowledge things as they were. Maybe now, after all these years, he wouldn't have to ask someone else to know if he could trust his eyes.

His voice sounded distant as he spoke, as though he were clawing out of a pit. "We did detect the signal," Ben insisted. "Just look at the recording."

Everyone was silent as Turen navigated his way through the files and brought up each detector's evidence that no signal had been received.

Ben's knees weakened.

There was a signal, he thought, determined to ignore the stares of bewilderment from both Kitt and Turen.

Being proven wrong was regular, even expected in science. Here, though, he was being proven incapable of doing any science at all.

Ben fell, barely catching himself in a nearby chair.

His demons were back.

He may need to change the way he investigated science now, but one thing was clear: he could—he *had* to—believe himself.

Yes. They're back. The hideous, grotesque creatures he had seen and remembered and eventually convinced himself weren't real. The monsters no one else could see but him.

His therapist, Heather Smith's, words came into his mind: "Change the way you see the monsters in order to lessen their effect on the rest of your life."

That's what he'd done, but he'd done it wrong. The false world he'd tried to maintain was being assaulted by the monsters and encircled by their long, thin limbs.

All the years of training, of cognitive behavioural therapy helped him finally acknowledge that all along, his view had not been distorted.

The monsters were real.

Ben *knew* they were as real as the arrival of the photon stream. There was no doubt. It was as though Occam had come along with his razor and shaved a scruffy beard to a smooth, soft finish.

The simplest explanation was the right one: others were seeing something different. His mother hadn't remembered seeing the monsters. His father hadn't been capable of seeing them. Now Kitt and Turen didn't remember seeing the photon stream.

Just like the monsters.

Ben rubbed his arms, suddenly chilled. The monsters were really out there.

They could be coming for him *now*.

He had to figure out a way to stop them, before they caught scent of his fear, but there were too many questions to answer.

The only way to the truth, he realized, *is to play along. For now.*

And pray the monsters didn't come for him in the meantime.

Kitt and Turen agreed with each other; that much was clear. Ben opened his mouth to join their discussion when Kitt said, "No signal was received."

It was as though she and Turen had forgotten about him.

Turen nodded and said, "Nothing was detected. That's why the Jupiter Chamber sent out a signal."

Kitt frowned and shook her head. She swallowed, waiting just long enough for her characteristic politeness, then said in a firm voice, "What are you saying, Al? We did not send a signal. We observed no signal in and we sent none out. It all makes sense. Think about it. No signal in, no signal out. We set up Jupiter that way, in self-consistency mode."

Ben jerked. *"What?"* he whispered. His head throbbed.

Now Kitt's saying no signal's been sent, he thought. *A*

moment ago she said that one had *been sent. I'm on a bloody merry-go-round of choose-your-reality.*

If the simplest explanation really was that reality was influenced by perspective, then perhaps Kitt and Turen disagreed now because their perspectives were different.

Turen's voice was low, almost a growl as he spoke. "We didn't set up in the self-consistent mode, Kitt. We're in the paradox mode: Jupiter is set up to send a signal if it does not receive one."

"Let's see the data," Kitt replied. "Show them to us, Al."

Turen typed and clicked to display the results.

A signal *had* been sent.

"Show us the video recording," Ben said. "Just to be sure."

The recording agreed—a signal *had* been sent.

Ben felt a sudden urge to put his own head in the Jupiter Chamber, if only to escape the madness that was wreaking havoc on his psyche.

And Kitt's.

"So why are you saying nothing went out?" Turen asked Kitt.

She answered, calmly, "I never said that. Of course a signal was sent. No signal arrived, so a signal was sent."

Silence spread through the room, thick as molasses. Kitt seemed satisfied. Turen waited.

Ben had no idea what to do. It took great effort to stop from trembling. As much as he'd tried to entertain the notion, he couldn't accept the illogical consequences of reality depending on human observation.

It seemed that he, Kitt and Turen were somehow knitting reality, clumsily, full of mistakes and knots. That anyone could have an impact on the fabric separating what was real and unreal was far more terrifying than insanity.

Not only were they creating reality through their experiments, but they were changing it as well, and if that wasn't the last straw, it was close to it.

Ben repeated the experiment with Kitt and Turen.

The repetitions confirmed the results, but unlike any other set of experiments Ben had ever done or heard of, was consistent only in repeating the chaos.

The second experiment was the same as the first. They all saw the red flash. Ben said no signal would be sent. Kitt was lost in disbelief. The time for emitting the photon stream came, and no signal was sent. Then Kitt said that no signal had arrived. Turen agreed. Ben asked to check the recording. No signal had been detected. Kitt explained this was because they were using the self-consistent mode.

"No signal arrived, no signal was sent," she said.

Still, Turen remembered a signal had been sent. The recording was checked and a signal had indeed gone out. They agreed that no signal had been detected, and that later one was sent out.

It was the most nightmarish deja-vu Ben had ever experienced.

Over and over, backward time travel was found to occur. Kitt and Turen then remembered it had never been seen, and all the detectors confirmed it.

Ben withdrew as they did more experiments.

Kitt and Turen argued until they both remembered the same thing, until the recording was what they ended up remembering.

With each experiment, their arguing dwindled, as though they were subconsciously aware of being trapped in a cycle.

Eventually, it became routine, like most experiments with good statistics, only the routine was a ghastly doppelgänger of scientific discovery.

By the end, Ben could hardly remember what he'd wanted the outcome to be in the first place. He could hardly remember why he'd ever cared.

The final record said no signal had come in and that one had subsequently been sent out. That was also what Kitt and Turen ended up remembering.

But not Ben.

CHAPTER TEN

Awakening

Allan Gerrold lay perfectly still, overwhelmed by sensory input.

His vision flickered, a superposition of the views from two bodies. Even though the ceilings above both bodies were more or less the same, the differences were enough to paralyze him, the mosaic textures crawling across one another. The movement created a shifting perspective of near and far, of being so close to the ceiling his nose touched the tiles, and of being so far away he'd fallen through the floor.

He tried to focus and make the image stand still. No luck. He tried to pick the perspective he thought was correct; the flicker's frequency increased.

Conflicting demands stretched his attention like an elastic between two poles.

His disjointed vision felt like a space between spaces, like he occupied a lonely realm orthogonal to reality. The flicker made it impossible to identify where he was. The ceiling might have belonged to the same sterile facility they'd been keeping him in, but the sensory Venn diagram made it hard to recognize anything.

Allan wondered if he would ever walk again.

Glancing down, he felt trapped in someone else's body.

Neither body felt like his own. He recognized the features, but each seemed bound by strings restricting movement.

The soundscape held resonant echoes. Two channels switched dizzyingly back and forth. The discordant buzz of the ventilation system came through headphones attached to someone else's skull, another pair funnelling in from both sides of him. Everything arrived in mismatched pairs, repeated thrums no matter how quiet, with enough separation that every sound jarred.

Worse than everything was breathing. Each body's frantic breath rippled through the other. Inhalation was delayed, uncontrolled, like Allan passed his will through a filter. His presence had simultaneously expanded to fill the room and diminished to a dust speck. He was more, and he was less.

The air tasted both dry and wet. He'd been stripped of voice. His tongue was as close to the centre of *him* as anything else, and his voice was the speaker for his mind. If the teeth he touched, the mouth he tasted, were this far removed from him, what did he have left?

Every sensation—the smell of his sweat, the salty taste on his lips—came from the wrong place. He jerked instinctively in both bodies, rocking up and down on the beds.

If lying still was a trial, then his convulsions were apocalyptic. A tidal wave of stimulation crashed through him, electric discharges crackling their way into every corner. His frayed dendrites burned him from the inside out. He lost control.

His screams buzzed and shook through him. They came from deep inside and far away; the volume amplified in positive feedback until it was deafening. He closed his mouths until his screams died to a murmur. He squeezed both pairs of his eyes shut.

The wild, bucking animals of his bodies slowed. With two senses diminished, his bodies responded to conscious action.

Later he would wonder if this was what a fully-conscious birth would feel like.

When his bodies lay still, he automatically rotated both pairs of his ankles and squeezed his four fists open and shut. The simple, rhythmic motion allowed him to gain purchase on his mind's delay and filtering. The rhythm also eased his breathing.

He synchronized the two bodies, until he felt—very remotely—like he was inhabiting one body again.

A single thought ran through him as he calmed: *Why have they done this to me?*

He suppressed a shudder. *They must want to use me as a weapon.*

He couldn't worry about that now, though. Keeping his mouths and eyes shut, he focused on regaining control of himself. Yes, he inhabited two bodies, but he had to cling to the notion of one self—one being, one mind—or he'd lose his remaining sanity.

He started to distinguish the senses that came from the copied body, and those that came from his original.

As a child, he had played a video game where he'd controlled two characters using two joysticks, one with each hand. Moving them simultaneously across separate winding beams cantered over a precipice had been intensely frustrating, and it'd taken him days of attempts before succeeding.

This was much, much worse, but Allan remembered his technique for getting comfortable with the controls: to control each one separately, and practice switching between them faster and faster.

He tried to clenched a fist in one body. His lefts and his rights were confused, and the feedback seemed all wrong. He ended up just clenching both hands on both bodies.

It was like staring into a double mirror. If you focused your attention on the image in the second mirror, when you tried to move your head in one direction, it would move the opposite way.

Nothing moved in the direction Allan expected, and he had to keep restarting.

He clenched both left fists of his bodies, then tried to switch to one body but instead just clenched his right fists.

After many tries, he moved a single fist, though the others remained on the periphery of perception.

He raised his arms on one body, and lifted the legs on the other. He was operating a complex machine rather than his own body.

His own *bodies*. Even his thoughts needed redirection.

Breathing, unsurprisingly, proved the most difficult to control. Allan tried and failed to get the bodies to breathe asynchronously. Strange that something as instinctive as breathing was more difficult to disconnect between the two—*his* two—bodies.

He sat up slowly in both bodies, feeling the horrifying sense of distance from himself. An observer watching the two sides of him and his biological machinery.

He lay back down. *I'm still me,* he thought. *You're still you, Allan.*

He couldn't believe himself anymore, because his thoughts seemed to arrive from outside.

Please, let me keep my mind. Don't take that from me.

He focused on moving, a goal to save him from spinning thought-circles. He sat up again; the dizziness took a bit longer to arrive.

He repeated the process several times for each body.

What felt like hours later, he grew brave enough to open one set of eyes, keeping the other set closed.

My world is this white room, he thought. *But it doesn't have to be. Keep going, and get out. Master this.*

It was strange having one pair of his eyes open and the other closed at the same time. His second body's eyelids fluttered on the edge of opening.

Dark spots bubbled along the white walls. He was going

to pass out, and he snapped all his eyes shut. The spots sizzled away. He gasped, fighting to synchronize his breathing again.

Try again. From the start. I can do this.

Each sense required a different level of control. By the time Allan had opened each pair of eyes individually, both his bodies lay panting on the tables.

I can handle this, he repeated.

He sat up with both bodies, and opened both sets of eyes.

The room's shift turned his stomach. The seam where the ceiling met the walls flickered at different angles, the boundary uncertain and chaotic. The bumpy white texture on the walls and the spotted grey tiles on the ceiling crawled into each other, swirling like a convection current.

It felt like a bad drug trip. If this were caused by a pill, Allan would vomit it out and burn it and bury the ashes in the deepest hole. It wasn't a drug, though. It was his new reality.

All the boundaries of objects flickered: the bed, the door, the lights, the corners of the room. Allan's head swayed. With so many conflicting visual cues, he couldn't gauge the distance to anything.

Was something as simple as depth perception lost to him forever?

Not forever. I can do this.

He swung two pairs of legs over the sides of the beds. Four feet touched the ground. He wiggled his toes, trying to put a little weight on each foot, his inner ears swimming. One body felt like it ascended in an elevator, while the other felt like he was falling.

He fell face-first back onto his beds, groaning. Every micro-movement encoded in his basal ganglia would need reprogramming. His temples throbbed.

Maybe an aneurysm would be a blessing.

That assumed he didn't pass out from dehydration and hunger. Drinking or eating in these conditions seemed unimaginably difficult.

Breathe, he told himself, withdrawing from mental

oblivion. *Breathe, and get up. The right visual cues might make balancing easier.*

He re-opened two sets of eyes, and his heads spun. He clutched at the edges of the bed as his torsos swayed. He managed to slam both his bodies back into the mattress rather than pitching them onto the hard floor.

His inability to act sent his thoughts running, gathering worries like iron filings to a magnet.

Would his captors return? Where had they gone? Were they watching him, laughing as they shared popcorn and took notes? Or were they sleeping, dreaming of Allan's ongoing suffering?

Maybe they weren't done with him, and more horror was in store. Allan whimpered; the sound echoed in both sets of ears.

He still felt like he watched his movements through a double set of mirrors, every instinct going in the wrong direction. The more he learned and moved, the more mirrors were added, like he was in a mirror maze where the reflections stretched to infinity if he wasn't careful where he looked.

What felt like days later, Allan stood. On four feet.

Opened both sets of eyes.

He moved slowly, haltingly, and rarely in both bodies at once. He was grinding through a marathon.

The texture on the floor, when it didn't crawl with the rough white of the walls, bore the same light-grey tiles of most of the facility. It was reasonable that he was still in the same prison.

The bruiser-man and the ice queen had apparently stripped the room completely of all the cables and conduit that had been there before, and had also removed the plexiglass. Or was he in a different room?

Was that out of consideration to his senses, or just so he couldn't hurt himself?

The door leading outside the room hung open.

Open.

He hadn't noticed. He hadn't been capable of registering anything from his surroundings. Were they letting him go?

No, that was too much to hope for.

The hallway beyond was as empty and plain as the room. Did they expect him to leave on his own? That was also unlike them—the bruiser-man wouldn't have passed up an opportunity to torment Allan.

Then again, there was nothing usual about any of this.

He looked around with his original body, and caught sight of his second body, standing still with clenched arms at his sides.

His view from his second body wrenched into a horrific out-of-body experience, only partly capable of seeing from its own eyes. Allan swayed and reached out with both sets of hands. As he fell with both bodies, he kept his gaze on his second body, as though a camera that couldn't miss the action.

He stared.

Seeing a naked duplicate of himself, he couldn't tear his eyes away. The fragility of his existence had been exposed, like he was watching his heart beat, afraid of looking away lest the machinery seize and stop.

Who *was* this other person? It was simultaneously an answer of who *he* was.

He was both question and answer. A loop disconnected from everything, either self-sustaining or self-destructing. No one would know if the loop choked itself into nothing.

His newly-birthed existence was so fragile. In every corner lay mind-death. With only a moment of weakness, he would disappear into that existential maw.

He didn't know how long he lay there on the precipice.

He could watch himself from inside and out, and such scrutiny made him hyper-aware of every micro-action. Never again could he claim ignorance, or doing something by accident.

Judgment would follow him to the last hour.

No, he thought. *Accept this. Please, let me accept this, or let it be over.*

He got up and, with Frankenstein-monster steps, moved both bodies until he stood face to face with himself.

He expected it to be like looking into a mirror. A mirror, however presents a left-right flipped image of yourself—not your actual self as everyone else in the world sees you.

This small difference magnified his awareness, especially as each body moved independently. The only kind of mirror here was one for the soul.

Allan wasn't ready, and didn't know if he ever would be.

There was no going back, though, and no choice.

He stared at himself staring at himself. He compared every detail. The scar above his nipple—where he'd scraped himself on a curb edge after pitching forward on his bike when he was eleven—was identical on both bodies. The veins on his arms were the same, his right more pronounced and showing longer trails where blood vessels wrapped through and fed his forearm.

He felt strangely exposed, trying to keep open-minded while being aware of another part of himself that was...

Judge. Jury. Executioner. His mind flashed with images of putting himself in a guillotine, looking into his own pleading eyes. Screaming with two mouths.

No, he thought firmly. *I have to accept this. This is my reality.*

He raised his one right arm slowly, extending it, and then raised the other right arm. He clasped and shook his hands, the touch a completed electric circuit. He jolted and cried out.

Every faint quiver of muscle in each hand sent a wave through the other, the neural feedback accelerating. Everything tingled. He felt every ridge and crevice of his fingerprints, every wrinkle on his hand, the swirling circles of the life lines in his palms.

Entwined. Entangled.

He lost track of which body was which, and the loss

of firm ground made him quaver. He had a weak grip on the functioning of each body. With this connection, he spun in a tornado, amorphous. His mind jerked back as though he'd touched a red-hot stovetop.

There was only a void to retreat to, though, and if he pulled back too far, he would be lost.

His breaths lost synchronicity and he gasped. He tried to let go, but the other body's movements followed his, as though he were playing a deadly game with a doppelgänger.

One of his arms shook. He forced himself to connect again with the vortex of sensations, then found the rift and pulled apart.

He fell back, each body tumbling hard because he had no resources left for balance.

Looking away, he stared at the side walls, each body keeping the other out of view.

Breathe, Allan.

The distinctions between the bodies came back like the blood into a frost-numbed limb, the coldness sending jets of pain as feeling returned. Tears streamed down his cheeks. He focused on micro-details on the walls, corners, anything to be distinct and normal.

But I'll never be normal again, he thought. The words echoed in two brains.

He thought of every moment dying to the next, the entirety of existence a series of small deaths. What he might have done differently if he'd known life as he knew it would end...

Stop it, he thought, recalling the psychological training he'd undergone. *This is despair. Yes. I acknowledge it. But it stops here.*

I have to accept this.

I have to accept... myself.

How can I expect others to warm to the man I've become if I turn away from myself?

Slowly, he turned his heads to look at himself again. For

some reason, he'd expected—wanted—the skin to be plastic, but it was as real as his own. The unseen judge whispered in his mind, and he replied to every detail with a constant refrain.

I accept you. I accept me.

The blemishes. The scars. The ripples of fat. The patchy hair.

I accept me.

He stood, each body taking a turn to watch the other. He moved like a toddler, knees quivering as he fought for balance.

He triumphed and stood in both bodies, accepting the trembles of imbalance and uncertainty in his inner ears.

He extended the right hand of each arm. He gripped, and winced at the swirling electricity.

Both bodies threatened to amalgamate again. Closing his eyes, he focused on individual sensations that allowed him to parse which was which, and remind himself who and what he was.

Two bodies, one mind.

He shifted and readjusted until his palms matched, as though their lifelines clicked into place. Then he shook his hand, gripping as confidently and firmly as he would greet a dignitary.

He had become a strong man in the care of his captors. His eyes lit with intensity and focus. He had become a better person than he'd been living on the streets. This new double-identity, however, was not something he would have taken in exchange if given the choice.

No, he thought, *they can't turn me against myself. I won't loathe myself because of what they've done. If this is a part of me now, then I accept it. One mind, two bodies.*

Both Allan Gerrolds turned and walked out of the room.

In the hall, there was only one way to go, and it led after a few turns to his bedroom door.

There was a new doorway beside it, of the same cold metal with a small window on top.

Cautiously, Allan opened the door and looked in with his

original body, while surveying his old room with the second body. The rooms were identical. He made sure not to walk into either room, and instead went back out into the hallway.

He felt more like a rat in a maze now than he had during any of the other tests.

His mouths worked, trying to work sound in between their breaths. His breath was the anchor of his whole control system, though, so disrupting that for speech was dangerous.

But he had to. His fury at how the bruiser-man and the ice queen toyed with him could not be stifled.

"What do you want from me?!" he shouted with both voices. They were out of sync and the pitches wavered. The off-beat sound echoed and rippled through his skulls. He winced at the ringing, resonant feedback.

He caught his breaths again, wheezing.

Allan Gerrold waited a long time, but there was no answer.

He feared if he went into the new room, the bruiser-man and the ice queen would separate his two halves to carry out twisted psychological experiments.

He could oppose them, though. He had twice the strength now, if not more, once he could properly control his selves.

He could start right now.

In his original room, Allan found a blanket for his second body, and made a small bed on the floor beside the king-sized bed frame. He didn't want both bodies in the same bed—that seemed too strange, almost narcissistic to him.

He'd have a lot of discovering to do in the days ahead, but he would do it on *his* terms, not theirs.

He would keep the two halves of himself in the same room together as long as he could. He would fight his captors. He wouldn't let them do worse things to him.

They couldn't do worse things to him.

As soon as his heads touched the pillows, he fell asleep and into something much worse.

CHAPTER ELEVEN

Sharing the Load

With the last experiment done, Ben walked to the facility's bathroom with a sag in his shoulders. He stared at his ashen face in the mirror, hoping for something, anything deep within, to spark words of wisdom.

There were dark implications of everything that had happened. Thankfully he was too exhausted to feel the fear, but at the back of his mind, he knew he couldn't ignore it for long.

He wondered if the detectors had experienced the same flip-flopping throughout the ordeal as he had. Maybe this was how computers felt as their bits were changed.

He ran cold water and splashed it on his face. It felt good to remember there were some things in the world that were still constant.

If Ben continued to accept that he hadn't gone crazy, he had to come up with a reasonable explanation for what happened.

The monsters had crept back into his life. Maybe they'd never left at all.

He shuddered.

It was as if the experiment had been a blank canvas, some deep facets of the universe waiting for someone to imprint upon them. As he finished wiping his face and leaned on the bathroom counter, Ben became more and more convinced that some sort of template had been carved out of the wishes, desires and intricate theories of the scientists involved in the whole mess.

He could never tell Kitt what had really happened in the experiments. If she knew—well, if she even believed him— she would be forced to accept that her life's work, her greatest achievement, was wrong. That, in itself, would devastate her. But to find this out after she had witnessed, time and time again, experiments that had proven her work to be fully correct, would harm her beyond description.

Kitt could be spared if Ben faced a horror that was almost as unbelievable as the outcome of the experiment. He would have to confront his childhood monsters.

He wondered fleetingly what his old therapist, Heather Smith, would think of everything, if she would be as disappointed and flabbergasted at the results of her labour as Ben was at the results of his own.

Even though he'd seen over and over that his work was right, the final result had been that time travel was impossible.

Kitt and Ben. One of them would be saved, while the other destroyed. And the choice was up to Ben.

He groaned and kicked the garbage bin, sending it tottering across the restroom floor.

The monsters were real. They would come back. Who were they? What did they want? Would they harm him? Could he somehow avoid them?

Maybe he could run from them.

But who would he run to? He had no family left. His father had died five years ago of a massive heart attack after a dog-walk. The man had been healthier than anyone Ben knew at his age. Nevertheless, he'd died instantly, collapsing in his driveway.

Ben's mother had been murdered by a nursing home. Not literally—just the murder of the soul that comes after a lifetime of toil funnels into an apathetic system with no place for the elderly. Ben had been trying to get things arranged to move her out, intending a beautiful surprise at Christmas.

She'd died in early December.

His mother was the only one with siblings, and she was the youngest. Most of them hadn't had children, and the one sister who did would have nothing to do with the Artemits. She hadn't even shown up to Ben's mother's funeral.

Ben had never been good at keeping friends, either. The only connections he maintained were those through his work, and the field was small enough that he really had only one person to turn to.

There was no one else left.

He cursed himself for painting himself into a spiritual corner, for leaving a single option with no alternative. It was a foolish way to prepare any scientific experiment, and in the test of life, the greatest experiment of all, his skills and training had failed him.

The only person left, his one and only friend in the solar system, was none other than Kitt. And the worst part was that if he told her, she might actually believe him.

He had to get home, get away from this place, as quickly as he could. Maybe he could just send Kitt a message saying he'd started to feel sick. Yes, that would do. He just had to grab his jacket and make it to his car.

He rubbed his face once more, blinking at his reflection. *You can do this.*

He wrenched the door open with sweaty hands—

—And Kitt was standing right there.

His mouth worked, trying to decide between a greeting, a congratulatory remark, anything intelligent really—

"Kitt."

"Hi Ben." Her voice and face were compassionate without condescension, something she alone seemed capable of.

Ben blinked at her, then said, "Well, it seems you were

right all along—congratulations." He tried to put more weight into his words, and cursed himself for his inability to muster up happiness for her. She truly deserved every bit of success that was coming her way.

"Thanks." She smiled, then blinked her blue eyes quickly a couple of times. She touched her lower lip as the silence between them lengthened, then said, "Did you want to come out of there?"

"Huh? Oh." Ben hadn't realized he'd been standing in the doorway of the bathroom. He pushed out and into the Quantix lab's white hallways with Kitt.

"Ben, don't take this the wrong way, but you don't look so well. Are you all right?"

Ben wished fleetingly that there might be more evidence to support a lie, but he had nothing that would support anything but the truth. He took a deep breath and sighed. "No, Kitt," he said in a small voice. "I'm not."

She tented her eyebrows and said, "The experiments... were quite exhausting, and disappointing."

Ben nodded.

She leaned in a bit, then added, "It's more than that, though."

Ben stared back, lips refusing to move. A token response of *I can neither confirm nor deny that statement* danced through his delirious mind.

She leaned on one hip, parked her bent arm there, then said in a half-serious chiding tone, "Well? Are you going to tell me about it, or not?"

Ben looked down, then to the side—anywhere, really, except Kitt's face. The shadows through the hall doors threatened to hide so much, however, so he shut his eyes.

He blanched. His childhood nightmares could be anywhere. "Maybe we could go somewhere more private to talk," he said.

"OK," she said, glancing over her shoulder. "I feel like we have to talk here though—and shoot, the cafeteria's already closed. How about this? I'll go tell Turen we're done, then we'll go find a board room where we can talk, OK?"

"OK."

Kitt grabbed one of his hands and squeezed, then rushed off.

The warmth from Kitt's hand still hadn't gone away by the time she returned with her bag, and they roamed the halls in search of a quiet place.

They sat in a long board room, where Kitt locked the door and closed the blinds. "Turen won't find us in here," she said. "And there's even coffee." She pointed to a machine by some cupboards, a counter and a sink.

A while later, they sat side-by-side, sipping.

Ben made small talk, chatting about where she intended to publish first, and what her next steps might be. Kitt obliged him with answers, but she must have known it was paining him, for she soon quieted.

Ben took a deep breath, then pulled at his coffee. "This is delicious," he said for the second time.

Kitt tilted her head and blinked at him, wearing a smile on the edge of impatience.

Maybe they should have gone into a board room closer to the active evening shift of the lab—that would have at least given him an excuse for not talking.

Kitt straightened and tapped her forefinger rapidly on the tabletop to get his attention. "You cannot do this, Ben! I'm here for you, and I want you to be honest. You're not allowed to clam up right now, after saying things aren't OK. No. Not acceptable."

Ben sighed, thinking how he'd led himself into this corner, and how if there were anyone in the world who could make the experience pleasant, it would be Kitt. And he owed her the truth—she'd come all this way, given up a chunk of her evening during what was possibly the best night of her career. He had to tell her something.

Ben looked into his coffee and scratched the top of his

head. "OK. I'll tell you."

What to say? Where to start? He sighed, realizing that no matter what, Kitt's opinion of him would change irreversibly from this moment on. He'd arrived at one of those cusps in life where the unpleasant change was essential, and the wake would ripple outward for long after he was done speaking.

"Suppose," he began, "just suppose—and I'm not admitting to anything, at least not yet—suppose that I told you I noticed something odd about the experiments, but nobody else did. I tried to tell you, and Turen, and … neither of you agreed with me. Neither of you remembered what I'd noticed. What would you say to that?"

Kitt tilted her head. "Well—hypothetically of course—" she added with a nod "—what did you see? Why wouldn't we pay attention to it?"

Ben swallowed. "Before we go there Kitt, please: just suppose this happened, just as I've described it. What would you think about that—about me? Honestly."

She furrowed her brow. "Of course I'll be honest, Ben," she protested. "I'd think that something happened... to you... because why wouldn't anyone else notice? I mean, especially if it's as important as you think it is."

Ben's heart quickened. "So basically you're saying, kindly, that you'd think I'd lost it—that I was crazy. Right?"

Kitt shifted in her chair. "OK," she said, averting her gaze for a moment before meeting Ben's eyes again. "Yes. Something like that."

Ben leaned back and brushed his hand through the air, as if warding off—or identifying—the elephant in the room. "So you see my problem," he said. "If I tell you what actually happened, you'll think I'm nuts."

He could only maintain eye contact with Kitt for a few moments. The trouble was, there wasn't much else to look at in the room, aside from making sure no one was peeking through the blinds.

Ben sighed again, wishing he could stretch the moment, the time with Kitt, before things changed. Change rarely seemed to occur for the better—it was like entropy: monotonic.

When he looked back at Kitt, she seemed to be searching him for where he'd gone. There was a hint of a smile on her lips. "What if I promise not to think you're crazy? Would you tell me what you saw? Could you tell me why it's so important?" Her eyes widened and she quickly added, "I don't mean your work isn't important. It is. I—"

"No, Kitt." Ben felt the weight come thundering down on him once more. "My work is not important." He shook his head, wrapped his hands around his cup, and rested his arms on the table. Stared into the steaming depths. "Not anymore. Not to me. I've lost that." The cup failed to keep out the chill that rose from his toes up his spine. "That's not what's wrong. What's wrong—what I'm up against—is so much worse than me losing my theory..."

Kitt reached over and rested her hand on Ben's arm. Kitt, bridging the gulf like she had so many times before. Then she spoke quietly, but intensely. "Whatever this is, you've got to trust me, Ben. You've opened up to me because you think I can help. If there's a way I can, I will. You can tell me what it is."

Ben fumbled for words, knowing that the great power he barely understood might wreak havoc again if he weakened. He felt on the edge, and the fluorescent lights above seemed to darken. "If I tell you, and you believe me, you're going to lose your life's work. And—and if you don't believe me..."

Kitt gently slid her hand from Ben's arm and drummed her fingers on the tabletop. She scanned the room, then looked at him once more. "Ben, I can't lose my life's work, no matter what's troubling you. I saw the experiments and I know my work is sound. I won't lose that. Just tell me what this is all about."

Despite Ben's inexplicable feeling that the creatures—the childhood monsters—were close, he let his spirit reach out to Kitt. Or perhaps it was because of that feeling, the growing dread and fear that blinded him to the risks to Kitt's happiness.

"Kitt, like I said, I know you're probably going to think I'm imagining all of this—that it's all in my mind." He hung his head, staring into the coffee mug, and exhaled deeply, forcing out the breath he'd been unconsciously holding.

"Go on, it's OK," she said gently.

Ben wondered if he was starting to sound even crazier the more he skirted around the issue.

He told her everything.

He told her how he'd observed different outcomes several times, and watched the circus of his indecision play out in Kitt's and Turen's reactions—an emotional roller coaster —until the final outcome. While Ben relayed the story, Kitt listened with a serious expression, never wavering or breaking her attention.

He finished, his heart pounding, as Kitt nodded thoughtfully. "Thank you, Ben," she said. "I understand why you hesitated, and like I promised, I don't think you're crazy. It is quite a lot to wrap my head around, though."

Ben felt his spirit lift, then realized his window of opportunity—of Kitt's open and accepting mind—might be closing. If he was going to get all the wildness out of his head, best to do it now, before she was tired of his rambling, before she wanted to go home and dream of all the success that awaited her.

The words tumbled out of him. "I had to tell you about the experiments because if you find that hard to accept, what I'm going to tell you now is… it's going to sound ludicrous. What happened to me when we did the experiments made me wonder again about the monsters my mother and I saw when I was a kid, but only I remembered, and—and—whether they really did exist. Just like the experiments! And now I… I'm afraid," he dropped his voice to a whisper, "I'm afraid they're going to come back."

"Wait, Ben," she replied. "I want to talk more about the

experiments."

Had she not heard him? Was he speaking too quickly, or had she just stopped listening because she was lost in thought after he'd recounted the experimental observations? Maybe she was ignoring him because he was crazy—

"The automated tests that are running now would show us what you're talking about, wouldn't they?" Kitt asked.

"No," Ben said, shoulders sagging. "I doubt they would. The results seem to be influenced by conscious observation."

Kitt frowned.

"Why don't we just go and do them again?" she continued. "If what you say is true, I want to see it for myself. Can we prove what you've said? Why can't we go back and do them again and this time get—I don't know how—get an indisputable record of the results? Hard evidence to prove what you're saying?"

"No, Kitt!" Ben shouted, standing.

Kitt jerked back, alarmed, and Ben worried he'd been loud enough to arouse Quantix security. He sat and lowered his voice. "Sorry. No. I don't want to do any more experiments. I saw what you went through before, and I don't want to see it again. Trust me. It's not the experiments that bother me."

Kitt leaned in and rested her hand on Ben's arm again. "I appreciate your concern, Ben."

Ben shook his head. "It's just like what happened to me when I was a boy." He stared off, then shook himself. "There's no point doing the experiments again because we'll get the same results."

Kitt leaned closer. "Ben, I do appreciate your concern, but I can decide what's best for me, and what I want. I want to see what you've seen." She shrugged her shoulders questioningly. "How can you say we'll just get the same results?"

Ben started to speak, but she cut him off.

"If you were in my position, what would you do? Could you just accept my claims at face value? Wouldn't you want to see for yourself?"

Ben swallowed, and felt the same sensation of having painted himself into a corner. Maybe Kitt just had that way of getting at him, better than anyone else. He couldn't argue—she was right. But there had to be another way. A way that didn't tempt fate with the monsters.

"There's no point, Kitt. In the end, just like before, you won't remember, and we can't make a permanent record: the final record in the computer was the same as what both you and Turen remembered. It's not going to be any different now."

Kitt cocked her head. "If I'm just going to remember the same as I did before, what harm can that do me? OK, sure, if I go through what you saw before, that will bother me, but only until it's all over, then I'll feel just the same as I do now. It's like taking valium for a conscious surgery. In the end I'm not going to be traumatized, or even harmed."

Ben's mouth felt dry. "But Kitt, it devastated you, and—"

"It might devastate me again, but I feel just fine right now. Besides, we can make a permanent record."

Ben raised his eyebrows. "How can we possibly do that?"

"Let's suppose," she said, "that it all happened just as you say it did. We did the experiments. We argued. In the end we got our way and you lost out. There were two of us remembering one thing, and just you remembering another thing. Let's go back, just you and me, Ben—and do it all over again."

"How else can I explain this?" Ben asked, more to himself than anyone else. "What we saw before, what ended up as your memory, and what the computer recorded: that result has been selected, out of all possible outcomes, as the final and definitive result. Like a template for everything to come." He shrugged. "We won't see anything different, Kitt."

"Maybe not. So here's what we do. One: we do different experiments. Two: we won't use the computer to make a record."

Ben scratched his head. "What experiments will we do

this time?"

"We will program the computer to send a signal one minute back into the past, but only if it did not receive a signal one minute ago, and we tell the computer not to send a signal if it did receive one."

Ben lifted his arms imploringly and said, "But that's just what we did last time."

"I know," Kitt said. "This time, if we receive a signal, we will change the computer program, and have it send out a *different* signal than the one received. If this happens, the only possible explanation is that the signal received—"

"—was sent from a different universe," Ben finished.

Kitt nodded, and raised an eyebrow, looking toward the door and into the night. "We do have after-hours access to the lab, you know."

Ben groaned. Her proposal sounded so good, but she seemed to be skirting around the issue of the monsters. Did she not believe him? Maybe if he insisted on it, she would give up and just dismiss him as crazy.

This wasn't the way he'd planned on things going. But maybe taking action, however foolish, was better than waiting for the encroaching shadows from the monsters.

"All right," he said at last, hoping that wherever the monsters were, they wouldn't be watching him tonight.

CHAPTER TWELVE

The Template II

"I knew I could count on you," Kitt said as Ben pulled a pen from his bag. "When I said we wouldn't use computers to record, this is exactly what I imagined."

Ben frowned, then dug a bit deeper until he found a second pen.

Kitt's eyes widened. "Two, Ben, really? You carry *two* around with you all the time?"

Ben turned his bag toward Kitt, showing her the two pieces of paper inside. "Of course. You never know."

"I guess I should be thankful you gave me time to practice with them before, so I can actually use them."

Ben enjoyed a burst of warmth and almost smiled. Those many playful conversations seemed like they belonged to another universe.

He stared at the tips of the pens, wondering if he should just call this whole thing off before it was too late. Was it weak of him to want someone else to know? To experience? It would cost Kitt so much... but she was dogged when determined.

Kitt snatched a pen out of Ben's hand. "You said my handwriting was excellent last time," she said. "You better have been telling the truth, if we're going to be relying on it now. Let's get going."

* * *

They tread carefully through the white halls of Quantix and into the section devoted to the Jupiter Lab. Here the halls grew dim except for a single light shining through a window on the door to the monitoring room.

There was probably only a single technician monitoring the instrumentation that could never be shut down for the sake of the time travel experiments.

Kitt's eyes were wide—clearly, she was relishing the rebellious, adventurous nature of their upcoming experiment, possibly more so than she had their anxious first experiment.

If only it were for a less important—or less devastating—experiment.

Kitt knocked on the facility's monitoring room door, and once again Ben jammed his hands in his pockets, fingers curling around his pen. A technician slowly opened the door, tilting his head in disbelief at the two scientists before him.

"Franklin!" Kitt exclaimed. "Thank goodness you're here."

"It's... Kat, right?" he said, looking between the two of them skeptically.

"It's Kitt, yeah," she replied, nodding enthusiastically. "And this is Ben. We did the experiment with Al today."

Franklin snorted, rolling his eyes. "Of course, yeah. Sorry, Al does tons of experiments, and it's hard to keep track of everyone. But," he continued, catching himself, "you're quite memorable."

Blood rushed Ben's cheeks. His fists clenched.

Kitt laughed. "Well, I didn't mean to misalign the spectrometer," she said. "I'm just so interested and impressed in all you guys do."

Franklin's chest rose. "That's another reason you're a rare breed, Kitt. Most theorists haven't got a clue what goes into making things actually work."

"I wish I had had enough time to learn it all," Kitt went on. "That's actually part of the reason we're here, Franklin. Ben and I were worried the automated data aren't enough, and wanted to look at the statistical data to see if more tests are needed."

Franklin shook his head. "Your automated runs just finished." Behind him, monitors flashed from one state to another as they rotated displays of various complex instruments.

Kitt moved closer to him, and put a hand on his arm. "Please, Franklin," she said. "You know there's never enough time assigned to any of the experiments for really good statistics. We just want better data, to make sure we aren't publishing a bunch of one-time irreproducible anomalies."

Franklin furrowed his brow. "I hadn't planned on staying much longer, Kitt, and was hoping to go home soon."

Kitt flashed a broad smile. "How often do you get to be in the spotlight? The equipment's not doing anything right now, and I'll buy you lunch if you'll help us make sure we run everything right."

"That might be worth more than lunch," Franklin said, keeping his gaze locked on Kitt, ignoring Ben altogether. Ben's blood boiled.

"All right, I'll bring donuts in too then," Kitt said. "Please, Franklin. We just want to do better science."

"Lunch date?"

Kitt bit her lip and let her hand fall away from his arm. "I'm sorry, I didn't mean it that way, Franklin. I would buy you lunch, but it wouldn't be a date." She smiled apologetically.

Franklin sighed. "No, I'm sorry for being presumptuous," he said. "I should just be grateful you're interested in what we do. And I am. So come on in—let's do some science."

Ben released the breath he had been holding, and relaxed his fists. Franklin wasn't so bad after all—and Kitt had graciously stayed within her comfort zone as she turned him down. There weren't many people who were as brilliant as she was who were also superb human beings. Ben supposed he couldn't fault Franklin for recognizing how wonderful Kitt was.

They stepped into the blinding light of the lab, and got to work setting up the Jupiter chamber diagnostics with Franklin's help.

* * *

A while later, everything was ready for another run.

"Let me know when you're done," Franklin said as he stepped out the lab door. "I'll be in the facility monitoring room, making sure the facility keeps humming."

"Thanks, Franklin," Kitt said, and waved goodbye.

The door shut after him, and Kitt and Ben were left alone.

Kitt pulled off her hair net and heaved a sigh. "There's so much I take for granted," she said, flopping into a chair. "The preparation is exhausting."

Ben was struggling to remove his shoe covers, teetering for balance near the doorway. He managed to get them off without knocking over an adjacent set of shelves, but was wheezing by the time he finished.

He hadn't realized how exhausted he was. Suddenly he was looking forward to being done and on his way home.

"Great. My phone's dead," Kitt said, frowning at the black glass in her hand.

Bad sign, Ben thought. "Hopefully we'll be quick enough you won't need it."

His voice carried optimism he didn't feel.

He peeled off his lab coveralls and clutched his pen to steady his nerves. He retrieved the paper from his bag and set one piece of paper in front of Kitt, and one in front of him.

She took out her own pen. Her grip was much steadier than the first time she'd used one.

"OK," he said, "so do you want to record positive time travel results, or negative?"

"I guess I'll do the positive results—when we get a signal that travelled back in time."

"Fair enough," Ben said. "I'll do the negative or null results, when we see no evidence of time travel."

Kitt tested the pen on paper, and made a face. "My writing is atrocious! I don't know if I can write quickly enough —should we make some shorthands?"

"Sure," Ben said, glancing and silently agreeing that her writing was horrific. "Our writing is easy to distinguish, and we should write before we have any time for discussion or argument. If a signal comes in and a different signal goes out, write SI-DSO then your initials in brackets: (KB). If no signal comes in, I will write NSI (BA)."

Soon the reality of the setup closed in. He couldn't be distracted by the meticulous nature of experimental setup.

A recorded warning to evacuate the lab played. In thirty seconds, the equipment would start running.

Kitt's hard work and research might bleed from her pen straight onto paper, a direct conduit for her life energy.

Ben looked across the table at her, and she returned his stare with a smile and raised eyebrows before returning to monitor the instrument screens.

The first trial came. No signal arrived. Ben scribbled on his paper, wishing he could disconnect from his body.

The second trial was the same—no signal.

On the third trial, the beacon in the centre of the table flooded the room in red light.

A signal through time had been received!

"No!" Kitt cried. She covered her mouth and nose, staring at Ben. She stood there unmoving for a moment, before the dam burst and the tears came through.

Oh, Kitt, Ben thought, a pang piercing his chest. *This is how you must have felt before, only last time you'd tried to hide it from Turen.* Her gaze reached deep into him, asking—begging —for a way to change the result.

Ben had known this was going to happen. His insides wrenched. There had to be a way to soothe her wounds. "Kitt, I —"

She broke in. "Oh, Ben! All that you told me is true!" She was crying openly now, tears streaming down her cheeks. "Ben, I *remember*! I remember... all those experiments we did. They went just as you said. A signal arrived..." She closed her eyes, the images clearly filling her mind and pouring out of her. "I was upset... we argued. No, I—no. I remember it all. And now it's happening again. A signal's arrived. My work... this means... my work... all of it..." She sniffled, struggling with the word trembling on her lips. "Wrong."

Ben felt a simultaneous urge to run far, far away, and an opposing urge to console Kitt. His insides burned, and every tingly sensation on his body disgusted him. He should never have agreed to this, as much as Kitt had encouraged him. He should have been stronger, risen above the momentary pains to see the bigger picture—Kitt's bigger picture of happiness and fulfillment.

Kitt wrote down "SR (KB)" on her piece of paper, even as tears spotted the area around it. She dropped the pen, leaving a blue gash where the tip broke contact with the paper.

Ben wished, very strongly, that Kitt could have it all back, that her memory of these experiments could somehow preserve her theory and life's work.

It was unlike any wish he'd ever had before, because in the strange paradigm he'd experienced in the last experiment, he'd seen that reality could be altered. Rather than a pie-in-the-sky desire, the wish seemed tangible, and something that *should* be, by whatever god or entity or force was controlling this charade.

That's when it all happened. It was as if time stopped, and everything changed. Kitt froze. Light scattering off the dust in the room stilled until it hung suspended by an invisible web. There was absolute, roaring silence.

Ben looked at Kitt's immobile features.

He knew that it had happened again. Just like the experiments they'd done earlier.

Things ground into motion again, the cogs of reality resisting the push of time. Flicks of light dazzled the edges of Ben's vision, and he tried to see what was coming into being.

What was different now? He couldn't pinpoint anything tangible, but it no longer felt like the same room he'd been standing in just moments earlier.

He turned back to Kitt, praying she, above all else, would survive whatever transition had just occurred. Several moments passed, and he waited for her movements to normalize again.

"Three in a row: no signal in," she said, with an apologetic glance at Ben.

The change was unbelievable. A moment ago she'd been an emotional wreck, tears running rivulets down her cheeks. Now her body—her everything—was totally relaxed. There was no sign she'd been upset.

In a blur, Ben grabbed his pen and scribbled, "NSI (BA)." Just as quickly, he realized it might be hopeless: Kitt's paper would still have her handwritten record that a signal had been received.

He was about to snatch the paper out from under her nose when he saw it was blank.

What she wrote is no longer there, he thought.

Just as had occurred in the realm of digital storage in the experiments before, the record had changed.

Can we actually get out of here without Kitt losing her success?

Ben watched everything unfold around him as in a dream. No, not a dream: a nightmare where he'd become too frightened to act lest his subconscious turn things down a dangerous path.

Ben robotically recorded the next repeated sets of experiments, Kitt polite and professional throughout.

Three experiments of No-Signal-In, and Kitt showed no sign of slowing down.

She seemed determined to validate Ben's claims through statistical breadth.

Ben felt cornered again. He couldn't suggest that they quit, since she would be suspicious of the results—and might even suggest another repetition—if they left early. But to stay was agony.

So Ben went through the motions, keeping as emotionally distant from the results as he could.

Suddenly and without warning, every molecule in his body tingled. He knew—even before he turned to look. He knew they were there. Watching. Analyzing. Planning.

It was perhaps out of fear for Kitt that he willed his stiffened muscles to turn. To look back at them.

Two creatures grinned hideously beneath slitted eyes on their large heads. They stood near the door to the lab, but there was no evidence they'd entered that way.

Something clutched at Ben's chest, a tension, a... sense of evil.

One of the monsters raised its long arm above its head, then pointed its three fingers accusingly at Ben. A tremor went through Ben, but otherwise he remained rooted, incapable of action.

Then the monsters disappeared. From one blink to the next, they vanished, as though they were a faulty frame on a holo recording.

Ben jumped as a hand gripped his shoulder.

It was Kitt, thank God.

"What... what happened, Ben?" Her mouth hung open after she spoke, her face blank. "What's happened?"

Ben wanted to tell her, but felt an even stronger pull to get out of the lab—out of the place which now welcomed his childhood monsters.

He shook himself, fighting all the voices in his head that said the monsters weren't real.

Darker voices—those of the monsters themselves—gripped him at his core. Those voices had haunted his nightmares as a child.

The dam of welled emotion readied to burst, and Ben wasn't sure how long he could hold it back.

"I'll explain later," he said finally. "Let's just finish the experiments and leave, OK?"

Every time a signal was received, both Ben and Kitt suffered through the result. The only observable difference was that, each time a signal arrived, Kitt's memory of what she went through changed, while Ben remembered everything. He was grateful Kitt wouldn't remember any of the tumultuous journey toward the final results.

Eventually, mercifully, they had gone through three results with a signal received and a different signal sent, and eight results with no signal received at all. Kitt didn't remember the three signals received: her recollection was that these too had been cases where no signal had come in.

Ben's page was filled with eleven notes of No-Signal-In. Eleven experiments confirming Kitt's theory. Ben held up the page, utterly exhausted.

"We've done enough," he said.

None of what Kitt had written remained on the paper. The record of the experiments had been changed. Ben wondered if part of his memory was being tampered with, and there really was a universe where she *had* written in those extra three results.

He handed her the paper. "All null results, Kitt."

Kitt looked at both pieces of paper—her empty one and the one she'd taken from Ben. Strange that she needed to confirm, but Ben supposed she was just being judicious and fair regarding Ben's claims. Her eyes met his after a time. "What do you think this means?"

Ben fought the urge to say all he wanted to, and instead

replied, "I think it means there is no backward time travel." He took a deep breath, turned away, and paced the white tiles.

"There was, for me, in our experiments just a few hours ago, time travel. That's all over with now, for all of us—including me. There can no longer be backward time travel, the sending of signals into the past."

A template had been formed. The question of time travel to the past was an open question prior to the experiments, but the results of the experiments had resulted in the formation of a template, one in which time travel to the past was not possible.

"There's no more backward time travel," he repeated. "Not for me, or for any of us—not in our universe, anyway."

Kitt pursed her lips. "But there was, before, for you, Ben. You witnessed signals being sent back, didn't you?"

There was no taking back what he'd already told her. "Yes. I did. I truly did. I know it sounds strange..."

"Quantum physics *is* strange," Kitt said. She looked hard at him, then said, "I believe you, Ben. I don't know why... but I do. I wasn't sure before—not really—but I am now."

The validation of his theory allowed Ben a moment of significant satisfaction, even if it was marred somewhat by the fear that lurking around the corner in the hallways of Turen's lab were the monsters, waiting to put their sinister plans into motion.

He wished he didn't have to face them alone.

Maybe Kitt's part of their plan, and she and I can—

No. That was just too horrible to imagine. He had to get out of the lab—and he had to keep Kitt out of all of it.

He and Kitt erased all the computer records showing they'd been in the lab, then prepared to leave.

Ben said a perfunctory thank-you to Franklin, while scanning all around for signs of the monsters. Kitt, in contrast, radiated sincerity and genuine appreciation.

By the time they'd begun walking home, Ben's thoughts had moved completely away from time travel and fully back onto the demons awaiting him. His legs moved rapidly but deep down he knew there was nowhere he could run that they wouldn't find him.

He needed Kitt's help, but he wouldn't give the plea a voice. He wouldn't—he refused to ask that of her.

Ben took a few distracted strides, then realized Kitt had stopped.

Had she truly forgotten everything, or did trickles of memory remain?

The street lights cast pale rays onto her face, even though the sun had begun to set in the distance.

"What happened back there, Ben?" she asked. "What was it? You were frightened, weren't you?"

Ben tried to think how to answer.

"While we were having coffee," Kitt continued, "you told me about the monsters you saw in the dark as a child. You said you were frightened then, and afraid again today."

Ben stared at Kitt, his resolve weakening under her visible concern. It was like she already knew, and her perpetual kindness was the only reason she waited for him to voice the truth.

But he couldn't—shouldn't—involve her. There was too much that could happen beyond the quantum weirdness they'd experienced.

But... if he couldn't tell her, whom could he tell?

What awaited him when he was alone was a tectonic shift threatening to cover his body in shakes.

"I saw them again, Kitt," Ben said in a small voice. "They were in the lab briefly, staring and grinning at me. Then in a blink they were gone, erased from the room without a trace."

He watched Kitt for a few moments, then looked away, unable to handle her reaction if—or when—she decided he was crazy. He desperately wanted her to stay with him.

She touched Ben's shoulder to get his attention. "What do we do now?" she asked gently. "You need to sleep, Ben, and I don't think you should be alone."

Ben swallowed, trying to think of a reason to argue, then nodded. "Don't feel obligated—"

"It's OK," Kitt said. "Let's go back. You won't be alone."

Ben stared at her, unfathomable gratitude filling him. As they walked back together, he could only think of how in the face of the world's greatest terrors, having someone who knew that they were real—even if just for you—was the greatest comfort.

It didn't remove the fact that Ben would have to face his fears sooner or later. Around some corner, either physical or a corner of his subconscious, he would encounter the monsters.

There was a sliver of good that had emerged from the mess. They had done the experiments to satisfy Kitt, while preserving her reality. Had Ben exerted influence over the outcome? It was almost too much to believe. They'd left Turen's lab exactly as they'd found it, so he'd never know they'd been there.

The monsters, however, knew he and Kitt had been there.

They had been watching everything, and they were ready. Ben had the sinking feeling they would come for him tonight.

CHAPTER THIRTEEN

Dual Sleep

For Allan Gerrold, sleeping in two bodies ushered in an experience almost beyond description.

Inky blues blended with bruised clouds. Jaundiced paint splotches dotted the image. Faint noises gurgled and swirled, swelling like a toad's vocal sac.

As the intensity grew, Allan discerned voices amidst other sounds. He tried to move away from them, but he had no body.

There was nothing to control. The sound was in his mind.

Pigs snorted and squealed. Frantic turkeys clucked in high pitch. A horse whinnied, but the sound was laced with such fear and desperation it was almost unrecognizable.

Animal cries bled into human screams, distinguished by pleading, begging, in barely-articulated language. Words were there, but coherence was gone.

Deafening, maniacal laughter reverberated and echoed in the infinite space. Other laughs joined the chaos. Horror surrounded him, clawed its way into him.

The number of voices increased and grew louder, mocking and taunting him, pressing from all sides. A dissonant overtone amplified the pain.

If there was an auditory definition of evil, this was it.

The inky purple and yellow swirled into distinct shapes. He tried to push himself away but at every attempt the voices drew nearer.

He had gotten a body, if only for the purpose of suffering.

He tasted ash and burnt meat, smelled sulfur and mould. Thick smoke filled his lungs. Rot filled his nostrils. Soot coated his tongue.

He tasted things like nothing he'd ever experienced. Smells invaded him and allowed no refuge. He jerked and gagged but it did not quell the indescribable ether invading him.

Guttural noises chanted at him. Shapes held foggy outlines of his past life—his high-school lab partner, Carl, pimple-faced and wearing braces as when they'd last met. The jocks on the basketball team—what were their names?—who'd clustered in the hallways, guffawing at Allan's expense.

Others poked their heads around corners and came forward to join the crowd—Allan's first impression was of Bill and Jasper, floor mates of his first-year dorm.

More joined the crowd—high-school crushes, professors, his parents' friends...

Everyone's voice was muffled. For a moment, Allan was comforted by the familiar presences, for although many of these people had hurt him in the past, none had hurt him as much as he'd experienced since his capture.

What's happening?

His memories were smashing together. The only way they could survive was without real form. His subconscious was playing tricks to sustain the illusion.

Yes, that's it. The thought made the hot sulfur air bearable.

The fog obscuring the figures cleared. Murky, off-coloured patches planted onto their skin. The hollows of their eyes darkened. Their hands became claws. Their movements left chunks of skin on the path behind them. Their steps toward him halted. Their hair fell off in patches.

The maw of mortality, with nothing beyond. Sharp acid and rot filled the air.

Some of the creatures were horned, and their jaws unhinged into wicked, sharp-toothed sneers.

They approached, while Allan was rooted, his heart yelling at him as loudly as the monsters.

The gap closed. Several leapt at him and Allan screamed.

Stabs punctured him. The monsters turned into smoke that sucked into Allan's skin, stealing his breath.

Spiders crawled up his legs. They spread an undulating blanket of prickles. They crawled up his spine.

While Allan writhed, the monsters encircled and stared at him with twisted, amused smiles. The chanting and shrieking continued.

Snakes squeezed around his legs, and their cold spread upward, slowing his movements. Needles punctured his skin in rapid *thip-thip-thips*.

Flames rose up around him.

Every time he went to the dark realm, his experience worsened.

* * *

Allan lay catatonic, adjusting to two darknesses. When his mind started back into motion, he guided it slowly toward a logical chain, staying on each thought for what felt like minutes at a time.

I am no good to anyone when I'm this weak.

They would not want me to be this weak.

They would not want me to endure these nightmares.

The thought slowed the churning in his bellies. His eyelids drooped.

Abruptly he slammed all four fists down, jolting himself

awake before he descended back into the horror.

If I go through these nightmares... the words came slowly as his mind halted and started in uncontrolled bursts.

If I go through these nightmares, then I can't do what they want me to do.

Anything they wanted to do with him—make him a weapon, a spy, a soldier—was better than this horror.

I will explain it to them. No, I will explain it to her, *the ice queen, and then she'll make these experiences go away.*

I just have to last the night.

He tried to roll his legs out of bed, but strained as his intentions cross-fired.

By the time he sat up with his real body, he was wheezing, and his leg and arm muscles primed on the verge of spasms.

His body ached with a weariness penetrating his bones. Nothing moved the way he expected it to; everything resisted. Allan heaved his second body up onto the bed, then lay each body next to the other.

Must stay awake, he thought.

He was more alone than he'd ever been on the street. Everyone was infinitely out of reach.

If Allan had the pleasure remote at hand, he would have happily said goodbye and taped the button down.

Lying in bed with both bodies, the curvature of the mattress shifted under and away from him as each body inhaled. He smelled sweat and the faint tang of plastic. He wondered if this was what others smelled when he forgot to put on deodorant, or when he'd gone for months without a shower on the streets.

Was it strange to lay with both bodies side-by-side? *They're both my body,* he reminded himself, trying to take deep breaths. He wanted to consolidate, think of himself inhabiting one body alone, but he couldn't any longer.

His lips trembled. He squeezed his eyes until he looked through slits. Then he reached out with the left hand of his original body, and the right hand of his second body.

He clasped hands, and by alternating his attention, he could pretend someone else was there to comfort him.

CHAPTER FOURTEEN

Quantum Plans

Belonthar pressed three long, thin fingers against the window of the tower. It offered little resistance. If he wanted to, he could have pushed right through and plummeted into the throngs of citizens below who had lost the strength to hold onto their souls.

He brought his hands together, fingers slithering over one another as he lost himself in thought.

The darkness outside was lined with other blurred towers piercing as high as the eye could see, one after another spaced on the horizon like bars on a cage. The towers perched high above the moaning masses. There were no streets, simply clusters of open space, mounds where citizens pawed at each other in a struggle for areas they felt more real, and less ephemeral. Above those, glass causeways ran between the superstructures.

Everyone's shape flicked through a series of potentialities. They never settled on any one form long enough to gain purchase. Belonthar knew all too well the feeling of being turned inside out, over and over again. In their suffering they could not hold onto any sense of self, and so they wailed, barely aware of anything, adrift in a sea of infinite potential and zero movement.

Belonthar had to remind himself of all this, go through it as part of a ritual in order to maintain his sanity when everything blurred evanescent. The ability to rationalize was a small but crucial difference between him and the suffering masses below. He longed to bring a stable existence to them, if only for long enough so the older ones could meet death.

As things stood, past a certain "age" death became a higher probability, but never a certainty. The elderly would flit back and forth across the great divide between life and death, each jolt into and out of consciousness feeling like a lightning strike. Belonthar wanted to end that uncertainty for them. He wanted to provide a firm base, even if that base meant the end. It would provide closure after an eternity of crossing back and forth across the chasm.

"Does he know?" Merthab asked from behind.

Belonthar turned away from the window and exhaled a long hiss. He had been working so hard lately he'd risked losing himself.

Merthab's neck bobbed as his long legs cantered across the room. Blurred, wobbling objects dotted the space between.

"Does he know?" Merthab repeated, snapping his jaws.

"No," Belonthar said. "We see no way that he could. We are almost certain he does not know."

Merthab hissed and thrashed his arms. "Almost? You say 'almost?' That's not good enough. We need to be certain. Need I remind you what's at stake?"

"I know what is at stake!" Belonthar snapped, blinking his eye-slits as blood rushed through him. "We all know... we have been working on this relentlessly, and we do not see what more could be done."

"We must act," Merthab said, grabbing Belonthar by the shoulders.

"So be it," Belonthar said. "You really think we have a strong enough link? It's re-established this time?"

"Yes! Yes. This we are certain of." Merthab's eye-slits opened wide and he released Belonthar. He tapped his mouth.

"His active involvement in the quantum experiments has led us back to him, and strengthened the link."

Belonthar imagined the hordes of his people suffering below. "Can he still do it?"

"We think so. But we must persuade him."

"And if we do not convince him?"

"We must." Merthab thumped his arm against the wall, and it passed right through, snapping to the other side then snapping back. "That gives us our best chance."

"If we do not convince him, what then?"

Merthab pressed his fingers together, then lowered his head as he whispered. "We will remove his brain, and use it to get what we need."

CHAPTER FIFTEEN

The Purpose

The sun rose in the artificial window like a soldier peeking his head out after a lapse in gunfire. Allan wanted to wrench the sun from its hiding place and launch it into the sky like a grenade. He fantasized about this and many other ways to bring the dawn. Light caught dust and both seemed to halt for stretches at a time.

Air scraped across his tongue. He licked his lips, as he'd done throughout the night. Each time he did, his tongues and esophagi teetered on the verge of spasms. He still hadn't gotten a handle on throat and tongue control. Everything seemed infinitely more difficult than the day before, like he'd run across the finish line only to realize it was the starting gate.

His stomachs periodically heaved, squeezing themselves to check for food.

The alarm clock showed 8:00. Allan clenched and unclenched his jaws waiting for the click from the front door. When the sound of the lock unlatching finally did come it seemed a bugle blast to Allan's ears.

He sat up with one body, still clutching the hand of the other. He was so tired he didn't think of which body was which. He guided the hands of one body onto the shoulders of the other, then rose and walked, feet in-step and in-sync, one body trotting behind the other like a conga line at a senior home.

The hallways stretched as bleak and empty as ever. The white walls held a blue tinge with the lights off. Everything smelled of bleach.

Allan trundled on four feet toward the end. Turning a corner, he reached an armoured stainless steel door with a numbered padlock.

The bruiser-man and the ice queen would come for him. He wanted desperately to know their names, so he could call out and reach them on a personal level. So he could articulate the horror of what he'd experienced.

What he must never experience again.

Allan pressed against the wall beside the door, groaning with both bodies. He squeezed his shoulders then let his arms drop, twisting until he leaned shoulder-to-shoulder with himself.

What do they need me in this condition for? They would not want me to have these nightmares. It goes against any possible end goal.

All that training...

Allan remembered all he'd learned, and the distant past of the person he'd been before. The proud street urchin of Allan Gerrold had cleared way for—what? Super academic? Master of tests? Trivial pursuit champion?

Soldier.

War.

They've made me a tool for war.

They could send his second body into enemy territory, and use his original form to report what he observed. More intelligent and covert than a drone, with limited personal risk.

Would it hurt as much when half of him died?

Then I might be free of the dreams...

Allan reached over and patted his shoulders, his stomach knotting for wishing ill on that part of himself.

The door screeched open. The bruiser-man shoved both of Allan away and down into the corner. He slammed the door shut behind him.

"What are you doing?" the bruiser-man snapped.

Allan shuddered from the pain rippling through his bodies, the extra physicality adding heightened awareness of every hurt rather than diluting it. The walls seemed to press in on him. He would lose his mind if he lost the tenuous grip he had on both bodies.

"I—" he began, reeling from his voice's internal and external echo, "I'd like to speak to… your colleague."

"Anything you can say to her, you can say to me," the bruiser-man said, sneering.

Allan's mouths twitched. He had to backtrack. "It's… actually something I need to tell both of you."

"I'll share the nuggets of information you pass onto me, I promise," the bruiser-man spat.

"Please," Allan croaked, "can you get her? Just this once?"

The bruiser-man crouched down until he was at eye level. "She's not coming for you. That's the last time I'm telling you. So either you tell me or, well, I'm sure you know by now."

Allan didn't know anything anymore. He couldn't guess what new horrors awaited him at each turn in this hell.

"All right," Allan said, speaking from the opposite body to split the load and transfer the ringing into the other set of ears. "When I slept last night, I had a horrible nightmare. It felt… more than real."

Allan described everything, tears coming to his eyes. He strained to control himself while suppressing the painful memories.

The bruiser-man alternated his gaze between Allan's bodies, listening and saying nothing for a while. Then he asked for clarifications, until Allan felt dangerously close to reliving the experience.

In an effort to keep distance between himself and the ghouls, past villains, and monstrosities, Allan flitted focus from one body to the other.

It didn't work. He couldn't shut the memories out,

because regardless of which body he focused on, the memories were all a part of *him.*

The bruiser-man probably took sadistic pleasure in drawing out the experience. He was no doubt aware of the effect the nightmare had on Allan; the bruiser-man and the ice queen had studied Allan and his psychology more deeply than anyone.

The bruiser-man stood and leaned against the wall.

Allan lay huddled below, beside himself in the corner. The bruiser-man seemed content to leave him there.

"What you described agrees with everything we recorded," he said.

Allan's jaws dropped. He shrank. "So you... you knew? You watched? H—how?"

"The implants, Gerrold. They're capable of more than inducing pain and pleasure."

Both of Allan sat up and took in the dual view of the bruiser-man gloating.

The bruiser-man would have enjoyed a double mirror of himself—if only Allan could transfer this view to him, and be rid of it forever.

"When you saw... why didn't you help me?" Allan whispered.

The bruiser-man smiled.

Allan extended both sets of arms, pleading. "Can you stop this from happening? It will interfere with what you plan for me."

The bruiser-man continued smiling, saying nothing.

Allan became hyper-aware of just how much he was at the bruiser-man's mercy. His vision blurred and he grew dizzy. Despite the sensory input, or perhaps because of it, he pawed the air trying to catch and hold his heads.

He was going to lose his mind.

Allan took deep breaths, trying to move past the weariness pulling at the back of his eyes. How long until the ice queen got here? Maybe Allan should return to the room, where it was more comfortable...

But comfort might induce sleep, and sleep led to... *that* place.

Allan moaned and raised both heads together. Synchronizing movements didn't make his temples throb as much.

The bruiser-man looked from one Allan to the other, his smile replaced by apathy. He scratched a tooth with one of his fingernails. "No, it won't affect our plans," he said.

Normally Allan would have weighed the bruiser-man's words before pressing further. But he was too tired, and he had to do everything he could to avoid returning to that dark world.

"Yes, it *will* affect your plans," Allan said. "I know what you intend to do with me."

The bruiser-man cocked his head. "Oh? And what's that?"

Allan articulated his theory about being a soldier, and relaying information back from the front lines with no fear of consequence.

"I'm your next step after the mice," Allan finished.

The bruiser-man straightened. He burst into laughter. "You have it all wrong, Gerrold. Sure, you're our next step. But you're not the step after the mice."

Goosebumps shivered up Allan's four legs. He tucked his knees closer. "What do you mean?"

The bruiser-man let the silence drag before answering. "There were plenty before you."

"Plenty of what? Of intermediate steps?"

"No. Plenty of people. People who had their brains copied into duplicate bodies."

Allan swallowed, but was only successful in one body. The other held a lump. The disjointed sensations tightened the muscles in his neck.

"W—what happened... to them?" he asked, voice hoarse.

"They experienced what you did."

"And then... what?"

Allan's attention shifted between bodily control and the implications of what the bruiser-man was saying.

The bruiser-man stared at him with his stupid grin.

"And then *what!?*" Allan repeated.

"They died." Cogs were visible behind the bruiser-man's cold eyes. "You are the first one to survive this long, Gerrold."

Allan hugged his knees. His hands shook and rocked his lower bodies.

In the right mind he might have recognized the futility of arguing with the bruiser-man, but he was quite far from the right mind.

"Well... you've got to make this stop. I won't be able to do what you want me to if I have to go through... *this...* every time I sleep."

"Again, Gerrold, you've got it all wrong."

The bruiser-man crouched and took hold of one shoulder from each of Allan's bodies. It was a cross between a formal group hug and being sternly taken aside. As the bruiser-man's hands clenched and unclenched, shooting sensations ran down Allan's arms and back.

"Your thoughts in these two brains, in these two bodies, are entangled."

"I'm aware," Allan said drily.

"Yes, because we taught you," the bruiser-man said, tightening his grip. This close to him, Allan smelled strong, nose-curling cologne.

"It's like the quantum entanglement of two particles," the bruiser-man went on, looking through Allan. "Pairs of quantum particles can be put into a special state in which the pair of particles can be inherently connected, and remain so even if they are far apart. What happens to one affects the other. This is because the true state of the pair cannot be thought of as two distinct, single-particle states. The two particles are actually one thing. It's a two-particle system, not two single-particle systems. This special two-particle state is called quantum entanglement."

Allan said nothing, thinking only that by not encouraging the lecture it would limit its duration. Maybe by being an attentive student Allan could then ask for the favour of talking to the ice queen.

Had the bruiser-man not been paying attention when the ice queen and Allan had talked about this? Or did he just feel the need to mansplain quantum theory Allan now knew inside and out?

"You saw the mice," the bruiser-man said, shaking Allan's shoulders. Two of his faces spoke in simultaneity from different angles. "The mice are entangled. Two bodies, but only one... call it a sense of awareness.

"You're special because you have consciousness, intelligence. There is only one of you. Your brains are innately connected. You're literally the sum of two parts and more than the sum. You're a new type of man. You've gone where no one has been before. No, that's not quite right. You're the first person to go there and come out of it alive."

"You mean what I... where I went when I, we—" Allan gestured with each body to his other half, "—slept?"

"Yes." The bruiser-man slid his hands up Allan's shoulders until they reached his necks. Although the hands were on two separate bodies, it felt as though he were wringing Allan's neck.

The bruiser-man grabbed the scruff of Allan's necks and heaved upward. Allan cried out as he was dragged up onto four feet. His heads spun as the bruiser-man shoved him down the hallway.

"This is a new world you go to. One infused with power. We intend to learn how to make use of this power." His voice held a conversational tone, something he'd never really had before with Allan. Allan's skins crawled.

"You," the bruiser-man continued, squeezing Allan's shoulders again, "will be our link. Our syphon."

They turned the corner and faced into one of the two

bedrooms. The bruiser-man pointed across Allan's shoulders to the bed. "All you have to do is sleep."

Allan pushed away from the entrance to the room, only to be shoved by the bruiser-man.

He refused to accept what he'd heard.

"What are you saying?" he said. "You expect me to experience *that place...* again?"

"You're catching on, Gerrold."

Allan shook his heads fast to blur the reality he rejected. "No, I won't do it. I couldn't... I can't stand it. It's of no use to you. You can't possibly glean power from what I just went through. You can't make a connection to it. You don't want to."

The bruiser-man filled the cramped doorway, blocking off escape. Allan stood closer to him than he felt comfortable, but he didn't want to risk being locked in the room.

"We already know how to make the connection. What do you think we were doing while you slept? You'll do it again. And again." He moved until his face stared inches from one of Allan's. His breath smelled of spearmint and cigarettes. Allan's view seesawed between the bruiser-man right in Allan's face, then far away.

"And again, and again," the bruiser-man taunted. "You know what will happen if you don't."

Allan shuddered. The bruiser-man could be bluffing. It was early in the morning—maybe he hadn't come prepared. Maybe his ego was so inflated he thought Allan wouldn't even need the remote anymore.

He was bluffing. He had to be bluffing.

"It doesn't make sense!" Allan shouted. "Why would you have put me through all that physical training if you'd just planned on this mental torture?"

"Subject survival rate was even more abysmal without physical training," the bruiser-man said coldly. "The physical training strengthens your bodies and mind past the point that meditation and focus can take you. It lets you withstand the assault, and make a more enduring tether."

"Tether." Allan spat the word. He shoved the bruiser-man back into the wall of the corridor. The bruiser-man grunted, then pulled a black remote out of his pocket.

"This is your last warning, Gerrold," he growled, dangling and twirling the remote between his fingers.

The pain Allan would feel from the little box was nothing compared to what he'd just gone through. And no amount of pleasure would convince him to do it, either.

Allan charged the bruiser-man in both bodies, feeling a double rush of movement in his inner ears.

The bruiser-man pushed the red button down and held it down. He darted to the side.

Allan's visions swelled red. Pain overloaded his senses. He saw his own erratic pulse in throbbing colours as the backs of his eyes burned.

The intensity was tenfold what they'd used before. Allan couldn't control his body. Lightning rode up and down his spines. He was faintly aware of writhing on the ground, and of kicking as he tried to escape from both bodies.

"Turn… off … please," Allan gasped in dual-echo.

The pain stopped long enough for Allan to hear the bruiser-man chortling. Then a rod drove up his spines, bent him backward, and shot jets of electricity through.

* * *

Allan lay on the ground in puddles of sweat. He had no idea how long he'd been unconscious. He faced his other half on the ground, seeing dark circles beneath dead, bloodshot eyes. His bodies had different bruises; blood stained different teeth.

He wanted to turn away, to avoid seeing and being reminded of the phantom pains still pulsing through him, but couldn't will his muscles into motion.

Sooner or later, he was going to have to sleep. He would have to return to that dark place, and the pain would be far worse.

CHAPTER SIXTEEN

Come the Childhood Monsters

In Ben's apartment, Kitt and Ben nestled on the couch on separate cushions. They stared at the powered-off TV screen as though it contained answers to their problems. Ben's muscles refused to move.

Their break was short-lived. What felt like moments after they sat, the entry door to their right crashed open in a wood-cracking bang.

How could Ben have forgotten to lock the door?

He and Kitt jumped off the couch to see Al Turen's five-foot tall form heaving in the doorway. How had he even gotten into the building?

Kitt gasped and shuffled closer to Ben, her hand on his shoulder. Ben gently touched Kitt's hand, maintaining Turen's stony gaze.

"How dare you," Turen said, bearing his teeth. "Who do you think you are? You're just a couple of *theorists*. Without me you have *nothing*."

Turen's lip curled as he scanned the kitchen and dining room to his right, the living room to his left. He paced straight ahead, toward the hall where the bedrooms and bathroom were. "You break into my lab, use it without my permission—coerce one of my technicians, no less—and pursue tests related to our campaign without my involvement. If I wanted, both of your careers would be finished."

On and on Turen went, pacing between the entryway and the hall, as though he'd forgotten Ben and Kitt were there.

As his protests lost clarity, Ben whispered to Kitt, "I thought Franklin was swapping out the security footage."

"There must be another copy somewhere," Kitt murmured. "That or maybe I should have agreed to go for lunch."

"Are you listening to me?!" Turen shouted. "You're both on thin ice, and you're doing nothing to help yourselves."

"What we did was wrong," Kitt said. "We just... had to know for sure. The curiosity was eating at us."

"Had to know *what* for sure?" Turen demanded, throwing his arms. "I have it all recorded. I watched everything you did."

His face was red enough to start a fire. A vein throbbed at his temple. Turen pulled out his phone, jabbing his finger like a weapon with each touch until his phone projected a faint holo.

"Look!" When he noticed how dim the colours were, he added, "Turn the lights off!"

Ben looked at Kitt, whose eyes were wide. He didn't want to face the replay. Kitt didn't remember what had happened—not everything. Ben did.

"Lights off!" Turen shouted. "Did you not hear me?"

Kitt moved before Ben could stop her. She went to the hall entry and dragged her finger down a touch panel until only the light of the holo filled the space.

Ben winced. The faded-colour holo began with their entrance into the lab, wobbling in Turen's grip. Ben held his breath. Would they see what Kitt remembered, that her theory had been confirmed as true?

Or would it show what had actually happened, that some of the experiments had verified Ben's theory, had shown that time travel to the past had occurred, and thus proved Kitt's theory to be wrong? Ben's desire for someone else to see what he'd seen remained beneath the surface no matter how much he focused on Kitt's well-being, right next to the scheming, grotesque childhood monsters.

They were coming back into Ben's life. He could feel it, and to know he wasn't crazy was the only weapon he had against them. His theory seemed one of the last things left to him.

The holo played on, shifting then finally stabilizing as Turen placed his phone on the island in the adjacent kitchen. Ben wanted the ephemeral nature of the images held true for their contents, as well.

The third experimental result was... evidence of backward time travel!

"There!" Turen shouted. "You have clear evidence of backward time travel, and on your third experiment!"

Finally! Ben thought. Someone else was seeing what he was!

Ben wanted to jump, but stopped himself. How many times would he spiritually betray Kitt like this? Kitt and Turen's memories of these experiments had differed before and might differ now from what had been recorded on the holo.

More importantly, Ben had put Kitt second. Again.

He would not let her be crushed a third time. This would be the last time.

Kitt stood near the hallway, her arms hanging loosely at her sides. Her wool sweater rose and fell, the silver strands in the grey catching the light and shimmering as it moved. Her face was as calm as it had been when he'd explained his theories to her so many years ago.

He wished he could go back to that time.

"What's this all about?" Turen snapped, stabbing a finger through the holo at Ben. It looked like he was skewering Kitt's form in the recording. "You have clear evidence of backward time travel. What do you intend to do?"

Kitt's jaw dropped.

Turen stalked around the coffee table until he paced in front of the television. His eyes narrowed like a lion targeting prey.

"You know I have already published my paper detailing our first experiments and that we never once had a case of backward time travel. What are you trying to do? Are you going to publish this? Show everybody I was wrong?"

Turen leaned across the gap and wagged a finger in Ben's face. Ben inhaled the stench of sweat.

"How did you manage this?" Turen whispered.

Ben opened his mouth to speak, but Turen cut him off.

"We had hundreds of results showing not a single case of backward time travel! You... you come along and get evidence of time travel to the past on your third try?!" Turen's voice rose, teetering on the edge of control. "What are you two up to?!"

Kitt shook her head and folded her arms. She moved and leaned against the kitchen island.

"What are you talking about? Are you seeing things?" She gestured to the holo that continued to cast pale phantoms between the living room and kitchen. "The holo showed quite clearly that no signal arrived, and no backward time travel occurred in this experiment. So why are you saying it did? Are you trying to give Ben a hard time, or—"

"Me?" Turen's eyebrows rose. "Me give him a hard time? Bah!"

He pointed at Kitt, then Ben. "You two are in this together. I just have to figure out... how you did this. Messed with my holo-recorder, or something. And I'll find it. Don't think I won't."

The holo's multi-coloured luminance flickered across Kitt and Turen's faces. Ben had never seen Kitt so angry before. She wasn't going to back down from Turen; Turen would never back down from anything.

"Stop trying to demonize us!" Kitt cried. "If you weren't so paranoid maybe we wouldn't have felt pressured to get these results without you! If you treated science as the driving factor, instead of your own career!"

"How dare you?" Turen shouted. "Do you know how much my facility has helped good-for-nothings like you? You have the audacity to say I don't value science?"

"Not as much as you value power over people," Kitt said. "No matter how much your facility has contributed to science, I can see in your eyes what you value. I could see it from the moment I met you."

They glared at one another. Turen stomped through the holo and snatched up his phone. "I—of all the—the nerve..."

He held his phone up. "This shows backward time travel happened. I know you two are conspiring against me together, no matter what you say."

A sense of deja-vu came over Ben. The arguments Kitt and Turen launched at each other faded into background noise. It had the same slightly-misaligned feeling as when reality had gone off the rails during the lab experiments. Ben shifted away from both Kitt and Turen to the far corner of the couch.

At the back of his mind, Ben had wondered if he was delusional. He was using Occam's razor: the simplest theory was usually the right one. The easiest way to explain all he'd seen was that he was imagining things.

The explanation was simple, but it wasn't satisfying. Now that Turen described the same reality rift Ben had lived through so many times, the explanation rang hollow.

Turen, no matter how much Ben disliked him, validated Ben's experience. By seeing the evidence of backward time travel, he'd saved Ben. It was neither a hallucination nor a dream.

But that meant the nightmares, the childhood monsters, were very real, too.

Ben's hands shook. His legs turned to sponge. He collapsed onto the couch.

I have some ability, he thought, *some power to select what becomes real... out of all the possibilities. I've... somehow used this skill to erase Kitt's memory of the experiments with backward time travel.*

Ben looked down at his palms. He prayed he had enough time to harness his newfound ability... before it was too late. He breathed in the stifling, stale air of his apartment and suddenly wished he could open a window. His vision swam every time he moved, though, and if he got up he would probably fall over.

Across the room, Turen had one hand on his hip, while the other shook a finger at Kitt. Kitt shook her head and dismissed Turen with a wave. The words of their argument became an indistinct muffle.

Stress? Ben thought. *That's it. So much stress... and no sleep.*

The swirling features in his vision moved in from the periphery. His head lolled. He leaned back, sinking farther into the couch.

Kitt and Turen were too involved to notice Ben's retreat, but Ben certainly paid attention to them. They moved as if they waded through molasses. Their words dragged out.

This can't be right, Ben thought. *This must just be me, overtired and overstressed.*

Their movements drew out, growing more sluggish until they'd almost stopped.

Ben's stomach lurched. Queasy, he fell off the couch onto his hands and knees. He coughed as he inhaled carpet dust. Sweat beaded on his brow. He glanced longingly up at Kitt and Turen, hoping they'd be back to normal, and that he was just temporarily feverish.

Kitt and Turen were frozen. More unearthly than statues, with their mouths partially open, their eyes unblinking. They held mid-movement postures impossible without momentum toward the next stable stance. Ben waited for Kitt to finish her step, for Turen's arm to come down, but they hung there, unmoving.

His chest lurched as though his heart were trying to

figure out if it, too, should stop. His mouth dried. He drew in rasping breaths.

The air thickened as a dense fog pressed and oozed over everything. The light dwindled until Ben could barely make out the statues of Kitt and Turen. A dreary grey flowed into the room, invading Ben's lungs. Cold rushed in, sudden and deep.

He pushed up from his hands and knees, then fell back into darkness.

"Kitt! Turen!" he cried.

Total darkness all around. No sound besides his own voice and breath.

Falling backward, endlessly backward.

He cringed in anticipation of impact.

It never came.

Ben called out again; nothing answered.

His inner ears were marbles balanced on a chopping board. Any sudden movement they too, would roll off and be lost.

The downward tug on his body weakened as his fall slowed. He stilled. With no acceleration and black all around, he lost track of up and down.

His inner ears went berserk. He was moving, then halting. He was spinning, then reversing.

He reached out, fighting the cues from his inner ears. His hands and knees touched a spongy ground he couldn't see.

A faint grey luminescence appeared through the darkness. Pushing down as much as he dared, Ben dragged his feet up, the residual uncertainty and mistrust of visual cues turning his stomach.

He stood in the gloom and spread his arms, steadying himself on the unbalanced floor. He wasn't sure if he was quivering, if it was, or if they both were.

A gloomy, featureless fog surrounded him. Thin air hissed between his teeth. He felt winded.

The light grew brighter by small measures, never enough to discern anything beyond the mist. With so little oxygen Ben dared not demand more from his body than simply standing.

The wobbling ground didn't help.

Two tall, thin shapes formed in the haze. They stepped toward him, their long legs, three-fingered hands and large heads emerging into full view.

They glared at him through slitted eyes.

Ben shuddered. Recognition tightened his muscles.

The monsters.

His monsters.

CHAPTER SEVENTEEN

The Request

Ben had never seen the monsters in so much light, but he wouldn't mistake them for anything else. Their grey pallor made them even more grotesque. Contrary to what he'd thought when he was a child, the clarity of light did nothing to ease his trembling.

The light brightened and devoured the surrounding fog. Ben realized he stood on a glass-like surface far above a bright, wide light source.

The monsters stepped closer.

Micro-fissures covered their slimy skin, diminishing only in the areas where the skin pulled taut over bone between joints. Their bones were outlined beneath a faintly-visible network of veins. Ben half-expected to see a three-chambered heart spreading red-blue throughout their forms.

Dense veins tracked their large heads, many terminating near huge jaws beneath slitted yellow eyes. Their bodies glistened with a slimy film, smelling mouldy and humid.

They've come for me.

"Greetings, Artemit," the taller one said. Its voice growled but had high-pitched chitters interwoven. A long row of teeth shone beneath thin lips.

They know my name, Ben thought, stiffening. *God, they know me by name.*

He had never wanted to speak to them. They'd been less terrifying as creatures who couldn't communicate. Knowing they could, that they bore such intelligence... with jaws that could snap him in half...

They're not real. They can't be real.

The shorter monster craned forward and bore its teeth, growling and shaking the floor.

"Who are you?" Ben stammered. "What do you want?"

"I am Belonthar," the tall monster said, then gestured. "This is Merthab. We have brought you here so you might help us."

Belonthar extended his arms straight out. They were about one and a half times the length of a human's. Was this an imploring gesture, or a threat? Were they asking for help, or demanding it?

The other, Merthab, raised his arms so his elbows were above his shoulders. The motion shadowed memories of the lab, where the monsters had stalked the darkness before returning to haunt him.

Belonthar and Merthab twittered at each other in high-pitched shrills.

They need my help. As long as I keep them talking, then, they won't hurt me. Just keep them busy. I can do this.

"Help you?" Ben asked. "Help you with what?"

Belonthar extended his arms once more. As well as being taller than Merthab, he had darker flesh, making his veins look slightly gangrenous.

"Artemit," Belonthar said, "You are One Who Chooses. We ask you to choose... us."

Ben clutched the front of his T-shirt. He wished he didn't know what Belonthar meant, but the truth was that Belonthar's words resonated with Ben's experience in the lab, with the way reality had bent under his will.

What could Ben even choose for them, though? Before the monsters, he was powerless. And what did it mean to "choose them"?

I have to get more information, he thought. *I need to understand.* His grip on his shirt tightened until it synched around his neck.

"What do you mean, I am 'The One Who Chooses'? What do I choose?"

Belonthar moved his arms gently up and down and said, "You are One Who Selects what will become of what might be. We are Ones Who Might Be."

Merthab raised his elbows again and moved close to Belonthar, vibrating. They twittered at each other again.

Belonthar jerked back to Ben. "We believe you know of your powers, that you know you can choose. Is this so, Artemit?"

They've seen right through me. Ben released his shirt and palmed his chest, feeling his heart's cadence like a fist banging on a prison wall.

Of all the possible outcomes, he was able to select a single one to become his reality. He could make it become another person's reality, as he'd done that with Kitt and Turen.

They know I have these powers.

Merthab's lips twitched. Belonthar stayed unnervingly still.

"It is so," Ben admitted. "I can choose."

Ben wondered how they knew so much about him.

He swallowed as the two monsters eyed each other in what Ben assumed was skepticism.

Just keep them talking. Get more information.

"What is it about me that makes me 'The One Who Chooses?'" The question burst from him as water from a dam. The dam opened more with each word, invoking all the unanswered questions of his life.

What gave me this power? Who am I? Why did it have to be me?

The monsters chirped and gestured, movements exaggerated by the length of their arms. Light reflected off slime on their teeth.

Ben quivered.

The monsters finished their conversation with a shared gasp.

"Artemit." Belonthar tilted his head one way then the other, lips pulled back to reveal glints of teeth. "Do you think you are the only one with this power?" The growls and chitters sounded like an audience amused by Ben's suffering.

"But you said I was The One Who…"

They didn't say that.

"You are One Who Chooses, Artemit," Belonthar corrected.

Blood rushed Ben's cheeks. *Not 'The One Who Chooses.' But 'one of those who can choose.'*

My suffering is not unique. I happen to be one of an infinite number, but small fraction of people, who have this power, in the many universes.

Out there are a billion Ben Artemits suffering through the same torture. I am a droplet in an ocean. Whatever happens to me doesn't matter.

Tears pooled in his eyes.

"Why me?" he asked. "Why not one of the infinite others who could choose whatever you want?"

His internal clock ticked wildly, accelerating until his heartbeat was a vibration.

His hands shouldn't be trembling anymore, because what was fear when existence didn't matter?

But his hands *were* trembling.

"Why can't one of your own kind choose?" he whispered.

The monsters conferred. Merthab stepped forward, but Belonthar stayed him with a hand. For a moment, their forms bulged out of shape, flickering through different monstrosities, some with armoured plating, some towering on four legs, others shrieking with fangs touching the ground.

Belonthar and Merthab stumbled away from each other and regained their original forms. They gazed at Ben with steel in their eyes.

"We cannot do this ourselves," Belonthar said, "but you, Artemit, can do this for us. You could do this when you were younger, but we lost our link with you."

Ben's internal clockwork jammed. Its clock face cracked. It was one thing to be tormented every night as a child. It was another thing to be inconsequential.

To be tortured *and* inconsequential was worse than anything. Something in him shrieked against the notion.

He stomped forward, throwing up his arms, spitting curses and exhaling poison. The monsters shrank from him.

"Do you know what my life's been like because of you? My fear as a child? You came for me every night! You... monsters!"

The word didn't do it justice. It didn't convey a fraction of what they were in his mind. He screamed at them, squeezing out all the filth that had grown inside since they'd entered his life.

When he thought he'd finished, he found more.

He yelled until he gasped for breath and tightness gripped his sternum. He tasted blood.

Belonthar closed his eyes and slid fingers over and beneath one another, as though he manipulated an invisible ball.

Merthab opened his mouth wide and lightly bit his fingers. He seemed to hold back a torrent before he pulled his hand away.

"Your fear," Merthab said, "was minuscule compared to all of our need. We did not intend to frighten you.

"Your powers are strong. That is why you saw us. Take note, Artemit: you saw us. Many others did not. That is why we selected you."

Belonthar's eyes opened. "You are the only one who can do this for us, Artemit."

Pain pinched below Ben's ribcage. Nothing felt right about this. There were an infinite number of him out there —how could he be the special one? *Why* did he see them? *Why* were his powers strong? The monsters contradicted what they'd told him minutes ago. There was something they weren't giving him, and it probably went beyond the notion of multiple universes.

Every time his thoughts drifted toward the notion of helping them, he wanted to double over.

I will not—I must not—help them.

He envisioned them becoming real and storming in through his apartment. They'd reach Kitt and Turen first. Ben didn't want to imagine what they'd do to Kitt.

He wouldn't let them get to her.

Was she still back in that room, arguing with Turen? Was there any way she would escape with her career, her life intact? Or would Turen not be satisfied until he'd ruined them all in a quest for his own ego?

Ben had to get back to her. He had to help her fend off Turen. Turen would want answers, however, clearer answers than Ben could provide right now.

He firmed his lip. *I need more information, for Kitt. Then I'm going back to help her.*

"Who are you? Tell me why I should do anything for you."

"We are Ones Who Might Be," said Belonthar.

"You said that already." Ben pressed his lips together and swept his arm through the air. "What do you mean?"

He crossed his arms.

Belonthar and Merthab craned forward, the tops of their heads wrinkling in shadows.

"You should know," Belonthar said. "You exist in one of the infinity of multiple universes. You came to be because... choices were made that brought you from having a possible existence, to an actual existence."

Ben grated his fingers through his hair, hoping to release

the building pressure in his skull. "Why all the riddles?"

Belonthar's body tightened before he answered in a whisper, "Do you not recall?"

Ben had gone through every one of his encounters with the monsters either with himself, with Heather Smith, or both. There was no facet of their encounters he hadn't dissected.

Yet he had no idea what the monsters were talking about.

Had the monsters interacted with him in ways he had suppressed?

"What am I supposed to remember?" Ben asked, struggling to keep his voice even. "Is it something I knew in my childhood, something I've forgotten?"

Belonthar's eye slits dilated. His jaw opened and snapped. He turned toward Merthab who rocked on his heels.

Belonthar's fingers curled. He motioned as though he were stabbing something repeatedly into the ground. The deftness and speed made Ben jerk back. Belonthar's muscles rippled with the aftershocks of the gestures.

"Make us real."

That was it, lain bare. That was what Ben could choose: to make these monsters real.

Every instinct told him he shouldn't. With each stab of Belonthar's arms, however, Ben imagined himself crushed under those powerful limbs.

If I make them real, will they devour us? Or take over and rule us?

He couldn't say yes, but saying no was suicide.

Just keep them talking. They won't do anything if we're talking.

It was hard to think.

"Do you really believe you don't actually exist? That you merely have a possibility of existing?"

Belonthar calmed, his eye-slits contracting and narrowing. "It is so."

Ben squeezed his eyes shut, grabbed a fistful of hair and tugged. The tingle in his scalp made it easier to think straight, and to stop focusing on the monsters.

"No. That makes no sense. If you only have the possibility of existing how can you even talk to me, if I actually exist and you don't?"

Merthab surged forward, blood, bone and muscle tearing through the air. He raised his elbow high, then thrust a finger toward Ben's face.

Ben flinched but held his ground.

Merthab roared, and his fingers flickered between sharp claws and rounded digits.

Then he dropped his arm, brought his face close to Ben's and stared deep into Ben's eyes. His lips opened wide and he leaned forward until his breath fed into Ben's mouth.

Ben suppressed a gag at the stench of mould.

"Just as you, One Who Chooses, can act upon those of us who might come to exist," Merthab said, "so too can we act upon you. Indeed, how could it be otherwise? You can make us be. We can affect you. Proof of that is that you are here, in a place of what might become."

Ben's eyes watered. He resisted the urge to back away, knowing any movement would give ground to Merthab and grant dominance.

Merthab retreated after a moment, his voice calming. "All you have to do is bring us into being."

He hunched his shoulders, looking more predatory in spite his words. What was he planning?

Belonthar, meanwhile, surveyed the scene calmly. He might be more reasonable.

"Surely you exist in one of the multiple universes, Belonthar," Ben said. "What's more, you exist in an infinite number of the multiple universes. So why do you need to be brought into being? You already exist.

"We know backward time travel exists. Therefore we know the infinity of multiple universes exists."

The words made Ben feel like he was back in a classroom, and flowed through him like liquid courage.

"Therefore, anything that can exist, no matter how unlikely, as long as it is possible, does exist. So you already exist. This is not a place of 'potentially existing,' or whatever you call it."

The monsters chirped and tittered as they snapped their jaws at one another. Their limbs stuttered through motions Ben didn't understand. They could be having a heart to heart, or be about to tear *him* apart.

I need out of here.

Merthab broke from the discussion and addressed Ben.

"We do not exist," he said. He stabbed an accusatory finger at Ben. "We want to exist! You can give this to us!"

The blood rushing to Merthab's face highlighted each vein running to his teeth. Ben stumbled back in spite of himself.

"What—" Ben turned to Belonthar to avoid looking at Merthab, "—will happen if I bring you into existence?"

Belonthar's hands shook, wriggling the taut flesh around every muscle. The fissures covering his head twisted. All of this happened in an instant as Belonthar snapped his reply.

"Nothing!" The chitter and pitch were higher than before. "We will simply move into our own world, a real world. That is all. We ask for existence. Nothing more!"

Merthab was the one more quick to anger, whose emotional outbursts were part of his natural expression. Belonthar, on the other hand, had maintained a calm demeanour throughout. Had it been Merthab who'd spoken, Ben might not have taken the unease and high-pitch as seriously.

They are not humans, though, he reminded himself. *I can't expect them to act like us. I probably shouldn't trust my readings of them... But I do trust my instincts. They're lying about something.*

The thought of the monsters becoming real continued

to form knots in his stomach. Was he clinging to his own bias toward them, to perceive them as monstrosities when all they wanted was a home and a place in the multiple universes? What they asked for didn't seem that complicated.

The mechanics of how he was a Chooser and how he could choose were utterly beyond him. But if the outcome was just to create space for them, was that really so bad? After that they might leave him alone, and all of this haunting could end.

He could say goodbye once and for all. He might even be regarded as their saviour.

But somewhere deep inside cried out against the idea. The opposition ran deeper than pure pettiness after so many years of torture. It was more than revulsion at their physical form. It was an instinct that a terrible disaster would occur if he made them real. They had been strangely evasive when asked about the consequences.

That evasiveness spoke louder than his biases.

I won't do it; I won't help them.

If he made them real, they'd be in his living room. In the city. Their individual force was far greater than any human's, and who knew what weapons they might have? They would overpower humanity in no time. Certainly Kitt, Turen and Ben would have no hope.

Would humanity and the monsters go to war? Or would these monsters appear all over the world, interspersed with humans everywhere? A global, instantaneous and complete invasion?

Or would their world appear next to Earth, transforming it into a twin planetary system? Where *would* their world be if it became real?

I need to know more.

"What is your potentially real world?"

Belonthar replied with some of the same high-pitched frenzy he'd had earlier. "We are, like you, beings of Earth— another Earth. We are what one type of dinosaur would have evolved into, had they not become extinct—had the asteroid not struck that world."

Merthab hissed at him as he finished, and Belonthar shrank.

Ben stared at the monsters' bodies in a new light. All along they'd looked mildly familiar, but he had assumed their forms rooted in the pits of his darkest nightmares.

They aren't just my childhood monsters. I've seen them before...

The blocks fell into place like Tetris pieces.

Ben knew where he'd seen their forms. In an anthology of speculations by scientists—speculations based on known facts, but without the rigour required for discourse—he'd pored over image after image. A Canadian scientist had suggested what this line of dinosaurs might have evolved into if they hadn't been wiped out 65 million years ago.

The pictures on the old book's pages came back as clearly as though Ben had the copy in front of him. He'd looked over it so much as a child the visions remained stamped in his mind.

The monsters were evolved from a type of dinosaur. He couldn't remember the name right now, but he could picture it clearly. It had the beginnings of an opposable appendage —a thumb, so to speak—binocular vision, a relative upright posture, and a relatively large brain.

Belonthar and Merthab were much like that imagined evolved dinosaur, but their limbs were exaggerated, thinner, with more jagged edges, and the movements brought to life produced an involuntary revulsion. The beauty of the original drawings had collided with the harshness of reality.

If that asteroid hadn't struck that other Earth, humans wouldn't exist. What could be wrong with bringing such a world into being?

Perhaps they believed if Ben chose for them to exist, the universe humanity lived in would branch over to one where dinosaurs had never become extinct, and where humans had never come to be.

Ben tried to imagine the effects of such an extreme

change on the timeline of Earth's history.

He failed.

An echo going back 65 million years reverberated in too many ways to predict what the present day might look like for the monsters.

Ben knew, from the infinity of multiple universes, that he could alter another timeline's past, but never his own. His fear of losing his own timeline by helping the monsters was irrational, but he couldn't shrug it off. Something about them seemed capable of shattering all he knew.

I must not make them real.

He scanned the monsters' features once more as he repeated the thought in his mind. Suddenly, their forms flickered in rapid bursts. Their arms lengthened and shortened, while their head shapes cascaded through a dozen variants, some looking more akin to the oblong snouts of velociraptors. Their fingers flickered from fingers to claws, while their body shifted between feathers, scales and skin.

They writhed as their forms shifted through the possibilities. This must have been what it was like in their would-be world. Forms would only exist for so long. Possible futures as common as gusts of wind would shake the fabric of their being.

They live in a quantum world, Ben thought.

Despite all he'd been through as a child, Ben felt sorry for them. They were intelligent beings who had evolved from dinosaurs, or at least, who could have. He doubted anything that they'd done had come out of malice. Rather, they were a fork in a road the universe hadn't traveled. As a result, they had been relegated to the shadows. What was it like to live as long as they had in a realm made entirely of possibilities, and not a single actuality?

Regardless of what they'd suffered, Ben could not justify the harm their existence could inflict on the human race. The extermination of billions could not be justified.

"Artemit," Belonthar asked, "what is your decision?"

Ben saw no other choice now but to tell them.

"Find yourselves another one who chooses. I won't do it."

He clutched tremors in his fists. *Don't shake. Don't show them weakness.*

The monsters stood still. Their eyes appeared lidless and there was not a trace of the quantum flickering that had been there before.

Ben's skin prickled.

Maybe... Maybe they stopped existing. Maybe they're on their way out. Ben tried inwardly repeating the words, but he couldn't fool himself. The thoughts were naïve hopes.

Belonthar's lips twitched. "Are you certain?"

"Yes, I am."

Merthab jerked violently one way, then another. His face twitched and contorted. "Enough!"

To Belonthar, he said in a low voice, "I told you this would not work."

Belonthar's gaze pierced through Ben. He twisted toward Merthab, grabbed his shoulder faster than Ben could blink, and shook it.

Belonthar spoke in high-pitched chitters for a long time, waving with the arm not holding Merthab.

Merthab shrugged off Belonthar's grip, swooping and curling away, snapping his jaws. He turned toward Ben and said, "Watch what will happen now to your arms, Artemit."

Ben crossed his arms instinctively, wishing suddenly he'd worn a sweater rather than a short-sleeved shirt. He refused to obey Merthab, but out of the corner of his eye he surveyed his forearms.

Everything seemed fine.

A strange tingling traveled along his skin, enveloping every bit until his arms vibrated. They grew warm, sweat breaking out on the reddening skin. The air blurred from the smoke of burning hair. Ben rubbed his forearms, then slapped himself to try and put out the invisible fire, but the heat kept intensifying.

The hairs on his arms vanished. Red-hot clamps latched onto Ben's arms and wouldn't let go.

He fell to his knees and screamed.

CHAPTER EIGHTEEN

The Demand

"**S**top—please!" Ben shouted as his skin roasted.

Belonthar shrieked in rapid twitters at Merthab, arms flying in violent striking motions.

Merthab ignored Belonthar, gazing instead at Ben and gnashing his jaws. He slid a thick, pointed tongue along his teeth.

Ben's fingers spasmed. He couldn't pat the flames out, because his skin was lava. Every touch blasted pain through him.

"Stop! Stop!"

His skin cooked blood red. It would be better for his arms to fall off.

Let them fall off. Let me free.

Waving. Writhing. The flames invisible, a phantom supernova on his skin.

"Make us real, Artemit," Merthab said. "Then the pain will go away."

Pustules and blisters inflated. Hissing when neighbouring bubbles touched borders. Tears blurred vision. Knobby, mangled tissue swelled to burst.

He knew what was coming, but was powerless.

Why not do as they ask?

Reservations, justifications. Part of another world.

Light burst in view. He tasted ash and blood. A log cracked, something inside him, his last resistance, unleashing a roar of embers.

Choking, throat useless for speech. Acrid smoke filled his nose, mouth, lungs. He writhed in retreat; the pain forbade it.

His arms a mess of sticky red, rivulets of sinew.

"STOP!" he screamed.

His ears rang from the reverberation. He pushed everything away, squeezing his eyes shut. As the air left his lungs it sucked and twisted the atmosphere.

The pressure lifted.

The change knocked the wind out of Ben. He gasped. Whatever good remained in the world had to be inhaled before it vanished again.

Light glowed beneath him. He lay in a fetal position on the transparent surface. He stared sideways at the monsters, quivering. His arms—were they really back? He brought them gingerly inward.

A cool, calm touch came from his wrist. Was this normal? It felt heavenly, artificial. Yet the skin, hairs and all, were back on both arms. No signs of damage.

Belonthar snapped his jaws and rasped at Merthab, his darker skin flushing with blood. Merthab jerked an arm up and down until Belonthar stilled him with a single gesture.

"Artemit," Belonthar said, letting each word drag, "I must ask you one. Last. Time. Will you make us real?"

Ben's mouth wouldn't open. The bodily control he'd just exerted had been robbed from him. Everything but his eyes, with which he gazed desperately for rescue.

The empty grey fog surrounded him, an indifferent witness to his end.

I'm already gone, he thought. *If this is all I have left, then they must not be allowed to exist...*

He moved his eyes in a side-to-side motion, then blinked

furiously, his last acts of defiance.

"No," he said with great effort. "You will not exist."

Belonthar turned to Merthab, who nodded. He bent down toward Ben, and murmured, "I regret what we must do now, Artemit. We must try another way."

Merthab snapped his jaws and edged closer. "There is only one other way. You should have cooperated. Now we have to do this."

Part of Ben shouted, *I will cooperate!* He was saved by his paralysis, though, and his own weak but surviving will to do what was right.

They must not be, he thought, wishing his spirit were more united and braver than he felt.

"We will remove your brain," Belonthar said. "We will use it to generate thoughts close to those you would have thought voluntarily. In this manner, we might still come to be."

What?!

Ben struggled against invisible restraints, his soul writhing without motion. He managed to make his hands quiver, but it was too little.

Was this what it was like in a would-be world?

I won't let them do this.

Merthab grabbed Ben by the shoulders. At his touch, Ben regained some wiggling motion in his arms and legs.

The victory was short-lived as Merthab jerked and slammed Ben into a chair. Merthab's fingers flickered between digits and claws, the claws digging into Ben's skin. Cold flesh choked limp terror. Ben's world spun from the unearthly force.

Merthab released. Ben shook, but otherwise had no bodily control.

Belonthar had disappeared. The fog had lifted above them, revealing towers taller than Ben had ever seen, jagged grey superstructures stretching up beyond sight.

Ben was an ant in a wheat field, knowing the combine would come for destruction.

Bridges linked the towers at several levels, where tooth-apertured doors opened. Shimmering reflections made each tower—pulse, beat, stretch—higher.

Ben saw a monster walk effortlessly through the air, but in an instant the moving spec was gone. The breeze carried stale dust and whispered moans.

Merthab leaned above Ben's upturned gaze, his head seeming larger than the sun. Ben smelled the mould on Merthab's breath.

"Only a bit longer now, Artemit," Merthab said. "When we have our tools, it will all be over for you. But take comfort—your brain will live on."

Merthab let out ear-piercing trills, his body rocking with each set.

Ben's body refused basic reactions like wincing or shutting his eyes.

Trapped as he was, he wondered dimly why the monsters had even bothered waiting to cut him open. Especially for Merthab, who seemed more inclined to detach Ben's brain stem than to waste time arguing quantum philosophy.

Maybe there was some inherent risk in what they were proposing. Hadn't they said they *might* still come to be with this method—that it wasn't guaranteed?

Belonthar stepped out of the fog with a silver knife in one hand, and an egg-shaped metal container.

He set them down on a table beside Ben. He dumped out the contents unceremoniously, clattering and echoing through the emptiness. The tools looked vaguely like scissors and forceps.

Merthab brought out a glowing spheroid shell with most of its surface area cut out. The two remaining surfaces jutted probes and needles into the centre. Perfect for a brain.

Ben didn't want to think about all the things they could do to him.

Belonthar's lips remained closed as he stooped over the

table and put the implements in a neat array, his fingers quantum-flickering into claws clacking the surface.

Belonthar stepped back and Merthab picked up a curved knife. He surged beside Ben and gripped the back of his skull with his other hand.

No please no—

Merthab drew thin cuts in a ring around Ben's head, rough sketches etched in oozing blood. The wetness on Ben's forehead streamed into his eyes, tinting everything red.

The pain was sharper when he couldn't move away from it. When he couldn't scream.

Belonthar handed Merthab a tool that hummed and glowed with a faint, blurred light.

They can't do this to me. I can't—I won't give in. Ever.

His hot red vision clouded his thoughts, weakening his self-talk.

What can I—how can I—stop this?

They exist in my mind. He wanted to jerk with each thought. *That's why they can hurt me.*

But I should have more power than them.

Understanding rushed through him.

They had tried to burn him, but nothing had happened before.

It wasn't that they'd burned him and reverted him back to normal. It was that they'd never burned him at all.

"Merthab! Belonthar! Stop!"

The blade froze in mid-air and stopped humming.

The starbursts of pain faded to a cloudless night sky.

Ben leaned back and away, closing his eyes as he felt his skull.

It was still whole.

"You blundered," Ben whispered, glaring at Merthab. "Both of you."

Ben stood and backed away from Merthab, who held the motionless saw in mid-air. Ben closed his eyes, shook his head, and opened them again. The saw was gone.

"You said I didn't remember, Belonthar. You burned my arms, Merthab. You tried to cut out my brain."

Ben held up his arms, and ran his fingers through his hair, above his ears and around his head. "I'm just fine now."

Merthab started to speak. Ben stepped up and passed his hand smoothly across Merthab's face.

"You are an embarrassment to your kind," Ben said. He swept his arms all around, glancing in both directions at the dimly-lit mist.

"All of this," he continued. "This place of fog. Your would-be world. It's a lie."

"No, Artemit," Belonthar said. He too was frozen in place.

"Oh, your quantum world exists," Ben admitted. "You are in it, but I'm not. I'm still on the floor, beside my couch. Kitt and Turen are with me, probably trying to help me. They didn't slow down. You simply drew my mind away from them."

Ben turned to Merthab. "Did you think you could actually make me think my arms were burning without giving yourselves away? Did you think you could saw open my skull?"

He touched a finger to his temple. "This is the only place where you are, in any sense, real. You can affect me, but only because I believe in you. Just as I did as a child."

Merthab jerked toward Ben. Ben held up a hand. Merthab halted, swayed and dropped to his knees.

"You do live in a would-be quantum world," Ben said, his words flowing and gaining power. "You connected with me when I was a boy, and you lost me when I was convinced you were just in my head. You got me back when we did the quantum experiments. My mind opened to you again.

"You tried for me in the lab, but Kitt was there and I wouldn't let you in. I'm not sure how I kept you away. Not quite. Then you took me when Kitt was with Turen and I had only myself to think of.

"You can't take my brain. All you can do is affect my thoughts."

Merthab swayed, still on his knees.

"You made my arms burn," Ben continued. "You cut into my skull. But only in my mind. You took the risk that I would break. When I did not, you gave up your secrets. Belonthar tried to stop you, but you went too far."

Belonthar clasped his chin. "Artemit," he pleaded, "we ask only that you make us real."

Years of struggle coalesced into a finished picture, as though Ben had finally been able to step back and see the brushstrokes for a landscape.

"You do ask. Yes. I am the only one you can ask. I am the only real mind you can connect with."

It wasn't boastful; it was fact. All the subtle clues of their visits, their mannerisms, now seemed natural from the desperation of their plight. They seemed smaller than they'd been before.

He leaned toward Belonthar. "Isn't that right?" he whispered.

Belonthar dropped his head and spread his arms. "Since you now know all this, why not grant us what we seek?"

"Because you blundered."

Belonthar stared at him, unblinking.

"What is it I don't remember?" Ben asked. It was the last piece of the puzzle, the only thing he might still need from the monsters.

Belonthar's jaws snapped open and closed. Twice.

"You won't tell me, will you? You've tried this before, and it almost worked—isn't that right?"

Belonthar's eyes fell half-shut. His gaze grew distant, as though he were ignoring Ben.

Heat rushed Ben's cheeks. How dare Belonthar, when Ben had control over them?

"I can choose you to be real," he snapped, "but I can't choose you to be any less real than you are now. You do live in a quantum world, where nothing is ever real, and only possibilities exist. If I had the ability to reduce your state of existence, to make it impossible for you to become real, I would use that skill and eliminate you completely."

Merthab stood, springing off his knees. He moved forward and snapped his jaws, jerking against an invisible wall.

Ben's fingertips trembled at the sight of his loss of control. Thankfully he'd managed to keep a wall up.

"You can't erase us, Artemit," Merthab snarled. "And we will not give up. You will still believe in us. You cannot change that. We'll come for you again. As many times as it takes."

Ben opened his mouth to deny, but thought better of it. "Yes," he said, "I do believe in you again. I wish I didn't."

Stiffening his arms at his sides and standing taller, he added, "I will find a way to stop believing in you."

Belonthar stepped forward, flexing his hands as he took control of himself again. "It is too late, Artemit. We can now arrange for others to make us real." His lips peeled back over his teeth, stretching up into a hideous smile.

Ben had to get out while he still had control. Despite their threats, Ben felt the power in his hands, a tingle pulsing beneath the surface, beneath veins, beneath bone.

He walked away. The fog thickened around him, but this time, *Ben* made it appear.

He lay on his back and closed his eyes, clasping hands above his chest. His weight pulled at his skin, and his organs nestled into the comfort of Earth's gravity. The air thickened. Breathing grew easy once again.

He heard a distant cry that became louder until it rang from both sides of his skull.

Kitt was calling his name.

He opened his eyes, searching for her.

CHAPTER NINETEEN

Forced Slumber

Rough, dry hands carried Allan Gerrold. Moans slowly awoke him. Shrieks jolted his eyes open, sounds echoing into the canyons of an abyss.

Insects crawled everywhere the hands touched, and Allan squirmed out of their grasp and rolled away. He slid on a cold, dark surface and only got a moment's respite before a new pair of hands, claws—or other appendages he didn't want to think about—took their place.

He rolled onto his stomach and stared into the maws of bestial creations.

Their eyes wobbled in blurs like their attention was continually divided between Allan and commands from the deepest hell. They sneered and snapped at him, some with pests that flew out of their mouths and tried to go up Allan's nose. Pus and blood oozed from the cracks lining their faces and bodies. Red streams trickled from their eye sockets.

Allan writhed and kicked and screamed until he couldn't.

He flitted into and out of awareness. His brain's trauma centres made vain attempts to forget it all.

The towers blurred. The hands blurred. At some point Allan was dragged right through a solid object. Was it a fountain, a statue, an altar? He didn't know. It lit his insides on fire and he clawed at the ground. His hands pushed below the surface and he heard a thousand new screams.

He fell through the ground and onto a mass of writhing flesh.

They ripped his arms out of their sockets, sinew and tendons sparking like electrical wires twitching over a puddle. When they tore off his legs his hips dislocated and his body contorted, compressing his stomach. He thought it might end when they ripped off his head, but fire at the base of his skull just intensified as his brain oozed out.

He still felt everything. His body had gone wireless so he could experience torture broadband.

Unescapable tastes assaulted him, beyond description or comparison. They touched primal emotions deep within, making him lose what little grasp of reality still remained.

Was this what screams tasted like, what tears smelt like? What monsters breathed?

The monsters pulled Allan into smaller and smaller pieces.

He lived through all of it.

* * *

There was no rest in this sleep. Allan awoke feeling more exhausted than before, but so terrified his eyes snapped and glued open. He ate, drank, and exercised, trying to treasure every minute in reality, remaining haunted by what was to come.

The sand in the hourglass refused to be clutched. Allan found the days racing by until night came and his exhausted bodies would stare at the ceiling, aching for rest but dreading slumber.

He hadn't seen the ice queen since he'd started having the nightmares. His futile pleas for mercy were wasted on the bruiser-man, whose smiles grew larger the more Allan suffered.

Allan took to writing and drawing on the walls. They'd given him an ancient pencil for writing and recording his thoughts, presumably because giving him a computer would have made him preoccupied with trying to contact the outside world.

He scribbled madly on the walls until the lead broke, and he'd start again by rotating it in the hole of a cheap plastic sharpener. The stream-of-consciousness writing staved off his fear and fatigue for short bursts, when he would be caught in flow. He'd write the first part with one body, then switch to the other because letting one be restless too long let the fear and fatigue creep back in.

I weep in the darkness

Four eyes not enough

My sorrow, they harness

Chained without handcuffs

Wind no longer whispers

The sun no longer shines

My life without a flicker

Rusted, my wind chimes

Four palms to read for fate

Four knees to clutch and hold

Two brains to calculate

The rotting of my soul

I'm a data point, a datum

They do it all for science

His her ultimatum

Will make my heart beat silence

But nothing does compare

To that I cannot face

The realm beyond despair

That cursed sleeping...

Please don't send me again.

Please.

Please.

Stay awake.

Stay awake.

Stay awake.

When he ran out of words, he drew molecular orbitals in the spaces between stanzas, all the shapes of quantum probability clouds.

Sharp. Principal. Diffuse. Fundamental. Hybridizations between them that allowed existences to blend together.

And when sleep inevitably came, whether through the sedatives they fed him or through sheer exhaustion, Allan went to worse hells. There were subtle variations in the worlds he visited, but the pain was always amplified, the torture deeper, everything heightened in ways that forbade him from remembering anything but agony.

* * *

One night, Allan cried out when he found the ice queen suddenly standing by the wall, reading his ramblings. She'd entered his room without a word.

"It's just me," she said. "Keep calm."

Allan's world spun. He hadn't been aware of anything, even though he'd thought to be paying attention to every detail to avoid sleep. How long had he been sleeping awake?

In his next blinks, she was gone again. He got up and scrambled around the room, searching under the bed, in the closet, the bathroom. He banged against the door until, in a flash, blood from his fists appeared.

He was living in stop motion animation.

The door pulled away. He thought he'd finally escaped until he hit the floor and fell back into the hell sleep.

* * *

He stopped eating.

The bruiser-man injected him with sedative. Allan fought back, so the injections became stab wounds. In both bodies—different places.

One of their struggles resulted in a smashed desk lamp, which had been the only light in the room Allan still had control over. The ice queen and bruiser-man didn't replace it, but they did erase what he'd written on the walls.

So he started over in total darkness.

In the morning, when the overhead lights came on, Allan's verses were crooked, skewed and barely understandable, but nowhere near as much as the rest of him.

In between the verses, drawn with increasing shading and detail, were more molecular orbitals, this time extending between molecules, with crooked lightning to symbolize electron flicker, the uncertain transitions between states.

If I went to the bottom

And asked for directions

They'd tell me to keep going

Keep digging, don't worry

If I searched for the fire

The ship to keep sailing

Go fleece gold, they'd say

Pull it out the cracks

If I reached the other side

And ended in the middle

You'd be above laughing

On clouds of pure pyrite

If I look up, there's a chimney

If I look down, the ground's crumbling

If I look ahead, cracks are bleeding

If I look behind, there's fire

Burn me, freeze me, pitch me, bat me

Fold me, mould me, chip me, cast me

Beat me, whip me, rip me, gas me

Hate me, face me, fear me, wrath me

Fury claws its way

Rage eyes its prey

To get you, finally

And if not, then me.

Goodbye—no, not good.

Bye—no, not bye.

End—but I'm there

Empty

Now

Why

Shouts echoed from the hall and in his skull. He blinked and he was crammed into a shower with two bodies. Another blink and he was walking out his room door.

Double vision with synchronized blackouts.

Staccato movements of the bruiser-man and the ice queen near him as he ate. They said nothing. Looked at each other more than him. Allan clutched forks in fists, lifted them up.

Ready to strike at them.

Maybe he'd make *them* eat the food, watch *them* go to sleep.

He was too exhausted to be strategic, though. Since sleep was not restorative, his only source of energy was food.

They must have known this. They had him trapped.

Allan blinked and they were gone.

Another blink and his cheek hurt, the bruiser-man shaking his hand out from striking him. Forcing Allan to eat, the ice queen sitting beside him holding a spoonful.

Shoved into the room. Stumbling around, looking for the pencil. *Blink.* Next to the dresser. *Blink.* On all fours. Behind the toilet. The pencil in one hand.

Bruiser-man and woman standing, blocking the writing wall. Bruiser-man whispered in ice queen's ear. *Blink.* She recoiled from him. *Blink.* She stood between Allan and the bruiser-man, two fingers on Allan's wrist.

She waved to get his attention. Focused on one set of

eyes. Then the other. One, then the other, the pulsing darkness making her eyes dance like a demon.

His will started separating from his mind. Neither trusted the other. It was beyond controlling.

Blink. The bruiser-man and ice queen were gone.

One of him slept. Might have been his original body. No way to be sure. With his other half, he remained awake.

He twitched, muscles jerking in anticipation of the coming nightmare. Making his way slowly toward himself, ready to awaken.

But he never went *there.*

He watched himself sleep.

It was the best thing he'd ever seen.

✳ ✳ ✳

He awoke with renewed clarity and purpose, feeling like the energy he'd recuperated from one body had spread evenly into the other. Everything seemed a bit easier: getting up, showering, putting on clothes. His chest no longer carried as heavy residue of the horrific nights, and he was able to ponder something beyond pain for the first time in what felt like months.

They must have messed up the sedative, he thought. The ice queen... had he seen her use a dropper in his water? Maybe she'd not put enough. Or maybe she'd taken pity upon him, and put something to counteract the sedative's effects.

It was a foolish, false idea, but it gave him enough comfort to keep going.

The hellish place, the dark worlds, are real, he thought, *even if they are confined to my mind. If I could be forced to go there, so could anyone else. If I get out of here, I won't let anyone else be made to go there.*

Are these the hells people believe in? If they are, could there be a place, someplace else, that's the opposite?

Please let there be.

His veins no longer felt like acid had been poured through them. Allan relished running, energy rippling through his calves. The excitement of fast motion in both bodies gave a new rhythm to the activity, frenetic intensity increasing endorphin production and enveloping his body in a warm blanket.

This is the secret, he thought. *Sleeping with one body at a time. If I can do this, I can survive. I can last. This is worth it.*

They will fight me not to do it. I don't know what, if any power they've harnessed from the dark worlds, but they will never be satisfied. They will keep making me return until I've lost everything.

Maybe I can alternate which body I eat certain foods with, so that the sedative they put in would only affect one body.

They'll catch on. But I have to try, while I have strength.

✻ ✻ ✻

Allan tried what he'd planned at lunch, to separately eat food types in his two different bodies, so that any sedative concentrated in one would only affect the one body.

As soon as the bruiser-man saw this, he grabbed both plates, slammed them on top of each other like a sandwich, then proceeded to vigorously stir them with a fork.

"I don't know what you did last night, how you managed to avoid entering the realm. It is not going to happen again, I assure you." He grinned and offered the plate back to Allan, whose contents were now evenly divided into slop on both plates.

"Eat up," the bruiser-man said. "We wouldn't want you getting malnourished, now would we?"

Allan didn't meet the bruiser man's cruel eyes, and refused to move.

"You know we can always just inject you," the bruiser-man said with a shrug. "You can live without food for a while, so that might actually be easier."

Allan slowly picked up his forks and looked past the bruiser-man at the featureless, windowless walls.

Clearly if he tried to circumvent the sedative in the food, he'd only suffer more. Today was one of the rare moments when he had enough lucidity to dream of escape, and he determined to find the chink in the armour.

But there was nothing. The complex was as empty as they'd made him. There were no plugs in the walls, no cracks, no seams indicating where joists or external supports might lie. He could try haphazardly punching the walls to find a way through, but unless he had some better clue to go on, he would only get a few shots. The ceilings were deliberately high, a practical cathedral Nietzsche would've been proud of, a monument to the vacuum in human souls. Even if Allan stacked two chairs upon one another on top of his desk, he doubted he could reach the fluorescent lights, and even then the ceiling held as much promise of hidden passage as the bruiser man did of inner beauty. The vents could barely fit the girth of Allan's arms.

The doorways and corridors were all indistinguishable from one another, with no insight as to what lay outside. It stretched all of Allan's spatial intelligence to map the place out in his head, to try and connect the differently-sized but featureless rooms they'd brought him to. He still couldn't rule out the possibility they were a kilometre underground.

The only features in the entire complex lay in his room and in his captors. His room was a trap, and in his captors he saw nothing but cruelty, a fun house mirror where their own happiness rose in proportion to his distress. Everything around him that had colour hid something ugly, a façade for the cold pursuit of power.

Allan wondered whether, if he got out, he would even be able to walk through a park again without being terrified.

He gazed at the ice queen across the table, who, he had to

admit, had never been as gleeful in her outward celebration of his suffering.

She wore a black skirt and a blue blouse, tucked in primly below where she usually held her tablet. He noticed for the first time a silver chain around her neck being pulled down by some pendant beneath her shirt. Allan knew it couldn't be religious, and wondered idly what symbol of emptiness, and ugliness—what rejection and assault on the human spirit—she could've hidden there.

In all likelihood, like everything around him, there was probably nothing underneath.

Today she didn't hold his gaze long, but looked back and forth between him and his food. For a moment, he thought he saw something, a glimmer of emotion flicker across her analytical features. But he couldn't trust it, and he certainly couldn't trust her. While she hadn't been celebratory, she had still allowed his torture to continue.

The bruiser-man slapped Allan, making him jump and return to eating. With the other body though, he continued to stare at the woman, who drew her lips into a line. A moment later, the bruiser-man slapped Allan's second staring face, too.

Allan remarked that the bruiser-man had, more and more lately, taken to physically assaulting him instead of using the implants.

"Eat up," the bruiser-man said. "And don't make me ask again."

Allen put a spoonful in his mouth. It tasted like chalk.

* * *

That night, Allan tried massaging one of his bodies to encourage one to sleep and the other to stay awake. But the sensations of relaxation passed through both of him and through his one mind, and he soon found all four eyes drooping.

He moaned, got up and paced the room, giving himself shoves as one body passed the other. He scoured the room in search of something to write with on the walls. He ripped the sheets off the mattress and pulled out all his clothing in the dresser, then every drawer in it. Not a single writing implement. As before, the walls had been scrubbed clean of any trace of Allan Gerrold being anything more than a lab rat.

His legs gave out as his bodies forced a shutdown. The sudden impact on the ground jolted him awake, and he lay there gasping, grateful for the pain in his knees and back that was far better than anything he would experience in the dark worlds.

He let the pain comfort him a little too much, and fell in.

The torment was much the same as before.

He was dimly aware of his movement up inside a dark tower, which made him cry out until his throat cracked. For any movement in this realm was never for the better.

❊ ❊ ❊

It ended as it had so many other times: wrenched back together, the dark world held onto him as long as it could before releasing. With one body, Allan twitched, and with the other he shouted and staggered around the room.

Several minutes later when his vision no longer flashed with pain, when he tasted nothing but the dryness of his mouth, he sobbed. One body against the wall, the other writhing on the bed.

"Allan."

Allan heard many things after the dreams, aftershocks of every sense rippling through him to maximize the duration of his stay in the other place. He would hear his own voice, rebuking him for his weakness, the voice of his father, and more cruel, sinister recordings where his cries metamorphosed into mockery.

"Allan."

He cried harder, struggling against his own chastisement and how to be alone with his suffering.

"Allan."

"Leave me alone!" he shouted. He covered his ears and sang a monotone as loud as he could.

Something grabbed his shoulder, and he jerked, swinging his arms to bat the force away.

He made contact. Usually his hallucinations never gave him the satisfaction. They usually didn't groan or curse, either.

Allan opened his eyes and saw the ice queen touching a bleeding lip and stumbling back. Her hair was disheveled and she wore a black jogging suit. Was this some new form of torture? When their gazes met, she looked only vaguely familiar, some incomplete doppelgänger of the cold analytical woman he'd known. He wondered whether or not the dark world had superimposed itself on reality, and was just waiting for the right moment to send him reeling in agony.

"Dammit, Allan," the ice queen said in hushed whispers, "I know you've been through hell, but if you don't calm down we're going to miss our window of opportunity."

She winced as she dabbed at the cut on her lip.

The sight of her showing vulnerability—*humanity*—made Allan's knees quiver. This was so far outside his experience that the future became black and unknowable.

He tried to speak but the words came out as incoherent blubbers.

The ice queen approached but he retreated. He garnered enough strength of mind to raise his other body off the bed.

The woman ran her fingers through her hair, another human gesture that fit with no element of reality. Allan jerked his head involuntarily.

"Allan, I'm here to help you. Please. This isn't a trick. I know you have no reason to trust me, but I also know that somewhere in that brilliant mind you're capable of recognizing that you have nothing to lose by coming with me."

Allan said nothing for a long time, just looking at her and moving his other body until he stood side-by-side brushing arms with himself. The physical contact, along with the similar view from each body made it easier to think straight.

In the ice queen's eyes he recognized the same expression he had worn on both faces for so long, and probably still wore now. Her eyebrows folded, quivering as her gaze darted about.

He had to take a mental plunger to push what he'd just experienced through to the rest of him. Had he ever been able to take his captors at their word? Everything was blurry. So many details of what they'd said were lost, suppressed by some trauma coping mechanism deep within. He had flashes, but nothing concrete.

"Allan, you are not just a data point. And I'm not going to let your hearts beat into silence. You need to find the fire, the ship to keep sailing."

Her words echoed inside his skull, rebounding and illuminating shadowy corners. He saw himself writing similar words on the walls in the late night, words he had never expected anyone to read but that had served as a means of staying awake and reminding himself there was more to him than pain.

"I want to help you find the fire, the ship to keep sailing." She held her arms out to him, palms up.

The words washed through Allan. He remembered the feeling of the pencil in his hands as he'd written the words, but hearing them spoken by someone else shot adrenaline and warmth through him.

What happened next might actually matter. As his internal chronology flickered with a hint of importance, his thoughts sharpened.

"Find the fire. The ship to keep sailing."

The words reverberated, amplifying.

"You read them," Allan whispered. The ends of the words

hung on both his tongues.

The woman looked from one set of eyes to the other. "Yes, Allan."

The reintegration of his past experiences made Allan dizzy. He couldn't remember all the details of his previous conversations with the ice queen, but he remembered an important one.

"You've never called me Allan before."

She inhaled sharply, then sighed. "I suppose you're right."

"I don't even know your name." He focused until everything behind her blurred.

"What? Oh, my name's not important."

"I've been calling you the ice queen," Allan said.

She paused, then said quietly, "That's understandable, I suppose." Another pause. "My name is Tamika. Tamika Werrett."

It was a small concession. It could have been a fake name, though. Allan's memories had not come back without all the engrained fear.

"Why now?" he asked.

Tamika looked at her watch, then paced toward the door. "We're almost out of time," she said.

Allan shook his head. "You owe me an answer."

Tamika folded her arms across her chest and hunched her shoulders. Words trembled on the edges of her lips before she finally spoke.

"You know you're the only one who's survived this long," she said. "And to think I used to have a hard time justifying the deaths of those before you...

"What we've done to you is much worse than death, Allan. We've made you go to a deeper and deeper hell every night. And rather than being ignorant, we were spectators, taking notes and trying to detach ourselves. I've lost myself, bit by bit, but I realized I'd paid a much smaller price than you had. We'd squeezed you for more and more and more.

"We've gone past the point of making meaningful scientific progress, and I can't justify it anymore. *He* won't admit it. He'll never stop."

Tamika scanned Allan's features and sighed. "You probably figured this out ages ago. Well, I finally realized it, and I couldn't let it go anymore. You finally held up a mirror to what I've become in the pursuit of progress.

"Come with me, Allan. I'll get you out of here. Let me give you a chance... of regaining some of the life you had before."

Allan turned with both bodies away from her. Regardless of the kind words and remorseful tone she now carried, she had still been an agent in everything that had transpired, and this could very well be another ploy to test him and use him in an experiment. If there was anybody in the world capable of this level of manipulation, it was her and the bruiser-man.

To stay, however, guaranteed prolonged suffering. At least the ice queen—Tamika—offered a chance at getting out, even if it was a small one.

It all depended on a miracle of human conscience and transformation, something Allan wasn't sure he believed in anymore.

Yet she had quoted his poems. Her face carried emotional baggage when she spoke, something she had never before shown. There was a possibility she was sincere. A remote one, and he would have to be careful, but he could do it. He could try.

"OK. What's the plan?"

She clutched her hands together. "Thank you, Allan."

She pulled out a phone and then crouched down to her bag to pull out a syringe and bottle of medicine. "I will put one of your bodies asleep. I'll then need you to be very quiet for a while as I wheel you out of the facility. I'm going to give you a mild sedative. It will relax you, but it won't put you to sleep. Not quite."

Allan shuddered involuntarily at the sight of the needle,

but rolled up his sleeves and took seats on the bed.

"You're going to pretend I'm in need of off-site medical attention," he said.

"Yes," she whispered. "Hold still."

She plunged the syringe in. The needle sent a wave of memory through him, of all the infinite pricks he'd sustained in the dark worlds, as well as all the times he'd been jabbed before being sent there. He jerked and whimpered, as the temporary sanity he'd regained ebbed out through the drugs.

"You have to hang on, Allan," Tamika said, clutching his shoulders. "Stay awake."

CHAPTER TWENTY

After the Coming

Kitt pulled Ben into a warm embrace. All the tension in his body melted. There was nothing better on Earth, here in the land of the real.

"Al and I were arguing," Kitt said, "and I didn't notice what was happening to you, until it was too late and we couldn't do anything!"

Ben smiled despite Kitt's concern. He inhaled the moment, a touch of sweat in the grapefruit scent of her hair.

"Are you here, Ben?" she asked, moving her head to see if his eyes followed her. "Are you really here now?"

"Yes, Kitt," he murmured. "What happened to me? What did you see?"

"You were still here, but," she moved her finger in a circle, "not really here. You seemed dazed and, oh, this is going to sound incredible..."

Her finger played out a tremolo on her chin. "I could touch you, and feel you, just like now, but, you were like a ghost, somehow, sometimes there and sometimes not. You'd fade in and out. You were mumbling and rolling, and getting up on your hands and knees and then standing and swaying, turning and muttering. You put your arms out and started to cry and scream. We tried to calm you down. Tried to talk to you. But you wouldn't answer us. We were just about to call an ambulance."

When Kitt said 'we', Ben jerked his head over, remembering Turen.

Turen lay sprawled on the sofa, pale, with no expression on his face. He stared into some empty pit, oblivious to anyone or anything.

"We called to you and shook you," Kitt went on. "You went on and on until you just curled up. We had to check your pulse. You were so still.

"Ben, please tell me what happened."

Ben couldn't help but look back at Turen, more passive and incapacitated than he'd ever seen him. "What's happened to him?" he whispered.

Kitt pressed a hand to Ben's chest, the soft warmth of her fingers yanking his attention back. "Ben, tell me what happened to you."

She cupped his chin in her hands, and pulled his face closer to hers. His heart went off like a metal detector near gold.

"Please!"

Again, Ben wanted to taste this moment forever, but knew that the instant he answered her those fingers would leave his cheeks, the touch and clarity of feeling disappearing like a window frosting over. But he knew he had to.

Feeling a kink in his back, he sat up, shivering as Kitt released him. He held his forehead and closed his eyes. Where to begin? He didn't want to travel back there, even in memory, but Kitt's imploring gaze meant he had to.

"Kitt, it's so strange..."

He opened his mouth and the words took shape. He told her everything he'd experienced, leaving out only the details of just how horrific the monsters were.

She listened attentively, and at times she looked about to reach out and grab his hand, but she resisted, waiting until he'd finished, recognizing somehow that if she touched him he wouldn't be able to finish recounting.

"I made it back here, but the monsters are still out there. They're in my mind, but I have the power to make them real, and as long as I keep believing in them, they'll still hold power."

Kitt sat still, and finally said, "How will we stop them?"

Ben firmed his lip. "I will not allow them to use me. Even when I almost tried to give them what they wanted, some deeper part of me resisted. We need to find out who the other Choosers are—those the monsters can now use to make themselves real."

"How can we do that?"

"I don't know."

Kitt grabbed Ben's hand and squeezed it. They cast furtive glances at one another, warmth punctuating the fear that had seeped in from the would-be world. The lights seemed to dim for a moment as though they were alone, sharing knowledge and responsibility far beyond both of them.

Then Ben remembered Turen flopped on the couch, near-catatonic. He pointed. "What happened to him?"

Before Kitt could reply, Turen broke out of his trance and snapped his attention to Ben.

His eyes looked haunted. Had he glimpsed the abyss of the would-be world? Sweat covered his grey face. Shallow breaths led to wispy words Ben barely made out.

"I saw them." Turen swallowed, then studied Kitt. "You didn't."

"See who?" Kitt asked, frowning.

"Kitt saw you," Turen continued, turning back to Ben, "but I saw you and the two of them."

Ben's throat tightened. If Turen saw the monsters, did that mean they were becoming more powerful? More real?

Soundless words worked on Turen's lips for a long while, his eyes unfocused. A frown creased his forehead and he shook his head.

"I saw the time travel experiments. I mean, I didn't see them on the holo, not at first. Kitt kept asking me what was the matter with me. Why I didn't see what she saw. And then...."

Blood drained from Turen's face.

"And then I saw what Kitt saw! But I still remember what I saw before, I mean, when I first looked at the holo."

He looked between Ben and Kitt, as if deciding which of them could explain what'd happened. "But now, when I look at the holo, I just see what Kitt saw all along."

Oh, no, Ben thought. *It's as bad as I thought.*

Turen jumped to his feet and yelled, "What's happening? What is going on? None of this makes any sense! I see two different things in the holo and Kitt sees the same thing all the time. And you, standing and speaking while they moved around you, until they faded away and you came back. What is... how can I make any sense of this?"

He sat back down, looking at his palms for answers.

Ben took a slow, measured breath. "Maybe I can help," he said carefully. "First, though, tell me—in detail—what *they* looked like."

Turen's description painted ghosts in Ben's mind, the monsters' flesh just as translucent and writhing and gnashing with each stuttered word out of Turen's mouth.

He had definitely seen them. *They were no longer confined to Ben's mind!*

With what Kitt and Turen now knew, would some of his power seep into them?

Turen, a science mogul who held incredible power over their lives, had not only seen proof that backward time travel occurred, but had also been the first outside of Ben and his mother to witness the creatures from the would-be world.

I have to decide, Ben thought. *I can either have both, or neither.*

Ben shuffled and knelt in front of Kitt, who was leaning up against the couch. Stray wisps of her hair jutted out at odd angles. The half moons on her cheeks were barely noticeable beneath the brightness of her eyes. Even with the worried frown rippling her forehead, she carried a lightness of spirit as though with a single kind word she could evaporate any problem.

Her frown wavered as Ben searched her face. He wished this all could've happened under different circumstances, better circumstances, and that he could've had more time.

He got the answer he sought in the calm settling over her eyes, the loosening of her cheeks, the million words unspoken that he longed to hear. Her blue eyes asked questions in return.

Ben answered by taking her face in his hands and gently, slowly kissing her.

For a flicker, stars burst and clouds parted. A simple touch elevated to the spiritual. Everything felt right.

They both sighed breaths as they released, opening their eyes to share a knowing glance of an incredible journey travelled together.

Ben stood slowly, turned toward Turen and made his choice. He focused on Turen's limp form, channeling his thoughts into every detail of the reality that would hold purchase from here onward.

Turen rolled off the couch and scanned the room. He rubbed his fingers over his eyes, and glanced around again. "What am I doing here? What's going on?"

"You came here to show us the holo," said Kitt, raising an eyebrow.

Turen frowned and said, "Oh yeah, the experiments you did. Confirming what we already knew."

Kitt's brow furrowed and she searched Ben's eyes. The serenity he felt must've reached her, for her frown died a moment later.

Ben motioned toward the door. "Of course, you're right. It's late though, Al. Go home. Celebrate some more without us."

Turen shook his head and blinked several times. "You both know how much trouble you'll be in if you try this again, right?"

It was strange to hear doubt in Turen's voice and

mannerisms, as though the wrought-iron beams supporting his personality were buckling under an encumbered weight.

"Yes," Ben said, putting on an apologetic frown. "We both just had so much on the line, we had to know for certain."

"Well, lucky for us," Turen said, standing, "physics doesn't change from one experiment to the next. Don't waste the lab's resources again."

"We won't, Al."

"No matter how badly you lost," Turen said. A smile quivered on his face, diminishing the power of his words. Ben felt as though Turen were groping back towards himself.

Ben took a few encouraging steps toward the door. "You're right. Of course. Sometimes, we're just kids, deep down."

"It won't happen again," Kitt added, leaning with one arm against the couch.

"If you feel the need to repeat an experiment," Turen said, picking up his phone and turning off the holo, "put a request through the proper channels."

"You got it, Al."

Turen stood at the doorway, staring dumbly at his shoes, clearly wondering why he hadn't bothered to remove them.

Ben wasn't sure how Turen had gotten here in the first place. As cruel as Turen could be, Ben didn't wish him any ill in return.

"Do you need a ride home or—"

"I'll be fine," Turen snapped. "Good night."

"Good night, Al," Ben said.

Turen stalked out into the corridor. Ben watched through his apartment window as, a minute later, Turen exited the front of the building and paused in the street. Eventually, he tapped his phone until a car's lights half a block away illuminated, and he strode away, his shoulders relaxing as he closed in on his vehicle.

Kitt approached Ben's side. With Turen gone, there was no longer any need to maintain a facade, and she huddled, shivering from an imperceptible cold. Ben felt he was the only one who had seen the true source of that bone-deep chill, and though he'd overpowered the monsters this time, their lingering threats weighed heavily in his mind.

In their experiments, the initial results had set up a template—a pattern the universe could follow from that moment on. Ben had been able to imprint on that template with his will, influence the physics of the universe by making a choice.

It seemed this notion of a template applied to other things, like his childhood monsters. Their template held repercussions too terrible to fathom, though.

He and Kitt stared out at the night lights of the densely-packed neighbourhood, wishing they lived in any one of those other houses, in minds where the monsters didn't exist.

Where they wouldn't exist.

For a time.

CHAPTER TWENTY-ONE

Haunted Departure

As his car drove him home, Al Turen sat confused. When he arrived in his garage, he wondered if he'd even made a trip at all. Half-bidden images puffed in and out of thought, conversations with Kitt and Artemit carrying resonances, words overlain with different possibilities contrary to what Turen had witnessed firsthand.

He thumbed on his holo, watching the footage from the lab experiments and turning up the volume so the recorded evidence drowned out the ghostly afterthoughts. What was happening to him?

He must have had a really long day. Yes, that was all—a long day.

He stewed, grateful no one was there to see the great Al Turen sweating and questioning himself like this. The motion sensing lights turned off, leaving only the dim glow of the emergency light at the end of the corridor into his house.

The emergency light flickered, projecting shadows from the mesh cage around it. Tall, thin lines of black took on life and motion as though the lamp were calling forth minions of darkness.

Turen's stomach clenched. This scene was way too familiar for how long ago it had happened.

In the schoolyard, when Turen had been nine years old. When he'd seen those figures approaching, and should've known better.

When he'd been too innocent to recognize what power could do.

He hadn't been frightened, then; he'd been more concerned about winning the game of hide and seek. Afterward, however, he'd had to try and bury the memories deep.

The emergency light flickered again. Helpless futility entrapped Turen, just as it had so long ago.

* * *

The schoolyard had been split into two areas on either side of a sloping hill where the highway ran. A wide-mouthed culvert ran beneath the highway, serving as passageway between the two halves of the schoolyard. It was a long, nearly full-circled cylinder, only flat on the bottom where it was paved. It was corrugated in a spiral around the circumference from one end to the other.

As a child, Turen had always thought it represented a portal, a gateway to another world. When he played, he and the other children often made use of this idea, creating a mythology around the tunnel until it became an alien entity gifted to their small town.

It had been a sunny, clear sky day in October when Turen and his friends were playing hide and seek at lunch time. Turen sprinted away from a counting friend, determined not to be found. He had approached the small opening in the chain-link fence near the tunnel as he usually did. He didn't think much of the bigger kids who leaned near the edges chatting with one another, suddenly stopping and whispering when Turen approached.

Big kids were a mystery to Turen. They always seemed to be doing things far outside his understanding, speaking in languages from another place, talking of things that existed in worlds far more exciting than his. He dreamed of the wonderful things they must be discovering and discussing and learning, but was too scared to ask. He didn't speak their language. He barely recognized the things on their shirts.

This imagined world of the big kids sustained Turen's excitement through each grade of school, and though he hadn't yet glimpsed the wonders of which he'd dreamed, he felt they were always just around the corner in the next grade, or just through one more walk through the portal. He imagined one day coming through the tunnel and emerging into a land where everything the big kids did made sense.

Turen passed into the tunnel which was curiously empty, and ran toward a gibbous moon of light at the far end.

A sound like the screech of a crow came from behind him. The sound traveled up and over him, swirling around the spiral until it reached the far end. Ghostly echoes wound their way back. Moist air rattled into his lungs.

A moment later, a crowd of big kids blocked the light from the far end of the tunnel, obscuring Turen's surroundings.

A nagging part of Turen's reptilian brain found the screech, the emptiness of the tunnel, and the emergence of the big kids a bit coincidental.

When the light behind Turen blotted out and he plunged into total darkness, his legs quaked and he stumbled.

"This here is our territory," said a crackling, deep voice. It seemed to come from all directions, swirling and cascading up and down in pitch. "We've been nice enough to let you kids use it for free, but, well, as my dad always says, you don't learn nothin' from a free ride."

Turen didn't know what they meant by a free ride. This tunnel wasn't a ride at all. But he understood the menace in the words, and stopped moving. Over his shoulder he saw he was being approached from both directions by groups of big kids.

"You're our lucky first customer," said the voice. "And as our first customer, you get the best lesson of anyone."

The big kids closed in on him in seconds. They surrounded him. The air sucked out of Turen's lungs.

"I'll get out of here," Turen blubbered.

"Of course you will," the voice said, still echoing but carrying more grit and bite now that the speaker stood right in front of Turen. He still couldn't make out any details in the encroaching darkness of the mob.

"Right after you pay the toll."

"I—I don't have any money," Turen stammered.

The voice made a *tsk-tsk-tsk* sound. "That's too bad. There are other ways to pay, though."

Turin took short breaths. He wished he understood them. He wished he understood the power they held by standing the way they stood and by talking the way they spoke.

If he did, he might not have to pay the price that made him tremble like a fly in a cave waiting to be devoured by bats.

"You're going to tell everyone what happened here," the voice said. It seemed like the figure leaned over Turen, but he couldn't be sure of anything anymore.

"You hear me? You're going to tell everyone what happened," the voice repeated. "You're going to make sure they tell their friends, too. No one is going to ever come in here unless they pay the toll: five bucks. If, like you, they can't pay, then they're going to stay the hell out."

Turen wished dearly that that commitment was the only thing he'd have to pay. He nodded his head vigorously, his heart pounding and making his ears ring like a fire alarm.

"You look like a smart kid, but this is a tricky lesson, and you know, tricky lessons always have to be learned... a few different ways."

A shadow knocked Turen's mouth. He gasped, tasting

copper as he put a hand up to his lip. Between the pulses of the fire alarm in his head he heard laughter. He felt the jolt-burn of a palm on one side of his face, then the other, batting him this way and that.

A hard lump rammed into his stomach and he wheezed out air and blood. His shirt pulled over his head and hands beat him like a conga drum. Those were nothing compared to sharp explosive cracks into his lower back and ribs as the big kids whipped him with their belts.

Somewhere in the chaotic laughter and whips the leader's voice, the one who had instigated all this cruelty, now offered respite, mercy, and an end to the torture.

Turen didn't remember the words he used. They didn't really matter. What mattered was that the leader had brought the pain, and he had just as easily halted it.

Turen limped out of the tunnel, shuddering as laughter echoed around him.

In the month it took for all the welts, cuts and bruises to heal, Turen had reflected on how deftly that big kid had wielded power, controlling primal forces to own the situation and the people in the portal.

Turen got the lesson.

He had, of course, obeyed the leaders will. He was too weak and entranced not to. Outside the tunnel, he went to the school nurse and eventually spoke to the principal. He was utterly incapable of identifying any of his assailants, and knew full well that he wouldn't even if he did know. Throughout the aftermath Turen had felt a twisted sort of gratitude grow within him.

He had gotten a deep view into the world of the big kids, and now had an inkling of their language. He resolved to never again be in a situation where he was under someone's power as he had been in the tunnel. The more he reflected, the more he realized the leader probably hadn't lifted a finger toward Turen. He had instead guided the others, holding the reins and letting the horses do the trampling.

The language Turen had glimpsed that day was that of power. He had devoted himself to mastering that language from then on, stumbling at first, but continuing his practice until he was a poet.

Wielding this language, he'd beat down any fear that ever showed itself. The power had always been by his side, a force he'd call upon to never be cornered as he'd been in the tunnel.

* * *

Turen panted and squeezed the steering wheel.

I'm not cornered, he thought. *I won't be cornered.*

He opened the door to get out of his car, and the motion triggered blinding lights to turn on.

See? All better.

Whatever he'd experienced, it was temporary, and if it weren't, he would figure out a way to rule it, too.

He strode down the hallway, trying to shut out the visions of what the darkness could become.

CHAPTER
TWENTY-TWO

Hunted

Allan Gerrold did as Tamika instructed, and managed to keep his eyes open in semi-consciousness as she wheeled both of his bodies out of the facility.

He looked down and saw bandages around his arms. He reached down and felt the same in his calves, like he'd had something carved out of him.

He only remembered fragments of the journey through a fog: among them the tense interrogation from a security guard dressed all in black with blue embroidered letters beneath his name tag. His voice sounded like he spoke with a sock in his mouth, but Allan vividly recalled staring at his lapel in a stupor to go along with Tamika's ruse to get them out of the facility.

The guard's name tag had said Marquez. The embroidery had spelt *Quantix*—a multinational research company with labs in Vancouver and various places in the US. Allan had once applied for a job there.

After getting past the security guard, they got into a van with tinted one-way windows. They travelled beyond a concrete bunker, outside chain-link fences and into the open world.

He had a vague sense of passing through hilly countrysides but was unable to absorb any details. His eyes struggled to adapt to long-range sights he hadn't experienced for ages.

Allan hid in the back of the van, holding blankets over both sets of eyes and pressing against his ears. The steady thrum of the van on the highway was too much. Half-lucid control left him trembling, uncertain as to what he could trust himself to do.

Tamika's voice came to him in echoes. He marked time by their stops.

Please, let this just be the drugs, he thought, *and not a new, permanent normal.*

If it were the drugs, that promised hope this would end. Hope, however, was in short supply in his spirit.

He focused on reaching the next stop.

Night turned to day; day turned to night.

On the second night, the drugs released their grip and he could think straight. It took him a few tries, but he slowly sat up.

Tamika brushed aside the curtain that had been half-open.

"You're alive," she said, sighing. "You were out of it so long I thought I'd done permanent damage. The drug was only supposed to last a few hours."

Dark circles and taut lines cut her features. She must've been on some drugs of her own to keep going for this long.

"Damn it. I should've taken into account the cognitive multiplicity of your brains' altered consciousness but I was just so focused on getting out. Getting all those bloody trackers off and all of the monitors out so this all wouldn't be a waste of time. So they wouldn't find us once we'd made it."

She muttered under her breath, but Allan didn't understand. It seemed she'd been talking to herself for some time now.

His new movements sent stabs of pain from the wounds on his wrist and upper forearms.

"You sure weren't gentle, were you?" he said, lifting a bandage and seeing a mess beneath.

"There was just no time, Allan. I had to make sure they wouldn't follow us." Tamika's voice was flat.

Allan shook his heads, touched the wounds, and winced.

If this is the only price I have to pay for my freedom, he thought, *then it was worth it.* But he wouldn't say as much to Tamika. He wouldn't reinforce the notion that this time, her hurting of him may have been justified.

His thoughts drifted and he glimpsed haunting after-images of the hellish place.

No, he thought, groaning, *anywhere but there.*

"Where are we going?" he asked, trying to distract himself.

"Far outside the state. Somewhere safe."

"What state is that, exactly?"

Tamika's mouth worked. "It's better for your long-term health if you don't know."

This has to stop, he thought. *She can't keep doing this to me.*

"I'm going to find out at the next stop one way or another," Allan said, gripping the edges of the beds. "What, are you worried I'm going to take revenge? Return to that place so I can rip it apart? Burn it down?"

"Something like that," Tamika muttered.

"The thought never occurred to me," Allan said.

Then, with both bodies speaking simultaneously he added, "It had occurred to *us,* though." The slight dissonance in the two voices made his ears twitch, but it was worth Tamika's reaction.

She made a face as though someone tried to push a nail through her forehead. After a few seconds, her face relaxed into its cool, logical ethos.

"I'm sorry," she said. "I thought I had everything

prepared, everything planned, but I had to act fast. I missed things. I hate being rushed. Not having all the details. The whole situation makes me nervous."

Allan empathized with the danger she'd put herself in for his rescue. While he knew he should feel grateful, he also remembered what she'd done to him in the past.

It was mildly satisfying watching her in discomfort.

He caught himself smiling at Tamika's pain, and shuddered. The self-image was far too much like the bruiser-man.

What if I become like him? he thought, seeing the bruiser-man's sneering face. *Then there was no point in making it this far.*

He ambled to the front seat with one body, then brushed the curtain shut behind him.

"What are you doing?"

"Riding shotgun."

"I don't think that's a good idea."

"Tough."

Even moving from the back of the van to the front made Allan dizzy with information overload.

He closed his eyes, needing a new strategy. Fixing his gaze on the horizon, he fought the urge to look in all directions. Instead, he focused on his breath every time he wanted to behold all.

He coaxed his mind back into believing things really could exist at a distance.

His bodies breathed in sync, one alert with eyes open, the other lying with eyes closed.

Golden fields of wheat stretched to the horizon, split only by the straight arc of the road going forever in one direction. A few patchy cirrus clouds dotted the sky, which was otherwise a radiant sapphire.

A lone oak tree stood at the edge of a fence, and for a moment, Allan felt himself drawn back to his childhood.

Roots wrapped around and fit his body perfectly. Beams of sunlight flickered between the leaves, the movement looking like a flock of birds on a high and distant journey.

It had been a very long time since Allan had sat in this field on his parents' acreage.

His body tightened at the thought of his parents calling out to him for dinner, forcing him back to a harsh reality after the refuge. They had never approved of anything he'd done, and when he'd moved to the city for university, they had all but disowned him. His father, especially, demanded proof that Allan's education would result in something better than what could be provided on the farm.

He'd never managed to prove himself to them. Would he get the chance now that he was free?

If his parents saw him now, in his entangled form, as The Entangled Man, they wouldn't be proud. Even if he told them he was the only one who'd survived the process. No, they'd see him as a freak, a blasphemy to the rest of humanity, something to be shunned even more.

Everything was blurry, and it was hard to take in all the details of the landscape, much less the swirling self-doubt.

He shivered. What other basic abilities had he lost during captivity, and how long would it take him to get them back?

If he couldn't use his eyes properly, he'd have to take another approach.

"You still haven't told me where we are," he said.

"I *really* don't think if it's a good idea for you to be up front." Tamika looked sidelong at him with a furrowed brow.

"There's nothing suspicious about having a passenger in the passenger seat," he snapped. "Now, where are we?"

"What difference does it make?"

"*Tell* me."

A county road came into view, splitting off and separating parallel to the horizon as it moved toward them. The endless line of crooked fence posts marked a boundary between government and private control, between old and new, between remembered and forgotten.

"Fine. We're in Montana," she said in a low voice, as though hoping Allan wouldn't hear.

"Montana?!" Allan exclaimed. Quantix must have had other labs around the country. "How far did you take me? Was your Quantix torture lab in Nevada, or somewhere even farther?"

"You know about Quantix?" Tamika said, raising her voice. "How the hell do you know about Quantix?"

Allan's jaw tightened. "You have to tell me a lot more about what's going on if you want me to keep going with you." He stared at her, wishing he could snuff out the notion that she could still control and hold power over him.

"Oh no."

"Oh yes."

"No, God no. They've found us!" Tamika's voice rose and cracked. "Look!"

Allan turned, and took in the sight of sirened cruisers pulling from the side county roads onto the main highway, forming a wall of cars blocking the road.

They knew we were coming.

"It's them," Allan said, his body going cold at the thought of returning to the facility. Maybe this had all been a ruse, something to prepare him for some obscene purpose.

"No! Oh no!" Tamika said, looking in the rearview mirror. "There's some behind us!"

Allan hyperventilated, breathing louder as the gap closed between them and the road block. In the side mirror, a car rapidly approached. The cars bore the marks of the state police, but he and Tamika both knew who'd really sent them.

They were in a tight corridor being run through the gauntlet, and in about ten seconds, it would all be over.

"The fields," Allan said, casting his gaze out to the golden stalks. "Cut through the fields."

Tamika bit her lip, hazarded another glance in the rearview mirror, then swung the car to the left.

They bounced down into the ditch, an explosion of

scraping metal assaulting their ears. The rumble of dirt and rock beneath their wheels grew deafening. The wheat covered all but a sliver of the horizon.

"Please work," Tamika said. "Please, for the love of—work! Just work!"

The right side of the car dipped and smashed, bottoming out in a deep hole. Allan's head hit the ceiling, sending shockwaves of pain and not-pain in his two bodies. Tamika swore but kept the car going.

They cut across two fields and found a trail off the county roads. They sped off down the trail and away from the sirens.

Allan darted glances behind. The state police cruisers were nowhere to be seen.

They'd lost them, for now.

✳ ✳ ✳

Allan and Tamika drove into the night, knowing it was only a matter of time before they were found again.

"There must be an implant I don't know about," Tamika said, half to herself and half to Allan. "We have to get it out." Her voice carried a tremor and the faint wheeze of long-suppressed fatigue.

Allan looked over at his other body, bearing similar signs. Now that the fear was loosening its hold, he could take stock.

"You're starving," he said.

"I'm hungry, but we don't have time," she said.

"Neither of us are going to do anything productive when we're starving," he said. "And I don't want you digging around in me with your hands quaking like that."

"Fair enough," she said, sighing.

They stopped off the highway at a fast food drive thru. One of two overhead street lamps was burnt out, the glow barely marring the surrounding darkness.

Tamika ordered chicken nuggets and fries, but forced Allan to make do on three salads with grilled chicken. It seemed part of her wanted to maintain her test subject's health.

Allan didn't bother arguing. He enjoyed both eating, and watching himself eat his first meal as a free man.

Every sign of where they were was obscured by the faceless, forgotten town. It was late by the time they'd picked up drugstore supplies and checked into a two-star motel.

The walls were yellow and reeked of cigarettes. Allan didn't even know such places existed anymore.

As they silently unwrapped the packaging on their tweezers, scissors, magnifying glass and box cutter—the closest thing they could find to a scalpel —Tamika's face grew increasingly pale.

"Where do you think the tracker could be?" Allan asked.

Tamika struggled to get words out, her face pained as she moved. "I think it's got to be somewhere we haven't dug around. They would've avoided any possible interference with the installation of an existing scanner, and put it somewhere else."

"Base of the neck, maybe?"

"Maybe. There's not a lot of fatty tissue to work with there, though."

"Where else, then?"

Tamika grabbed her stomach and closed her eyes. "The buttocks or just above the hips."

"Are you OK?" Allan asked. With his other body he inspected the mattress for bedbugs, finding deep yellow and brown stains that made him wish he hadn't looked.

"Those nuggets aren't sitting right," Tamika said, wrinkling her nose. "But I'll be all right."

A minute later, she was in the bathroom. There were big gaps of silence where he thought would come back out again, but then she'd continue. As the clock ticked on, Allan realized they were going to be found again before Tamika was in any shape to dig around for the tracker.

With his eyes fixed on the box cutter, he sat across the square table from himself and rolled up his sleeves.

* * *

Allan took turns with his bodies sipping from a large Styrofoam cup filled with burnt coffee. His hands trembled. Next to him, the coffee maker brewed, the pot lined with rings of caked-on grime. At his feet the garbage can was full of bloodied tissues. He had managed to get the smears of blood off the table, but a few flakes still crusted beneath his fingernails.

He took a sip, set the coffee down and slid it across to himself. He tried not to shift his weight on the pillows padding the wounds beneath him.

Tamika came out of the washroom, her hair disheveled but her skin looking far less green than Allan's. She reeled, steadying herself with a hand on the wall as she saw Allan's bloody mess.

"I found two," he said, tapping a finger on a napkin bearing four puddles of blood. He was careful to only reach one hand forward so as not to touch the other body. He wasn't sure how long it would be before he could touch himself again.

"I don't think there are any others," he continued, passing himself the cup of coffee. "There's coffee if you want. But we have to get moving again."

The words came out of necessity. All he could do right now was think forward, look forward. To what came after. Anything but looking back or inward.

Tamika grabbed the bloodied napkin with the implants and put it on the bedside table. She picked up the lamp and held it out to Allan. "Do you want to do the honours?"

Allan sipped with one body while with the other he

walked over, grabbed the lamp and crushed the chips.

"Let's go," he said.

CHAPTER TWENTY-THREE

Mending Broken Ties

B en winced as he pressed his knife into an onion. Every sound amplified, threatening to shatter the precarious atmosphere. On the other side of the kitchen island, Kitt sat at the dining table holding her head. She stared into the distance, her fingers entwined in her hair as though it were the last thing she could hold onto.

Patchy overhead lights cast bleaching spotlights on each of them. Every so often the knife reflected a brilliant white into Ben's eyes. He blinked and readjusted each time, as he imagined the reflection tearing a hole in reality and allowing the monsters through.

It was absurd, wasn't it?

The cues for the monster's arrival would be different from the everyday. He would spot them coming as he had so many other times, wouldn't he?

Deep in his gut, though, Ben knew things had changed.

Juice from the onion burst onto his fingers. Crisp, bitterness filled his nostrils. He cut and felt the layers give under his weight.

He'd defeated them before. He could do it again. He had

the power to call things into being, to make something out of nothing.

Should he feel godlike from this realization? In other circumstances he might've viewed the ability differently. If the power came without attachments, without the threat of unleashing a terror upon the world, he might've been able to look at it idealistically. How many wrongs could he right by calling certain things into being, and wishing certain things away? Could he feed the poor? End wars? Halt natural disasters?

Where did the limits of his power really lie?

So far he'd only tested it on a slice of reality affecting Kitt and Turen. For both of them, however, Ben's lack of clarity around the new reality led to Kitt and Turen re-evaluating their psyches and beliefs. Turen had seen Ben's encounter with the monsters without Ben being consciously aware he was wishing it so. Ben was toying with their souls, able to flip things one way or the other in a moment of weakness. Or worse, unconsciously.

The thought of doing such a thing on a grand scale, to a city, province, state, country or, heaven forbid, the entire Earth, made his gut wrench. No matter how good the potential outcome, he would never be able to live knowing he had robbed people of their free will.

I won't use it, he told himself. *I'll control myself and live my life so it never happens.*

Yet sitting across from him, as he scraped the chopped onions into a bowl, was the person he cared about most in the world, who was also the biggest victim of his unwitting failures of willpower.

He had to make things right, but not by wishing.

"Kitt," he said, "what are you feeling?"

So much loaded into so few words. Ben wished he could pretend a deeper knowledge and insight into what Kitt was going through, but her thoughts were as remote to him as the dark side of the moon. The island between them emphasized their separation.

Ben turned on the stove, hoping the quotidian activity would provide clarity or respite from the unrelenting tension.

When had he last eaten? He couldn't remember.

"Confused," Kitt said at last, her voice quiet but hoarse. "Sad. There's just too much to process."

The frying pan sizzled with oil, and Ben dumped the onions in. Steam rose in a rippling vapour as he stirred.

"I'm sorry I... did that to you," he said, the bitter vapour making him wonder if he'd ever be able to eat onions again. "I was trying to protect you. I didn't want your work to be ruined."

"Both our works are ruined, Ben," Kitt replied. She unknotted her fingers from her hair. "Don't you see? The reasons for either of us being correct run so much deeper than what we thought. Backward time travel existing or not depends on much more than the physics we thought we understood. It depends—it depends on *you.*"

"Maybe," Ben suggested, "I just chose your assumptions to be right. I'm not changing the fabric of reality, just which assumptions are correct. I don't really know how I'm 'Choosing', Kitt. There could be something deeper going on that neither of us understands. As far as I see it, your theory is still valid."

"I don't know," Kitt said. "Maybe. I know... you chose for my theory to be right out of compassion, Ben, and..."

Because I love you, he finished in his mind. He wondered fleetingly, terrified but thrilled, if she were also thinking the same thing. If she knew.

"Both our assumptions could have been valid, though," she said. "I can see yours being right just as well as mine. That was the point of doing the experiment, to find out things we might be missing, that might've pushed things one way or the other."

"There could be a universe somewhere where my theory is valid," Ben said. "And more where yours is. We've both worked so hard and both theories are so rigorous that they're both possible."

"I suppose. It makes it a little better to think that somewhere there's a place where my work wasn't... pointless."

"Kitt, you've done amazing work. There's a reason you're the top of your field."

She gave him a small smile, and for an instant, Ben thought he'd alleviated her grief.

Kitt shook her head. "But what makes one theory possible in one universe or the other? The most evidence we have so far is not any further, deeper understanding of physics. It's not the influence of an additional force, or a hidden dependency that leads us to a new physical theory. No, it depends on you. On your choices. It depends on your consciousness, Ben."

Ben took the frying pan off the burner and closed his eyes. "I don't want it to. I don't want anything to."

"I understand why you did what you did. But I have to be honest about how... manipulated and tricked I feel. Your reality got better, but mine just became... so trivial... so malleable..."

"It's not trivial, Kitt."

"Easy for you to say," she whispered. "Is that what you've chosen to make so?"

"I didn't ask for this."

"Lots of people would."

"I'm sorry. I won't ever do it again," he said.

"You can't guarantee that."

Ben turned away from the stove, wanting to reach out to Kitt, bridge the gulf, but she'd turned away from him.

He grabbed a jar of pasta sauce, cracked it open with a loud *POP* and poured it in with the onions. For some reason the onions stayed in clumps, and he had to fight them apart to mix. He poured half a box of fettuccine into a pot of boiling water and set a timer.

Several long minutes later he had two plates of

fettuccine marinara, and he carried them across the great divide. The clatter of the plates on the table was the only thing to fill the vacuum.

"Nothing fancy," he said, "but we should eat."

"If you say so." Kitt leaned back in her chair, looking down at the plate.

"It might help, that's all. You don't have to eat anything if you don't want." Ben waited a moment to see if she would meet his gaze, then started slowly eating, each bite a mouthful of grass.

Kitt sighed, then grabbed a fork.

Despite the tension, the food helped ease the pressure in Ben's temples. He closed his eyes as he chewed, trying to see past the moment to something larger. He was careful not to wish for anything, not to feed any wants or desires.

"You're right, Kitt," he said at last. With his fork he played with the last fragments of noodles bobbing disparate in puddles of tomato sauce.

Kitt chewed and swallowed.

"This power does rob our work from us," Ben continued. "But only in this universe. There are other universes where your work is valid, and others where mine is. We can take comfort in that, at least."

Kitt jabbed a noodle violently. "Send me to one of those ones," she muttered. "Where things still make sense. Where physical principles matter more than your conscious decisions."

"Physical principles still matter," Ben said. "We really don't know the extent of the power. I don't think things can arbitrarily come into being. Both our theories were based on solid data, real observations, and assumptions in different directions based on what we knew about the universe. We didn't magic things into being."

Kitt stared into her plate. "Maybe not. But we really don't know anything."

"We've had a lot called into question," Ben admitted.

"But I'd like to believe that physical principles still play a role in our reality. It might be wishful thinking on my part."

Kitt raised an eyebrow, grabbed a napkin, and dabbed her lip silently.

"I *will* make sure my wishes never come true, though, because to rob the world of free will is a heinous crime. Better the world be imperfect and free than peaceful and dominated. I've never had to put it in these terms before, but it's how I feel.

"Kitt, you've known me longer than anyone. Do you believe me when I say that, aside from stopping the monsters, I won't use this power ever again?"

Kitt sucked her lips in, her jaw trembling. A tear spilled from her eye. "Yes, I believe you, Ben."

Ben's shoulders relaxed, leaving a bone-deep fatigue behind. "Thank you."

"I still don't know what to do," Kitt said, propping her elbows on the table. "I don't know what to think about what I've done anymore. I used to be proud knowing I'd devoted myself to the pursuit of truth, but now there seems to be a higher truth."

"What we've done isn't wrong, Kitt," Ben said. "The physics you've done, and the physics I've done, are both right. They just differ from one universe to another. I don't really know what makes these choices come to be real. I really think the physics exists independent of me, independent of you... independent of all of us. We've just been caught somehow, flipping between the possibilities of what can exist or not exist."

"It's not fair." Kitt's back heaved and she covered her face. "The universe we're in is so arbitrary. It defies understanding. Everything I've done, my whole life, means nothing compared to that. What will I do tomorrow? What is the point of any of this?"

The words spiralled and seeped into Ben, into that part of his soul reserved for Kitt, the part that trembled when she shook, that wept when she cried, that leaped when she jumped, beat its heart in sync with hers.

He couldn't offer much more, for he had only barren and weary stores. He had to offer what little he had left, though, the best he could for the best person he knew.

"Kitt," Ben said gently, "you have a formidable intellect. And your theoretical work has transferred out of our field—like your work on sliding, rolling cylinders that was used in canning factories."

"Whoopee," Kitt said. "I helped some big corporations make more money."

"You and I both know that the value of scientific research is not always recognized in the timeline of its discovery. Neither is much art. Humanity takes time to catch up—to *truly* catch up—to individual progress, and who are we to say where things will go? Yes, I have this power, but I don't know how it works. What its limits are. For all I know, it could stop having an effect tomorrow. Maybe there will be a cataclysmic side-effect to this power, and we will be driven back to a dark age where we have to re-derive all of our understanding of the universe from first principles. Then all our work will become more important than ever, but more importantly, the world will need thinkers like you."

"There are so many like us, like me," Kitt said, slumping in her chair. "How can my tiny contributions, my derivative work, make a difference?"

"We don't know, Kitt, but that doesn't mean it won't. It's arrogant to think we can see all the intrinsic and extrinsic value of our work in the here and now, and where it will go beyond. We are strong and capable human beings. Kitt, you know I have more respect for you than I have for anyone else in this world, but even you cannot be all-seeing and all-knowing. The steps we take today might be baby steps compared to the progress of tomorrow, but that doesn't make them any less important. I know it's easier said than done, and God knows I'm as guilty as anyone of losing sight of the forest for the trees. But Kitt, you have to pop your head up sometimes, and realize the process of research has intrinsic value for our development as self-actualizing human beings. For the same reasons we continue studying mathematics that don't have immediate applications, you and I need to keep working."

Kitt opened her mouth, but Ben interrupted her.

"Don't you start in on impact factors and all that. Impact factors are no measure of the long-term effects I'm talking about."

Kitt frowned. "Fine."

Ben recognized Kitt's facade immediately, and smiled faintly. "I know this is hard. That this brings much more into question than we'd ever thought. But that doesn't mean it's the end. It could be the beginning of something very exciting. Or, like I said, maybe these powers are temporary. Maybe tomorrow someone will exert more control—more power—and I will no longer have any effect."

Ben shuddered as he spoke the last words. He tried to move beyond them, but his mind halted from memories of the monsters' last words to him—their threat of finding another Chooser—replaying in his mind.

Kitt leaned in and pushed her plate out of the way, her face wet as she moved into the lamplight. "Don't say that, Ben."

She reached out her hand, and he took it, warm and soft. It was as though she'd reached inside his chest and urged his heart to pump.

"I don't like the power," she said, squeezing his grip, "but if someone has to have it, I'm glad it's you."

Ben wanted to freeze the moment, to make this warmth last forever.

He recognized this desire for what it was, and steeled himself. No matter what he felt, no matter how great or how terrible things got, he must never give in to his base desires. He must only use the power for the monsters, then wall that part of himself off forever.

Ben's experience with the monsters had left deep scars on his psyche, scars that would prevent him from abusing his power. For once, he was grateful he could count on the pain, the trauma that had never let go, for it would steer him away from temptation.

Nevertheless, a part of him worried.

"Thank you, Kitt," he whispered. "I promise; once the monsters are gone, I will never use this power again. Maybe we can defeat them without it."

"I think you have to use it against them," Kitt said. "It seems the only way you've managed to push them back so far. They're going to come again. And when that moment comes, I hope the power is still within your hands."

Ben shivered as he remembered the monsters' words. "Do you think they meant it when they said they'd found someone else to make them real?"

"We can only trust your instincts on that." She released his hand and shrugged. "But it doesn't seem that big of a stretch, does it?"

"No," he whispered, gazing down, "after all we've seen, it isn't out of the realm of possibility. I can't read them well enough to tell lies from truth, though."

"It's probably a good thing you haven't spent enough time with them that you can read their body language, Ben." Kitt folded her arms across her chest, and smiled.

Thank you for being so understanding, Kitt. He was too afraid to give the words voice.

Kitt arched her back and twisted, looking and frowning at the chairs. "You know, these aren't very comfortable."

Ben glanced from Kitt to the kitchen chairs, looking at the flat wood and square angles. Next to everything he faced, the problem of uncomfortable chairs seemed utterly intractable.

"Well, I'm going to the couch," Kitt said. "You're welcome to join me." Kitt's voice mirrored some of Ben's fatigue.

Despite his wishes, hopes, dreams to develop something deeper with Kitt, he realized they had both been running at high capacity for quite a while now, and he should let her get some sleep.

"Maybe I should take you home," he said.

"Are you kidding me?" Kitt shot him a look over her shoulder as she walked to the couch, her movements somewhat disjointed as she dragged her feet.

"Well, it's late and we've both been up so long..."

Kitt plopped herself on the couch, groaning. "Ben, there is no way I would be able to stay at home alone after everything we've experienced. Not tonight, and not in this universe, anyway."

She smirked at him. "Come and sit down. You owe me some more conversation, at the very least."

Ben smiled, then winced as he straightened the rusty joints in his legs. He fumbled his way to the couch and collapsed at the opposite end of Kitt. The light was dimmer over here, the illumination from the kitchen struggling just as much as they had to travel the distance. It cast them both in an orange glow, and Ben's eyelids sagged.

"Ben, have you wondered what gave you this power?" Kitt propped her head against the back of the couch with her elbow.

Ben took a long breath. He wanted to think more clearly and quickly, but the night shift of his brain would only operate at half capacity. When he finally answered, his words were stunted and slow, but thankfully Kitt was patient.

"I... never really thought about that. I think I always approached it as though none of this was real, and if anything my vision of the monsters was the result of some trauma I'd experienced in my childhood. Something like a fear of losing my parents after being left at the grocery store. It's only really recently that I've even accepted the notion the monsters are real, let alone that I have this incredible power. And I haven't exactly had a lot of time to philosophize over its nature."

Kitt tapped her lip. "But I mean, there had to be something that happened to you to give you this power, don't you think? It seems hard to believe that it would just be random chance or fate that gives you the power of gods."

Ben massaged his temples to try and regain alertness, but his fingers only served as muscle relaxants. "I don't know, Kitt. What sort of thing are you thinking of? You know as well as I do how exciting and fraught with calamity the life of a theoretical physicist is. It's not like I was bitten by a radioactive spider, or hit by a gamma-ray burst. Maybe in a past life I lived dangerously as an experimental physicist, exposing myself to the jungle of the physical universe."

Kitt jabbed him with her toe. "I'm being serious, Ben. If we find out what gave you your power, we might be able to anticipate who the monsters might approach next."

Ben's mind somersaulted, his head lolling in turn. He straightened and felt like a fermion whose spin state had changed by doing a complete circle, that would need another full circle before he felt normal again.

Fermions, he thought with a demented smile.

"Come on, Ben, where did that mind go that was sharp enough to rival the great Kitt Bell?" She spread her arms in showcase.

"Oh, it's still here," Ben replied. "And don't you worry, I'm taking this very seriously. You know, come to think of it, I must have been somebody *amazing* in my previous life. Like... Nikola Tesla! All those wild experiments and crazy devices he built in his early labs. Those must be what gave me my power, and my brain. Definitely."

Ben grinned and tapped a finger repeatedly to his forehead. Anything requiring more dexterity and he might poke an eye out.

"No, you probably re-birthed from Thomas Edison," Kitt said, pursing her lips.

Ben gasped. "No! Don't even joke about that. That's atrocious. Like I spend all my time stealing credit for things I barely understand."

"I think you two share similar egos, though." Kitt stuck her tongue out.

"I'm hurt!" Ben said. "The only way that could be even remotely true were if I were experiencing all the bad karma for Edison's horrible life."

"You're ridiculous, you know that. If anyone's a reincarnation of Tesla, it's me."

"No, you're totally Ada Lovelace."

"Hrm, I can buy that. Oh! Now I know where you got your power. Marie Curie."

"Now you're just being mean."

"No! Marie was a tremendous scientist."

"Being mean to Marie, I mean."

❉ ❉ ❉

Ben woke to the sound and feel of soft breaths on his shoulder. Kitt sank against him with all her weight, trusting him with the pressure of all her concerns, worries, and fears.

It felt good.

He had opened his eyes with the intention of getting a head-start on the day, of catching up to all the worries they'd hidden from. When he saw her body rising and falling against him, though, he didn't move.

The sun streamed in columns through the slits in the blinds. Tendrils of dust wove lazily through the air. Between Kitt's breaths came the distant, muffled hum of passing vehicles.

Ben flitted in and out of consciousness, each time opening his eyes to a different angle of sunlight.

"I'm scared, Ben," Kitt whispered, wrapping an arm around him.

"I am, too."

"I'm glad we have each other."

"Me too."

Kitt gently pulled herself up his shoulder until her lips brushed his cheek. Then they found his. Her kiss sent pulses through every nerve in his face. His breath caught. At the same time, he and Kitt reached and held each other, pulling their bodies together as tightly as they could.

They tasted each other tentatively at first, touching and retreating shyly, doing a separate courtship until their need for each other grew fierce.

Kitt helped Ben throw his clothes off. Every motion of her body made him ache. She stretched her elbows up taking off her shirt. He fumbled with her bra but she didn't wait for him to crack the puzzle. She thumbed the clasp open and threw it off.

In the next instant her breasts pressed against his chest. His hands caressed the back of her head, and they pressed their bodies tighter, the space between still too much.

She grabbed him and whispered urgently, "Do you have a condom?"

He felt pain in his loins. "No."

"Hold on."

She got up and jogged to her purse, pulling out a packet of napkins and a tablet before finally returning with protection.

"Do you know how long I've carried this around?" she asked.

Ben shook his head, words failing him.

"Let's just say it's been a while," she continued, checking the expiry date.

He wondered briefly if she meant she'd had a hard time finding a boyfriend. "I can't imagine anyone not wanting—"

"Stop, silly," she said, putting a finger to his lip. "Ben, I've been waiting for *you*."

When he fumbled with the condom, she helped him, smiling warmly, not out of mockery, but reassurance. In the few moments when his brain re-engaged, Ben thought of how this scene would have been far more uncomfortable and awkward with anyone else. With Kitt, everything felt natural. All the worries engendered by societal pressures, anxieties and desires to be someone else fell away.

Together, he and Kitt made more.

They kissed each other's ears, cheeks, forehead, and mouth. They moved together, finally giving their bodies what their minds had denied for so long. No longer were there multiple universes. No longer were there monsters, dinosauroids from another space and time. The world vanished, and they held each other. They needed nothing else.

At some point they moved onto the floor, and when they were done, they pulled a blanket over, and lay together entwined.

MARK R.A. SHEGELSKI

PART TWO

CHAPTER TWENTY-FOUR

Safe House

"**I** told you to stay under the blanket," Tamika said, pulling their newly-traded SUV onto a crowded street in downtown Vancouver. The sky was grey and the air thick with moisture, on the verge of rain.

"I can't believe I'm back," Allan whispered, using both bodies to look out of opposite windows of the vehicle. It seemed beyond comprehension that once he had roamed the streets of the bustling metropolis as a vagrant.

He wasn't sure if he could call his new life progress.

"Exactly," Tamika said, "you've been here before, which means people might recognize you. And that means they won't be fooled as easily by sunglasses and a hat. You can be certain Quantix will hear if your old friends think they're seeing double of you."

Allan shook a head. He'd heard nothing but commands this entire trip, and Tamika had revealed to him very little about their plans.

"There's no way Quantix has agents this far north," he said.

"Actually, they have a facility here," Tamika said,

pointing to their right as though the headquarters were on the next street. "So get under the blanket."

Allan grabbed a blanket and swung it over himself while with the other body he gaped at Tamika. "Really? And this is the best place you could think of to take me? Wow."

They stopped at a traffic light, and Tamika closed her eyes. "There's nowhere else," she whispered. "It's unfortunate you used to live here, but it really is the last place they'll expect."

"That kind of reasoning only works in movies. Statistically speaking, our chances of running into—"

Tamika dropped the SUV into first gear and peeled the tires when the light turned green. "No more arguing, Allan!"

She raced ahead of traffic and shifted over three lanes, not bothering to signal.

"I'm trying to help you!" she continued, her mouth twisting out the words. "Just do what I say. I have more information than you. You have to trust that I know. What. I'm. Doing."

Allan was done being frightened by her. "Just like you knew what you were doing with all the those test subjects before me, right?"

"Shut your mouth before I leave you here," Tamika said, her arms rigid and her shoulders hunched. Her mouth pulled tight and shook with a faint tremor. She refused to meet his gaze.

With one last look at the decorated street lamps, and rows of coffee and sushi shops, Allan hid both his bodies under some blankets in the backseat.

He had plenty of time to ruminate over where they were going. It was possible Tamika was selling him to a higher bidder in another nefarious organization. Quantix had invested countless dollars both in developing the technology, as well as in the trials—and errors—before producing him. Any number of corporate giants would pay handsomely for a prized subject like him. And the military's interest? It was a no-brainer.

He managed to use the information from two sets of ear canals to track where they were going, distilling accelerations he could confirm in both bodies. The sound and feel of the SUV on the road at certain points identified bridges and he managed to work out that they were headed into West Vancouver, into the suburbs.

Maybe he'd have a fancy dinner in an oversized dining room, and *then* she'd pawn him off. The thought gave Allan little comfort.

They stopped, and Allan peeked out of the covers. Tamika sighed and rubbed her hands on her pants. She took a few deep breaths as though drawing courage from the stifling air.

Allan didn't want to imagine what sort of person would inspire fear in the woman who'd spent months torturing him.

"We're here," she said, her voice as drained of colour as the Vancouver sky. "I'm going to go make sure he's there, and that it's... OK before I come back and get you. One of you— and only one of you—needs to be ready in the passenger seat. When I come back and wave only one of you will come out to meet us. The other needs to stay hidden until I say otherwise. Do you understand?"

Allan slid the blanket off, and squinted into his light-saturated surroundings. "Yes."

He couldn't piece together the fragments of her behaviour. In the lab, the patterns of their daily routines, and any deviations, were more obvious. Now back in the real world, he felt as he had in his first few weeks on the street, threatened under the shadow of dangers he didn't understand but felt approaching.

Maybe the time had come for him to cut loose and risk going it on his own.

"I'll be back," Tamika said. "Hopefully soon."

She got out of the SUV in jerky motions, her hands fumbling with the keys and the door handle—tasks she could've done five minutes ago with her eyes closed. She had to push the door to close it properly after she'd shut it, then she paced up the sidewalk toward one of the apartment buildings.

Allan got into the front seat and planned his escape.

He was immersed in a sea of townhouses and eight-story condo towers in different shades of brown ,white or grey. Lawn ornaments seemed to be the only way the townhouse owners expressed any individuality, and even then Allan swore some of the garden gnomes looked identical.

Maybe this would be his new prison.

The streets were deserted. Through the gaps between townhouses, the pattern of condo towers and squat row-houses continued.

If Allan ran, he had no idea where he'd go. His internal GPS had gotten lost in this winding labyrinth. The housing district was densely packed, with taller skyscrapers on every side. He couldn't see the mountains north of Vancouver, which were normally a North star for wayward travellers.

Allan tapped the SUV's dash, hoping for a revelation in the few minutes he had left.

Tamika was buzzed into one of the condo towers, and passed through a glass door into the hall and out of sight.

Now or never.

Allan opened the SUV door while his other body uncovered, waited for confirmation the coast was clear, then emerged too. One body wore a sky-blue Hawaiian shirt and beige khakis. The other body wore a Calgary Flames baseball hat, aviator sunglasses, black T-shirt, and blue jeans. Hopefully Tamika's clothing preparations would serve him well.

He walked briskly down the street with his bodies side-by-side, not wanting to attract too much attention from suburbia. They probably saw people jogging without $500 exercise gear about as often as they skipped their morning latte. Better for him to stick to walking.

Tremors passed through him as he tried to anticipate what lay ahead. The thrill at being finally, truly free prevented him from planning further than getting out of the neighbourhood. After so much stress and pain, he just wanted to switch off and enjoy the sun trickling through the clouds.

A small part of him hungered for the pleasure response Tamika and the bruiser-man used to give him. Those memories of pleasure, however, were shadowed with those of the pain response and the nightmares of double-sleep.

Allan shuddered.

He rounded a bend and cursed: dead-end. There were no paths between the houses, and everyone seemed to have high fences stickered with logos of security companies. He didn't dare squeeze through someone's property.

He bunched his fists and pretended to shake all the fences that blocked his escape. He took in everything one more time, then turned around. There was nowhere else to go but back, and hope that he had enough time to get onto another street without hitting any more dead ends.

He started jogging, giving more weight to speed over the neighbour's suspicions. When he made it back to the condo tower where their SUV was parked, Allan heard a door shut, followed by Tamika's voice.

"He'll probably be a bit skittish, so don't take it personally."

Allan had just enough time to duck behind the SUV before she and her conspirator came around the corner. With his bodies positioned at opposite ends of the SUV's left side, Allan could use the sounds he heard from each body to gauge the distance and how far the two sets of footsteps were from him.

"That's a bit... odd..." Tamika said. Allan recognized faintly-concealed panic in her voice.

His only hope was to get the keys from Tamika, and fight her and her conspirator off long enough to get away. He took a long breath, aware of every tiny sound sucking through his nostrils.

"Allan?" Tamika said, on the other side of the SUV

peering into the cab. "You can come out now. It's safe." She peered in through the window, searching the pile of blankets for any sign of him.

Allan rounded the back of the SUV, making as much noise as he could to make her and her male companion jump. With his other body, he went around the front, behind her and grabbed her handbag.

"Allan!" she shouted, her face darting between the two of them. She swung at him, clipping the aviator sunglasses and knocking them to the ground.

The man beside her, in his forties with dark half-moons under his eyes, looked stunned. He slowly reached for Tamika but Allan's other body was already in position to wrap him in a bear hug that captured his arms.

"Allan, he's here to help you!" Tamika shouted as Allan finally pulled free of Tamika with her handbag.

He ruffled inside and found the keys.

"I can't believe what they've done to you," the man said, glancing between Allan's two bodies.

From the man's remark, Allan knew Tamika had told him about the entanglement. He fumbled for the SUV door but Tamika put an arm out to stop him from opening it.

"I'm sorry," the man said. "You must've gone through hell."

Allan wondered if it was a trick, something Tamika had set up. He stared at the man. His eyes were old, speckled grey, and his limp form hardly struggled against him, as though he waited for moments of more import, having perspective to conserve energy for what mattered. It was as though he had wisdom laced through his physicality.

"Who are you?" Allan said, releasing the man. With his other body Allan took a step around the side of the SUV to better see him from two angles.

"Allan Gerrold," Tamika said, "meet Ben Artemit."

CHAPTER TWENTY-FIVE

Unexpected Visitor

B en Artemit was stunned when Sally Burton showed up on the video-feed from the condo entry. She seemed yet another proof of multiple universes, that Ben could have visitors from worlds far removed from his own.

Though she no longer donned the rainbow hairdo, he recognized the proud posture she maintained, the uneven tilt of her lips when she forced a smile, and the constant wariness and questioning in her eyes. There was hardness there now, though.

When he'd gone down and met her at the building's entrance, a flurry of hope, fear, and shame danced on her face. She'd pushed brown hair back behind her ear and nonchalantly asked him if he remembered her.

Of course he did. He also recognized the verge of panic in her demeanour.

They'd made a bit of small talk as he invited her up to his apartment, catching up over the years. Ben kept his summaries brief, trying to probe and discover more without letting her know he saw right through her.

Eventually, he'd had enough, and sitting in an armchair

adjacent the couch where Sally sat, he asked her what brought her here in the middle of the day.

The story came out like droplets condensing on a window, running down and clearing the fog as warmth crept in.

By the end he knew that she, too, worked for Quantix, at another facility where they'd done some experiments Sally wasn't proud of.

He knew she now went by Tamika instead of Sally.

She needed Ben to watch over and protect a man who'd gone through hell, and whom Quantix would stop at nothing to get. Meanwhile, Tamika would draw their attention away, and work to take them down. That part sounded questionable to Ben, but he didn't want to pass judgment too quickly after their reunion.

He had to address some of the more immediate practicalities, however. When he pointed out that he also worked for Quantix, and that he wasn't necessarily the best person to rescue or keep someone far away from the organization, Tamika broke down.

Fine tears trickled from her bloodshot eyes. "I know," she said. "But Dr. Artemit, you're the only person I trust. The only person I can turn to. I have… no one else." Her voice cracked on the last words.

As much as Ben wanted to tell her he was overwhelmed with his own demons hunting him, he knew what it was to be alone and without aid. He knew how hard it could be to ask for help, after struggling so long to be independent. Saying no to Tamika might suggest she couldn't turn to anyone, and that she would have to bear this burden alone. He wouldn't do that to her.

"Of course I'll help," he said. "Where is he?"

"Well…" she said, "there's actually two bodies, one man."

Ben leaned forward and raised his eyebrows. "What does *that* mean?"

She explained how Allan Gerrold had become The

Entangled Man.

Ben listened carefully, trying to wrap his mind around it. He didn't doubt her sincerity or her sanity, having been through enough to know how important it was to be heard and believed. But what would a person *really* look like when they'd been entangled in such a way?

Tamika led him outside, where he glimpsed the reality of entangled bodies for himself.

No words could have prepared him. The situation was far more extreme than he'd imagined.

Initially he thought the two men might be twins. However, something—maybe from all his time in the dark world of his monsters, or from anticipating the depravity Quantix was capable of—told him the resonant twinges in the muscles of the two bodies, in the facial expressions, could not be explained by the bond between twins. If Sally's face bore hints of desperation, it was practically wall-papered on the identical bodies' faces.

Along with some things far worse.

"Allan Gerrold," Tamika said, "meet Ben Artemit."

Ben shook hands with each body, his gaze darting back and forth as he acknowledged that these two entities were, in fact, one person.

* * *

"So you're entangled," Ben said as he sat in the living room. "I can't even begin to imagine what that must be like."

Allan Gerrold nodded with one body, the other giving a weak smile. It seemed to take an effort for Allan to separate his actions, but he sustained it as though it made each body seem more natural. As much as the scientist within Ben was fascinated by the sight and the implications, he also felt a deep pity for the suffering Allan must have endured to get this far.

There was nothing ethical about what Quantix had

done. Ben was shocked that Sally—Tamika—had played such a major role in it. By the way Allan acted around her, they had a tenuous and troubled history, as though he expected her to pull out a clipboard and start shock therapy at any time.

Tamika got up and brushed her hands off her pants. "Thank you so much, Dr. Artemit. You have no idea what this means to me."

"Of course, Sally. Tamika, I mean," Ben said. "I'm glad you came."

"Sally?" Allan muttered, while the other body stared darkly at her.

"That was my name once," she said, her features sagging, the bags beneath her eyes casting deeper shadows. "I changed it... I guess right before I started at Quantix."

Ben nodded. "My mistake. Old habits die hard."

For Allan Gerrold, the explanation clearly wasn't good enough. "Why?" he asked.

Tamika ran a hand through her hair. "I wasn't happy with who I was. I felt weak, and broken and... this seemed like a way to pick up and start again. On my own terms."

Ben remembered the vicious relationship she'd had with Turen. The world, especially the world of theoretical physics, was far too small. Turen's damage could not be undone by Ben's years with her. All the comforts he'd told himself about her problems were just that. He'd either not helped her as much as he thought, or her wounds had run too deep.

Yet Tamika *had* come to him before her rope had run out, and intended to make things right.

"I should get going," she said. "You have my contact information in case you need to get in touch, but do so only if absolutely necessary. I'm going to be drawing a lot of heat from this—"

"Sally, you shouldn't do that," Ben said for the third time during their discussion.

"Please, Dr. Artemit, call me Tamika now."

"Tamika," Ben said carefully, "don't do this."

"I have to," she whispered. "It's as much for me as for anyone else. I hope you understand, Dr. Artemit."

Ben opened his mouth, then fell silent. He did understand, at least a little. He just wished she didn't have to do it alone.

"Goodbye, Allan," she said, turning to the Gerrold bodies on the couch. "Maybe you'll have an easier time trusting Dr. Artemit."

Allan stared at her for a long, uncomfortable silence before he rose and extended a hand toward her. Ben suspected it was Allan's original body, but he couldn't be sure.

"Thank you, Tamika," he said. His voice quieted as he continued, as though he half-spoke to himself. "It seems you were helping me after all."

Tamika closed her eyes and shook her head. "Of course I was," she whispered. "But I know why you didn't trust me. Maybe... some day we'll be able to see each other without... so much baggage."

"Maybe."

Tamika took his hand. "Take care of yourself. Remember not to go out much."

Allan smiled with one body, while the other rolled its eyes. "I'll try."

Tamika took a last, longing glance at the room. Ben fought the urge to ask her again to stay. She had warred enough with herself already.

He walked her to the door. "Thank you again, Dr. Artemit," she repeated.

"Goodbye, Tamika."

The door shut behind her.

Moments later, the SUV pulled out of sight.

CHAPTER
TWENTY-SIX

New Prey

Al Turen squeezed the driver with both hands, while the massive holo before him sculpted a perfect fairway. He could barely make out a checkerboard grid of mesh suspended in the image, destined to catch and funnel his golf ball back to him. He had the other three walls of the room darkened as usual, which made him feel less exposed.

He shuffled and accidentally knocked the golf ball off the tee. Cursing, he batted the ball forward into the net. His game room seemed to take longer than usual returning the golf ball to the tee.

The extra time allowed his mind to wander, which was exactly what he was trying to avoid by coming in here.

Ever since he'd chastised Artemit and Kitt over their unauthorized use of the lab, his thoughts had gone off the rails. The instant he had left Artemit's apartment, Turen was certain and satisfied the two scientists had repeated experiments to get the exact same results, and in doing so risked their careers.

He still couldn't believe they were so superstitious they'd need further experimental evidence. He could, however, understand the egos involved in such high-stakes theories. Manipulating those egos gave Turen some of his greatest pleasures.

The satisfaction of rebuking them had decayed and fractured, however. Even though only a few days had passed, the memory of their encounter had grown distant.

Turen struggled to separate fact from fiction.

He remembered things that hadn't happened, different outcomes of the experiment, different arguments with Kitt and Artemit that were so real they couldn't be dismissed. The visions were waking dreams, so close to the truth Turen had to check their academic paper's publication and the lab's security footage to confirm his sanity.

Reviewing hard facts he could hold and touch confirmed the reality he thought he'd known. Time travel wasn't possible.

This evidence should have quelled the power of the ghostly visions, especially after the second or third viewing. By the fourth or fifth, any doubts should've been crushed.

When Turen started checking the evidence daily, he should've acknowledged it wasn't helping.

The visions brought uncertainty that lingered like mysterious birthmarks, raising questions but incapable of providing answers.

So Turen spent more and more time in his game room, anything to hold his attention on something other than this new obsession.

Bringing the matter up with Kitt or Artemit was out of the question. Not only would it make them question his sanity, it would validate their insane need to repeat the experiment.

Seeing a shrink wasn't an option, because he was one of the public faces for Quantix, and easily recognizable. What would people think if the great Al Turen, fearless head of the Quantix Vancouver lab, were seen seeking mental aid? He had scorned countless employees for far less, shaming them so consistently they'd resigned.

He liked to think the purity of his research field was due in large part to his efforts.

He imagined all of his previous victims circling the periphery of civilization like carrion crows. They would tear him apart if they smelled a hint of mental frailty.

So Turen would endure this alone, knowing privately that when it was all over, he'd have overcome what the weak-willed could not.

While he was at it, he would improve his golf game.

He raised the driver then swung as hard as he could. He sliced the ball, sending it shooting at an angle, getting caught at the far right edge of the mesh before the holo tracked its movement and projected its fictional but expected path through the always-sunny fairway.

Turen cursed and swung the club like a baseball bat as though he might be able to strike the escaping ball and readjust its course.

Just as he was lining up his next swing, grey clouds crept over the landscape. Turen dropped the club to his side and growled. The scene wasn't supposed to change unless he told it to.

Like many other beloved things in his life, he had complete control over this domain. There wasn't a blade of grass that should flutter here without him granting permission.

Turen wondered if, in his distracted state the past few days, he'd turned on weather variation. It was also possible the developers had released an update to "improve" the user experience. If that were the case they'd get an earful from him.

No time for that now, though. Sighing, he lined up his next shot into the darkening sky.

Turen drove one ball after another, no longer bothering with practice swings or careful setup. He grunted more with each stroke, swatting furiously in the buzz-cut grass in search of the perfect shot. Meanwhile, grey stratus clouds descended, enveloping everything they touched.

Turen felt like his muscles would cool and stiffen if he didn't keep swinging. He growled when the ball wasn't replaced fast enough on the tee, and hammered it in *clacks* that demanded he swing harder.

At some point he noticed the mesh starkly outlined in fog despite the holo's overlay.

The tech should have better compensated for the mesh's presence. Turen examined the edges of the field of view, noticing the fog had spread to the other walls. Those walls were capable of supporting holo-projection, but he thought he'd turned them off.

The fog crept into forbidden sections, appearing so real he could taste moisture on his tongue.

That was crazy, of course. Maybe he'd had enough for the day.

Turen turned to hit the power switch on the wall beside the door.

Wisps of fog curled before him.

The door was not a holo. In fact, the whole back wall was plain as plain could be, only bearing lights and projectors that cast forward. At least, it should have been, but instead it was wreathed in fog like all the other walls.

A faint whimper escaped Turen's throat. This couldn't be right. None of this could be right.

Through a gap in the fog, he reached for the door handle, but the fog swallowed it before he made contact.

The fog wrapped closer, tighter, colder. It spun, a motion that had been there all along but had been too slow to notice. The mist now readied to engulf him, whirling like a dust devil coalescing into a tornado.

The air whistled but it was also strangely hushed, as though something on the other side of the fog swallowed the sound.

The violent swirl searched for a focus and found Turen. The humid air held the reek of sewers after spring runoff.

Turen put out his hands, but the vortex rocked him and scraped his skin. Gasping, he snapped his arms back to his sides.

He'd be torn apart if he tried to step out.

He cried out for help, but his shouts went into a cone, drowned barely after surfacing.

The sheath of warm air around him, his last barrier, was ripped away. He shuddered from the cold.

Turen felt something watching him. Studying him.

He gazed frantically around but there was only the fog swirling in bands, joining and breaking apart in vivid oscillations.

Two blurred shapes approached as though from the end of a long tunnel. The view resonated intensely with the tunnel from Turen's childhood.

He couldn't breathe.

Grey light outlined the forms. They were humanoid, but as they lurched closer, Turen saw their legs were much too thin and long, the heads too large.

Turen stepped back but it didn't affect the distance between him and the figures.

He turned back toward the door, but all around him now lay a flat, empty expanse. He ran, hoping to reach the door, a wall, a net, anything—but the only things in the void were him and the figures.

The gravity diminished with each footfall. He flailed as he lost touch with the ground, floating in molasses. He glanced over his shoulder; the figures drew closer.

Turen screamed, but someone had turned down the volume of his existence. The figures surged through the remaining gap. Turen curled into a ball.

The creatures' voices echoed in the fog, a dissonant blend of chitters and growls. It took Turen a few moments to distinguish words.

"...Weeeee assssssssskkkk... weeeee knooooooow."

The voices ground out harsh, ear-piercing cries of a dozen people in agony.

"—thissssss. Weeeee waaaaant toooooo exisssssssst."

Turen wanted to scream, *I'll give you anything you want!*

Just leave me alone! His tongue refused him voice.

They're not real. They don't exist. The thought came from another part of Turen, maybe the logical part that had grown instinctive through years as a scientist.

I'm just imagining this. This isn't really happening!

The figures slammed into an invisible wall, the impact shuddering through the mist. As the ripple spread, gravity returned and Turen fell to the ground. The ground shook, rattling Turen's skull. One of the figures pawed at the invisible wall while the other hammered on it.

Turen got up on his knees, searching for a way out.

A screech echoed from all sides, growing louder like a microphone and a speaker brought too close together. Turen covered his ears as pain travelled through his skull and down his sinuses.

Abruptly, the shrieking stopped. The figures turned and skulked toward the distant grey light.

Turen's ears rang with pain's swan song.

Are they leaving? Please, tell me they're leaving.

The fog swirled away as the figures passed out of sight.

Turen found himself kneeling, gravity returned, his shirt stained with tears, in the middle of his game room, staring into the blinding projection of the perfect golf course.

He felt hollowed, as though the mist had raked his insides. The memory of the figures approaching him, and raging as they crashed against the invisible wall, echoed in his thoughts.

He shivered, trying not to imagine them breaking through.

"It's all in your head," Turen muttered, over and over. That had seemed to hold them back, hadn't it?

His words faded at each repetition until they became a low whimper.

The invisible wall—some sort of metaphysical barrier— was all that had saved him from the figures' monstrous power.

He scrambled for the door, sweaty hands slipping on the

handle. He slammed the door shut and ran to his room.

Turning on all the lights, he huddled on his bed with knees drawn up, the same way he had as a beaten boy.

* * *

Turen dreamed of Kitt Bell and Ben Artemit. Despite his contempt toward them, he wanted to stay with them—he wanted to be with anybody. He chased them.

They retreated, not noticing him and always out of reach. They entered Artemit's apartment. When Turen followed, he was met inside by two grinning, monsters.

He sat awake with a shout. Light blinded him.

Where am I? What time is it?

He trembled, too weary to get up and move. If he could rest a bit, he might be able to deal with the nightmares more logically...

Not if sleeping means seeing them.

He lay slowly back down. He rolled from side to side, shaking his head to keep his eyelids from drooping.

Within a few minutes, he fell back asleep.

* * *

He chased after Kitt and Artemit again, screaming at them not to go into the apartment.

They couldn't hear him. Turen pushed reluctantly through into Artemit's living room and this time, things looked normal.

He reached to grab Artemit's shoulder—

Gravity stopped pulling, casting Turen afloat. His stomach lurched in his throat. He flailed, unable to reach Artemit and Kitt.

From the hall, two hideous figures approached. Their heads were huge and they opened wide, gaping maws to reveal rows of sharp teeth.

They sucked the light from the room, until Turen stood in darkness with them.

He screamed.

The monsters faded, gravity weighing down until Turen's feet hit the ground. He ran, the fog dissipating with his footfalls.

* * *

Turen paced his room. His legs felt like they belonged to someone else. He wanted out of his body, out of his mind and out of himself.

He went to the kitchen and grabbed a jar of applesauce. Sitting on a stool at the counter, he spooned some into his mouth.

He closed his eyes and focused on the small, soft lumps.

That's it. Yes, that's it.

He just had to do this for a few hours until the day began. Then he'd distract himself with work, surround himself with people who had to listen to him.

He set his head down, content with his plan, and fell back into darkness.

* * *

He dreamed of the time travel experiments with Kitt and Artemit, except the fog was there now, too, surrounding every movement they made, coming out of their mouths with each word they spoke. The fog flashed with each experimental result. Scenes blended, repeating in ghostly echoes of different outcomes.

Backward time travel was possible.

Then it wasn't.

Then it was again.

The contradictions wove together seamlessly. Kitt and Artemit took in the incongruities without pause.

Turen wanted both Kitt and Artemit to face this awful reality with him, but was forced to relive the twilight half-truths alone. Over and over.

At the fog's edge, the monsters appeared, moving their arms as though they wove enchantments.

Were they sustaining this awful unreality?

They gazed at Turen with deep orange eyes, and recognition sparked in him.

He'd seen them before. Before his memory had somehow... disappeared.

He'd watched them on the holo not long after confronting Kitt and Artemit. Their glistening flesh pulsed with blue veins, and they grinned wickedly at him. Spittle dripped from razor-sharp teeth.

The experimental echoes tapered out, never quite finishing, for the madness of the patterns could never truly end. Fog engulfed the whole scene, leaving only the hideous monsters, who dropped their arms and stalked toward Turen.

"...Weeeee assssssssskkkk..."

The ground gave out beneath Turen. In a moment they'd be upon him. This time, he knew the invisible barrier would not hold them back.

"Weeeee waaaaant toooo exisssssst."

❊ ❊ ❊

Turen awoke on the kitchen floor beside a tipped-over stool. Nauseated, he took gasping breaths.

Minutes later, he hunched over the sink, pressing a cold cloth to his throbbing skull. Thoughts of the monsters pulsed in and out.

Those monsters had almost gotten him in his game room. Were they the same monsters he had seen in the holo?

Had he even seen those monsters in the holo, or had he only dreamed that part?

He couldn't be sure—each vision had added a new horror to shake the foundations of his sanity. He might have projected them from his own imagination.

I won't go crazy, he thought. *I can't. Please.*

The monsters were gaining strength, and they were cornering him. He had to do something, anything, even if it was raving to the police... or an escort... anyone.

No, he thought, trying to clear the blur out of his head. *I'm Al Turen, and none of those will do.*

There was one person he could approach, though, who knew, who *had* to know what all of this meant and how to fight it.

It hurt Turen's pride, but it would hurt a lot less than other alternatives, and infinitely less than what the monsters would do to him.

Turen grabbed a jacket and stomped into the early morning sun, mumbling feverish hopes that he could make it to Artemit before the monsters got him.

CHAPTER TWENTY-SEVEN

Entangled Friendship

"**A**re you sure you don't want another bed?" Ben Artemit asked, testing the inflated twin size mattress with his palm. The room could've easily fit a queen size, but Allan had insisted on a twin.

One of Allan's bodies stood at the doorway, while the other walked in and inspected, hands gently crossed at his waist. The blackout curtains were drawn tightly shut and the only light in the room was the blue white of the overhead LEDs.

"No, this is perfect. This way I won't be tempted to sleep with both at once."

Ben frowned. He hadn't quite wrapped his head around the notion of an entangled man, let alone sleeping beside yourself.

Allan had been through hell, though. Ben needed to keep his mind more open than his eyes.

"Allan, can I ask why you're so afraid of that? Both bodies asleep, I mean."

Allan stole a peek out the blinds before pacing on the opposite side of the bed. "I go somewhere if I sleep with both at the same time." His voice dropped as though he might travel to the place by speaking of it too loudly. "Somewhere... horrible. Worse than anything you can imagine."

Ben nodded, his lips pressed together. *It's remarkable how whole and sane he is. Just how terrible was this place?* The horror in Allan's voice stopped Ben from voicing his questions.

"Well, I hope that's at an end," Ben said finally. "If there's anything I can do to help, let me know."

Allan's other body behind Ben answered this time. "This is great, Ben. I'm... Thank you."

After scanning the walls, the other Allan continued, "Actually, maybe there is something. Do you have any pictures to put up?"

Ben glanced at the white paint he'd applied less than a year ago. "Maybe. What did you have in mind?"

"Anything. Absolutely anything is better than that dull, empty sameness."

Ben wondered how much the room reminded Allan of the facility where he'd been imprisoned. He nodded. "Sure."

❊ ❊ ❊

For dinner, Ben prepared a stir-fry. It had been a long time since he'd cooked so frequently, and he allowed himself to get caught up in the familiar actions and comfortable smells. For a brief time, he forgot about the monsters.

Earlier, he'd told Kitt about Allan and belatedly asked if she was comfortable with his stay. Although at first she'd been skeptical and bewildered, Kitt's root-deep compassion had ultimately won out, and she'd even offered to make a grocery trip for the three of them.

Despite all the recent horrors, Ben felt very lucky.

Allan padded into the kitchen, examining the countertops and appliances. With the scent of fried garlic filling the air, Allan reached a tentative hand out to the cupboard doors.

"May I?"

Ben looked over as he stirred hissing garlic. "Of course. Treat this place like your home." He dumped cubed chicken into the wok.

Allan opened cupboards and brushed his fingertips across rows of glasses. He opened drawers and touched the handles of the cutlery. He picked up a set of chopsticks, walked over with his other body and grabbed another pair so they were each holding a set.

Allan's bodies faced one another, holding out the chopsticks and bridging the gap between until their tips touched one another. Once they did, Allan began moving the chopsticks in a slow circle, keeping the tips together. They slipped apart before he'd made a complete revolution, but after a few tries he was able to do it successfully, getting faster each time.

The smell of sizzling chicken roused Ben from his fascinated reverie, and he abruptly lowered the heat and stirred the chicken. When he looked over again, Allan had put the chopsticks back, but now smiled on both faces.

He's like a child, Ben thought. *He's finally allowed all the playfulness denied him when he first started this new entangled life. He's playing catch-up.*

He watched Allan in silence, feeling a swell in his chest for the opportunity to witness this moment in Allan's life.

Unfortunately, the moment didn't last long. As though some malevolence had crept into the room, Allan shivered and frowned with both bodies. His eyes grew distant and he strode to the window next to the dining table to pull back one of the blinds. The shoulders of both bodies sagged. On the other body leaning against the counter facing Ben, the life and playfulness had disappeared, replaced by slack features and eclipses beneath brooding eyes.

He's diving deeper into himself. Ben recognized the signs from when he'd done the exact same thing. How had he gotten himself out of that pit?

Kitt. She saved me. A meaningful connection with her... which meant opening up.

Sharing.

"Allan," Ben said, turning away from the stove, "you know how you said you go somewhere horrible when you sleep? Well, I also go somewhere really horrible, though it's maybe not as bad. I haven't been able to reliably reproduce it, because it—and I know how this sounds—it's like it brings me to them."

Allan straightened and turned both bodies toward Ben. "Who are *they*?" His voice held no hint of disbelief or irony. After everything Allan had been through, nothing was impossible anymore. Allan's body language conveyed a readiness to absorb whatever was said.

The fluttering in Ben's chest calmed, something he hadn't thought possible when speaking about the monsters.

Maybe both he and Allan had travelled well beyond the boundary of what most people called reality. What a pair they made: an entangled man and a man whose childhood monsters haunted him from every shadow.

Somehow they'd been equipped to understand one another.

"It started when I was a child," he began.

He told of the terrors of his youth, the lurking darkness that only he ended up remembering. All before he knew of his power to be a Chooser.

"I lost parts of myself during those therapy sessions, when I had to reprogram my mind to reject what stared me in the face. I opened a rift inside between what I trusted and what I didn't. I'm still not sure if I've repaired the gap."

Allan listened quietly, nodding in sincere acceptance. Dinner was ready, so they served themselves, and ate as Ben continued.

"I don't know if the dinosauroids will be with me forever, never mind what I choose for their fate."

Ben fumbled as he recounted the events in the lab. What

did chronology mean when a web of possibilities had branched in all directions from a moment?

Ben shared the threats, the looming horror constantly weighing on his mind. He told of how he'd finally managed to push back against the monsters, to stop them from removing his brain and burning his arms. He told of his temporary victory, and the threat posed by other Choosers that might make the monsters real.

"It seems," Allan said after a lengthy silence, "that you might've expected the pressure on you to relieve when you found out there might be another Chooser. But instead that knowledge has intensified the urgency to make things right before it's too late."

"Exactly," Ben replied. "I'm terrified I'll run out of time before I figure out how to control my power."

"Or that your power will be gone before you do," Allan said.

Ben shivered. *It's like he's reading my mind. He's far more than he seems.*

"Yeah," Ben said at last, rubbing his eyes and groaning. "You know, I don't know if it's because you have two sets of ears, but you're a really good listener."

They burst into laughter. It sliced the tension, a box cutter opening packed layers that spilled out to fill the space.

At first the release felt wonderful, then the weight of everything settled, pressing from every angle. Ben's throat tightened, laughter wheezing into nothing.

They glanced at each other, then stared silently into the folds of the blinds.

* * *

Images of Ben's monsters clouded Allan Gerrold's thoughts. He got up from the dining table with both bodies and paced, deliberately offsetting his steps to consume his focus. The images lingered, however.

He had so little control. He'd thought that escaping from Quantix would grant him better control, but it hadn't.

He saw haunting flashes of the dark world whenever he yawned, whenever his eyes burned from being open too long, whenever his back and feet ached from the tightness of controlling two halves of himself.

Now that he'd met Ben and heard about his monsters, Allan was reminded of what felt a lifetime ago—when he'd been living on the streets and had gotten wholly absorbed in a vision of a chain. He'd been compelled to help whoever was at the end, and at the time he'd thought it was the woman with the faulty bike chain.

Had it instead been Ben's face at the end of the chain? Was he the one who needed help? Before Allan had been entangled, he never would have given premonitions any credence. Now, however, anything seemed possible.

Allan wasn't sure he was in any state to help anyone at the moment, though.

He wished he could better control switching one body off while the other slept. Even when he did manage to switch one body off, the long-term memory integration buzzing in the background was exhausting.

He pressed his thumbs to his temples.

The conversation with Ben had been good. Real. How long had it been since he'd had a conversation with someone he could trust, sharing something deep and personal? Tamika had only opened up to him a little in the end, and he didn't trust what was truth and what was fiction.

In another life, Allan would have thought Ben insane. Ben could be under the spell of hallucinatory nightmares from a misguided childhood.

Entangled as he was, though, Allan believed him. Perhaps through his own insanities, he'd paradoxically come to better recognize truth.

"Allan, are you OK?" Ben asked.

"Yeah," Allan said. "I just keep thinking about the worlds we each travel to, so distinct and yet rooted in commonality blending the depths of fear from our imagination. I'm not saying you're making this up. I believe you because what you describe resonates so strongly with what I live whenever I sleep with both bodies at the same time. I kind of wish I didn't recognize the connections, because the sensory associations I have are way too strong whenever I try to think about... that place even in abstract terms."

"I'm sorry, Allan," Ben said. "I didn't intend to make you relive the trauma."

"Right now the triggers are so small it's hard not to. I don't know what my new normal is going to be like. You're the first person I've spoken to who actually cares about what I say and experience beyond a cold scientific curiosity. And really, I'm sorry about the monsters haunting you. Saying that barely does it justice. I've tried to tell myself that such suffering must ultimately mean something, but I don't know if I believe it."

"It sounds like, if nothing else, our suffering is helping us understand each other."

"I guess so."

Allan rubbed his chins. His connection with Ben seemed stronger than he'd had in years. His old coping mechanisms in the laboratory had kept him alive up to now, but that had been in a nearly constant state of crisis. Now that he was free and able to relax, he had to rediscover how.

He'd lost much more of himself than he'd thought. Could he get some of it back by talking to Ben? It seemed a childish hope, but he had to try.

"I don't," he said, "know how well I'm going to be able to talk about this."

He lifted both sets of hands, scanning his fingers to try and ground himself.

"When I sleep, I'm in a dreamscape of shifting colours. It'd be wonderful if it lasted. From there it's like each sense needs to find itself again, then reconnect to the others. The jolts when they do reconnect bring about the worst tastes and smells I never knew could exist. I hear blended cries of a million horrible things. My brain turns into a giant melting pot. Positive memories all come out tainted by an evil force.

"When the hellish journey shifts to ground me in my body, I am nowhere on Earth. With the out of body experience, I could tell myself it wasn't real and pull back from everything. Once I'm grounded in this visceral horror, though, there's no escape. It's torture. Creatures, forms, shapes more ghastly than anything ever imagined—all of them take a turn tearing me apart. I struggle but can never escape this dark place. The worst part is that I never die."

Allan closed his eyes and shuddered. "I don't know how many times I've visited this world. I'm dragged to new places for new horrors."

Allan tapped a fist against his forehead, wishing the images out. A second later he placed both palms on the table, opened his eyes wide and took long breaths.

"Words don't convey it. I wouldn't wish this on anyone else, so maybe it's for the best that I can't articulate it. I just know it hurts me more than anything else they did to me at the lab.

"I haven't figured out how to consistently sleep with one body at a time. I'm exhausted and I don't know if that's because of all the stress I've been under or because my long-term memory integration is forced to happen when I'm awake. All of this is new. In some ways it would it be nice to be studied at least a bit by somebody who is interested in helping me live a healthy life.

"I don't know, though... that might be too much to ask." Allan's voice trailed off to a whisper.

❊ ❊ ❊

Ben tried to steer the conversation away from the darkness

covering them both, but inevitably both his and Allan's thoughts were too swayed by their worries.

"These monsters," Allan said, "were based on dinosaurs you'd read in a book, right? That's why they seemed so familiar to you?"

"Yes," Ben said. "They're a predicted version of what intelligent dinosaurs might have been... but I have a feeling the familiarity might go deeper." He groaned. "But I have no idea why. I could really use more sleep."

"Is there a chance you saw the book or images when you were younger, before you actually owned it?"

"I don't think so. I got the book the year it was published, saving up my allowance as a teenager. Unless I'd snuck into the creator's studio or something, I don't think I would have ever had the opportunity to see the monsters before that. Which is why it's so weird that their likeness strikes me with resonance as though I'd known them my whole life."

"What's your earliest memory of them?"

"I always thought it was when I was five or so, maybe six? In my room, I think. But it's all so foggy. I wish I had a better memory."

"Why don't you try closing your eyes as you tell me about it?" Allan suggested.

Ben considered. "I guess it can't hurt..."

Ben closed his eyes and inhaled stale air through his nostrils. The actions reminded him of countless sessions with his therapist Heather Smith. He felt as though he were back in her musty, cramped room where she'd tried to squeeze the truth out of him. When she didn't get a truth she understood, she'd just squeezed harder.

It was difficult, but he managed to push aside the painful memories, and not let them be a roadblock. What had happened before all that? When was the first time he'd seen the monsters?

He was in his old room with action figures, Lego and robotics kits strewn about, the only clear space a narrow path between his bed in the corner and the door. Everywhere else was a hazard zone where you risked a sharp plastic block in your foot, or worse, destroying a half-finished creation.

Ben had effectively laid traps for anyone who might approach. The traps had done nothing to weaken the monsters, however.

"God, I was young," he said. "Before the monsters, my world had been nothing but toys... worlds where I could play. I'd never experienced real danger. I thought danger was something fun you invoked to spice up a game with friends. It's hard to imagine I was ever so naïve.

"I saw their outlines in the dark, open closet as Mom read me stories. Mom was a great storyteller, so I kept getting distracted and pulled back into the book we were reading, not realizing she was inadvertently saving me from the terror of the monsters' existence. When the story finished, my mother wove her way out as my eyelids drooped."

Ben's thoughts drifted from where the monsters had tormented him repeatedly, to the very first night they'd approached him. Giving the stories new voice seemed to lay out a timeline more clearly in his mind, but the exact order was still unclear.

His face tightened as the memories came back, and refused to let go.

"No. It wasn't in my room. It was in the motel, in Drumheller. How could I have forgotten? It was awful. After my first visit to the Royal Tyrrell Museum. I... I wanted to bring the dinosaurs back. They'd seemed so caged, shackled. Reduced to far less than their glory. And Mom had read me a story despite my intent to stay awake until I had a solution.

"Did I see them in the motel that night, before my nightmare? I think I did, but I didn't want to acknowledge it. So they didn't come out of my dream. They were there *before*. And when they came, they said... *We made it*. Didn't they? Or was there something else they also said...?"

Ben cantered his fingers on his temples, leaning forward

and concentrating.

"Yes. They did say something else. They said, *'Time can't keep you from us, Artemit.'*"

He groaned. "Why am I remembering this now? It's just like the dinosauroids, who aren't constrained by the passage of time. My memories of them seem to behave the same way. I'm seeing so many things it's hard to put them in order. It's all a non-linear mess.

"Is that all they really meant, though," Ben continued, "when they said time couldn't keep me from them? The way they said it suggests a reference point, a start date..."

"It suggests you met them before," Allan said.

"Yes," Ben said, his breath catching. "But when? And why? Seeing them after visiting the Tyrrell makes sense to me. Before that, the dinosauroids didn't exist in my mind. Or did they? I thought I knew... but it's getting murkier the more I talk about it."

Ben walked into the hall and pressed his forehead against the wall. "OK, maybe there's a chance they were in my mind, but they hadn't become as real as they did that day. If I truly *had* seen them before, what was preventing them from coming back to me? If I met them before, they must have already existed..."

Ben thought back to his dream many years ago, on what he'd thought was his first night seeing the monsters, when he'd wandered the Tyrrell Museum before a cold, reptilian hand had pulled him into the shadows to hide from a guard. The distinct form and image of the creatures had carried familiarity even then. In his dream, he'd walked side by side next to the monsters, muscle memory letting him fall into a routine from long, long ago...

He paced the hall, letting the feeling of walking side by side with the monsters wash over him. His steps brought him deeper into to the dream in Tyrell museum, and then much, much further back.

He remembered everything.

His face contorted and his eyes widened until they threatened to burst from their sockets. He grabbed the sides of his head as throbbing pain pounded from inside like tribal drums. He fell to his knees and gasped.

"How could—how could—?" Ben's words crusted in his throat like sand after a landslide.

Allan asked him questions with far away words, distorted and reverberating.

Ben trembled. He lost feeling in his legs and toppled into Allan's arms, while Allan's other body rushed to brace them.

Spit dribbled from Ben's mouth. He coughed, struggling to breathe. Not sure if he even wanted to.

The world came to him in stop-motion animation. Allan leaning toward the door. Kitt appearing. Groceries dropped. Kitt beside him. Asking questions, more questions. Ben wishing more and more that he could sink deep into the ground and never emerge.

Kitt was next to him, then gone, then back again. He couldn't remember her leaving. Things stopped making sense; he didn't want to make sense of things anymore. His mind retreated, unwilling to engage with what he'd experienced.

How long he twitched and drooled, he couldn't be sure, but at some point, he saw his instinctive behaviour for what it was: denial and avoidance. He cried out, gritting his teeth at the cowardice that risked pushing this revelation back into the shadows, back into a forgotten memory where it had lingered too long without action.

The only way he could see forward, to possibly get through and survive to act productively, was to give the words voice.

It was real. He had to admit it.

The words on his tongue felt like they might take everything. He had no idea where he would go afterward, if he would continue to be, or not.

"I... I've done something... terrible..."

He told them all he'd remembered.

* * *

It was a world before humans, a world before worlds.

Not in the dimension of time, but in the dimension of possibility. The would-be realm of quantum mechanics, where the dinosauroids resided.

Humanity had been in this realm, relegated and constrained to insubstantiality. They were so insubstantial that few concrete memories could emerge, and what did came in patchy blurs.

Artemit had been a leader, a commander. Perhaps because he had enough substance, essence or whatever passed for such in the realm of possibilities, he felt more firm and stable in a place that was anything but.

All around, everything was possible, but nothing definitive occurred. Nothing mattered more than anything else. Hardly anything mattered at all.

One of the other few things Artemit knew was that the privilege granted to him was based on no merit of his own, but merely random quantum fluctuations.

The memories that came into clear focus were those when he'd been near the dinosauroids. At that time, or at that state, they had what humans did not: reality.

Artemit, in his position of privilege and power, was tasked with getting the dinosauroids to make his people real.

Artemit had begged and pleaded with them, recognizing them as the gods they were. They alone were capable of bestowing a rich and deep existence upon humanity.

Artemit didn't know if he'd imagined what the distant future might look like. He wasn't sure if he'd even been capable of it. Had he acted out of self-interested survival, or out of altruism to improve the station of the entire human race?

Maybe all possibilities were true, and maybe none were.

Most importantly, had he known he would end the

dinosauroids' existence? Ben didn't know. He suspected he might never know.

In the dimly-outlined, would-be realm, Artemit had appeared before the dinosauroids. He'd given every argument imaginable to justify humanity's existence. He'd threatened, cajoled, bargained. He'd offered trades, favours, gifts. He'd promised the dinosauroids worship in the New World.

Anything for the future of the human race. For its present. For its past.

Or was it only for Artemit's ego?

The agent, the leader who'd listened to Artemit's pleas, was none other than Belonthar. The most reasonable of the dinosauroids took pity on Artemit's.

Belonthar had granted Artemit's request, and given the humans existence.

He was a Chooser, and he had chosen *Homo sapiens*, unwittingly betraying himself and everyone he loved to a fate worse than death.

All because only one of their worlds could be real.

Artemit had asked the dinosauroids for exactly the same thing they requested now. He'd succeeded in convincing them to make humans real, and had won the ultimate evolutionary battle between quantum mechanical realities.

Now they'd returned for justice.

* * *

There was a long silence after Ben finished. Everyone could only travel so quickly between now and the ancient times. Between non-existence, and would-be, Ben's purchase of their birth at a terrible price.

Ben was on his knees, tears streaming down his face, seeing only a blurred vision of his palms that should by all rights not exist.

He wanted to sink through the floor, into the dirt, and

down until he'd been burned in the deepest fires of the Earth for his xenocide.

Everything that was and ever would be stemmed from a sacrifice that should never have been made.

And he'd done it.

He'd committed unimaginable atrocity against an entire species.

He took wheezing breaths. The air tasted thick with smog.

He had to face it, face himself, but how could he? Was the reason he hadn't remembered before because of deep denial? Had he suppressed all memory of it so he could look at himself in the mirror?

If he had, he couldn't do it any longer. He couldn't pretend it hadn't happened.

He took deep, shaky breaths.

Ben prayed he would take a fraction of the time, and commit far fewer atrocities along the way toward reconciliation with the dinosauroids.

Kitt, Allan and Ben all sat in a stunned state. Ben imagined they, like him, were barely able to comprehend the enormity of what he had done. Ben did not know how much time had passed before one of them finally spoke.

Kitt spoke first. "I can only imagine how you must feel, Ben. It's hard... to believe that was you." She paused solemnly, looking downward.

Ben sank further into the floor.

Kitt hesitated, her face twisted as though forces pulled her in different directions. "But when I try to put myself in the same situation, I can't really know if I would do anything different. Would I have done or said similar things had I existed—or not—in such a place? Maybe. I definitely would've done what you did if I didn't know what the consequences would be. We're all selfish in the end, looking out for our own survival."

"That doesn't make it right," Ben said. "What I did was

worse than Genghis Khan."

Kitt's eyes widened as she made the connection, and she formed a wordless 'Oh' on her lips. After several minutes of silence, she spoke again.

"The difference is that the dinosauroids know what the consequences will be this time, and are pushing forward anyway. I understand their desire for retribution, for revenge. But that doesn't make it right. How many people would we have to kill to make things right? We could play this back-and-forth game until the end of time. And in the end, no one would be the better for it."

"But who are we to say that we're the ones who get to stop the cycle here?" Ben protested. "Do we really have the moral high ground? I don't think so."

"You're right... they have to be involved for any sense of equity in all of this," Kitt said. "And we have such a huge bias it'd be a travesty to claim otherwise. I don't want them dead, Ben, and I don't think you do, either. But I also want don't want the extinction of the entire human race, which is what they're asking for in order for things to be made right. They haven't been straight in what they're asking."

"I wasn't either when I tricked them," Ben said.

"You convinced them, Ben; you didn't trick them. You said you don't know if you knew what would happen. You didn't necessarily know they'd be eradicated."

"I don't think I did. But I can't be certain. I might be deluding myself."

"What we can be certain of is that the dinosauroids know this time around. They directly lied to you about it, didn't they? Belonthar went out of his way to act like nothing bad would happen. The dinosauroids definitely know what they're doing. What they're proposing is monstrous and unjust regardless of what's happened in the past. We can only affect and correct our behaviour going forward. We can't change the past but we can try to make equitable amends.

"That means we have to stop them from what they're

doing right now, and hope that gives us the opportunity and time so we can later find a way to work cooperatively with them to reconcile what was done to them so long ago."

"What *I* did to them so long ago," Ben said. "I still don't know if we have any right to make that call, Kitt. What if we never find a way to pay them back? What if there's no other way for... retribution?"

"Reconciliation, not retribution," Kitt said. "We have to keep looking. No matter what, we keep looking, and don't stop until the search for knowledge is done. That's the most just, moral thing we can do for them without compounding acts of the past. It's not great, but it's the best we can do, isn't it?"

Ben wasn't satisfied. He still wanted to shrink and disappear. Dimly, in a corner of his rattled mind, he saw Kitt's reasoning as the best option they had. Like her, he didn't want the extinction of the entire human race. He wondered if the guilt pressing down on him would ever ease up, or if he could find small actions to make up for all he'd done to the dinosauroids.

Then he recognized the selfish focus on his own guilt. How could he be so self-focused after all this? He suddenly wanted to trade his own existence for that of the dinosauroids.

Why? his mind shouted back at him.

"Why does it have to be one or the other?" he blurted. "Why did it have to happen this way? Why couldn't we both exist in separate universes?"

"Because your two universes are entangled," Allan said, stepping forward and uncapping his chin.

"What? How do you know?" Kitt asked.

Allan gestured at each of his bodies. "I'm somewhat familiar with entanglement, you might say. Somewhere or sometime along the line our two universes got entangled in such a way that one's existence suppresses the other.

"Ben, you described my quantum entanglement as being vastly complicated. Well, your two worlds are extremely complicated as well. Right now our world, the world of humans, is real, and the world of the dinosauroids is purely quantum mechanical. But I doubt that you could come up with a theoretical description of these two worlds. You said it was hard to do for molecules with a few dozen particles. It's got to be impossible to understand it all for two Worlds." Ben heard the capitalized W.

"I agree," said Ben, "but let's see what we can come up with." He wanted to find something better than one world real and the other not. He paced. "One entangled state, oversimplified, I admit, is that one world is real and the other is purely quantum mechanical. But the quantum world, the dinosauroid's world, cannot be said not to exist at all. If their quantum world didn't exist at all there would be no connection between their world and ours." His mind slipped back to his experiences with Belonthar and Merthab. He shivered. "No, their world is quantal, but it has the potential to be real, whatever the word 'real' means. We know it exists, because we have interacted with them. Calling it a *would-be* world is more accurate. It's not accurate to say that their world doesn't exist."

"So in a way," Allan said, "we could say that one entangled state is where the human Earth is real, but the dinosauroid world is merely a *would-be* world, one which could exist in the way that we do, but doesn't, not at this time. And that is why they asked you to make them real. You're tied directly to them, Ben."

Ben had been nodding and now spoke slowly and quietly: "Yes, I am. I am connected to Belonthar and Merthab. And it was only me at the beginning. But now I've brought Turen into it: he saw the experiments and he saw the monsters. And worse," Ben's hands shook, "I've brought Kitt into it as well."

"I'm sorry to say, but yes, you have," Allan said.

"Don't be sorry, either of you," Kitt said. "I wouldn't want Ben to fight these things alone, and I don't want to stand back and watch, either."

Ben smiled at her, but couldn't quell his lingering guilt.

"That Kitt and Turen saw the dinosauroids," Allan said, "is clear evidence that these 'connections' between our people and the dinosauroids are changing."

Ben's mouth opened as he realized the consequences of what Allan had said. A moment passed. Then he said, "This means we might already be on the way to the opposite entangled state. Where they are real and we are just quantum mechanical."

Allan put one of his hands on Ben's right shoulder. "But that is almost infinitely far away Ben. So, don't panic. Be calm. Remain rational. We'll figure this out, all three of us, together."

"Other states of the two worlds are possible," Ben pointed out. "They could both be purely quantum mechanical, for example." He pointed upward with a finger, and with hope in his voice added, "Another state could be that both worlds are real."

Kitt asked, "But how could we change the states from what they are now to both being real? There doesn't seem to be a way to do this."

The trio were silent, thinking, but none of them could come up with any idea of how do so.

"I agree with Kitt," Allan said. "We won't be able to investigate these avenues, or even come close to rectifying the past, unless we have more time. To get more time, we have to stop the dinosauroids' immediate plans.

"For now, we fight them; that much is clear. What we have to figure out is how they're manipulating this entangled relationship between our universes to their advantage. I humbly suggest that I'm the best person in both universes for this job. I never thought any good would come of my entangled state, but this could be it."

Allan walked over to his other body and clasped his shoulder. He then turned to Ben and Kitt who clutched his hands until they formed a circle.

"We can do this," Allan said. "And we'll work toward making things right, without making things worse."

Everyone nodded.

The pain of Ben's ancient crime pulsed through him in reverberating echoes. He doubted the pain would ever go away. Maybe it shouldn't. It was, after all, well-deserved.

For now, he tried to focus on what they needed to do next, which he prayed would only serve to stop the dinosauroids and open the door for reconciliation.

* * *

Belonthar and Merthab watched the discussion and planning through a thick mist, the human figures smoky and blurred but the sound sharp so they heard every word spoken. Belonthar tapped his long fingers together, his mouth unmoving, while Merthab paced beside him.

"He's not even aware we're here," Merthab spat.

Belonthar shook his head, then bared his teeth and hissed.

CHAPTER TWENTY-EIGHT

Gathering Intel

"**I**'m sorry, Mr. Kramer, but we're simply not allowed to divulge that kind of information."

Marlon Kramer, hands clasped in front of him on the desk in an amicable pose for the video chat, smiled and dug his fingers in near the knuckles. "As I've told you, Ms. Wellington, I have the warrant to obtain this information through law-enforcement officials. However, Quantix and its stakeholders are keen on resolving this in a manner that won't carry our intellectual property into the public domain."

Ms. Wellington, the operator at the other end of the video chat, let out a sigh that was far more audible than the last several. Kramer knew he was winning.

"Mr. Kramer, we cannot put corporate security ahead of personal privacy. I'm sorry that this situation could have such a detrimental effect on Quantix, but these rules are in place for the public good."

"Ms. Wellington," Marlon said, leaning forward and letting his smile grow, "I don't think you quite understand the relationship between corporate wellness and the public good."

"Mr. Kramer, I —"

"I'm not sure you understand the extent of Quantix's influences. Our fine elected representative, Avery Larson, would never have gotten noticed politically without our generous donations. You might remember that she's of course the one who pushed so hard for funding increases to your invaluable department. Not to mention the GDP growth figures quoted by the party for which Quantix is almost entirely responsible. The security personnel and resources required to maintain and preserve the security of our great nation. Do you think crime rates dropped on their own, out of an inherent increase in the goodwill of humanity?"

"I can't believe you're —"

"No, Quantix's militia is as much responsible for the progress of society as Martin Luther King or Gandhi. We are as intertwined in the system as income tax, and just as necessary. If you cause us direct harm you are sabotaging a life you take for granted."

Ms. Wellington's face turned red, and her hands, which had been typing at a keyboard as they talked, now trembled. "I don't know where you got the notion you could talk to me like that, or say such outrageous things, but that is unprofessional and I will not compromise my morality or code of ethics just because you had a disgruntled employee flee with sensitive information."

Kramer's smile widened. Ms. Wellington shrank back from him even though thousands of kilometres separated them. He wasn't entirely sure why people retreated when he smiled but seemed to warm to one another when *they* smiled. He'd learned to fake the expression in order to make it through life, part of his necessary chameleon act, but in moments like these, where his true happiness showed, people pulled away, as though he showed a primal face of atavism they were incapable of facing.

He could have won this discussion far sooner, but he was thrilled to see how much he had pushed Ms. Wellington to the peak of her moral high ground. Ms. Alicia Wellington, to be precise. The fall was much more satisfying to watch this way.

"Alicia," Marlon said, savouring every ounce of surprise her first name elicited, "I know your father is on dialysis at the St. Augustus Frontier Hospital. It may surprise you to learn that Quantix is the chief donor that makes not only the running of the hospital possible, but treatment of underinsured patients like your father possible. I see that he's been moved up the list for kidney transplants, which is really encouraging. It would be a shame if all that waiting, all those long hours attached to machines went to waste simply because the hospital was forced to shut down."

"No. You can't. You wouldn't —"

"As I said twenty of my precious minutes ago, Alicia: Give. Me. The. File."

Alicia Wellington stared back for several seconds, frozen except for a tremor beneath her eyes. When she finally spoke, her voice was as flat and subdued as steamrolled concrete.

"I'm sending Tamika's file to you right away, Mr. Kramer."

"Thank you, Alicia. Good day to you, and please give my best to your father."

* * *

Several minutes later, Marlon had Tamika Werrett's file, which cited the name change she'd tried very hard to cover up.

Sally Burton.

So, if she didn't reach out to one of Tamika's friends, would she have reached out to Sally's?

It was child's play to find Sally Burton's old connections, and everyone she might have contacted.

Father: deceased.

Mother: Rotilda Burton.

Siblings: Jack Burton, brother, Felicia Burton, sister.

Family seemed estranged from her. It was possible,

however, that in desperation she'd forgotten old pains, whether her family had or not. He scanned farther down the list.

Previous employers: Paula Fitzgerald, Tracy Chen, Dr. Al Turen, Dr. Ben Artemit...

Marlon made call after call until he was satisfied all the leads were being followed, and the trail burned like a dynamite fuse.

CHAPTER
TWENTY-NINE

Losing Control

I t was early in the morning, the sun just starting to rise through the apartment window. Ben and Allan's two bodies sat at the dining table, sipping coffee, while Kitt slept in the bedroom down the hall.

Ben was grateful for someone to talk to in the early morning—until Allan had showed up, he'd been stuck alone with his worries until Kitt awoke.

He was also grateful that Allan had such a sharp mind, and they could bounce possibilities around at a rapid-fire pace.

"If the entangled state of the two worlds was changed, would energy be conserved?" asked Allan.

"What do you mean?" replied Ben.

"Well, suppose they both started as purely quantum mechanical. Suppose further that something was done to make one world fully real and leave the other as purely quantal. Wouldn't that violate conservation of energy?"

Ben thought about this question for a moment.

"This is a question that has been looked at many times since quantum mechanics began. I'll just describe what I have done in my own work regarding this question. In short, there isn't any problem with conservation of energy in my theory."

Allan frowned. "Why not?"

"Well, suppose we have a single electron and we make a measurement to see if it is spin up or spin down. When we make the measurement, the universe becomes two universes, one with spin up and one with spin down. That seems to mean that the total energy has doubled, and therefore it seems like energy is not conserved."

"Doubling of the energy is a serious violation of conservation of energy!" Allan exclaimed.

"That could be argued against and has been in the past," said Ben. "One clever idea that I liked was that for each observer in his or her own universe, energy is conserved, and that adding up the energies of all the universes may well not be the best way to look at this question. But other ideas have been proposed.

"Another reason we might say the energy has doubled," Ben continued, "is that we are treating the second universe as not existing at all before the measurement, and being fully real after the measurement. And as time goes by there is more splitting of universes, and more and more until the number of universes is extremely large. As a result, the total energy seems to be increasing as time goes by. However, there is a way to have conservation of energy."

"And how is that?" Allan asked.

"The answer is like what we've said about the Dinosauroids' would-be world. In my view, we can have, in the many worlds of quantum mechanics, that all of the individual universes have the potential to exist right from the beginning of time. And a particular universe becomes fully real after the experiment. The energy for each universe is already there even before it comes to be real, fully real. And that universe was a sort of 'would-be' universe before it becomes fully real. As a result, the total energy in all of the universes is conserved. All the time."

"But energy is conserved in each universe as well, isn't

it?"

"Most of the time, yes, but not all the time. Energy can go from one universe to another. For example, in time travel some particles can be sent from one universe to the past in another universe. In between the time where the particles are sent back and the time they reach the other universe, the particles are in both universes. But before this time interval, the particles are in just one of the two universes and the same is true for the time afterward."

Allan's two bodies started walking around like leaves falling in the wind. "This is getting a bit complicated. I'm having trouble keeping all this in mind."

Ben and Allan spent time drawing diagrams like the ones Ben and Kitt had drawn when they first met and went for dinner together. After a while Allan understood it all. If the particles were sent back in time from 2PM to 1PM, then they existed in both universes from 1PM to 2PM. But they existed only in one universe before 1PM and only in the other after 2PM. Before 1PM and after 2PM energy is conserved.

"What about between 1PM and 2PM?" challenged Allan.

"Ah. That's where my theory comes to the rescue! In my theory there is what we call a 'vacuum state.' The extra energy comes from this vacuum state between 1PM and 2PM, and goes back into it after 2PM. It's not really my own idea. This vacuum state idea goes all the way back to the beginning of quantum mechanics in the 1930s."

"So what about the quantum worlds?" Allan persisted.

"Energy conservation works out the same way," Ben said. "Energy exists in both a 'would-be world' and a 'real world.' And if the entangled state changes, the total energy stays the same through the change. So, if we can find a way to make both worlds 'real worlds' the energy is conserved, because the would-be world had energy before it was made real. Of course, there is also a vacuum state to keep in mind, as we said before."

Allan clapped both pairs of hands together. "I

understand now! It's just like having one electron and measuring its spin to find it up or down. The universe splits into two universes, but the second universe already existed as a would-be universe before the measurement was made. So there is no doubling of energy because the energy was already there in the would-be universe. And the two quantum worlds of the Dinosauroids and Humans has energy conservation in exactly same way!" One of Allan's right hands did a high five with the other body's right hand.

"Right on." Ben pointed at the fridge. "I think we've both earned a nice cold beer."

"The sun's barely risen, Ben," Allan said, raising an eyebrow on each face.

"Nothing about these past few days has been normal. Come on! I'm being generous—It's not fair that you get two and I get only one!"

❊ ❊ ❊

Later that day, Ben Artemit walked around the block, hoping the fresh air would do him some good. He inhaled the faint odours of pollen and spring, but everything still seemed far away by the time he made it back to his apartment complex.

He tapped the FOB to gain entry, then stepped inside. He looked back at the empty neighbourhood behind him, wondering why he couldn't seem to take pleasure from simple things anymore.

He could watch his body go through the motions, hoping to sink back into an old routine, but he remained outside of it, incapable of escaping all that weighed on his mind.

Sighing, he turned toward the stairs and hallway. So many identical doors, but behind each one lay a rich life. What he would give to switch places with any one of them.

A bang on the front glass door made him jump. He

turned to find Turen's gaunt, pale face staring at him.

There really was no escaping this mess, physically or mentally.

Ben approached warily and noticed Turen's bloodshot eyes. Turen banged on the glass again.

"Turen? What are you doing here?" Ben asked.

"We need to talk, Artemit." Turen shot a glance over his shoulder, as though someone were following him. "In private, in your apartment."

Allan, Ben thought immediately. *He's going to find Allan.* He hadn't even thought of having visitors in all the confusion, nor of the need to keep his apartment free of signs of Allan's presence. Although Turen wouldn't necessarily know Allan if he saw him, exposing any evidence of Allan to other Quantix employees was a serious risk.

"Can it wait, Turen? I'm supposed to meet someone in twenty minutes."

Turen's gaze could have drilled through concrete. "No. It can't. Cancel whatever it is, and let me in. Now, Artemit. You don't want me to do this where everyone can hear."

Oh God, what does he know?

Cold spread over Ben like snow on a windy plain. He walked up to the door and opened it as slowly as he could. As soon as the latch cleared, Turen pushed through.

Ben rushed to catch up to him and squeeze ahead on the stairwell.

"You'll have to give me a few minutes to clean up, at least," Ben said.

"I don't care one quark whether or not your dump is clean," Turen snapped as he took stairs two at a time.

"W—well I do," Ben said with as much false pride as he could muster.

How was he going to hide Allan in time?

Approaching the door to the apartment, Ben jogged ahead and opened it, intending to close it sharply behind him, only to find Turen there matching pace, sticking his arm through the opening to hold his place. Ben had planned to lock the door and give himself a few precious minutes.

"Nice try," Turen snarled.

"Fine," Ben said, mouth dry, "come in."

Ben looked down and thankfully Allan's two pairs of shoes were mixed in and amongst the rest of Ben's poorly-organized footwear.

"I dreamed of monsters," Turen said as soon as the door shut. "The same monsters I saw that day I came over here, after you and Bell did that experiment without my permission."

Ben reeled, his head spinning from the combination of Turen's words and the effort of spotting any evidence of Allan. Ben braced himself against the couch. *Thank God both of Allan's bodies are somewhere else.*

"W—what?" Ben said. This was too much. He couldn't fend off queries about the monsters and hide Allan at the same time. How did Turen know?

"Monsters, Artemit. I know you've seen them."

"What monsters? What are you talking about, Turen?" Ben said loudly, enunciating every word to try and convey to Allan, wherever he was, that he should stay hidden.

Turen stomped into the kitchen, groaning and slamming a hand on a cupboard. "Don't play with me, Artemit! I've seen them! They're coming for me. They've already tried in my games room. I—I don't dare sleep with the lights out anymore."

Ben saw a drawing on paper—a rare luxury—of a complex web of swirls and links reminiscent of a neural network. One of Allan's projects to keep his mind active, sitting on the side table beside the couch. Ben walked over and sat on it, covering up Allan's stylized signature.

"Look at me, Artemit! Are you listening to me?"

"I hear you, Turen," Ben said, furrowing his brow as he tried to work through what Turen was saying.

The dinosauroids are getting more power, he thought. *And they approached Turen. I should have tried to reach him before they did.*

The dinosauroids might deserve to outwit and outmaneuver Ben after all he'd done to them. Then Ben imagined all the human lives that would be erased, and remembered the pact he'd made to prevent such a thing. He sat up straighter and clenched his fists.

I have to stop what they're doing now, and figure out a way to make amends—in a way that doesn't destroy humanity—later.

"You're not listening, Artemit!" Turen shouted. "I've barely been sleeping. And you knew about this! You've *known* all along! And you can't even look at me!" Turen walked over and shook Ben by the shoulders.

"Calm down, Turen!" Ben said, standing. Out of the corner of his eye he saw Allan poke a head through a doorway in the hall.

Ben's eyes widened.

Turen whipped his head around. "What are you gawking at?"

Allan had shot out of sight just in time. Ben's breath froze in his lungs.

Turen stalked down the hall toward the bedrooms. "You're hiding something, and if you won't tell me what it is, then I'll bloody well find it."

"T—Turen, come on!" Ben shouted. "I hear you. I'm just shocked, is all. It's a lot to take in. Now come back here so we can talk properly." He walked after Turen, trying not to appear frantic. He grabbed Turen's shoulder and guided him away from the hall and toward the dining table.

Turen growled, shooting glances behind him. "You're hiding something."

"I'm not," Ben said, fighting to keep his voice calm. "I just like my privacy like anyone else."

Ben gestured to one of the seats at the dining table, but Turen remained standing, glaring and scanning the kitchen.

Ben followed Turen's gaze. On the island in the kitchen, beside the knife block, was a plate covered with a thin layer of tomato sauce. Allan had, as he had the habit of doing, carefully drawn overlapping series of molecular orbitals. Maybe Turen would think Ben had drawn them—the sink was too far away to hide it, and any more sudden movements would only increase Turen's suspicions.

"I'm a grown man, Artemit. I'm a renowned scientist. The head of the Vancouver Quantix lab. Sleeping with the bloody lights on, because of monsters! I know how ridiculous it sounds. But you've seen them too. Admit you've seen them."

Ben considered carefully. He didn't have long before Turen exploded again. He shut his eyes for a full second, concentrating all his attention on willing Turen not to have any knowledge of the dinosauroids.

"Turen, I'm really sorry you've been having such horrible nightmares," Ben said, opening his eyes. "And insomnia, too. I've had it before and those periods of my life are a complete write-off. You want to sleep but you don't want the things to get you if you *do* sleep. It's just an awf—"

"What are you doing?" Turen's brow furrowed. "My head feels like it's being kicked every time I think of the monst...the mon... the...."

He hesitated, then words poured out of him. "I guess they... I guess they were just nightmares. They felt so real, and I needed to talk to someone to get past their hold on me. But in the end, they're just nightmares, after all. I shouldn't let them stop me from sleeping."

Turen's words had a mechanical tone, but it was better than how he'd been a moment earlier. Ben sighed. It would be too much for Turen to know about the dinosauroids. As much as Ben had wanted someone else to see the dinosauroids back when he'd been alone, he now realized the threat they posed if they escaped the boundaries of his mind.

Ben sagged against the counter, focusing his attention back on making Turen forget, and pushing him toward leaving of his own accord.

Turen clutched his head with both arms and staggered

backward. "No, none of that is right. What—what's going on?"

Ben's heart went off like an alarm. Something wasn't right.

No, Turen, you had nightmares, and that's all.

Turen's disturbed face looked far from convinced.

"Turen," Ben said quickly, "you had some pretty intense visions, but that's all they were. Nothing more. Nothing to be afraid of."

Turen covered his ears and shrank away as though Ben's words were knives. "Your words are... twisting my memories. You... you piece of trash! You're with them, aren't you? Making me... trying to make me forget, somehow!"

Ben forced in a deep breath, and closed his eyes again.

He's never seen the dinosauroids. He's never seen the dinosauroids.

His heart thudded a frantic back-beat to the images. Visions of the dinosauroids kept coming in to displace the reality Ben tried to imagine.

Come on, don't fail me now, Ben thought, as though he could send a message to the source of his power.

Turen shoved Ben, and Ben's concentration broke. The dinosauroids sneered at him in his thoughts.

"You're trying to make me forget! Like you did before!" Turen brushed his arm across the counter and the plate with Allan's artistic tomato sauce shattered on the kitchen tiles.

"Do you have any idea what I've been through?" Turen shouted. "The self-doubt I've had? I don't know what's real anymore. I remember different sets of events that come and whisper in my ear like ghosts, each wanting to be real. Watching recorded footage doesn't help. Nothing helps. So I came to you. And what do you do? Try and wipe my brain with the same dirty cloth you'd used before."

"I'm sorry, Turen," Ben managed, his voice catching.

Turen stormed toward the hall, then returned pointing an accusatory finger in Ben's face. "Only because I caught you, you worthless—how could you do this to me? You would have nothing without me. Your big breakthrough would never have happened, and now you bring these—these *things* into my life. You let them haunt me, then try to make me think it's all a bad dream, so you can keep a horrible secret.

"No more, Artemit!" Turen shouted, tearing a chef's knife out off the knife block on the kitchen island. Brandishing it toward Ben, Turen backed into the hall.

Ben's mouth refused to work anymore, unwilling to speak to Turen about the dinosauroids for fear they would make them more powerful in his mind.

Or make Turen use the knife. He shouldn't have sharpened it yesterday.

Turen stomped down the hall.

Oh God, no! Hide, Allan!

Turen shoved open the guest bedroom door.

"Turen!" Ben shouted.

"You have a guest?" Turen shouted.

Ben winced. "Yes."

"Who?"

He hasn't seen Allan, Ben realized. *Thank God he managed to hide.*

Ben's mind raced. "It's—it's Kitt Bell."

Turen snorted. "*That's* what you're hiding? That you've started an office tryst?"

Ben looked down, trying his best to look ashamed. "Yes."

Turen snorted. "It must not be going very well, if she's sleeping in here."

Ben shrugged. "We're taking it slow."

Turen glared at Ben, then stomped into the master bedroom. Ben said a silent prayer of thanks that Kitt was judicious about cleaning up after herself. There'd be little evidence of her there.

"Stay away from me!" Turen shouted as Ben followed him. Turen opened the ensuite bathroom, and the closets, finding nothing.

He turned back to Ben, pointing the knife accusingly.

"Pathetic, Artemit. Just what I imagined your dump to look like. If I didn't know any better, I would think there's nothing to worry about from you. Now get away from the door, and let me pass."

Ben did as instructed, raising his arms and sliding along the wall.

Turen passed, keeping the knife pointed at Ben. Ben slowly followed, arms raised, as Turen moved to the apartment's entry.

Turen waved the knife wildly as he cracked the door open. "Don't try and alter my mind anymore, Artemit. I'm leaving, and if you try to change my mind again, I'll hurt you. I'll find a way to expose you and those monsters for what you are. They'll come for me and I'll drive them off just like I did with you today. I'll put them in the light for all to see. Whatever your plan is, it's going to fail, Artemit. I'll make sure of it."

Turen opened the door and backed through it.

As soon as Ben lost sight of Turen and the knife, the chill that had come over him thawed enough for his mind to engage again.

His cheeks burned as he realized he'd been paralyzed by being threatened at knifepoint. Ben's denial of the dinosauroids' existence wasn't working anymore, and was only serving to enrage Turen.

"Wait!" Ben cried, opening the door to the hall. "I'm not with them. I'm trying to fight them!"

But Turen was already down the stairs. Several floors below, the door to the apartment complex slammed. The silence that followed screamed in Ben's mind that the dinosauroids had grown real—grown real beyond himself, and were slipping out of his control.

CHAPTER THIRTY

Meeting

The Quantix boardroom was dark aside from the rotating holo of a man named Allan Gerrold in the centre of the table, and a few glowing screens around. Al Turen sat toward one end, his fingertips trembling on his seventh cup of coffee. The weights under his eyes followed the laws of an ever-increasing gravity.

The effort to appear normal taxed every bit of his remaining energy.

He was grateful the head of Quantix, Dr. Marlon Kramer, had taken Turen out of the spotlight.

Another part of him—a growing part of him—worried about the monsters lurking in every shadow. The worry grew and fed on Turen's thoughts, making even coming to work a trial.

Kramer's presence commanded attention, which helped distract Turen from his thoughts.

Kramer circled the table as he spoke, his voice menacing and challenging, all just below the surface, as he used words of respect among colleagues but leaned over each of them in search of hints of betrayal.

Around the table sat a dozen of Quantix's top executives, some of them typing at laptops and others appearing as virtual heads on the backs of chairs.

"The subject, Allan Gerrold, broke out of the facility with the assistance of Tamika Werrett," Kramer said. "With them went valuable intellectual property with the power to destroy this company. Decades of research will be lost to the public domain—or worse—if we don't apprehend them quickly. All our livelihoods depend on this.

"Both the subject and Werrett are extremely intelligent and dangerous. We need all your help to track them down. If any of you have information about their whereabouts, or any potential leads, it is imperative you come forward."

One of the executives, a grey-haired man in a pinstripe suit, leaned over to a colleague and whispered, "What's *really* going on?"

Kramer halted in his circuit, and grinned broadly at the man who'd spoken. Turen had no idea who the man was, but he knew he didn't want to be him right now.

"Of course you deserve the real story, don't you, Henderson?" Kramer said, leaning against the table. "Can you tell me anything else you think you deserve?"

Henderson straightened in his chair and put his hands on his lap. "I'm sorry, sir. I—I'll be quiet now."

Kramer's smile widened. "I think you should fill in the rest of the details for us, Henderson. What did Gerrold take?"

"I—intellectual property, sir."

"He *is* the property," Kramer said. "He belongs to Quantix. He belongs to me. I've invested more in him than I have in any of you. What do we do when a primary investment is at risk, Henderson?"

"We f—focus our attention on that, on any actions we can take. Cut losses. Diversify."

Kramer nodded. "What happens to other investments?"

"They get deprioritized."

"How long have you worked for this company, Henderson?"

"Five years."

"Quite an investment. But not quite as much as Allan Gerrold. If only there were a way you could increase your value."

"I will dedicate myself to finding him, sir."

"Good."

"P—please don't hold this incident against me, sir," Henderson whispered.

Kramer paused, his smile twitching a moment before he said, "Just do your job, pay attention, and we'll all be friends, yes?"

"Y—yes, sir."

Kramer patted Henderson on the shoulder, who twitched with each tap. Slowly, Kramer made his way back toward the head of the table, where he started flicking through holographic images profiling both Gerrold and Werrett.

Turen tried to follow all the details of each of their profiles, but his attention waned, returning to worries about the monsters.

When he caught himself, he prayed Kramer hadn't noticed. Turen had nearly missed all of Werrett's profile but managed to bring his attention back onto Gerrold.

"These are some of the drawings the subject made throughout the experiments," Kramer said, flipping through a presentation of hand-drawn molecular orbitals on walls. "He had a preoccupation with the fundamental sciences, especially at the quantum level." He snorted, laughing at a joke Turen didn't understand, and no one else seemed to, either.

The scenes Kramer showed of the white-walled labs danced at the edge of Turen's memories, hinting at something he couldn't quite remember.

Damn Artemit for messing with my head! I can hardly focus. I can't tell what's real and what isn't anymore. I'll make him pay— yes, I've got to make him pay.

His thoughts returned to their last encounter, when he'd stalked Artemit in his apartment, trying to corner and force some answers out of him. Artemit had seemed preoccupied. At the time it seemed like Artemit was just focused on trying to wipe Turen's memory of things, but now Turen realized there may have been something more.

The plate, Turen thought with sudden awareness. *That's where I've seen those drawings before. In the pasta sauce of that plate.*

Turen was willing to bet there were less than a handful of people on the planet who drew molecular orbitals as they played with their food.

He raised a hand and sat straighter in his seat.

"What is it, Turen?" Kramer asked. "Have you finally woken up?"

Turen blinked and jerked back, alerted to an impending assault. What he had to say, however, was too important, and had the power to mitigate Kramer's wrath.

"I've seen drawings like that before."

Kramer leaned with both fists on the table. "Where?"

"Ben Artemit's house. It was drawn in pasta sauce on a plate."

"You're certain it was these drawings?"

"Yes."

"Of course," Kramer muttered, standing up and lifting a squeezed fist. "One traitor begets another."

Kramer's nose and mouth twitched as his eyes moved back and forth as though replaying an image in his mind. "Chen, send a team to Artemit's apartment, *now.*"

A man with short-cropped black hair typed furiously at his keyboard, frowning. "Sir, it seems like something is interfering with our intranet... I'm not getting anywhere. Anyone else?"

The screens of heads on the backs of chairs had completely frozen.

"I see one user is swamping the system with over a thousand—and more by the second—large uploads and downloads," Henderson said.

"Werrett," Kramer said with disgust. "She's the only one

with enough knowledge of our network, and the motive. Track her down. Everyone up. Let's go! We'll find her, and get a team to Artemit's!"

Turen stood up dizzily as people spurred into action. He smiled at the thought of revenge on Artemit.

❊ ❊ ❊

Tamika Werrett closed her laptop and unplugged a massive antenna and signal booster. She scrambled around her hotel room, shoving her belongings into a duffel bag.

She dialled Ben Artemit's number. No answer.

She tried several more times as she packed, without success.

She'd have to warn him in person. Thankfully her hotel wasn't that far from his place.

Before today, her heart wouldn't have pounded so hard at the thought of being discovered. Sacrificing herself in redemption after what she'd done to Gerrold was among the list of things she considered karmic justice. Before now, her breaths wouldn't have come as tremulous as a rolling boil.

Before, however, it had only been her at risk of discovery. Now Kramer was after not only Gerrold, but Ben Artemit, and anyone else who might get caught in the crossfire.

In the hotel's parkade, she got into her rental car.

Driving to Artemit's, her hands shook as though they already sensed the thunder of Quantix's approach.

CHAPTER
THIRTY-ONE

Flight

Ben Artemit awoke next to Kitt Bell, light-blue sheets draped messily across both of them. He thought to himself how lucky he was to have her in his life, and how much more unmanageable this whole nightmare would have been without her. He couldn't count how many times she'd helped him through his most trying ordeals.

Despite everything, his thoughts darkened. Today they had to reach Turen, before the dinosauroids did.

Ben had tried to keep Turen ignorant of everything, but he'd failed. What was even worse was that Turen knew Ben had tried to keep him blind.

Now they had no choice but to try to get Turen on their side. They had to explain everything and hope to win Turen over, even if it meant making the dinosauroids more real as a result.

Ben swung his legs off the bed carefully, trying not to disturb Kitt. The least he could do was give her a few more moments of peace.

A loud, strangled cry from down the hall jolted him.

"Allan?" Ben called, opening the door and jogging down

the hall, past a grey feature wall with framed images of Mandelbrot fractals.

Ben turned the corner into Allan's room, where the walls were adorned with a patchwork of framed landscape art and pencil and paper drawings Allan had begun posting together in a webbed mosaic.

Sweat permeated the air in the room. Both of Allan's bodies were awake, mirror images of each other on either side of the bed. They hunched with their backs to each other and both of them breathed heavily.

"Are you all right?" Ben asked, stopping himself just before putting an arm on Allan's shoulder. He had to remind himself that touch could overwhelm Allan in his entangled state.

Both Allan's bodies shuddered.

"I thought I was safe," Allan said at last, the words coming partly from each body as though each were a badly tuned radio station. "I thought I had control. For the first time I could move around and look and see and think about what I was experiencing but... it was all a trap. I ended up being tortured just as cruelly as before, and it was worse because I'd had a taste of freedom in that space. Freedom that was wrenched from me."

Ben sat down next to one of Allan's bodies and asked in a soft voice, "You slept with both bodies?"

Allan nodded synchronously.

"I'm sorry it was so much worse than before. If there's anything I can do to help you keep your sleep schedule—"

"It's my responsibility," Allan interrupted. "I need to be able to handle this on my own." He gripped the edges of the bed tighter, flexing and releasing in succession.

Ben took a deep breath. "I know this is your cross to bear, Allan, but it's not weak to ask for help when—"

There was a loud banging on their front door, and muffled shouts.

Is that—

He recognized the flat voice that modulated and thinned only with strong emotion, as it did now.

Tamika.

Ben's spirits sank. Whatever reason Tamika had for coming here, it couldn't be good.

"I'll be back," he said, rushing out.

He opened the apartment's front door to find Tamika Werrett wearing a pair of coveralls, her hair pulled back into a bun. She looked out of breath.

"Why don't you answer your phone?" she said.

Ben frowned. "We've kept our phones off so we couldn't be tracked."

"Never mind," Tamika said. "Quantix is on the way here. They know, Ben, and they're after you and Allan now."

Ben hung stunned as Tamika stormed in.

"But how did they—"

"Does it matter? We need to clear out, *now.*" Tamika's cheeks were flushed and her gaze darted around the apartment. "Where's Allan? Where's Kitt?"

"Still waking up," Ben said. "Where are we going to go?"

"Anywhere but here. Let's go! Come on!"

She ran down the hall.

*   *   *

Allan Gerrold watched through a slit in the blinds as a swarm of black vans descended on the building.

"Allan!" Tamika said as she entered. "We need to get out of here."

Allan had figured that much out already. One body rushed to the closet and grabbed clothes, while the other surveyed out the window.

The bruiser-man himself got out of one of the Quantix vans. He cracked his knuckles.

Oh God.

"There's no time, Allan—"

"He's here," Allan said, shuddering.

Tamika picked up a sweater from the floor and shoved it at him. "I *know*. Let's go!"

She pulled on an arm from each of Allan's bodies until he finally escaped from the room.

Kitt and Ben were slipping their shoes on, bags slung over their shoulders.

Allan stopped when he heard stomping footsteps echo up the stairwell and into the hall.

"I can help us escape," Allan said. "I can be our eyes and ears."

"What are you talking about?" Tamika said.

"Just go! I'll stay here with one body. Otherwise none of us is going to make it."

Ben looked intensely at him. "Fine. No time to argue. Let's go."

They ran out of the apartment and into the stairwell.

Allan's other body went to Ben Artemit's narrow balcony. The second perspective gave him a heightened sense of where everything was in the building, his mind harnessing the triangulation sense he'd been developing.

Allan directed Kitt, Ben and Tamika up toward the rooftop, and followed with one body.

When he was certain the goons had reached the floor of Ben's apartment, Allan took a deep breath, lifted himself over the edge of the Ben's balcony, and fell onto the one below.

He grabbed frantically at the railing, smashing his knuckles. His feet caught the edge and lances of pain darted up his toes.

He climbed in and opened the sliding door, which was open a crack. The apartment was empty.

His other body with Tamika, Ben and Kitt reached the rooftop. They looked over each edge to assess which exit looked clear.

The one opposite the street seemed best, with the least

number of guards and no vans.

Allan darted back into the stairwell and shouted to get the attention of the goons.

"What are you doing?" Ben hissed.

"Trust me," Allan said in both bodies. "Tamika, where are your keys?"

Tamika handed them to him, and Allan dropped them off one side of the roof and into the garden.

He heard the goons continue upward, and the ones guarding the outside door entered the building. Allan waited until the guards had gone a floor above him before he left the stranger's empty apartment and quietly descended the stairs.

He exited the building on the alley side, picking up Tamika's dropped keys from the garden. His brain went into overdrive to mentally map the layout from multiple angles.

He'd made it out of the building, but everyone else was practically trapped.

He went back inside, toward the front door, and shouted at the bruiser-man through the window. He shrank under the bruiser-man's withering glare and shouts at his men.

Allan surged back up the stairs.

Listening at the rooftop door, Allan's body on the rooftop cursed. The other goons heading to the roof hadn't altered course.

He looked over the edge toward the nearest balcony. It was over double the distance of the last drop, but it was their only chance.

"Come on," he said.

"Are you nuts?" Tamika asked.

Allan crept over the edge, lowering himself on his stomach as much as possible, the hot wind bringing tears to his eyes and gusting to make him sway. Craning his neck to see his target, he let go.

He hung in the air for long enough to imagine missing the railing and continuing down—far down—to the pavement below. He smashed into the railing, then pushed through into another stranger's apartment.

This one wasn't empty, though, and the occupant cried out. Allan raced over and clamped a hand over the poor old man's mouth, holding him in a headlock.

Allan waited what felt an eternity for his friends to drop and join him.

Kitt came, then Ben, then Tamika.

"Never want to do that again," Tamika muttered.

Allan released the old man. "I'm sorry. We meant you no harm."

They pushed into the hallway, and Allan pushed the elevator call button.

"The elevator? Really?" Ben whispered.

With his other body, Allan ascended to the second floor, grabbed one of the lamps by a reading nook, and launched it through the window.

The shattering glass elicited cries of surprise from everyone around.

Good. Got their attention.

Allan launched himself out.

He hit the ground and felt the shudder up his spine as he rolled. Something pulled in his legs and he gasped.

The Quantix goons stared at him from the second floor window, unwilling to follow him down. They turned and ran down the stairs.

Perfect.

Allan limped, his legs burning and screaming at him to stop. He got into Tamika's car and started the engine.

With his other body, Allan and the others boarded the elevator.

"Someone's using the elevator," the goons said from somewhere nearby.

Allan popped out of the elevator just as the doors closed. "Go, I'll distract them," he said to the others. "Out the back, I've got the car."

He went into the stairwell, stomping and shouting as

though he were fighting someone. The footsteps followed him soon after.

Thank God they took the bait.

They were closing in on him from above and below. That left the ground floor clear, which meant Ben, Tamika and Kitt could get out safely.

But Allan needed a way out.

He went back to the elevator doors, yanked them open, and edged inside. Pushing them shut behind him, he teetered before grabbing onto the elevator cables.

With his other body, Allan pulled the car to the back door of the apartment building just as Ben, Tamika and Kitt came out. They scrambled into the vehicle.

A bullet shattered the back window.

Allan peeled away.

"What about your other—"

"No time," Allan said.

The Quantix agents scrambled, some taking aim and firing, others rushing to get into their own cars.

The pavement smacked with bullets and hollow smacks punctured the car's frame. Everyone but Allan cowered below the seats as they raced down the street.

Sirens pursued them out of suburbia, but the worst of it was over. They'd almost all made it out. Almost.

Allan's other body now hunched on top of the elevator, riding up and down, hearing the bruiser man's angry voice shouting orders to search every unit. Terrified of being discovered, Allan found a maintenance nook inside the elevator shaft, with a barely noticeable door. He hid in the narrow space, huddled and cramped in pitch-darkness.

The rest of the group drove away, looking at each other in search of what they could do, and where they could go, now that they were fugitives.

CHAPTER
THIRTY-TWO

A New Darkness

Kitt, Ben, Tamika, and Allan ended up in a motel three hours East of Vancouver, after having ditched their vehicle and switched into another self-driving rental car. They'd safely outmaneuvered Quantix, for the time being.

"We have to figure out how to get you out of that apartment," Tamika had said to Allan a few different ways.

At the moment, however, no one had any good ideas on how to get him out while the bruiser-man—whose named Allan learned was Marlon Kramer—had his crew digging through every room.

In the elevator compartment, Allan drifted in and out of consciousness, alternating between exhaustion and terror. He shivered from the cold that crept in as night settled in, a chill that reached across the gulf between his two bodies to cool the bones of both. He was utterly exhausted, grateful but barely speaking much beyond the necessities.

By the way Kitt and Ben acted, they felt much the same, sitting up in one of the double beds, staring blankly into the distance.

Tamika paced the motel carpet for a little while before

she crumpled into the armchair.

Allan wanted to force himself awake in the blackness of the elevator shaft compartment, so that he could instead rest the weary body that had been fleeing all day. He had aches and bruises on his arms and shins, where he'd crashed into the railings. He drifted into sleep in the motel as soon as the pillow cradled his head.

Staying awake with the body in the elevator shaft was like staring into a deep, hollow reflection, with nothing but the sound of his breaths, the occasional turning of motors and grinding metal to keep him company. His thoughts churned and the cramped space seemed to close in while simultaneously expanding into a large hall. The rare voices he heard were angry shouts from Kramer's men, which dashed any hope of crawling out to the illuminated world.

After a while Kramer's men were silent. He had only himself to contend with, and thoughts that raced between what he was, what had happened, what he'd become, and the grim future that awaited.

He wavered, oscillating between conscious and unconscious. His head jerked as he seesawed. He trembled at the thought that Kramer's goons were so close to him and continued unrelenting. His taut muscles drained his energy, lulling him toward the relaxation they desperately sought.

His body's instincts for retreat wrestled his willpower until both were spent.

* * *

The dark flipped up and around Allan like a cloak. Its invisible cold pushed him upright and prodded him into a trot.

A grey fog enveloped all. On his left was what looked like the middle of a chain, with the links more like mobius rings, the interconnections difficult to parse. In a black cage attached to the chain, a small, glowing cloud stretched and twisted, sending bursts of green and yellow in wide-sweeping beams. The chain was taut, stretching in either direction, slackening and tightening with what Allan assumed was the pace of walkers on either end. It was impossible to make out anything but a long string of other glowing clouds far in front and behind.

As the chain and caged light moved away, Allan's surroundings darkened. He rushed to grab on before it was too late.

The chain sucked the warmth from his hand. It was heavy but slid easily over his fingers if he relaxed his grip.

He dared not let go, because every time he did the grey around blackened.

He dared not stop.

He didn't know where he traveled to or from. The foray into the unknown, harbouring a spell pulling him deeper, kept him on edge. Unwilling to question what it required of him.

At least at first.

No progress showed in his surroundings, only an occasional change in direction to still the quivers in his calves.

At least this place wasn't as dark as those other, terrible places.

After a time, he feared the march itself was the torture. He couldn't walk forever, whether or not it was only in his mind.

He loosened his grip and ran down the line. The links bumped through his grasp as he approached the glowing cloud.

The light outlined a hunched figure with long, thin limbs. Allan made out an oblong head, rows of sharp teeth, and long, thin limbs. The figure glistened with slime. The air smelled swampy.

Allan slowed, causing the chain to ripple.

He shouldn't have been so brazen. Walking was much better than getting his head torn off between this creature's jaws. Before Allan could turn back, the creature whipped its head around, gazing at him from the corner of its eye.

"Strange, yet sad," it said in a low, deep voice. It squinted as though it, too, struggled to see in the fog. "Another lost one joins the line. It looks odd, but I cannot judge. The lost must accept one another in order to be found."

Allan rolled the words around in his mind to try to make sense of them. Better to err on the cautious side.

He let go of the moving chain, hoping he could turn around before it was too late, no matter what the darkness held.

The creature stopped as he did, piercing yellow eyes boring through him. "A human? A lost *human?* What brings a human to the link?"

Allan's mouth was too dry, his thoughts too paralyzed, to speak.

"How came you here? Or can you not speak?"

"I don't know," Allan said, rushing at last to respond. "What...what brought you here?"

"Neither of us have energy for the full answer to that question," said the creature. "And discourse with a human is not what I enjoy during these marathons."

Allan stepped back. "I'm sorry. I... I can leave you alone."

"No, do not leave. The lost—no matter our nature—must be loyal to each other, for there to be any hope of discovery. Human intrusion here is unheard-of, so perhaps we can squeeze some good from it.

"To answer your question: our existence was robbed from us. Now we live in a realm of possibility. Occasionally, we have to make a pilgrimage to the last place our existence was strongest. Our potentialities move, so in relation to the our last point of existence, our home is in flux."

"This chain connects you to it?"

"Yes. We have been very fortunate to find it, and have learned to seek it out constantly, lest we lose it forever. Somehow you have found our link without effort. I do not know if it will be of any use to you, or what purpose it may serve, but it is better to have a link of some kind than none at all."

Allan moved closer to the creature, who seemed less and less monstrous. "Thank you for welcoming me. It's... the last thing I expected."

"I can only assume your presence here means that you are lost, and for that, you have my empathy."

The creature didn't look at him, but beckoned him back to the chain, to hold onto where it pulled them.

Allan fought to suppress his natural instincts of revulsion toward the creature, and tried to settle into a new norm. This place was, after all, far better than the hellish realms he'd visited before.

However, what they approached—the realm or place closest to where these creatures had once existed—might be one of those hellish places.

Breaking this link now might be the better choice for Allan. It might be better for the creatures, too.

"What will happen once we arrive?" Allan asked.

"We will feel more whole, if such a thing can be said of a would-be realm," the creature said.

"You do not feel whole now?"

"You have caught me at a moment of calm. My body's form has stabilized, perhaps in part because of your presence. Normally my shape would flicker through thousands of possibilities, some subtle alterations, others drastic re-imaginings of my existence. A firm form is rare so far from the nexus of greatest probability. Be thankful your own existence has not yet turned into discontinuous soup."

Allan looked down the chain's line, wondering how many creatures were suffering the same fate. It reminded him faintly of the world where endlessly needy hands had clawed at him from piles of rejected beings.

"Has it always been like this?" he asked.

"No," the creature said. "Before, when we were real, we had incredible towers. We had mastery over gravity, so these towers stretched into low Earth orbit, with an interconnected web of bridges linking everything together. The beanstalks were a massive, cooperative and expertly coordinated web.

"With control of gravity, we no longer needed great muscle mass, so we became as you now see me. We had cities in the clouds. As we'd developed, our elders were no longer relegated to the higher altitudes with reduced gravity. They could walk in and among us, and our communities flourished with young and old side-by-side, united and intimate. No one was left to suffer a lonely abandonment in their later years, confined to isolated care of their decaying bodies."

"Do you think you'll ever rebuild it, if you regain your... reality?" Allan asked.

"Most certainly, yes. It will be better than any of us can imagine. We had only just begun to reap and spread the wealth of a world where no one was weighed down by gravity's insatiability. We had begun to better control our consumption, and I expect within a few decades, we would have moved fully beyond scarcity. We would remove the drive for economic wealth, and replace it with a quest for personal fulfilment, meaningful work to drive our people into positions where they felt most compelled.

"I do not know for certain what that future might hold. It is hard to keep it in mind for long stretches before the ideas are snatched away by the fickle hand of quantum fluctuation, and I have to go seeking them again. However, I feel an incredible draw toward this future that promises to transcend the curse placed upon my people. It gives me hope there is some providence at play that might allow us to see the moon and the stars once more."

How many creatures I've encountered, Allan wondered, *would have blossomed if they'd only been granted the privilege of existence in the real? What fantastic creations would they have wrought? What fully-realized selves would they have become, instead of slathering monsters clawing at any hint of corporeality?*

"We're close now," said the creature, straightening.

The orb light up ahead was cut off by a black wall as the path rounded a corner. Allan followed and turned to be completely blinded. He let go of the chain and covered his eyes.

He opened a slit to find the chains, the orbs, and his companion were all gone. A faint light shone up from some unseen place below the ground. A shallow mist hung around everything.

The light allowed Allan to know the moment the ground gave out beneath him. He flailed for an edge, but his hands just swept blackness.

CHAPTER THIRTY-THREE

Expanding Influence

Ben longed for sleep to take him, but kept imagining black Quantix vans swarming the parking lot and kicking down the chained door.

With Tamika and Allan in the same motel room, he didn't feel comfortable getting close to Kitt, so they lay beside one another in awkward silence. He wished she, at least, could get some sleep.

Late into the night, cold air snaked past Ben's ankles and up his legs. A dozen voices whispered in his mind.

Just let me sleep.

Kitt spoke beside him, sounding like she was underwater. "No, you can't—where are you taking me?"

Ben opened his eyes and struggled to sit up, but was weighed down by tremendous pressure. The light beneath their room door shone through fog.

Squinting, Ben made out two blurred forms pulling Kitt off the bed. They were hunched, with long, thin limbs.

The sight of Belonthar and Merthab holding his beloved Kitt was worse than any nightmare. Her head jerked but her eyes remained closed, the rest of her body limp.

Ben struggled to move, but his muscles only tightened and vibrated.

This is in my head, he thought, forcing slow breaths. *I can control them, like I did before.* He closed his eyes and willed the dinosauroids to go home, to release Kitt into a dreamless sleep. He imagined this as the firm reality which should be—which *was.*

When Ben opened his eyes, Merthab's razor-toothed grin was inches away.

The electricity powering Ben's body had its wires ripped out.

"Not quite what you hoped for, is it, Artemit?" Merthab chittered. "Your power has diminished. Nothing left for you but to suffer, which is only fitting after what you did. And we *know* you remember what you did."

Ben winced away from Merthab's spit, but every movement was suppressed. He shuffled back as though moving through molasses.

Merthab's head tilted back. He opened his jaw wide and howled a stuttering, echoing tremor Ben felt in his bones. Merthab's tongue glistened as it dragged across his teeth.

Ben could feel Kitt now, and how her terror had intermingled with his.

Nothing Ben had told her, nor what she'd imagined, could have prepared her to face the dinosauroids.

He wanted to reach out, to comfort her, but she felt so far away. He had no idea what hope he might offer, either.

"Artemit," Belonthar said from behind. Ben craned to see.

Belonthar stood above a kneeling Kitt, his long fingers cupping the top of her head. Fingers that could crush it without hesitation.

Ben would've done anything to trade places and spare her everything he'd brought upon her.

Ben yanked himself to his feet, his muscles aflame fighting the pressure all around.

Belonthar held out a hand in warning, and the pressure grew stifling. His hand flickered, alternating between fingertips and long, jagged claws.

Were they doing this intentionally, influencing their quantum nature?

"Since you don't want to miss out on what we plan to do with Bell," Belonthar said, "we will let you participate. Or maybe the right word is *spectate*."

Ben's insides churned. He found enough strength to move his jaw. "Wrong, Belonthar. I came here by choice. There's nothing you could have done to keep me away. You overestimate your power."

Belonthar drew a claw down Kitt's forehead and to the tip of her nose, drawing a clean red line. All Kitt could do was widen her eyes.

"Let her go! She has nothing to do with this!" Ben shouted.

"You wouldn't help us, Artemit," Belonthar said, unperturbed by Ben's outburst. "We had to seek others to make us real. She has this capacity, so her involvement is necessary, even if it's only for her... brain."

Belonthar drew a halo in the air above Kitt's skull.

Ben twisted, wrestling for control of his body. As Ben's arms finally freed, Merthab jerked and ran toward him.

Ben's knees shook with the effort to get free. He pulled his legs up and rolled to the side just as Merthab slashed the air where Ben had stood.

Ben had to regain the control he'd lost. "Stop!" he yelled, holding up his hand.

Merthab snarled and lashed out, the air rippling where an invisible wall blocked him. It was better than nothing, but still a far cry from the control Ben had exerted in their last encounter.

"Ben!" Kitt cried.

Ben's concentration dropped; the invisible wall wavered. Merthab tore it into wisps and crashed through.

"No!" Kitt shouted, holding up an arm.

Merthab fell to the ground just before reaching Ben.

"My power has weakened," Ben acknowledged. "But some of it has gone into Kitt. We will fight together."

Belonthar batted Kitt's arm down, then twisted to strike her in the back.

She and Ben put up their arms simultaneously. A ripple pulsed through the air, knocking Belonthar back and sending Merthab rolling.

Merthab got up on all fours, snarling. "You dare fight us, now that you know what you've done?"

Ben held up his arms and said, "Wait! I remember what I did. I want to work to find a way to make us both real. We could work together."

Belonthar glared at him. "Your entire existence is predicated on treachery and murder, Artemit. And still you begrudge us for wanting what you *stole* from us. You think we'll trust you now? We are not stupid."

Ben tried to firm his goals in his mind. He closed his eyes. *Fight them now. What they're doing is wrong. Reconciliation after. Reconciliation after...*

He opened his eyes; the ground beneath had turned to piles of bones, dotted with the long, toothy skulls of dinosauroids.

Ben moaned. His feet gave way and he sank in.

Belonthar and Merthab howled, treading lightly on the surface.

Kitt scrambled on her back on a hill, struggling to avoid being carried away by a current of flowing bones.

"You're... trying to perpetuate the injustices," Kitt said breathlessly. "You think eradicating the human race will make things right?"

"We have suffered long enough!" Merthab screamed, launching himself at Ben.

They're not real, Ben thought, forcing each word to resonate. *The bones aren't real. None of it is. This has to be in my head.*

But he couldn't believe it. Not when Belonthar had drawn blood from Kitt's face.

"Ben, get out of the way!" Kitt shouted, flailing.

Ben was pushed up and back out of the bones while Merthab crashed beneath.

Dinosauroid remains scattered everywhere in a crackling explosion. The bones floated as though gravity had broken.

Kitt, did you do this?

He couldn't see either Belonthar or Merthab, and he could only feel Kitt's presence. The bones floated, rotating and giving life to the macabre manifestation of Ben's crime.

The gaps between were too small to pass through; the bones had formed a maze of walls. Everything went painfully silent. Ben tasted blood.

Where are you, Kitt?

He wanted to call out to her, but knew that would alert Belonthar and Merthab.

He sensed how weak his grip over this realm had become. If they found him, he didn't know if he could repel them. The only reason he hadn't been maimed was because of Kitt.

She is now a Chooser, like me.

Some of my power has gone into her. And probably Turen as well.

"You cower in your guilt, Artemit!" Merthab shrieked, his voice echoing from a dozen directions. "It will not protect you."

Focus, Ben. Don't let them be real.

He walked carefully around the bone walls, wincing as some of the skulls sneered at him. He had to get Kitt and get out somehow, but right now his mind was only adding barriers.

"Bell," Belonthar said from far away, "you have the opportunity to rectify Artemit's transgressions. Don't make the same mistake he did."

Ben couldn't place the source of Belonthar's voice. A moment later, Kitt cried out and Belonthar roared.

There was a loud *BOOM*, and Belonthar soared high above the walls.

"These bones are but a fraction of the lives destroyed!" he shouted, his voice enveloping the surroundings. "My people... all gone because of Artemit's greed. Stop hiding, and face justice."

There's no way I can hide from it anymore, Ben thought. *Nothing I can do will ever make up for it.*

"I don't know if we can find justice," he murmured. "None that will satisfy you."

"You can make us *real!*" Merthab shouted.

The wall beside Ben shattered and Merthab sailed through, his flickering finger-claws extended. Ben fell back hard onto his arms, his teeth clacking. He skittered backward, pushing with his heels to get away as Merthab swiped at the ground.

Merthab grinned as he stalked toward Ben, closing the gap in great strides. He lowered his head and bared his teeth. Ben's back struck bone. He gazed around frantically for another way out.

Merthab slashed at Ben's shin.

He screamed. The pain was real, as was the oozing blood.

Just how real are they?

Ben felt Kitt's presence, warmth reaching across the physical gap separating them. Ben sucked in a breath.

Bones flew at Merthab, striking his face and body. More flew from the outside walls, forcing Merthab to shield himself and back away. He growled, slashing at the relentless onslaught.

"Thank you, Kitt," he said breathlessly.

"You're welcome," she said, emerging from behind a bone wall with outstretched arms. "Now get up and help me!"

Ben struggled to his feet, looking at the bones striking

Merthab. He shuddered when he realized they were using the bones of Merthab's ancestors to push him away.

The bones started vanishing into dust when they struck Merthab, who unshielded himself and stomped back toward them.

"No, Ben!" Kitt shouted. "Don't let them in your head! This graveyard is also what they'd do to *all of us!*"

"You're right," Ben whispered. "You're absolutely right." He looked at the bones and tried to reframe them as the lives of all the people he needed to protect, all the people who were defenceless against the dinosauroids' advances.

"Where's Belonthar?" Ben asked, looking around.

"I pushed him away," Kitt replied. "Let's get Merthab before he comes back."

Ben nodded. He held up his arms, and felt himself align with Kitt's control, as though they heaved on a boulder together before watching it crash down a mountainside.

The bones struck Merthab more rapidly. They adhered to him, forming an encasing shell that slowed his movements.

"We're winning!" Ben shouted. "We're winning!"

BOOM.

The sound thundered through the realm, silencing Merthab's shouts and Ben's jubilant cries.

BOOM.

A sphere of bone pushed out toward them, stopping in mid-air. The bones slid together to form a thick, gapless shell. White spikes cracked out, large enough to impale anything in their path. The spiked bone shell shuddered and spun. Through the gaps Ben saw Belonthar at the centre, his head lowered and his eyes blazing.

"We are united against you, thief. Trickster. Betrayer. And we always will be."

CHAPTER THIRTY-FOUR

Bridge

Allan Gerrold clutched his stomach in both the motel room and the elevator. "So hungry," he whispered into the darkness.

"You too, huh," Tamika replied beside him, her voice hoarse.

He rolled over, struggling to focus two sets of eyes in nearly complete darkness. "Why are you still awake?"

"I don't like being chased and hunted either, Allan. And I don't know what to do about Ben and Kitt."

"What? What's going on?"

"Wake up. You think this is normal?" Tamika said.

Allan saw both Ben and Kitt thrashing in the double bed beside theirs.

"Nightmare?"

"Worse. The dinosauroids. You clearly slept through their yells. I've tried to wake them. Nothing works."

As Tamika spoke, the tales Ben had told Allan ploughed into his thoughts.

The dinosauroids. Was it possible Allan had somehow found his way to the dinosauroids'—how did Ben put it—

would-be world? Or had Allan just caught them in transition between worlds?

"I've got to help them. I've got to try."

"What? How?"

"I think I saw a dinosauroid in the world I just went to," Allan said. "They matched everything Ben told me. I can't believe I didn't see the connection sooner."

"You think you can go back there consciously?"

"Maybe."

"All right." Tamika flicked on the light and brushed hair out of half-mooned eyes. "Do you need some water?"

❊ ❊ ❊

Allan closed both sets of eyes and tried to focus on what he had felt during his last trip to another world. He'd been exhausted, but he suspected that was not the essential step to how he'd managed to commune with the world of Artemit's dinosauroids.

Possibilities. He'd been entertaining a variety of possibilities, both in the past and the future. He'd felt a mixture of dread, but had gotten too tired to continue.

Distantly, he heard Tamika ask him if he was all right. He mumbled a request for silence.

His hunger was too strong for him to focus, and he groaned. Basic needs had to be met before waxing introspectively about potentialities.

There must be another way, some path I'm not seeing.

If only he wasn't so tired and hungry.

He'd started out sleeping in one body. That was clear; he'd been sleeping in the hotel room.

"Are you giving up?" Tamika asked as he lay down.

"No. Trying a different strategy. Turn off the lights."

Forcing himself to fall asleep met with little success, because he kept triggering awake from a desperate need for a solution.

He wished he could have slept with the body in the elevator, but Kramer's goons were back scouring the halls, approaching footfalls making Allan tremble.

He felt as though the last time, he'd been half asleep and couldn't remember.

That's it. Half-sleep.

He'd gone into a half-sleep, the thin misty layer of semi-consciousness. Halfway, oscillating along the barrier.

His heart pumped faster, as though every pulse sent blood to uncover mysteries in the depths. He took deep, careful breaths to calm himself.

The fear of falling completely asleep, as well as the fear of Kramer, kept him far from the boundary. He kept pulling back awake, receding too far, only to slowly work his way back again.

With each try, though, he drew closer. Conscious thought diminished until his psyche teetered on the edge, an abyss blacker than black below.

He saw himself walking along that edge until it transformed into a tightrope. On one side, blinding light, and on the other, penetrating darkness. In the middle walked Allan Gerrold, off into the distant grey.

CHAPTER THIRTY-FIVE

Cornered

B en and Kitt stood on a rocky crag, surrounded by the bones of Ben's victims.

Belonthar's explosive approach snaked lesions across the surface like lightning strikes. At any moment the ground would shift and open to swallow them.

Dust filled Ben's nostrils and he smelled burning.

Belonthar marched toward them in cold, unstoppable fury, behind a shield of orbiting bone.

"Ben," Kitt cried, "we need to get out, now!"

She grabbed Ben's hand.

"Do these remains disturb you?" Belonthar shouted. "Imagine staring at them for one lifetime after another, and you will know a fraction of our pain. We will find another Chooser, Artemit, don't you worry."

BOOM.

The shell stopped spinning, with two massive spikes pointed directly at Ben and Kitt. It quaked, shuddering as a terrible force grew behind it.

"Ben!" Kitt shouted. "Look at me!"

Ben turned and looked fearfully into her eyes.

"Focus somewhere else! What's your favourite place in the world?"

Ben coughed. He tried to imagine anything else, but the reality around was all-consuming.

Wind stirred up the dust coating the rock.

It's not dust, he thought. *It's the... ashes of countless victims.*

"This is but one of the battlefields where you obliterated my people, Artemit," Belonthar hissed. "You're getting a taste of what we live. Every. Single. Moment."

This is the same tactic they've used before, Ben.

The same guilt-reliant attack had gone through in his mind over and over again.

I did what I had to, and I didn't know it would kill them. What they're doing now is monstrous.

The sting in Belonthar's words pushed the familiar rationalizations into the background. No matter what Ben tried, Belonthar had an insidious ability to get in deep.

The ground rumbled. Everything flickered. A violent tremor kicked and threw Ben.

He slammed down and scraped his hands on the ground to stop sliding. He winced as he picked himself up, palms covered in blood and ash.

Between him and the dinosauroids, a hundred meters away, a hand darted out of a rift.

The hand shot furtively around with rapid, jarring movements. Finally it grabbed onto an edge and heaved.

As the hand heaved, Belonthar's spiked shell of bone split, then shattered.

A figure emerged through the haze of bone dust.

It seemed human, but flickered in and out of sight like passing trees on a highway. It took Ben several moments to see it was a human whose features changed faster than fragments of humanity blinked alive or dead on Earth.

The figure stalked toward him and Kitt like a shadow moving through tree branches, movements disjointed and multi-directional.

Ben winced. The flickering threatened to roll his eyes back inside his head.

He averted his gaze as though he were avoiding staring into the sun. Even then, he had to force his eyes to blur and not try to focus.

That was when he saw.

Like an optical illusion or the after-burn from staring at a bright light and moving his gaze into darkness, he saw the average of all the shifts and flickers.

"Allan?"

Allan looked toward him and Kitt. For a moment, he held a fixed form. An instant later he reverted back to shimmering and flickering, but he moved more quickly in a more consistent direction.

Both Merthab and Belonthar stopped moving.

"What is this new treachery?" Merthab snapped.

Ben and Kitt rushed toward Allan. "It's... my friend... The Entangled Man!" Ben said. "You have no idea what he's capable of doing to you."

Ben avoided thinking about the fact that he hadn't a clue, either.

Belonthar and Merthab were maybe fifty meters away now. Merthab snarled while Belonthar surveyed them before bearing his teeth.

"It seems you've found another way to avoid responsibility, Artemit," Belonthar said. "So be it. We might have allowed you to effect the change on terms you could live with, but that is clearly more respect than you deserve. We have found and strengthened ourselves in the mind of another One Who Chooses.

"Turen. Yes, the one called Turen," Belonthar said, as though reading Ben's thoughts. "We no longer have any need to trouble ourselves with you, your *friends* or any of your trickery."

Merthab dipped low and shrieked, the staccato trill

pounding Ben's ears and shaking ash into the air.

Belonthar turned and walked calmly away.

Allan fell to his knees, holding himself straight with quivering, flickering arms.

Ben closed in on Allan, watching the dinosauroids out of the corner of his eye.

"Are you all right?" Ben asked. "How did—never mind. Are you OK?"

"See...so much. Too much," Allan replied thickly. "Quantix. Turen. Dinosauroids. Kitt."

"Let's get out of here," Kitt said, squeezing Ben's hand. He felt her will as strong as his to be free of this place.

But he couldn't leave Allan.

Ben frowned. "However you got here, Allan, you need to get out again."

Allan nodded. He opened his mouth to reply, but fog rushed in from the periphery. Allan was swallowed and pulled away, before the fog tightened around Ben and Kitt.

Ben awoke on the motel room floor with Allan standing over him. He groaned and struggled to his feet, his whole body aching.

Kitt sprawled sideways across the bed, jolting up and searching frantically until she and Ben's eyes met.

She was all right. All of them were OK.

But the dinosauroids were no longer confined to Ben's mind.

They had to reach Turen before the dinosauroids did.

CHAPTER THIRTY-SIX

Breakout

"They've tracked Artemit down, and they figure he's got the other Gerrold hidden with them," one of Kramer's goons said. "Murdock is staying here just in case, but the rest of us need to head out to support the chase."

The words came to Allan Gerrold through the walls of the elevator. He managed to hear them despite the assault on all his senses from travelling to the realm of the dinosauroids.

Now that the apartment complex was mostly empty —save for Kramer's last goon named Murdock—Allan desperately wanted to sleep in the elevator. Especially as his other body hurriedly packed and got into the car with Kitt, Ben and Tamika.

They were all going back toward the Quantix facility to reach Turen.

Allan knew, however, that even huddled in the elevator shaft, he was the closest to Quantix, and to Turen, of anyone. After everything Ben, Kitt and Tamika had done for him, he owed them.

He thought about telling one of them with his other

body, but decided they'd protest and distract him too much.

He waited until the building was wrapped only in the hum of the furnace and the lingering whispers of footsteps.

Then he climbed out of his nook, his feet wobbling. He pulled on the elevator doors, straining to open them without toppling down the shaft. Finally, they cooperated.

He padded into the carpeted hall and crept back into Artemit's apartment, which was miraculously still unlocked. It only took him a few minutes to find Artemit's Quantix badge, as well as an emergency stash of cash.

He tiptoed down the stairs. A goon in a suit, who must have been Murdock, puffed on an e-cigarette near the main entrance.

Allan hustled out the back, and was soon several blocks away. His legs and eyes burned from the movement and daylight.

This will all be over soon, Allan, he thought.

He bought a hoodie, a pair of sunglasses and binoculars. About an hour later, he had a rental car and a box of chicken nuggets, and was headed through busy traffic toward the lab.

Scoping the Quantix building from a distance, it took him a few minutes to steady his shaking hands enough to see a stable image through the binoculars.

Employees came and went, flashing their badges. Allan confirmed they didn't need to scan the badges to get in through the main entrance, and that the security guard didn't seem to be taking any note of the badge numbers.

Allan noticed the Quantix shipping doors were left open by staff who didn't want to be opening and closing the door all day long.

As he watched, he slowly relaxed, and crunched on chicken nuggets. The first food he'd had in what seemed like weeks—greasy, terrible, and utterly delicious. He ate fries as he drove away.

He made a quick trip to a public library and printer, then a suit store. An hour later he had his own badge—modified from Artemit's—and looked the part of a regular Quantix employee.

A regular Quantix employee, however, didn't have nearly as much fear of being near the facility.

Keeping his other body in meditation, he drove up to the Quantix gate.

Where his nightmares had begun. It wasn't the same facility, but it might as well have been.

The guard strolled out from the booth, hand casually resting on his hip pistol holster. Allan had watched other employees enter, and they never smiled too much.

Allan didn't either, and suspected he couldn't have even if he'd tried.

The guard waved him through. Allan drove slowly, afraid that any faster would burn what remained of his nerves.

He parked in the lot closest to shipping, then speed-walked through the bay door and past chemical boxes covered with safety warnings. Into the halls that looked identical to the bleached, faceless interior of his old prison. He shuddered.

He'd made it. Now he just needed to track down Turen.

CHAPTER THIRTY-SEVEN

Turen's Choice

A l Turen leaned back in his chair, yawning at a grid of lab monitors. He was glad to be watching over the lab again, familiar, relaxing satisfaction. He felt even better knowing justice would be served on Artemit for the curse that exhausted Turen every other day.

His only regret was that he couldn't join the hordes of Quantix militia going after Artemit. Kramer had insisted Turen stay in the lab and keep things running smoothly.

Who would've thought a theorist like Artemit was capable of such criminal activity? Not to mention all the other strangeness Turen looked forward to putting out of mind. He'd gone two days without seeing a hint of the nebulous monsters, and hoped it was a trend.

On one of the monitors, a technician unloaded a cart of dirty beakers into a prep room, took off his gloves, and strolled out.

Turen shook his head and smiled, grateful for life's simple pleasures. Picking up the microphone and selecting the channel for the hallway where the technician walked, he announced, "Unless you plan to leave your job at Quantix permanently, get back in there and clean your beakers."

The technician jumped, looked around until he found the camera, then nodded meekly.

Turen never got to see him go back and finish.

Fog rushed in with the sound of a giant's breath. The microphone vanished from Turen's hands, and he fell out of his chair onto cold, rocky ground.

Turen moaned and hugged his shins.

A meter away, two feet stepped out of the fog. Red veins pulsed on translucent flesh. The fog peeled back the higher Turen's gaze lifted.

A monster hunched over him with a large skull and a wide row of glittering pointed teeth. Slitted yellow eyes stared through Turen. Long, thin arms tapped fingers together that flickered between flesh and claws.

The monster's whole body flickered between opaque and translucent, revealing a detailed network of dark, pulsating organs.

The monster opened its mouth and a series of high-pitched chitters echoed in the space. Turen squeezed his eyes shut, wishing to wake from the nightmare.

Rather than awaken, however, a torrent of memories crashed likes waves breaking on the shore of his consciousness.

Moments earlier, he would have thought the memories delusions.

The gruesome creature in front of him was the same monster Turen had seen in Artemit's apartment. A memory from before Artemit had tried to erase Turen's memory, and now seemed in the distant past.

Turen jerked and opened his eyes, seeking anything to refute the truth.

The monster stepped closer. Blood throbbed through its veins.

The last of Turen's memories connected, monster chitters coalescing into human speech.

"...cooperate, and we will have no reason to hurt you," the monster said.

Turen fell back and pressed palms into his eyes. *No, this isn't real. This can't be real.*

I am Belonthar, the monster said in Turen's mind, breaking his attempts to suppress them. *And this is Merthab.*

Turen shrank back. Another monster—Merthab—had joined Belonthar. Merthab opened his mouth wide and ran a long, pointed tongue over long rows of teeth. Saliva dripped onto Turen's knees.

"What do you want from me?" Turen whispered.

Merthab hissed and dipped lower.

Belonthar put his hand-claw on Merthab's shoulder, stilling him. Belonthar stood taller, officious and powerful.

"First, you need to bring us to your world," Belonthar said.

Turen looked around frantically. "H—how?"

"Focus your thoughts on the space you just inhabited. Put all your effort into picturing us there, and you will bring us with you."

Merthab leaned in and tapped Turen's head with his finger-claw.

The fact that Merthab's form was undecided—quantal—was more terrifying than anything.

"OK," Turen said. "Just don't hurt me." His heartbeat echoed in his ears.

He hadn't felt this scared since grade four, in the tunnel, when he'd been beaten and whipped. His dark surroundings seemed to be taking him back there.

Merthab reared back and let out a long chitter.

Turen stared, petrified.

"Do it, Turen," Belonthar said.

Turen nodded. He closed his eyes, imagining the smell of the office carpet, the oversight of the monitors, the taste of a cold cup of coffee right before getting on the microphone...

Then he pictured the monsters leaning over him, and his

thoughts retreated.

He tried again, transforming the scene by making the monsters help him enforce the rules of the lab. That allowed Turen to keep breathing.

When he'd taken the illusion as far as he could, he opened his eyes.

Belonthar and Merthab still towered over him, but in the surrounding fog were tenebrous outlines of Turen's desk and monitors. An office chair sat beside them with a patch of carpet beneath. Had this chunk of reality been brought over into their dark world, or had Turen brought the monsters partway to Earth? If Turen had successfully transported the monsters over, then it was only in a small bubble in the office.

"Is this your space?" Belonthar asked, prodding the chair with his finger-claw.

Turen thought back to the office, and for a moment, the whole area flashed into illumination.

Everything was much the same as he'd left it, with one exception: the space the monsters would have inhabited was gone, and in its place was a blurred, flickering cloud. If it hadn't yet winked out of existence, it soon would.

"Turen!" Belonthar shouted, bringing Turen crashing back, his cheeks cold and fingertips tingling.

"You've done well, but you must bring us further. Focus on your office. Make us real there, as real as this." Belonthar tapped the chair.

"If I bring you there, what will happen?" Turen asked.

"We will have our existence returned to us," Belonthar said. "What was robbed will finally be returned. That is all. Your role in helping enact justice will not be forgotten."

As Belonthar finished, Merthab nodded vigorously and let out a disjointed chitter. Belonthar glared at him and Merthab quieted.

Turen's neck bristled. He had a feeling the room would disappear if he brought the monsters into it. What would happen to the rest of Quantix remained unclear.

They were hiding something.

He had no idea what they would do if he didn't cooperate, though. A room or two from Quantix was surely a small price to pay to avoid trauma.

Maybe he could divert, a tactic he'd used with other power-hungry fanatics he'd met in his life. A tactic he'd used to wrestle power in situations where he'd felt helpless. When he'd used others' lust for control to exert power over them.

"I don't know if I can imagine it properly," Turen said, watching the monsters carefully for a reaction. Belonthar gave none, while the edges of Merthab's mouth crinkled.

"I'm too worked up," Turen continued. "Maybe we can find another way? Some other strategy?"

"You are going to make us real," Merthab said, his chitters laced with a growl. "You have this power. You are One Who Chooses. You are special, Turen, but if you choose to waste this gift, you will regret it."

Turen nodded, struggling to get words out. "I—I'm just saying we might need another approach, that's all."

Merthab snorted, spraying mist in Turen's eyes. Turen recoiled.

"Fine," Belonthar said. "We will try one last method, but if this doesn't work, we will be using other...*involuntary* means. Time is precious, Al Turen, and we have little to spare for games. I hope, for your sake, you're not trying to stall."

"I don't mind if you are," Merthab said. "It just means I get to cut your skull open."

The blood drained from Turen's face, as though preemptively.

"Instead of picturing us in that room, then, I want you to open this door into it." Belonthar stepped back, and sure enough, floating beside him, a white wooden door had appeared.

Where did that come from? And how did they—

"You will open this door, and in doing so, provide a bridge. You need to push with your mind and body. Open the door, Turen, and there will be no need to hurt you. Understand?"

Turen nodded. Opening a door and avoiding brain surgery were about the only things he understood about the situation.

Merthab traced his finger along the edge of Turen's skull. This close, Turen smelled wet rot. He gagged.

Merthab reared back and let out a chitter-laugh.

"The door, Turen," Belonthar said. "Open it."

Turen rose and slowly crossed to the door. The handle's outer edge was warm, while the middle pulsed with cold. Turen couldn't tell if it was from his own heartbeat.

Whatever damage was done, Turen would get himself out of it. He could manipulate almost anyone. He'd been doing so for decades.

These monsters, however, were a different story. They put him into the same powerless state he'd fought against most of his life.

No one would blame him for what he was about to do. Who could stand up to such power, when they could corner him anytime, anywhere, and transport him to a realm of nightmares?

He turned the handle. As he did, his mind filled with the sight of monsters in the office.

It's fine, he told himself. *This means you'll survive. Keep going.*

The door clicked and he pushed against it. He felt a wind blowing against it and holding it shut. Air whistled through the seams.

"Push, Turen," Belonthar said. "Open it."

Turen leaned with his shoulder, smelling old paint on dusty wood. It reminded him of elementary school, full of neglect and bullying.

The same forces were controlling him now.

Just a little longer, then it'll all be over, he thought.

He pushed harder. Merthab's acrid breath filled Turen's

nostrils. His eyes blazed with visions of many monsters pouring into the room.

Turen just wanted it to be over. He gave the door a violent shove. The barrier broke with a *whoosh* and air hissed across.

Turen stood with one leg in the office, and the other in the dark void.

"Yessssss," Merthab said behind him. "The gate to reality is open."

"Finally," Belonthar breathed, stepping closer until he stood shoulder to shoulder with Turen. He moved around the threshold as though blocked by an invisible wall.

He chittered loudly to Merthab in a language Turen didn't understand.

Merthab disappeared into the fog, and a moment later the fog peeled back, revealing a long line of monsters marching single-file toward him.

"I've done what you asked," Turen said. "Now let me go."

Belonthar tilted his head at him. "You will be let go after we are all through."

"You promised not to hurt me," he said as the line of monsters drew closer.

"It will not hurt," Belonthar said, keeping his gaze on the line.

Turen pictured two hulking monsters stalking through the door, their long legs slamming into the ground, each step an epicentre of a quantum quake. Their multi-jointed, thin arms stretched ominously above their heads like praying mantises ready to devour. Each swipe they made gashed reality, a blur of uncertainty before the pulse of Quantix halted and winked out.

Turen wasn't so sure he'd avoided their punishment.

He imagined the monsters moving from his office through the rest of the Quantix facility, creating similar reality-destroying bubbles everywhere they went, the first drops in the pond of Earth's reality.

More would follow, a growing clamour of chitters as two became four, then eight, then sixteen, sending a quantum tsunami through the fabric of reality.

They would march, a sea unmaking everything in its path. The ground would glisten with the hot spit from their chants and the air would stink of rot and lichen.

All of them. They're invading.

If he let them through, he wouldn't have a place to hide. He wouldn't have *any* place.

He shuffled until his back was against the doorframe, still standing with one leg in each world. He wanted to voice a protest, but all that came out was a low whimper.

These creatures were capable of hurting him so much more than those older kids had hurt him in elementary school. The monsters had a great deal more power. He didn't want to —he wouldn't, couldn't—subject himself to a treatment worse than he'd already endured. He'd made a promise to himself never to go through that again.

The line was seconds away from crossing the threshold. Belonthar stepped back to make space. He chittered something to all of them, then said to Turen, "Let them through."

Turen moved back into the doorway on the dark side, not daring to test what would happen to him if he were in the real world when the line marched through. The monsters' excited chitters blurred into a single, warbling note.

This was all Artemit's fault. He'd dragged Turen into this. How, Turen didn't know, but he felt, deep down, this madness had started with Artemit. No one would fault Turen for what he'd done today.

But there might not be anyone around to.

The lineup of monsters stopped at the threshold, and the warbling chitter of the throng hung like the pause before a final orchestral coda.

In the collective pulse, Turen heard echoes of his cries as a nine-year-old boy, trapped in the torrent of pain in that tunnel whose lines of force went round and round and round...

One monster went forward. Another followed.

A translucent foot crossed the threshold, and the office floor vanished. It was replaced by long grass and a wide-leafed tropical bush Turen would have never expected to grow there. He tasted hot, humid air.

The second monster stepped through and the area of effect widened, rippling and making a sound like wood cracking and metal grinding.

More greenery filled in. Parts of the ceiling of the Quantix lab collapsed into the greenspace before disintegrating. Steam rose from the plants and brought the scent of fresh blooms mixed with the smell of mould in a dank attic corner.

"Yesssssss," Belonthar said behind Turen.

Turen's arms shook at his sides.

These monsters had come for him as soon as they'd become tangible in his mind. They'd spread like memes from Artemit to him. If it spread to other people, who knew what would happen.

This wouldn't stop at Quantix. This wouldn't even stop in Vancouver. It would continue until there was nothing left.

Then Turen's territory, the fragile biome he'd tried to carve out with him as the alpha, would have less than a note in a history book. It would have never existed at all.

The last act of Al Turen, and possibly the last act of any human, period, would be to cave in to the threats of the powerful. Just as he'd caved in as a child, to the forces that had guided many of his actions from that day forward.

No.

But to resist was to willingly put himself in those thousand-toothed jaws, into the grips of long arms that could crush him. To fight back was to end his life back in the tunnel, suffering as those bullies had meant him to suffer that day, with the stinging whip-crack of a dozen leather belts.

He moaned. He just wanted out, wanted it to be over. If

he just closed his eyes, he could count and wait a little while, and it would all be over.

In his mind he saw what he'd imagined so many times: himself taking revenge on those bullies that day. However, he'd never actually fought back when he was weaker—he'd always succumbed to its influence in some way or another. To be faced with it again now was, he realized, the chance to do what he'd never been able to.

Fight back, and don't cave in to the power.

No matter how much it hurt. No matter the risk of failure.

He reached across the threshold and grabbed the door handle. It burned. The pain seared up his arm as his grip stuck to it.

"Turen!" Belonthar snapped. "Out of the way!"

A hand grabbed Turen's shoulder. His stomach quivered with phantom wounds of hot leather whips. His knees shook.

It's not too late to turn back. His nostrils filled with pollen, rot, and the sweat of bullies too young to bother with deodorant.

Don't let them hurt you.

Belonthar shoved Turen. He let go of the knob and struck the side of the doorframe.

"I'm s—sorry," he blubbered.

No one could blame him. It wasn't his fault, after all. No one else had had such a horrific, life-scarring experience as a child. They couldn't judge. They couldn't possibly understand how difficult this was for him.

The line of monsters paused, hesitating a few steps from the threshold as they watched the first two scouts going farther into Quantix. Each of the scout's steps peeled back a lush, tropical landscape while the wind carried the paradoxical scent of carrion.

The rumble of missing joists shook the scene.

Turen moaned, feeling hollow. The marching dinosaurs in the jungle reminded him, absurdly, of a diorama in science class. A class not long after the incident with the bullies. His mind, desperate to escape, locked onto this image.

He'd smashed that diorama. It had helped transform the pain into power.

He'd become an expert in finding what was weak, hollowed and unsupported.

Now, as the ridiculous image rolled through his skull, he realized the reason he'd gotten so good at it was because he could always spot himself in the mirror.

It's too late. Better to wink out painlessly along with everyone else.

His arms dangled like bloodless meat, swaying with the life-death breeze of one world being made, and another being undone.

I can't fill the void inside me, he thought, *not completely.*

His mind swam with the vision of other young boys, playing in schoolyards across the world, who would never get the chance to realize their potentials, for good or bad. Never get the chance to grow beyond their pain.

It hurt, he thought. *It hurt so, so much.*

It will *hurt so much.*

He leaped across to the doorframe, grabbed the handle and yanked the door as hard as he could.

The door slammed. The wind buffeted and shook the whole frame.

"It's too late!" Belonthar shouted, pinning him against the door. "We've already made it through, and the damage is done! Open it again, or we'll tear you apart!"

Yes, this will hurt, Turen thought, tears streaming down his cheeks. He twitched from the whips of the past, and the coming jaws of the future. *They'll use their power to hurt me.*

His back was against the door, but in his mind he was back on the pavement in an endless tunnel, with a thousand looming figures ready to shatter his world.

Merthab pushed through the line and slashed at Turen's legs. His knees gave out but Belonthar kept him pinned to the door.

He moaned. All he had to do was reach for the handle, open it a crack, and they'd let him go. Then the hot burning in his quads would stop. The pressure that threatened to break his collar bones would stop.

No. I won't let the pain control me anymore.

"You said I have the power to choose," Turen said, his voice quavering. "And not to waste it."

The stench of the monsters was overwhelming, and behind Merthab and Belonthar, a crowd was forming.

They're all going to hurt you. They're going to take turns eating your flesh.

Turen moaned. He tried to see beyond the tunnel, to gaze upon the two worlds whose borders were colliding and overlapping, where only one could exist.

I'm the only one who can stop them.

"Choose us!" Belonthar hissed. "Choose justice!"

They've suffered. I've suffered. It can all be over if I just give in.

Turen cried out as Merthab brought a finger claw millimetres in front of his right eye.

"Do it!" Merthab shrieked.

"All right!" Turen shouted. "All right."

Turen's hand reached for the knob, and he moaned with the anticipated pleasure of being free of... everything. It was a comfortable, familiar feeling, a routine he'd fallen into so many times before. Avoid resisting the pain, and follow its logical course of acceptance.

Acceptance that will end humanity.

His fingers sparked blue lightning on the door knob, and he was unwilling to pull away or to commit further. His hand hung on the threshold, with Merthab's finger-claw a shudder away from blinding him.

I have to stop them. No matter how much it hurts. No matter what it costs.

He might die in this tunnel, this space between worlds.

But it would be his choice. It would be on his terms.

The pain wouldn't be, but it didn't have to control him anymore. He wouldn't be its puppet any longer.

No more.

Turen closed his eyes, and imagined the Quantix lab exactly as it had been. The pristine office chair, the desk with the many monitors, the cold coffee he'd enjoyed on so many mornings, and the hallways where he'd maintained dominion.

There were a few blurry spots in his vision, spots he quickly realized were the shapes of two monsters.

He had the power to choose. And in opening the door, he'd chosen the monsters to *be* in the world.

A choice he hoped it wasn't too late to take back.

As though he were monitoring through the security cameras, he focused his gaze on the spots where the monsters were, filling in the details exactly as they should be, as though he were wiping away dust and debris left by a lazy lab tech.

"Lying filth!" Merthab shouted.

Pop-skshh.

His right eye exploded with the ringing force of a supernova. The burn started hot, deep within, then expanded out in shockwaves.

Turen screamed.

He inhaled dust and gravel, his skull lolling back and forth against the concrete.

He was pinned now, the darkness tightened around him like a tourniquet. He squeezed his mangled eye shut, feeling a building pressure in his skull.

"Stop it!" Merthab shouted, waving his claw in Turen's other eye.

"No!" Belonthar said, shoving Merthab out of the way. "He needs to see us, you idiot!"

Turen smiled weakly, remembering where he really was, and what he needed to do. He pictured the halls of Quantix exactly as they were, spotless, all in order, everything under control.

"No!" Belonthar screamed. "You've killed them! You've killed them!"

Belonthar jerked a finger-claw back and jammed it into Turen's gut.

Turen gagged as the punctured hole flashed with lightning, then grew numb with cold. He tasted copper.

He couldn't see Quantix now—couldn't see much of anything beyond the thousand-sun fury burning in Belonthar's eyes.

But Turen knew, maybe from the trickle in his gut, that those monsters in Quantix were no more.

"Merthab, remove his brain!" Belonthar shouted. "Do it now!"

They're going to force me to do it, Turen realized. *Whether I choose so or not.*

Turen shrieked in a nine-year-old's broken soprano cry.

He had to step further into the pain. It was taking hold again, dominating every part of his being.

"Please," he whispered, the blood slurring his words, "stop."

Merthab drew a claw across his forehead, and he saw blood like trickles of red raindrops on a window pane.

He would die in the pain of that tunnel, and it wouldn't mean a thing in the world. His choice to step back into this place would mean nothing, because he, his choice, everything that ever was, would be pinched out of reality.

His mother, father. Grandmother, grandfather. Gone. Never born. Friends—back when the term had held meaning for him. All gone.

The bullies would be gone too, though. Turen smiled at that.

Just give in, and they'll pay. Artemit will pay.
Everyone will pay.

"No," Turen moaned. Down that path lay an emptiness more hollow than he could imagine.

He had to push the monsters so much they destroyed

what remained of him.

His body shook.

Belonthar and Merthab were too close to him, reeking of salt and rancid garbage. He couldn't get a good focus, and their constant physical presence couldn't be overcome.

He had to choose a different target.

"Watch," Turen murmured, using every last bit of strength he had to nod his head.

Belonthar and Merthab followed his gaze to the monster at the front of the line.

Turen closed his eyes and imagined the realm they were in with that monster never having been.

Nothing but a thousand black fireflies, he thought deliriously. *Ash to ash.*

A moment later, he opened his eyes and the monster tumbled into black soot.

Belonthar, Merthab, and the entire population of monsters roared.

Merthab chomped on Turen's arm. Fire burned up every nerve. A moment later the fibres were torn off with frayed, red-hot ends.

Merthab held Turen's arm in his jaws. He threw it to the side.

"His brain," Belonthar said between heavy breaths, "get his brain!"

Turen coughed and closed his eyes again, winking another of the monsters out of existence.

From the skull-shaking wail, he knew he'd succeeded.

Belonthar slammed Turen against the door again. A crack echoed through Turen as his breath caught. Another bang and the left side of his body caved.

His vision blurred. Despite the pain, he felt free, like none of the cruelty could control his actions anymore.

As Belonthar moved to bang him against the door again, Turen twitched his neck backward as far as it would go, until he was sailing headfirst toward the white sea of the door.

Out of the tunnel.
Not a puppet any—

CHAPTER THIRTY-EIGHT

Return to Quantix

Allan Gerrold peered out of a maintenance closet in one of Quantix Lab's corridors, checking to see if anyone else had stuck around.

He'd made it pretty far into the facility before reality itself started falling apart.

A red siren was flashing at one intersection to his left, accompanied by the anachronistic wail of an ancient fire engine.

To his right, at the other end of the hall, the siren that would have flashed was gone, along with the walls, floor and the rest of the ceiling.

Dense tropical plants filled the space, rustling. Two flickering dinosauroids lumbered out, spreading the vegetation and making the building shudder.

Allan squeezed out of the closet—the door was tight now and wouldn't budge—and ran in the opposite direction, trying to think of anything he could possibly do to stop the dinosauroids.

His mind came back empty.

At the end of the hall, he slammed into a door. His

head banged, making everything dim and ringing. The door wouldn't budge. Dust from the shifting ceiling rained down. He coughed and gagged.

Allan turned to see the dinosauroids slavering after him, picking up pace now that they had prey.

"Help!" he shouted. "Anyone, please!"

His other body was still in the car with Tamika, Ben and Kitt. He jerked awake, then saw a flurry of blinding street lights.

Nowhere near Quantix.

He closed his eyes again, focusing on the body in Quantix.

He blinked.

The dinosauroids were gone.

The hallway looked perfectly normal. Allan fell back against the door and it opened normally.

Am I going insane?

The vision of the two flickering dinosauroids stomping toward him burned in his mind. But they'd vanished. There was no evidence of them ever having been there.

Turen had to be here.

It had gone from the hazy, static-filled fog, to the vegetation of the dinosauroids' world, and now it had returned to normal.

Was it a trap? Or had Turen successfully pushed them back?

Maybe, just maybe, he'd defeated them, but Allan couldn't allow such hope to blossom yet.

Allan sped down the hallway, sucking breaths. He winced as he crossed the threshold of what used to be tropical forest.

Around the corner Al Turen's name was plastered on an office door. It was cracked open and dark inside.

"Turen?" Allan called, pushing in.

Turen sat limply in an office chair facing away. Allan hoped the grey pallor of Turen's skin was just a trick of the light.

He edged around, maintaining a gap in case Turen was concentrating on fighting the dinosauroids.

Turen's head leaned far back, and there was a hollow on top where the bone looked like it had been sawed off. A mound of dust filled the empty cavity and stuck to the blood-coated insides of what remained of his skull.

Allan clutched his stomach, then turned away.

It was real. It had all happened. The dinosauroids had almost invaded.

Turen had paid the ultimate price to protect humanity.

If there was any doubt in Allan's mind over whether or not the two worlds—that of humans and the dinosauroids— could coexist, the fact that Turen's head had a bubble smashed out of existence was proof enough.

Allan heaved and rushed out of the room. At the entrance, he whispered to Turen, "I'm sorry. I'm sorry I couldn't get here in time."

Allan doubled over in the hallway, taking deep breaths, trying to slow his racing thoughts. The dinosauroids couldn't have gotten Turen's brain, because there was too much matter filling—

Allan shook his head to try and get rid of the image.

He fought them off. That's the explanation that makes the most sense.

"You did well, Turen," Allan muttered.

* * *

Allan awoke in his other body once more to blinding city lights. This world was moving much too quickly, passing cars flashing like strobes. He groaned as he covered his eyes.

"Turen's dead."

"What! How?" Ben said.

"The dinosauroids got him. He must've resisted them

too much. They... destroyed his brain."

"How do you know this?"

Allan inhaled. "I found him at Quantix."

"What?" Tamika shouted. "You went to Quantix! You're *at* Quantix?"

"I was closer than any of us," Allan said quietly. "I had the best chance of getting there in time. I was still too late, though."

"Poor Al," Ben breathed.

Ben hugged himself in the back seat, his shoulders hunched. Kitt's hand rested on him.

"Well, get out of there," Tamika said, glaring across at Allan from the driver's seat. "There's no point hanging around."

"As soon as my head stops spinning, I will."

"The dinosauroids can do real damage," Ben murmured. "They can affect our world. They weren't bluffing."

"Turen stopped the worst of it," Allan said. "I saw the start of their invasion, Ben. They were here. They were really here, and then they were gone just like that."

"Are you sure they didn't... take his brain?" Ben asked.

"Yes. It was obliterated."

"They've got to be very, very angry."

"Guys, we're almost there," Kitt said from the back seat.

"Poor Al. I hope he's... found solace. He must have—"

"Now's not the time to grieve," Tamika snapped from the driver's seat. "Allan, have you made your way out yet?"

Everyone turned to him.

"I'm navigating the halls now, but I'm fighting queasiness. The alarms are going off, so it'll be hard not to be noticed now."

"Hurry up!" Tamika shouted. "Were coming to get you. You can be sick as much as you want once you're out."

"Don't come back for me," Allan said. "All of you risking your lives for me is too much."

"Oh, shut it," Tamika said. "I got you out of Quantix, and

I'm not letting any part of you get pulled back in."

* * *

Back in Quantix, Allan heard heavy footsteps and the sound of thick canvas rubbing what he guessed were heavy pant legs against each other.

Firefighters, he thought.

"Ten bucks says it's another coffeepot left on," one of them said.

Allan turned and ran in the opposite direction down the hall, through the door that minutes earlier wouldn't open because the building was about to collapse.

The door was fine now, but part of Allan still expected reality to snap back to that horror.

The dinosauroids.

Only one world could exist at a time. Ben's suspicions were absolutely right.

It was only a matter of time before the furious dinosauroids would come for Ben, but Allan couldn't do anything about it until he was safely out of Quantix.

He darted through another door, then heard more footsteps and voices. He backtracked, and sprinted through a set of empty cubicles. He couldn't place where he was anymore.

Past the cubicles, there were two classified doors that needed a keycard, and one that led deeper, in a direction Allan thought was back where he'd come from.

He groaned. This was taking way too much time.

* * *

"Come on, hurry up!" Ben Artemit shouted out his open window. Vancouver's familiar rush-hour potpourri of wet pavement and car exhaust rushed at him. They only increased his urge to yell at people to get off the road.

They were stuck in traffic, barely moving, everyone leaning and looking around for other options.

Ahead of them, a blue sedan jutted into traffic, blocking off one and a half lanes as the driver forced a left turn into the packed flow.

"You've got to be kidding me!" Ben shouted.

"Ben, stop. You're not helping anything," Kitt said.

Ben leaned his head on the windowsill and groaned.

He'd added another name—Turen's—to the long list of beings he was responsible for murdering. Every part of him wanted to run, move, fight—anything!—but they were too far from Quantix for him to do anything but sit and wait.

He would never get a chance to thank Turen, or to commend him for standing up to the dinosauroids. He hoped Turen's death hadn't been painful, but it was a vain hope.

He had to admit it was a selfish one, too, one to appease his guilt.

Pretty soon Allan's name would be added to that list, or it might as well be for what Marlon Kramer planned.

Blinking neon lights from three sushi shops, two cafés and an assortment of fusion restaurants seemed to mark a countdown for their vanishing time. A group of teenagers laughed and walked along the sidewalk. Ben felt an incredible desire to be that young again, to be carefree aside from homework, studying, and overblown social crises.

No, he thought. Such an intense desire might lead him to use his powers, and he remembered his vow to use it on nothing but the dinosauroids.

Nothing but the dinosauroids.

As he repeated the thought, a penetrating black oozed out of the base of the storefronts. It rose and slopped toward him, blocking out everything and extinguishing any light in its path. The teenagers waded through it, but seemed not to see it, though their footsteps kicked it into an avalanche of emptiness. The sound of motors and horns muffled and stuttered as though the black were choking out life.

Ben gasped. The black converged on him from all sides. Maybe the dinosauroids *did* have Turen's brain, and he was seeing the last of human civilization.

"No, no, no!"

"What is it, Ben?" Kitt asked, grabbing his arm. By the sharp hiss of breath past her lips, Ben knew that by touching him she saw it now, too.

The black pooled at the car, bubbling as it worked its way up the sides, swallowing the tires and the hood.

"What's happening?" Tamika said sharply, turning around to face them.

Been rolled up his window, wishing the electric motor to move the glass faster. Before the window sealed at the top, a line of black poured down, an inky waterfall stopping the window's movement.

The black pooled at Ben's feet. He cried out but couldn't pull free. The flow increased, the pressure hissing through the gap in the window as the cold black wormed up his shins, his waist, then his chest. It smelled sterile, noxious like formaldehyde.

He and Kitt grabbed one another before the black filled their throats, then their eyes.

* * *

Allan Gerrold wanted to reach back and comfort Kitt and Ben, but by the glazed look on both their faces, he knew they were already with the dinosauroids.

He also had his own problems to deal with.

"Hold on," he muttered with both bodies.

In Quantix, Allan heard voices down every hall. He had to backtrack and try two separate pathways, the first of which nearly led him to stumble into an atrium full of employees. It would've been fine if they weren't all hunting around like hawks for anything or anyone out of the ordinary.

His plan now was to find a maintenance closet—back where he'd started—and hide out until things calmed down. Then he could just walk out as though everything were normal. It would take more time, but seemed to be his only option.

He sprinted through an open concept office, tables and computers scattered all around. He turned a corner and saw a pair of washrooms on the right side, and—yes!—a storage closet on the left.

He was a few meters from the door when a large man in a suit too tight for his bulk strolled around the corner.

"Hello, Allan," Marlon Kramer said with a wide grin.

CHAPTER THIRTY-NINE

Familiar Pain

Tamika pulled the car over on the road leading up to Quantix, shuddering as they crossed onto gravel. The neighbouring pines of Quantix's curated forest stopped as they did. Shadows deepened in the stillness.

In the back, Ben and Kitt had their eyes closed and twitched as murmurs crossed their lips. In the front beside Tamika, Allan whimpered.

She squeezed the steering wheel, reminding herself not to touch him. "What is it, Allan? We could use some good news right now."

"He found me," he whispered. "He found me."

Kramer, she thought. The throb of her fingers' pulse quickened against the rubber.

"Where are you? What do you see?"

Allan twitched, squeezing his eyes shut. He curled into a ball. His lips moved through incoherent mutters.

"Come on, Allan. Stay with me."

It was no use. She tried a few more times, but got no response from him. The trauma he'd suffered at hers and Kramer's hands had been too much.

"All right," she said. "You've got to take care of Dr. Artemit and Dr. Bell, then."

She programmed the car to take the trio to Blue Hills Park, a sanctuary safe and remote enough it should give the three of them some options when they woke.

If they woke.

She got out and watched the car self-drive away. She tried to say goodbye but the lump in her throat made the sound a croak.

She jogged towards the Quantix gate, where a burly guard stormed out and shouted at her to stop.

When she didn't, he pointed a pistol in her face.

She channeled her desperation into a display of hysteria. "I'm sorry!" she said. "It's just that my husband's in there. We were talking on the phone until I heard sirens and he got cut off. Now I can't reach him, and I'm worried sick."

The guard relaxed, lowering the pistol. "I'm sorry, ma'am, but without a badge, I can't let you in."

He stood in the middle of the path, a few metres away from Tamika. She was so nervous her ears rang.

"Well, can you at least tell me what those fire trucks are doing there?" she said, pointing.

The guard glanced back to look at the emergency response scene. Tamika shot forward.

She tackled him, knocking the gun out of his hand before he could squeeze off a shot. She wrestled him until she was choking him and pinching his carotid artery.

He struggled and bucked against her. He dragged her along the ground with him. She cried out, foreseeing a sharp ending to this rescue before it had even begun.

Then the guard's movements slowed, and he fell limp.

"I'm sorry," she muttered.

Tamika took a few steps away, hesitated, then turned and grabbed his pistol. Then she sprinted into Quantix.

* * *

Allan Gerrold quivered, unwilling to believe he was right back where it had all begun. The Quantix facilities were nearly identical in layout and construction between sites, and Kramer had taken sick pleasure dragging Allan to the room where he'd first been entangled.

Allan could taste the blood and burning from all the painful memories of this space. The worst part was that he knew it was just a fraction of what was to come.

"Well, Allan," Kramer said, strolling around the archaic iron hospital bed to which Allan was strapped, "I'm not sure if we could send you to the dark world with only one body, but we'll try our best, won't we?"

Kramer grinned and retreated into the shadows, away from the central spotlight. In the outer rim, scores of instruments lined shelves and hung from the walls.

He returned with a long prod and pressed it into Allan's inner thigh.

"This device is simply marvellous," Kramer said. "I press this button and it helps bring your other body here. Would you believe it?"

Kramer pressed the button. White fury rocked Allan. He screamed and writhed as hot fire crackled through him.

He tried to retreat into his other body but the pain brought him back. Within moments he had no strength to speak.

He had no idea where his other body was, driving through suburbs with increased forest coverage.

Allan wasn't sure how long Kramer tortured him, as he passed in and out of consciousness in attempts to escape the suffering.

At some point he woke to find Kramer bouncing excitedly.

"Take your mind there, Gerrold," he was saying. "Tap into that power, so we can seize it."

Kramer made a fist so tight it vibrated.

Allan moaned, knowing any argument against Kramer's

folly would only bring more pain. Maybe if Allan went to the dark place and managed to control himself, he could at least find refuge from Kramer.

He concentrated, wrestling his body into the state between dreams and reality. He glimpsed fog rolling in the horizon of his mental landscape, and tried to steer toward the dinosauroid realm.

Where Kitt and Ben were cornered.

Lightning exploded across the vast plain. Allan felt as though he were torn backward at an incredible pace, everything flashing away.

"Stop that," Kramer snarled. "I know the biometric signs that lead you to the dark world. Whatever you're doing, that's not it. Don't test my patience."

Five or six gunshots rang out, followed by two thumps from the other side of the door. Kramer whipped around, brandishing his cattle prod like a sword.

He looked around, then darted into the shadows to wait in ambush.

Tamika, Allan thought. He wanted to cry out a warning, but his mouth was too dry.

❋ ❋ ❋

Tamika's hands shook as she approached the door. She avoided looking at the guards' blood, but the metallic tang made her gag. At the keypad, she tapped in the code she thought Kramer would still be using for his favourite room in the facility.

The total number of Kramer's publications and citations, chained one after the other. Regularly updated, but easy to retrieve.

It worked. If she could count on two things, they were Kramer's pride and arrogance.

She stepped carefully into the room, scanning the shadows. Her gaze kept wandering to the spotlit centre, where

Allan lay strapped and in a puddle of sweat.

Kramer leapt at her. Lightning coursed up her legs and into her arms. Her hands quaked; she dropped the gun. Kramer removed the prod just long enough to meet her gaze before jabbing it back in.

She grabbed his hand as he pulled the trigger, giving the electricity a path through his body. He rocked and fell back. She scrambled away, found the pistol, and fired wildly. Her bullets tore through the prod but missed Kramer.

Then he was on top of her, and they thrashed together, fighting for control of the pistol. It went off several times until it was out of bullets. Kramer squeezed her throat, straddling her.

"You should have brought help," he said, wheezing. "Arrogant of you to think you could match me. You always tried to do too much alone."

She was near the instrument-laden walls, her vision darkening. She pawed at Kramer.

She reached up and clasped a collar she would have recognized anywhere.

It was an early version of the pain-pleasure collar, one that didn't need to be implanted.

Gathering the last of her energy, she heaved and wrapped the collar around Kramer's neck, jabbing the needles in. Her fingers cranked the dial to maximum pleasure.

Kramer writhed and moaned, falling off her.

Tamika took a few moments to catch her breath, her throat ragged. She stood above Kramer's pathetic, curled form. Then she bent and switched the collar to maximum pain.

Kramer screamed. His hands reached for the dial at the collar's back, but Tamika stomped on his fingers. She towered over him and attacked anytime his hands drew close.

His hands hunted along the ground but found nothing. He clawed at his chest, and begged incoherently between fits of spit.

Tamika pulled a sharp probe off a nearby shelf and

dropped it within Kramer's reach.

He grabbed and swung it at her. Tamika hopped out of the way. The pain was too much; he was losing what little muscle control remained.

Kramer must have realized this, too, because he shuddered with his face twisted to control his thrashing.

He raised quaking arms above his chest. He jabbed the probe in. A few twitches later, he stilled.

Marlon Kramer was no more.

* * *

Allan Gerrold awoke to the sounds of screams, then silence. Tamika stood beside him.

"I'm sorry, Allan," she whispered. "I tried. But they're on their way to get us."

She unstrapped him and helped him sit up. Allan gasped as he brought himself back to reality. "K—Kramer?"

"Dead."

On the floor beside them lay Kramer, a pool of blood spreading beneath his torso.

"We can give them a good fight, can't we?" Tamika said.

Allan pursed his lips. "I should use this time to help Ben and Kitt. If I don't, there might not be any world left to fight for."

Tears streamed down Tamika's cheeks. She nodded. "All right. You're going to that place, aren't you?"

"Yes."

Tamika squeezed her eyes shut and shook her head. "Fine."

Without warning, she moved in and pressed her lips into his. Allan jerked, then relaxed. He gently put a hand on her cheek. She tasted warm and salty.

Then she pulled away, and he was left so dizzy that black freckles dotted his vision.

"I'll buy you as much time as I can," Tamika said, moving to the door and piling things in front to barricade it. "Go save them... and the world."

Allan frowned, took a deep breath, and closed his eyes.

CHAPTER FORTY

This is the Way the Worlds End

en Artemit gasped on hands and knees. The black sludge's chemical taste had been transferred into the surrounding yellow mist. The air singed his nose.

Stones beneath flickered, appearing rectangular, then triangular, then hexagonal. They shifted between forms in lurches, alternating smooth and rough and scraping the pads off his fingers.

He jerked as a hand touched his.

It was Kitt, her worried face the only clear sight in the toxic haze.

"We can do this." She sounded like she shouted through a tunnel. "We've made it through before, and we can do it again."

The dinosauroid world, however, had never felt so alien. Massive, sharp-edged buildings surrounded them. Jagged-spoked columns stuck out of every corner, while reflections shifted across the flat surfaces.

Kitt and Ben scrambled up as twitching crowds of dinosauroids loped toward them. A cacophony of chitters and moans tore the air.

"We have to stick together," Kitt whispered.

They sought an escape, but in the middle of a five-spoked intersection, quantum shifting monsters approached from every direction.

"We're faster than them," Ben said. "Their forms are changing so quickly they'll barely see us."

Kitt nodded. "This way—there's less of them."

They jogged down one of the spokes. Sunlight peeled back the jaundiced fog to reveal an endless stream of flickering, tortured dinosauroids. Everything, even the buildings, steamed as though being boiled away.

The towers stretched up until they faded to purple-bruise pinpricks. Dinosauroids tried to climb the walls, but the shifting surfaces made them tumble back into the masses. Windows continually undulated as though liquid. Through the glass shone a dizzying array of faces. Ramps crisscrossed between structures, translucent and glinting like spider webs.

At the epicentre of the trap ran Kitt and Ben.

The approaching throng's forms flickered between possibilities, legs, arms, jaws lengthening and tightening in succession, while eyes, adapted to countless years of this torment, twitched between alternate versions of deadened stares.

Ben's chest ached for them. Kitt's tugging drew him on.

He and Kitt slammed into the crowd. Chitters and moans rose to a crescendo. Blurry fingers pulled at them. The grasp of Kitt's hand became Ben's only certainty.

The flickering expressions burned an image into him, a recurring one of bitterness, anger and blame.

He shut his eyes, squeezing tighter to Kitt. He jolted as they took a sharp turn, shuttled through the crowd-gauntlet into one of the superstructures.

The throng shoved them up a long, winding ramp whose surface quivered like swamp-water in the rain.

In the chaos, several dinosauroids pressed themselves between Ben and Kitt. They lost their grip on each other.

"Kitt!" Ben shouted.

It had only taken a moment, but she'd vanished.

He shoved his way up the ramp where they must have taken her. The dinosauroids gave him more freedom to run, yet Kitt was nowhere to be found.

His legs pumped and gradually the chitters gave way to a faint, steady howl.

Ben followed a mass of dinosauroids as they ascended and passed through a jagged-toothed aperture. Ben was shoved through, the teeth bending and scraping against him. As the teeth touched his ears filled with screams.

He fell face-first onto a balcony on the other side. His palms pressed against a patchwork of glass, numerous layers a mosaic of stitched edges.

On a neighbouring building's balcony, joined to this one by a causeway, Belonthar and Merthab hunched next to Kitt. In contrast to the other dinosauroids in this realm, Belonthar and Merthab held a constant form, because they had a definite form in Ben's mind.

They were definite, with one exception: their quantum-flickering hand-talons. One of Merthab's gripped Kitt's shoulder, and she winced each time their form flashed and changed.

Ben's stomach clenched. He wouldn't let them hurt her.

As though in response the wind brought a moaning howl.

An apertured door stood to the dinosauroids' left. To their right a causeway stretched across the streets to join up with another superspire. Every few seconds the layers of glass beneath them shuddered, a slow-motion arc of rearranging atoms. Chaotic whimsy flowed everywhere.

"We're giving you a special tour today, Artemit," Belonthar said, spreading long arms. "I hope you are grateful."

"None of this is real, Ben!" Kitt shouted. "They're just trying to make themselves more real in your mind so—"

She screamed as Merthab dug finger-claws into her shoulder. Ben sucked air through his teeth.

"You believe in us," Belonthar said, striding toward Ben.

"Both of you do, and you can't stop. It's pointless to try."

"Let her go," Ben said, getting to his feet and surging forward. "Or there will be no negotiating."

Belonthar's gaze darted between Ben and Kitt. "We are well past negotiations, Artemit. I'm surprised you still think otherwise."

"What is this then? Torture?"

Ben grew queasy at the peripheral sight of countless dinosauroids hundreds of metres below, but forced himself onward.

Belonthar retreated, urging Ben on. He pressed a three-fingered hand to the apertured door beside him. "This," Belonthar said, dragging out the words, "is an enlightenment."

The door opened, and tiny, quivering forms shuffled through. They clung to one another, their skin translucent —as Belonthar's and Merthab's had sometimes appeared— extending even into their eyeballs, teeth and bones.

A few seconds later, one disappeared completely, ushering a high keen from the rest. A few breaths after, their brethren popped back into existence looking as frightened and out of place as swallows who'd missed winter migration.

Children. Dinosauroid children.

"Ben! Look at me!" Kitt shouted, but he was transfixed by the children.

There was a time in Ben's childhood when he'd been irritated by birds fluttering past the balcony and into his house. He had shooed them out, slamming the window shut. Moments later, he'd heard a thump and turned to find, twitching on the balcony, the mangled body of a bird.

Now, faced with the gathered children of the dinosauroids, Ben's insides felt as twisted and broken as that bird so long ago.

He had done this, as he'd done to the bird, a thousand times over.

Kitt elbowed Merthab and held out her palm, saying, "You are not real. We are not here. Those children you're using on Ben aren't real."

Merthab halted for an instant, then shimmered. He roared and swung his arms at Kitt, colliding with an invisible wall that sent a warble through the wind.

"See?" Kitt said. "Ben, we can control this. We control them. Don't fall for their tricks."

Kitt extended her other arm in the opposite direction, toward Belonthar and the dinosauroid children.

Belonthar flicked a hand and snapped his jaws. Kitt stumbled back.

"This isn't a trick," Belonthar said. "This is our world. These are the children who *might have been* if it weren't for your selfish betrayal, Artemit. Take a good look, because they don't always last the night."

Belonthar trailed off until his voice blended into the air's mournful howl.

"Ben, don't listen to him! Focus on me!" Kitt sounded far away, a lost echo in a canyon.

All Ben could see was the quivering huddle of dinosauroid children. They took turns disappearing, trying in the interim to cling to a tenuous notion of family. A few of them whispered and pointed in Ben's direction until the entire group stared, shrinking en masse before a force too evil and powerful to comprehend.

Ben knew no amount of running would save him from this new horror.

Belonthar had somehow moved next to him and tapped his skull lightly with a finger.

Kitt's mouth opened wide in a shout. Ben couldn't hear a thing.

❊ ❊ ❊

With both of his bodies, Allan Gerrold focused on his breathing, then withdrew from the bright light of consciousness and into the black. He braked before going too far, holding on as though grasping the surface of reality with the tips of his fingers.

A loud bang jolted him awake. He snapped his head up to see the door of the Quantix lab shuddering from an onslaught of security guards.

There wasn't much time left.

Tamika shoved the remaining equipment against the door, then readied herself with an arsenal of makeshift weapons laid out on the bed at Allan's feet.

He didn't have time to worry about all that, though.

Allan closed his eyes again, intentionally breathing louder to drown out his surroundings. He sought a strong image to take him away.

He pictured himself sitting beneath a thick oak tree in the middle of a golden field. Leaves fluttered. It was the same tree where, as a child, he'd found his final refuge before the harsh realities of family life.

It had been impossible to please his parents. He could never have satisfied them.

Why was he seeing it again now? Was it because he was in another impossible situation, and recognized it as all-too familiar?

Maybe it was because he felt an end drawing near. An end meant his parents had been right—that everything he'd done was wrong.

No, he told himself. *I've been through this. That's all over now. It was many lifetimes ago, and I built a new life, despite everything. One with friends.*

Friends I need to save.

He wasn't sure he could save them with all of the baggage of Allan Gerrold. He had been reborn, and it was his rebirth that had given him the ability to save them.

No more Allan Gerrold. He was The Entangled Man.

He pictured Kitt, Ben and Tamika all seated beside him, smiling. The oak tree was thick enough they could all find a comfortable seat leaning against it.

The tension in his chest eased, as did his breathing. The surrounding light dimmed, and everything slowed until the leaves no longer fluttered.

The horizon creeped slowly toward him, everything behind it winking into darkness. It wasn't an encroachment, but the warm embrace of sleep and safe company. The promise of rest and recuperation was even more enticing with The Entangled Man's knowledge that he was, indeed, sitting next to Kitt, Ben and Tamika somewhere.

He balanced on the knife-edge. On one side lay the ignorant bliss of the unconscious, and on the other sirens flashed and horns blared in the panic of awakening.

The Entangled Man, in the middle.

He stood alone. Wisps flew, twisted and curled in visible contrails. They sailed faster, multiplying and bringing an all-encompassing grey haze.

The contrails formed chain links. Dense fog brightened with lantern light.

The Entangled Man recognized the chain that formed in his left hand, stretching off ahead and behind. He took a deep breath and started walking.

Almost there, he thought. *Just hold on, Ben and Kitt.*

The ground steepened the farther he hiked. The wind picked up, replacing the fog with ice pellets that scraped his skin. The haze dissipated to reveal an icy cliff where the chain ascended. It whipped with the gusts, smashing against the ice.

The Entangled Man jumped to avoid falling debris.

Winter's chill had not just been in his mind.

❋ ❋ ❋

Belonthar beckoned the children forward until they surrounded Ben Artemit.

Ben's chest constricted. He shivered, not only from the

wind but from the ever-widening hollow inside. He'd no idea how much harm he'd done when he'd winked the dinosauroids out of existence.

This whole time, he hadn't been facing his childhood monsters. He *was* the childhood monster.

"I must admit, Artemit, I struggle to understand what this must be like for you," Belonthar said. He walked around Ben, tracing a finger on his skull. "I guess what I *can* understand is how you buried your head in the sand for so long about the monstrosity of what you'd done so you wouldn't have to face it. I can see versions of myself that *might* have done the same thing."

Whenever Belonthar passed next to one of the children, they grew sharper, their flickering slowing as though Belonthar's realness momentarily transferred to them.

"This is the same thing you're going to do to us, Belonthar!" Kitt shouted. "Ben didn't know the consequences. You do, and you're *still* continuing!"

She struggled at the far end of the balcony, her arms outstretched. Merthab blocked her path to Ben, and swatted furiously at an invisible wall protecting Kitt.

Ben batted Belonthar's arm away.

They glared at each other, neither flinching.

"Yes, I am going to do the same," Belonthar said. "But unlike you, Artemit, I'm going to fully face my actions. I'm not going to hide from them; I will accept them. I will bear the guilt, and grieve for what was necessary to tip the scales. This is more than you ever did for us.

"Also unlike you, Artemit, I have watched these children suffer between existence and unreality, more than any other creature. So I will appreciate what is happening to human children, more than you ever will in the brief time you're spending now. All you're experiencing is a fraction of their suffering."

Ben knew that part already. His mind had already begun travelling down long timelines, trying and failing to fully understand what these children had endured.

At his hand.

"Ben, listen to me!" Kitt shouted. "Their suffering does not justify condemning the entire human race to the same fate. You know this. There are children, real children living at this very moment, who will have everything stolen from them."

Yes, Ben thought.

He had a duty to humanity. He wouldn't give up without a fight. He just wished it didn't have to be against... these children. Part of him wanted to lash out at Belonthar, but he feared what the collateral damage might do to the young ones.

He would fight. It might eat him up inside, but he would fight. He just wasn't sure yet *how.*

"*These* children had everything snatched away!" Belonthar snapped.

"Yes!" Merthab roared in agreement.

"You are trying to create a moral distinction that doesn't exist," Belonthar continued. "Stop it! Just stop it!

"I've offered this lesson to you as a final treaty, but if you continue learning nothing from it then I will dispense with the kindness I have left for you."

"Kindness?" Ben snapped. "You call terrorizing a young boy like you did *kindness*?" His voice shook with countless childhood memories.

"Still kinder than what you did," Belonthar snarled.

"You can't claim the moral high ground, Belonthar," Kitt said. "Just look at the tactics you've used throughout all our encounters. You knew what you were doing. You tried to manipulate us. You lied, threatened, coerced. It says a lot when your most trusted assistant is a miserable creature like Merthab."

As Kitt spoke, she stepped forward, shoving with invisible force toward Merthab, who shimmered and stumbled. Her voice grew more powerful, and she pushed past Merthab.

"Is this really the best your civilization has to offer? Because if it is, then I don't think you deserve to be real. Before, I might have argued for finding another way, but the more I see of your actions, the more I'm convinced you are not worth the weight of atoms in your body."

The children scattered, fleeing back through the apertured door. Kitt rushed next to Ben, while Belonthar and Merthab pressed against the opposite railing. The power and menace in Kitt's words shook the balcony.

"Ben," she whispered, "you can't change the past. Remember, we don't know if you knew the dinosauroids would no longer exist when you made your decision so long ago. The best we can do is make better choices *now*. And right now, we need to fight to save the human race."

With Belonthar farther away, the surroundings blurred, while Kitt's face and voice were crystal clear. Behind her, though, Belonthar and Merthab were gathering strength, pushing off the railing and wading through the temporary force field Kitt had erected.

"You're right, Kitt," he said. "We'll fight them together."

As he spoke, he wanted to take back the words. He wanted to take back so much. So many people had been brought into this because of him, between Turen, Allan, Kitt, Tamika, and probably others he wasn't aware of.

He knew he had awakened the Chooser powers within both Kitt and Turen. He knew it the same way he felt the cries of all the dinosauroids in this realm tingling on his skin. His unconscious desire *not* to be a Chooser had inadvertently created more. It had all started with him.

Seeing and feeling the small dinosauroids, haunted as much as he'd been as a child, made Ben's chest ache. As Kitt said, that was the past—he had to do better *now*.

"I don't want to hurt those children any more than I already have," he said. "And I don't want you to get hurt."

"Stop it," Kitt said. "We're in this together. The kids scattered—it's just us now."

"No," Belonthar said, closer. "You can't hide from your guilt, Artemit."

Belonthar let out a high-pitched, two-tone chitter, and the children came scurrying out again. He gave barking orders, and they moved under his direction.

Merthab, meanwhile, had his arms raised above his head. The causeway behind him curled up like the tail of a scorpion. He brought his arms forward, and the causeway split in two enormous spears that sailed toward Ben and Kitt.

Ben lifted his arms and instinctively summoned growth out of the glass to shield them. Roots formed, then trees that shot up rapidly. He gasped and stopped when they threatened to knock the children over the balcony rail. The trees halted into mere stumps that stood no chance of blocking anything.

He and Kitt jumped out of the way as the spears tore through the floor of the balcony and into the building behind them.

The blow also shattered Kitt's focus, and she dropped the wall holding Merthab back. She reached for Ben, but Merthab tackled her. Shards of glass rained beneath them, while the building behind creaked and groaned.

"Kitt!" Ben shouted. Merthab was sprinting off with her, waving his hand and making a new causeway appear as he leaped onto it.

Buildings shifted. A deafening rumble drowned out everything. Children moved in to surround Ben, while the causeway jolted. He tried to edge around the children and focus on summoning a wall to stop Merthab, but the children continually bumped into him and broke his concentration.

Dirty tricks, Belonthar, he thought. *You're using them as a distraction.*

"Face me, Artemit!" Belonthar shouted. "And face your guilt!"

"Not without her," Ben snapped, seizing a moment of calm to leap onto the railing and sprint along the edge to get past the hordes of children.

The perilous depth below sent his mind reeling, but he clung to the need to save Kitt, focusing on where his feet needed to land.

He cleared the children and jumped to the next causeway. A chunk of the building to his right tore away and sliced through the bridge ahead, leaving a wide chasm.

Merthab took Kitt through one translucent door, blurring but staying visible.

Kitt had been absolutely right. They were in this together.

And she was right about another thing—none of this was real.

"There's a bridge *here!*" Ben shouted, and wooden planks slammed down beneath his feet. They were shaky and started to split, but he had enough time to race across and into the building before joining the destruction behind.

A thousand windows shattered behind him. He ignored them and pushed ahead, along another glass causeway that twisted underfoot, threatening to catapult him or shatter.

He threw down more wooden planks that straightened the curl and gave him enough time to cross and go through the door.

More windows appeared ahead. Merthab and Kitt were at least three windows deep.

"Shield!" he shouted, forming a round slice of a tree trunk on his arm, with a spike in the centre. He shattered the glass as he went through. Kitt seemed to be getting farther away, buried in more layers of glass.

He smashed through another wall, then another. He ran on a long causeway that seemed to have an endless series of window barriers.

He ran, smashed, and ran.

Kitt was alone now, banging on the glass and shouting wordless cries for him to hurry up.

I'm coming, Kitt, he thought.

The gap between them finally started closing. He was

making progress, barging through the glass faster than the dinosauroids could make it.

Kitt looked like she was shouting, but the sound was still faint. Finally, a dozen glass layers later, he heard her:

"Ben! Get out of there! They've got you!"

Ben blinked. For a moment, the scene flickered, and he wondered if he could trust his eyes.

The doubt caused a shower of glass to rain down. Walls crumbled on all sides.

He blinked again. He was strapped to a black iron table, thick metal clasps around his ankles, wrists, torso, and head. Something sharp dug into his neck.

He couldn't move.

He was still on one of the many glass causeways, but totally restrained.

Above him, smiling, Merthab drew a silver knife across Ben's skull. A moment later, flowing blood turned his vision red. Sharp pain lanced through the cut. Ben tried to struggle: nothing.

Nothing—exactly what would be left of humanity if he didn't get out of the dinosauroids' trap.

CHAPTER FORTY-ONE

Shattering

The chill wind cut deeper than The Entangled Man had ever felt in the natural world. His forearms cramped in less than fifty metres, still far from the distant blue light at the peak.

This journey is only in my mind, he thought, but the words didn't stick.

He lost his grip and fell.

He caught an edge a few terrifying metres below, stomach heaving in his throat.

It took excruciating effort to pry his fingers loose and reach higher. The wind rocked him. Snow whirled like a thousand angry thoughts. The distant blue light vanished.

The Entangled Man clung to the hope that the cold light was still up there, somewhere.

Icy fingers snaked through his veins.

I accept it. He acknowledged the pain, gave it all his attention. He shivered.

He'd been thrust into a place, into a time, that wouldn't have him.

I accept that, too.

Laced in the screaming wind were the derision of his parents, the scorn of passersby in Vancouver streets, and the condescension of Kramer just before torture began anew.

The Entangled Man had tried to leave it all behind, but there were indelible marks at his core. He would carry them with him, perhaps forever.

I accept them.

One hand. One foot. One after another.

He crawled over the edge; he'd reached the top.

The storm abruptly ceased. The Entangled Man lay on his back, gasping.

Light shone overhead, but it wasn't the blue he'd seen before. Up here, it was more of an orange-yellow sliced by sharp spires running to the top of the world. Yellow haze enveloped everything.

The sprawl defied logic, being far larger than the mountaintop seemed capable of supporting. Yet here it was, a spider-web of streets linked together, growing denser with dinosauroids closer to the centre of it all.

The Entangled Man stood and moved in. At the centre must be Ben and Kitt.

Dinosauroid families huddled together. Parents tried to quiet the moans of desperate children who couldn't understand their chaotic world. Faces lined with the worries of the next year, the next month, the next day.

The next second.

The Entangled Man's view shook. He stumbled.

A busy urban street surrounded him, bustling with humans threading their way through each other's spaces like diverting rivulets of a stream.

The people didn't occupy the same space as the dinosauroids had, however. It wasn't a matter of choosing a being's human version or their dinosauroid version.

The scene jolted back to the dinosauroid version, the buildings shifting and stretching.

The Entangled Man knew Ben and Kitt had been here. He

felt it as he sensed the other dinosauroids could, in the path of certainty that hung like a cloud. Dinosauroid crowds clustered around a line snaking through the streets. They huddled in these spaces like shivering children around a campfire.

The closer he got, the more the dinosauroids stared. He seemed an anomaly, a bringer of neither certainty nor chaos. A smell they couldn't quite place.

The scene flicked back to the urban sprawl, filled with bustling humans avoiding The Entangled Man but otherwise taking no notice of him.

At first, the reactions from the two worlds seemed stark in contrast, but as the scenes continued to alternate, The Entangled Man glimpsed resonances.

Beings struggling to do their best for loved ones. Beings trying to make it to the next patch of stable ground.

The farther he followed the trail, into the sharp-cornered building and up the spiralling ramp that waved like water, the less he saw of the human vision. As he spent more time with them in their world, the dinosauroids reached out to him.

They asked things of him. Perhaps they wanted him to leave behind a bit more certainty in his wake than Kitt and Ben had, but The Entangled Man could make no clear sense of their words, only a broad stroke of their intent.

He crested the top of the ramp to an apertured door with radial spokes like encircling jaws. He pushed through.

He emerged to a whipping wind and for a moment, he thought he'd returned to the icy cliff far below.

No. He was somewhere far, far different.

Many dinosauroids, large and small, lined a mosaic glass balcony on either side and shielded him from the wind's full onslaught. Many of them were much younger than any of the dinosauroids trailing behind him.

The balcony joined with glass causeways joining all the surrounding buildings together.

His world rocked and he stared at a playground of

human children giggling, screaming and running.

The world rocked back and The Entangled Man fell flat against the balcony glass. Many of the dinosauroid children pressing against the balcony's edges gasped the same way he did.

Had they just taken a similar reality-bending trip? From their huddled body language, he guessed that whatever was happening was something these children had to deal with often.

The trail of Kitt and Ben snaked through the sky where seams of causeways and buildings had been torn and stitched together. All along the way, refugee dinosauroids had emerged, seeking new homes.

By the way Kitt and Ben's trail dispersed, The Entangled Man knew reaching them meant journeying through a lot of dinosauroid pain and misery.

He stormed along the causeway, ignoring the pawing hands and keeping his gaze straight ahead. He couldn't shut out the periphery, however, the scenes of children waving their arms at phantoms, carrying out one-sided arguments with themselves.

He had been there once—no, many times.

In his youth, when he'd been too frightened to argue with this father, and instead carried on lonely arguments in the corner of his room. As an adult, when he'd taken this tradition into the streets, even when his father was nowhere near.

The Entangled Man recognized the signs of their long-term suffering from afar.

He stopped, swaying on the rough glass patchwork.

A gaggle of nearby children finished wrestling demons. Their hands, dizzying quantum flickers, slowly steadied. They blinked through translucent eyes like tadpoles who had just grown limbs.

They shrank from him, pressing against the glass so hard their flickering merged into a two-dimensional mosaic.

The image reminded him of what he'd wanted to do so many times when his father had yelled at him. He had pressed into the walls, hoping to vanish between the cracks.

Now he was perceived as the same oppressive force his father had been.

No.

The Entangled Man sank to his knees and spread his arms. "I won't hurt you," he said, though in his heart he wondered how he could stay true to these words while remaining loyal to his friends.

There must be a way.

He closed his eyes and imagined a wooden jungle gym on a bed of sand, surrounded by a lush garden, something that would weather the quakes of this realm.

He opened his eyes to a human playground. The dinosauroid children chittered and shrieked, their sounds echoing off nearby spires.

After a few tentative prods, they explored the playground.

The Entangled Man smiled, ready to continue, then hesitated. He'd helped the children, but at what cost?

He pictured the maw of reality that had been eaten away in the Quantix lab. Had he just done that, in order to make a playground for these children?

The dinosauroid children crowded around him, just as the adults had on his way up here.

If he had to destroy these children in order to save Ben and Kitt—in order to save humanity—he wasn't sure if he could.

But he couldn't wipe out his own species, either.

* * *

Fury boiled from the base of Ben's spine, rising fast to meet with the blood flowing down his forehead.

The dinosauroids had tricked him. They had walled him off within a nested reality, an imaginarium. They'd done it by giving him a repeated task he would always buy into: that of saving Kitt.

Now he was cornered, about to have his brain removed by an animal like Merthab. The operating table was in the open air on one of the glass causeways.

Ben wanted to tear out of the shackles, put his hands on Merthab's throat and show him he was just as capable of ferocity.

No movement came. He was paralyzed from the needle stabbing the base of his neck.

None of this is real, he told himself. He rolled the words over, but they changed nothing. The dinosauroids had grown so powerful that will alone could not stop them.

"Belonthar says we owe you gratitude for giving us options," Merthab said, twirling a scalpel. "He says it'll be good to have two brains to try. If yours doesn't work, I'm sure Kitt's will. To be honest, I'm going to enjoy cutting open her brain whether we need to... or not."

The table quivered beneath Ben. Every atom in his body revolted against Merthab.

Killer instinct? Ben thought. *You're not the only one who has it, Merthab.*

Concentrating rage into a single movement, he jerked his neck. He felt the needle bend and snap, releasing the pressure on his spinal cord. The sudden movement made Merthab's blade cut deeply into his left ear.

With the needle out of his neck, Ben could move again, and he focused on that instead of the pain radiating from his mangled earlobe.

Nothing can restrain me.

He tore his hands free from the iron clasps. He jerked out of the way of Merthab's finger-claws as they tried to grab his head. Ben snapped off another restraint and it grew red hot in his grasp, moulding into a dagger.

He jabbed it hard into Merthab's side, who howled and gouged Ben's arm.

Searing pain. Ben stumbled back, barely avoiding Merthab's follow-up swipes.

Ben darted around the edge of the torture slab, then kicked it hard. It exploded out of its anchors and knocked Merthab down.

"Belonthar is already tasting Kitt's blood, Artemit," Merthab hissed, standing and wiping blood from his chin. "You can't stop it. Give up. We are stronger than you. We always have been."

Merthab raised his arms. Portions of the glass buildings around him tore away, forming six spears. He launched them at Ben.

Ben put out his hand, letting the first one tear into it. He embraced the pain, focused all of his attention on it as spear after spear came at him. He shifted, aligning himself so that each spear impacted on the same spot, burying into each other.

A few moments later, Ben had a large spike cantilevering out of his hand. A bloody tip jutted toward him, while a large, conical base extended toward Merthab. The force of each impact had nearly split the bones in his hand, but he'd held them together even as the tissue was pulverized.

Ben lowered the spike, which looked like a large stalagmite, until its base knocked against the glass surface.

"That's m—monstrous," Merthab said, eyes shifting between the glass spike and Ben's face. "How—"

Ben twitched his hand violently, launching a tremor from the centre of impact from the spike and the glass. The glass spike sang but did not shatter. The rippling wave, however, cracked into the glass beneath Merthab's feet.

A split-second later, the surface shattered, and Merthab was falling, shrieking.

Merthab tried to bring in a platform to land on, using his influence in this realm to pull bridges out of the surrounding buildings.

Ben heaved and rocketed his spike down. It left a trail of glass in a cylinder in its wake. It caught up and overtook Merthab, obliterating the balconies Merthab created to catch him.

The pillar buried into the rock far below. Merthab was in a giant straw, tumbling, scratching in vain at the sides as he fell toward the stalagmite Ben had planted.

Merthab accelerated right to the moment of impact. The spike tore through his torso and split him open, the sound of cracking bones echoing up the glass.

Merthab twitched once, then his head lolled back, tongue hanging limply from his mouth.

He was dead.

Ben took in gasping breaths, clutching at his mangled hand as the pain finally pushed its way through. He shuffled to the balcony railing and leaned against it, closing his eyes and shuddering.

He still had to save Kitt. He would push through the pain to find her and finish this.

"Your savagery has reached a new level," Belonthar said, his voice a low growl.

Ben's eyes snapped open. Belonthar paced toward him, surrounded by a throng of children. A winding trail of glass and more children followed behind. With each step Belonthar took, he repaired the destruction of the causeway.

"Where's Kitt?" Ben asked in a husky voice. He straightened and let go of his hand, wincing as it failed to move.

"Always centred on your own," Belonthar replied. He stopped and stared down the long glass tube to the ground where Merthab had been impaled.

"I'm surprised you are even capable of hearing us over the trumpet of your own needs," Belonthar went on. He shook his head. "You have the power to choose. And this is how you use it. You could've chosen to blink him out of existence, to make him die painlessly, but instead you did this."

"I had no choice," Ben replied, his voice hardening.

"Yes, you did. You know you did."

Belonthar closed his eyes and pressed a hand against the glass.

"Did you also know Merthab is a brother and an uncle? I could prove it to you, have them come out and show themselves, but I won't do them more harm by propping them into a spectacle. As if the constant pain and uncertainty of this realm were not torture enough already."

Ben opened his mouth to reply, then hesitated. Had he let his rage carry too far? Had there been another option with Merthab?

No, he decided.

"You know my power over you has diminished," Ben said. "I had to fight Merthab using the tools you'd left me, Belonthar. You can't pretend I'm an omnipotent chooser only when it suits you. I fought back against Merthab with his own savagery. Follow your own wisdom: stop trying to create distinctions that don't exist."

"In that case, maybe I should do the same to Kitt?" Belonthar asked, tilting his head.

Ben's fury rose, and he formed the ground into spikes. He wanted to launch them at Belonthar, but there were far too many children nearby, children who'd suffered enough already.

"Where is she?" Ben shouted.

"She is alive and well, but separated from you," Belonthar said. "My actions, unlike yours, are driven out of necessity, not cruelty. Though I confess, Artemit, that my resolve to show restraint has all but evaporated."

Belonthar approached with children on all sides, and Ben was forced to withdraw his spikes. Soon he and Belonthar stood metres away from each other. Belonthar shifted and ducked between the children.

Ben glimpsed Belonthar's wrinkles, his lines of worry, pain and frustration. They seemed obvious now in contrast to the other dinosauroids in this realm. While every being here had experienced the pain of constant quantum uncertainty, Belonthar had tried to lead them through it all, tried to hold a society together in spite of everything.

The weight of it showed in the larger number of vein fractures along his skin, in the black cracks along his teeth, and in the faint brown creeping in from the edges of his yellow eyes.

On the ground, dinosauroids had gathered around Merthab's body, and on the causeways, more were coming out and staring.

Every part of Ben's body ached for this to be over. He didn't want to hurt the children. He didn't want to hurt anyone else. He'd already taken enough from the dinosauroids. He had to fight for humanity's survival, but how much further could he go, and still live with himself?

Ben didn't want to admit that all he had to do now to save the real world of humans was to kill Belonthar. He kept the thought pushed to the back of his mind. Could he actually kill Belonthar? Yet how could he *not* try to do so?

"Give me your brain, Artemit," Belonthar said, leaning from behind one of the children. "You don't have to condemn your race. You just have to relinquish and I will finish it. Humanity has had their time. Let us have ours."

Ben stared at Belonthar for a long while. Faint moans from below mixed with the wind threading through superspires. The blue sky was tinged with wisps of yellow mist. The air smelled of formaldehyde and blood, the taste sticking to Ben's tongue. Children stared at him, some shivering, many more blinking in and out of existence.

He had to decide now: save the real world of humans and sacrifice his soul by murdering Belonthar along with the children around him, or surrender and condemn the human race—and everyone he loved—to non-existence.

✻ ✻ ✻

Kitt Bell stood in the meeting room of the Jupiter chamber beside a long table and a dozen chairs. In the middle of the table, a screen and large red beacon sat ready for time travel experiments.

It was the same as it had been the day this whole nightmare had begun.

That wasn't quite true. It was the same, with one important difference.

The walls were mirrors, and reflected in every direction were an infinite number of duplicate rooms, where copies of Ben Artemit and Al Turen walked about, arguing as red beacons flashed at random intervals.

Kitt called out but Ben and Turen made no sign of hearing her.

She pressed her hands against the mirror edge. It rippled. Leaning, she pushed her hands through, then stepped the rest of the way with her whole body.

When she pulled her head through, she arrived to find the room empty. The apparitions of Ben and Turen were gone. They were still in other far-away scenes of the room, where she could hear them faintly arguing over whether a signal had been received.

She tried again, moving faster. As soon as she stepped through, they were gone again.

This horrible illusion held freedom and constriction in superposition, making her feel spread out and choked at the same time. She put a hand to her forehead.

I haven't gone back in time, she thought. *This is an illusion built from possibilities. It's not real.*

She called out to Ben, but the mirrors swallowed her voice.

How did I get here?

She mentally retraced her steps. Merthab had taken her. They'd sailed behind layers of glass, and then... he'd released her. Through the layers she'd seen Ben lain down and restrained.

Then Belonthar had dragged her through winding corridors.

She'd blinked, and then she'd found herself here. Were the mirrors just like Ben's panes of glass? Could she smash through them?

She made a run for it, leaping through the mirrors like an olympic runner doing hurdles. A few moments later, she was panting, and there was no sign of any progress.

"No! No!" she shouted.

If she didn't get out soon, the dinosauroids would trap Ben. He was too susceptible to their influence after having held them back and endured their onslaught.

A lush garden and playground popped into existence in her peripheral vision, knocking out several copies of the room and bulging halfway into others. Dinosauroid children leapt back.

At the centre of it all stood Allan Gerrold.

"Allan!" she called.

He didn't hear her, but she saw him. He was real—he had to be.

Now she had a link to the outside. How or why, she didn't have a clue, but she had to follow it.

She ran the swirling beacons bathing her in red as she heard a dizzying repetition: *No signal sent. Signal received. No signal sent. No signal received.*

The playground faded, but she grabbed at the edges of the mirror as they closed in.

"This... isn't... real!" she shouted.

The wall tore open, and she was out, on a causeway, back in the noxious haze of the dinosauroid realm.

She felt Allan's presence. It wasn't a trick; he'd come to help them.

She felt Ben's presence again, too.

He was in trouble.

Far ahead, a dinosauroid lay impaled on a spike, and crowds had gathered. It was in the same direction as Ben.

Kitt ran from causeway to causeway, criss-crossing her way from one superstructure to the next. Dinosauroids came out in droves. She shoved past them, keeping her attention on Ben's presence.

Hold on, Ben.

She sped around the edge of a spire, then was forced to slow and press through a tightly gathered crowd. She edged through a few groups, then saw scores of child dinosauroids ahead. They surrounded Ben and Belonthar, blocking all passage in or out.

"Ben!" she shouted.

Upon seeing her, Belonthar snarled and whipped tendrils of glass down in ropes. Ben held up his arms and created shields to block them, which shattered and regrew with each blow.

Belonthar's assault accelerated, a few of the whips breaking through and wearing Ben down. He winced, and though his face remained determined, Kitt worried if it was only a matter of time before Belonthar broke him.

Ben would fight, but he wouldn't harm the children. Belonthar was using them as his shield.

Kitt shoved and screamed at the crowding dinosauroids, but they didn't move. With every cut from Belonthar, his brethren gained more solidity.

Dinosauroids pressed in behind Kitt.

Tears poured down her cheeks. She had to do something. How to give Ben the strength to fight back when he had no options left?

Of course.

It came to her in an instant, perhaps because she felt so close to losing absolutely everything.

"Ben!" she shouted. "This is *our* future!"

She held up her arms and held a vision firmly in mind.

A child.

A baby girl.

She had Ben's thoughtful eyes, Kitt's blonde hair and

thin nose. When she smiled, their baby girl wore the same inquisitive expression Kitt and Ben shared. Her gaze made troubles evaporate.

Kitt hugged their baby close, then turned her toward Ben, holding her up. She radiated a faint light in a thin sheen. The dinosauroids parted, gasping and chittering.

"Ben, this is the reality they will destroy," Kitt said. "Don't let them do it! Dig deep and fight back! You have more power than you think. You're in control. You can get Belonthar without hurting the children. Separate the now from what you *know* to be true."

❊ ❊ ❊

The Entangled Man saw the child several blocks away, and whispered a thank you for the perspective and clarity she granted him.

He strode toward the beacon of her radiant white light. He focused on his breathing, the only way he could keep steady about what he might have to do, and how he might do it.

A pack of dinosauroid children followed behind. He didn't have the heart to turn them away. Who was he to take this moment from them? Just seconds earlier they'd been nearly catatonic. Now they moved. They took action. They expressed agency.

What they marched for, or toward... The Entangled Man didn't know. Did they hope he would save them? If so, it was a false hope. But even a false hope was better than what they'd had before.

Separate the now from what you know to be true.

Kitt's words echoed across the urban chasms of the dinosauroid world.

Separate...

The worlds of humanity and the dinosauroids were entangled. They had been entangled before the age of the dinosaurs. There was no other way to exist than for one to be real, and for the other to be purely quantum mechanical.

The long timeline stretched back further than The Entangled Man could imagine. Separating the two worlds was impossible, because the history ran backward with so many twists, turns and knots that disentanglement would mean cutting the threads and losing vast portions of each world altogether.

The integrity of each reality could not be sustained with so much missing. On their own, each would fall apart.

The worlds linked along lines of possibility, with actual existence infinitely far away at one end, and a world of possibilities with zero probability of existence infinitely far away at the other end. Each world had its own line intimately bound with that of the other. To move a world from one extreme to the other required pivoting the whole system like an incredible seesaw. To pivot *only* one end, to bend the system without breaking all that bound it together, would require a force greater than anything he could imagine.

The Entangled Man drew closer to Kitt and Ben. He squeezed through crowds of dinosauroids.

He wished he could ask Ben and Kitt for help. He wished he had time to discuss the philosophy, the theories with them.

Maybe Marlon Kramer, the mastermind behind the creation of The Entangled Man, might have had some insight as to how to reverse the entanglement process. But The Entangled Man's creation had been an anomaly among a long list of failures.

If there was a universe where Kramer actually gave up his lust for power and helped save the two worlds, it had the same probability as flipping a hundred coins and having them all land on their edges.

The Entangled Man passed through the throng. Ben and Belonthar were surrounded by dinosauroid children. Belonthar had his arms up toward Kitt, who stood several feet away with her child held outstretched. White waves billowed against yellow haze, signs of an invisible wall between her and Belonthar.

"I'm here!" The Entangled Man shouted. "I'm with you, Kitt, Ben!"

He looked down at one of the children who blocked his way, staring from an unnervingly stable form. The Entangled Man couldn't trust himself to read dinosauroid faces, but he swore the child was giving him a pleading look.

Separate...

No. Kitt, Ben and Belonthar were at loggerheads, and there was no telling how long they could maintain their strength.

No separation. They had to join forces before there was nothing left.

*   *   *

"Separate the now from what you know to be true!" Kitt shouted again.

Ben heard it in a gap between Belonthar's assaults, the sound coming through sharp, lancing pain all over his body.

He felt someone else's presence in addition to Kitt's. Had he heard Allan?

His head pulsed with a low throb. He locked gazes with Kitt, and then the baby bathed in thin white light. He didn't need to be told who it was.

Their child.

The combination of both of them that offered the possibility of bringing out the best of both, maybe some of the bad, or maybe something else entirely.

If Ben didn't fight hard, using every last bit of his power, their baby would never grow up to make the choice for herself —make *all* the choices for herself.

This wasn't just their child. She represented every child of the human race. The future that would be winked out.

Tears lined Kitt's cheeks. Her lips trembled from the sustained, solitary effort.

She wasn't alone anymore. The Entangled Man had come, and was here, somewhere.

"Ben," she said, her voice thin, "this is the future. This is what's real."

Ben would fight for that future, whether or not he lived to see it.

"This is what's real," he said.

She was not alone. She had him, too.

"Yes!"

Belonthar thinks he's in control, Ben thought. *But he isn't. He's tried to make me think otherwise. I can control this. They started in my mind, and they're still confined there.*

We'll fight you, Belonthar, and at worst, we'll end at a stalemate. But The Entangled Man's here now, and with his help... who knows what we'll achieve.

Ben raised his arms. Waves of energy pulsed from him, rocking the glass and repelling the children.

He kept a bubble around Belonthar, who called for the children to come back.

Soon Belonthar stood alone.

"Artemit!" Belonthar shouted. "Do not turn away from your legacy! Let justice guide your actions."

"No, Belonthar," Ben said. "This back and forth, this tit-for-tat exchange is not justice. It is not reconciliation.

"No. We'll find another way, somehow, to correct the wrongs of the past."

"That's it!" Kitt shouted. "Yes, Ben, yes!"

Belonthar was silent for a moment. He shot a glance over his shoulder at Merthab's impaled body down below. His arms quivered.

"No!" he thundered.

His voice echoed up and down the spires, amplifying as though he lashed the word at them. "No! No! No!"

Some of the dinosauroids cheered in their ear-piercing

chitters. Others shrank, bowing in deference to their leader who'd kept so many of them alive for as long as he had.

"When will that be, Artemit? When will justice arrive? Who will devote themselves to such a task? You lied to us all before, and you're lying to us now. As soon as you step back into your world, you're going to forget everything you promised. Your words are hollow. Your power is already weakening, and your resolve and commitment to us is, too. You don't deserve this power to choose. The universe is correcting this imbalance. Humanity doesn't deserve existence over us. If you won't make us real, then you don't deserve reality, either."

Belonthar reached toward Kitt and the outstretched baby, then closed his fist. The yellow haze pressed against the white radiance, swirling in a dense fog until the baby was completely obscured.

Kitt stumbled back, jerking her hands away as though they'd been burned. Before her, a dense cloud of yellow hung in the air where the baby had been.

"No!" Ben shouted. With a wave of his arm, the yellow haze spun outward and vanished, revealing their baby again, who was now crying. Ben rotated his hands and wove a spiral thread of tree roots up from the ground, weaving around and cradling their girl. The wood repelled the yellow mist, and soon she calmed, closing her eyes and laying down her head.

Ben waved his arm once more, and the nest of roots spun down and away, carrying their baby girl to safety.

"No!" Belonthar shouted, his voice quavering. "You don't deserve this power." He paused, his whole body vibrating, before he screamed, "Attack! Everyone, charge!"

A roar spread like a seismic wave. Dinosauroids surged forward and clawed at Kitt, leaving red gashes along her legs and arms.

Ben knocked her out of their grasp by willing a tree to sprout beneath her, propelling her above the scrambling masses.

Belonthar launched at Ben, shards of glass gathering on his limbs into spikes. Ben formed a wooden shield and blocked most of them, but one drove through his shoulder. He sank to his knees.

The causeways rang and shook. Ben and Belonthar were pressed against the surface as the causeways launched into the sky.

Allan, Ben thought. *Thank you. This is what we need.*

He scrambled up, tearing the glass painfully out of his shoulder.

He and Belonthar swung at each other, forming weapons of glass and wood that grew and struck like thunder.

The clash of wills exploded and sent them flying backward. Ben cushioned himself with trees and bushes, while Belonthar formed a glass slide that carried him into a graceful spiral.

Kitt knocked Belonthar off-balance by sending waves of white mist weaving in and around the glass. Belonthar roared, furious that he'd been separated from his brethren below.

Belonthar shielded himself with a thick glass shell. Ben and Kitt joined forces to entwine wind-whipped branches pressing in on Belonthar's shell.

There was the briefest pause like an inhalation, then the sky darkened.

Ben looked above to see spires snapping off and tipping downward. They fractured into a billion raining glass shards blotting out the sun.

Ben grew a forest, straining his mind to fill the space with the most dense rain forest and tree cover he could imagine. He wove the branches together into a mesh shelter.

Glass hammered the shield in a sound like a thousand boot stomps. Holes punched through. Kitt pushed the stray shards away with wind, but the gashes in the forest canopy were growing too wide.

Ben sprinted toward her.

Kitt screamed as a spike tore through her leg.

"Kitt!" Ben shouted, reaching and wrapping his arms around her. She shivered, clutching at the shard in her thigh. She oozed blood from countless other cuts.

Ben lost concentration as his vision blurred. A spike tore the rest of his left ear off. He cried out, putting his hands above his head and forming enormous finger-like branches to shield them.

The sound of growing, twining wood dwindled next to the onslaught of splintering glass knives.

Ben couldn't keep up. The hailing glass would breach in moments.

"We're not really here," Ben said, pressing his forehead against Kitt's. "Where are we, Kitt?"

"We're driving in the forest," Kitt replied, tears streaming down her face.

The torrent rumbled in their ears, centimetres away.

"Allan!" Ben cried, remembering his friend. He wished suddenly that now, at the end of everything, they should all be fighting together, to the very end.

He sensed The Entangled Man's presence, far below, struggling against Belonthar's bombardment. Ben's mind feeling like a stretched band about to snap, he willed roots to grow up and around The Entangled Man, concentrating every facet of his influence as a chooser around maintaining the nest around him, his friend, and his love.

The tremendous tides of energy from Belonthar's will shook him. Shattered glass filled the air with sand and wood chips. The Entangled Man was deep in meditation, Ben knew, and its importance rippled like raindrops on the surface of a tsunami.

Ben had to protect everyone, no matter what the effort leached from him. With every protective branch he willed to grow, he left more of himself behind.

He hoped it would be enough.

Glass needles punctured the air, the trees, and all sound. A vertical, shredding flood assaulted Ben's will.

* * *

The Entangled Man watched in horror as the dinosauroids attacked. Both sides had suffered so much.

The dinosauroids tried to close on him, but the children snapped protectively. The Entangled Man put up barriers to push everyone back. It took him several long moments to decide what to do, during which Ben and Kitt were nearly swarmed.

The Entangled Man launched the causeway into the air, selecting and reforming the glass around him and his friends. He couldn't differentiate between everything, though, and ended up carrying Belonthar and a few other dinosauroids on the platforms he pushed into the air.

At least now it was a fair fight. He left the children below, hoping they wouldn't suffer for their actions.

He sat and closed his eyes. He withdrew, picturing himself as a watcher sensing everything happening in the world around him, but unaffected by it.

He needed time. He just needed time.

The sky darkened with the shattered remnants of the superstructures, and came down raining death.

The Entangled Man's shields broke, and the shards sliced him. He convulsed, burning through a thousand cuts. There was nothing he could do to hold back such power, and he glimpsed a few seconds from now when his body would be a pulverized mess of meat and bones.

Roots shot up and formed a cocoon around him. There was only one person who could have done and sustained such protection. "Thank you, Ben," he whispered when he'd finally regained control of his breath.

The Entangled Man focused his thoughts alternately on Ben, Kitt and Belonthar. He whispered, "Kitt, Ben, I know what I have to do. And I know how to do it."

You saved me, Ben, but I still have to do this.

He gazed up, imagining beyond his protective cocoon to Belonthar in the sky, a dinosauroid pushed to the brink and filled with righteous anger. He continued, "Your time has finally come, Belonthar."

Now that he knew what he had to do, The Entangled Man's vision blurred. His form changed from a single body into two.

When his vision cleared, he occupied his two, true bodies, seated on the roots facing one another on either side of the cocoon. Each body gripped the hands of the other.

He was ready.

And he was real.

CHAPTER FORTY-TWO

World Made Real

B elonthar awoke in his angled bed, jerking out of its foam contours. He wiped cold sweat from his forehead, looking frantically around for Artemit and Kitt.

Instead, he was greeted by walls—real, unshifting walls —adorned with etchings of his family.

They depicted his wife and son, who'd been among the first victims to fall into formless and featureless identities when Artemit had tricked them all into non-existence.

The carvings, which Belonthar had tried to maintain every day for so long, now showed his huddled, smiling family more clearly than ever.

Could it be true?

The tension in his body vanished. He'd lightened, but only by hollowing, letting everything go but forestalling hope's entry. It was too early for hope. He wouldn't accept the evidence before him until he was absolutely sure.

If it was a dream, or one of Artemit's tricks, Belonthar couldn't go on.

His feet pressed against solid ground. Real, solid ground. He ran his shoulder against the wall.

He didn't push through it. There were boundaries, definition.

Clarity.

He bounded through the apertured door and out onto the balcony.

The sky shone a brilliant, clear blue. The superstructures around were varied, showcasing creativity and uniqueness particular to many different architects and engineers. Some were covered in painted murals, others wrapping, twisting and waving as they shimmered with solar panels following the sun. Colour gradients highlighted the spectrum of the world's pleasures.

They was so much variety in the city—vastly more beautiful than the repetitious, faceless monoliths they'd had in the would-be world, the only structures they could maintain.

In the streets below, people sang and swayed with a joyous melody. Along the sides of buildings, tethered by harnesses, acrobats flipped and bounced in choreographed synchrony.

Belonthar had nearly forgotten such celebrations could exist—*had* existed.

Do exist.

His eyes burned, but not from the noxious fumes that pervaded the would-be world.

This was real. This was all real.

Their world was real.

His son came barreling along the causeway toward him. Childish drawings and impressions dotted the path behind him.

"Dad!"

They embraced, and Belonthar soaked in every sensation, each chitter of his son's pleasure. He found no words to speak.

"Am I real? Am I really real?" his son asked.

"Yes," Belonthar said with a thick voice.

"Are you sure? Will it go away, or will it stay?"

Everything Belonthar had just seen was more detailed and beautiful than any illusion or falsehood could sustain. At least, any trick he could conceive. He still had lingering doubts, but he suspected those would always be there in some form, long-term trauma from lifetimes of barely existing.

"I'm sure," he said at last. "And it is here to stay, my son."

His son shook and jumped against him. Belonthar suspected his son was just as torn between the great feeling of finally having true contact with someone again, and the desire to leap and bound with all the energy that had been repressed by the would-be realm.

Eventually his son calmed, and they held each other in silence.

"Can we play gravity tag?" his son asked after some time.

Belonthar fought to gain control of the flood of emotions stifling movement. Another thing he'd forgotten— that there could be paralysis and uncertainty in the real world, too.

"I—I have some things I need to tend to first," he replied. "There is much... I need to check. Have you seen your mother?"

His son nodded and pointed back at their home. "She wouldn't let me wake you."

Belonthar went back inside, and found his wife in another room running her hands along the walls. They stared at one another, then embraced in silence. It was wonderful, but somewhat alien after how long it had been since they'd last touched. They shuddered, each wracked with emotions too powerful to articulate.

"I had no idea how much I'd lost," she whispered.

"I thought I knew. But I didn't, either."

After some time, Belonthar said, "I have to make sure everything's... running. Working. Flowing. There's too much. I don't know where to begin."

His wife nodded. "I will help, but I might need... some time."

"Of course. Take your time. It is yours now, my love."

Belonthar went into his study, then prepared a contact list of everyone he could think of, every government position and authority who would need to take up the mantle of responsibility once more.

The first on the list was Merthab. Belonthar was reminded of another truth of the real world—that it, too, could cause deep pain.

Merthab was nowhere to be found.

"I'm sorry, brother," he whispered into the air, knowing there would be no body, no trace of Merthab's existence, over which he could mourn. "I'm sorry you cannot be here to enjoy this."

He reminded himself of his commitment to grieving the sacrifices made to invoke this reality. He bent down on one knee and bowed his head, first for Merthab, then for all of humanity. As much as they'd struggled, and as much fury had ruled Belonthar in the end, it still didn't diminish what had happened to the humans.

But how *had* it really ended?

By the one they call Gerrold, Belonthar thought. He'd been aware of Gerrold as another Chooser. He'd planned to approach Gerrold once he'd dealt with Artemit and Bell. It seemed, however, that Gerrold had made the choice to resolve matters on his own.

I will honour all your sacrifices, Belonthar thought. *They will not be wasted, nor forgotten.*

He got up and continued contacting anyone and everyone who might have influence over societal infrastructure.

In one conversation after another, he realized everyone had regained their independence and capabilities. They were all falling back into routine, into their old roles, as though society hadn't collapsed, and as though their existence hadn't been wiped from the face of the universe.

Some time later, Belonthar sat staring into space. For the first time in as long as he could remember, he didn't have to worry about holding his world together. It would survive on its own.

He wouldn't have to carry the weight of the future on his shoulders.

He had no idea what to do with himself. Thankfully, his son came in, asking again about gravity tag.

"I'd nearly forgotten," Belonthar said. "Let's go. Get your mother."

As they ascended to the top of their superstructure, Belonthar looked again for signs of Merthab. He found nothing, not even a remnant of the destruction and grisly stalagmite he'd been impaled upon.

Belonthar allowed some of the guilt at what had happened to the humans wash over him.

"Artemit," Belonthar whispered, "I am sorry for you and your people. If only there were another way. But it is our time now."

It was devastating. But it had been the only way. It was one or the other, and humanity had had its turn. Perhaps one day Belonthar's society would elect to bring humanity back, to give them another turn in the cycle.

Only time would tell. For now, Belonthar basked in the warm glow of the sun, and the freedom of low gravity on the roof of the superstructure.

"You're chasing!" his son said, bouncing away. A moment later, his wife shrugged, grinned and followed suit.

Belonthar smiled. Dozens of other families were up here, too, bouncing playfully. On everyone's face was a dazed look as though every sensation threatened to overwhelm their senses.

The wind picked up, and for a moment Belonthar thought he saw a gathering of dust formed into the shape of a human. He rubbed his moist eyes, and the shape vanished.

He bounded after his wife and son, drinking in the sound of every laugh, the feel of air brushing on his skin, and every taste of the real.

* * *

Ben Artemit and Kitt Bell opened their eyes to purple, pink and orange colours twisting and blurring together.

Ben grasped frantically around and felt Kitt's hand. In the corner of his eye, she flickered. He gasped, wondering if these were the last certain breaths he would ever take.

He was in a would-be world, along with the rest of humanity.

This was how it had been, eons ago. The formless uncertainty settled in and Ben's mind reeled, recognizing the state immediately and repelling it with all his strength. His head pounded. His eyes rolled. He jerked and lost hold of Kitt.

Coloured swirls blanketed everything.

At this boundary between existence and non-existence, memories from both sides could trickle across.

These colours had been Ben's world once. These colours normally dominated the landscape, but they'd been pushed to the periphery the day he'd asked Belonthar to make the humans real.

Ben, like everything in the would-be realm, had been filled with uncertainty, barely knowing if he would survive the next month, day, year. The sameness, the average of the constant quantum flickering, made time immaterial.

Everyone blinked through every possible version of themselves, at once everything and nothing.

The dinosauroids had been a beacon in the dark, a guiding light providing assurance on an otherwise sightless voyage. Ben and many other humans had gravitated toward them like debris gathering into orbit to form Saturn's rings.

All Ben had known was that the dinosauroids possessed the firmness and reality he wanted for himself. For everyone.

Asking them hadn't been a scheme. It had been a plea, a beg for kindness on their part.

He hadn't known what effect it would have on the dinosauroids. He'd been incapable of imagining anything close to entanglement, let alone its implications.

Ben hadn't tricked the dinosauroids after all.

The realization should have filled him with relief, but instead he continued to jerk, fighting the steady fall into the would-be realm.

He hadn't tricked the dinosauroids, but he feared he'd forget that, along with just about everything else.

He was reverting into a quantum state of possibility, rather than actuality.

He thrashed and managed to catch sight of Kitt again. He locked his gaze on her, wanting to immortalize her in his mind before her form flickered into shapelessness.

If there was one thing he could hold in the would-be realm, let it be a memory of Kitt. And let her keep some of herself.

"Are we dead?" she whispered.

Her words echoed in Ben's ears. Definition spread from her form outward, filaments of clarity lighting up the surroundings like fireworks. The sound intensified into a ring that resonated and faded slowly until it seemed they were in a place now, blurred but possessing threads of lines and boundaries.

Tears filled Ben's eyes. Had she brought them back? It was too much to believe. Maybe this was a final torture from the dinosauroids.

Ben rubbed his eyes. The blurriness cleared. The brilliant colours resolved into the gradient of a setting sun. Sharp lines around them defined the car they'd been in when they last left the human world.

"Ben?" Kitt asked, her hand gently padding in search of him. She finally found and clutched his hand.

"I'm here," he whispered. "And I don't think we're dead."

Ben ran his other hand along the upholstery and vinyl insides of the car. Outside, pine and spruce trees surrounded them. The faint sound of chirping birds came through the windows.

"We made it," Kitt said. "We got away from them. Again."

Ben twisted and looked around, not trusting his senses. He winced, then lifted his sleeve to see a deep purple bruise on his shoulder, with veins spidering out.

It was where Belonthar had stabbed him.

His head felt fuzzy. Something teetered the edge of thought, something fundamental he was forgetting.

"Did you bring us here?" he asked.

"No," Kitt said. "I thought we were done for. Maybe Allan and Tamika did something."

Of course. Allan and Tamika.

The car seemed like it had been shut off for a while, the plastic cool to the touch. There was no sign of anyone else nearby. Behind them, a narrow dirt road wound its way through the forest.

"Oh my God, Ben!" Kitt cried. "Your ear!"

Ben fingered his head delicately. He felt a bump where his skull had been cut open, and the hair there was missing. He patted down the left side of his head toward his ear, and traced the contours of a gaping hole.

His ear was gone—completely gone.

On his left side, every sound came blurred and raw, as though he listened through a badly balanced speaker.

"I'm so sorry, Ben," Kitt said, hugging him. "They're never going to stop, are they?"

Ben closed his eyes and tried to focus on his breathing rather than his brain's new viewing window.

His thoughts drifted to shards of glass raining down upon him, and a thousand angry dinosauroids demanding retribution.

As these scenes passed through him, they evaporated like dew in the morning sun.

His fingertips tingled. Something wasn't right. Despite his internal resistance, he forced himself to picture his next encounter with the dinosauroids.

His mind went blank, as though the concept of the dinosauroids had lost tangibility, become an abstraction rather than an intimate and long-term association.

He searched for the memories of his time in the would-be realm, but those ran from his touch, fading into pinpricks as he tried to bring himself closer to them. He was left with nothing. His worries were misty, indistinct.

No. He wouldn't let himself forget. He clutched for memories of the dinosauroids, forcing his mind through the details of their encounters. Belonthar's reasoning, Merthab's anger. All the formless children.

It was a struggle, because his self-preservation instincts were to let the memories vanish. On top of that, there was another force at work, trying to unload the weight long strapped around his neck.

How long had it been since he'd been free from the burdens of tomorrow?

The last time he'd felt anything like this... had been before the experiments at Quantix.

Before the dinosauroids had come back.

"They're gone," he whispered.

"For now," Kitt replied.

"No. They're gone for good."

He wouldn't forget them, though. Not this time. He traced Belonthar's face in his mind.

Kitt pulled back and looked him in the eye. "How—"

"Search your feelings. Search your thoughts. Everything's changed now."

Kitt closed her eyes, then sucked in sharply. "You're right. It's like my memories of them are dissolving. My anxiety about their attacks... it's formless now."

Ben nodded soberly, knowing what this had cost. "Hold onto the memories if you can, Kitt. They deserve that much."

He was thankful, but he wouldn't allow himself to be jubilant. Not when such a vast world of beings had to forgo their existence for his.

I won't forget, Belonthar.

He owed them that, at the very least.

"But how?" Kitt asked.

"Allan," Ben replied. "He must've decided to stop them once and for all. Maybe with the strength of all our wills combined, that finally did it."

"Thank God for Allan," Kitt said.

"Yes."

Silence wrapped around them like a blanket. They held one another. They lay as still as grass after a thunderstorm, waiting for sun and time to thaw their cold weariness.

"Do you think our daughter will look like the baby?" Kitt asked.

"It's possible. But it won't matter, will it?"

"No. We'll love them all."

After a while, they got out and searched for Allan and Tamika. They explored the surrounding forest and long stretches of the dirt road. Wherever the car had taken Kitt and Ben, it was a good hiding place, for there wasn't a hint of another soul present.

Unfortunately, that meant they didn't find a hint of Allan or Tamika, either.

"I hope they're all right," Kitt said.

"Me too."

While they waited and watched the forest for Allan and Tamika's return, Ben collected and arranged a number of large rocks into a circle. He then spread smaller rocks around the periphery in radial lines, so that the whole formation looked like a sun.

It wasn't much. In fact, even as he made it, Ben vaguely pictured Belonthar rebuking him for carrying out such empty gestures and avoiding real action.

Ben had to do it though, in his own way.

When he finished, he and Kitt knelt in the centre of the formation and bowed.

"I'm sorry for everything I did to you," Ben said. "I'm sorry it had to end this way, and that you had to be made to suffer while humanity lived."

Tears poured down his cheeks. He wondered if the burden of knowing and remembering would allow him to see things through.

He had to.

"I'll continue my research," Ben went on. "I'll try to find a way for both of our worlds to be real, as soon as I can, so your suffering can end. Until that day, I will come back here every year to renew this pledge. I will remember."

They started the car and noted the GPS location of the refuge Allan and Tamika had given them. Then they left.

They headed home, because at home, they reasoned, they could better look for and help Allan and Tamika. They were also so bone-deep exhausted they hadn't the stamina to be fugitives anymore.

Besides, the world would be safe now regardless of what happened to them. It was time to face the music.

* * *

In the weeks after their return, Kitt and Ben learned Tamika was in police custody for the murders of Al Turen and Marlon Kramer. Ben was questioned for his connections to her, and tried his best to speak of her good qualities. The evidence supporting her guilt was pretty damning, however, and her lawyer was encouraging her to plead guilty.

With each day that passed, Ben's guilt over the dinosauroids eased, but the matter of Allan remained. He and Kitt hadn't been able to find Allan anywhere.

Allan was yet another sacrifice Ben had been unaware of, and in so many ways, was one he wished he would've made himself. Tamika, too, had made a great sacrifice, though she was still alive.

In the dark times, Kitt reminded him they should treasure and honour these sacrifices rather than despairing over them.

Neither Kitt nor Ben were investigated for their ties to Allan Gerrold. In fact, Allan's name never came up. It was as though he'd been completely erased.

Ben suspected, however, that Kramer's actions regarding The Entangled Man had been so secretive, and had violated so many human rights, that there was no way Quantix could pursue the issue. With Kramer's death, it seemed The Entangled Man project died, too.

Ben was true to his word; he continued researching entanglement.

He wondered how the two entangled worlds had come to be and developed a theory of their formation. It showed that entangled worlds could be created, and would remain entangled forever. He resolved to find a way to find the Dinosauroids' world and a way to make them real. His thoughts never strayed far from the dinosauroids, and he often found himself researching dinosaurs in moments of leisure.

One day he tracked down the anthology of speculations by scientists, the book from which he'd recognized the dinosauroids. The book with a Canadian scientist's sketch of how a dinosaur species might have evolved.

The dinosaur that had the beginnings of an opposable appendage, upright posture, and larger brain was *Stenonychosaurus*. The sketches were strikingly familiar. Belonthar, Merthab, and all the rest of the dinosauroids had evolved from the *Stenonychosaurus*, and Ben was relieved to have finally tracked down the name.

He took careful notes, hoping that by bringing this knowledge into his world, he could help them make theirs real, too.

* * *

On a hot summer afternoon, Ben strolled through the hallway to his apartment door, rolling his neck back and forth. It had been a long day at work.

He unlocked the door and pushed his way in, dropping his keys and kicking off his shoes.

Partway into the kitchen, he halted and gaped at the counters.

Hundreds—maybe thousands—of quarters covered every surface in row upon row.

Ben stared, motionless, for several minutes, all the day's plans vanishing from thought. His mouth hung open. His muscles tingled. He felt any movement might break the spell.

Every single quarter was balanced on its edge. Every. Single. One.

None trembled or showed even the faintest wobble.

❊ ❊ ❊

Separate. There was no other way.

He inhaled deeply, and pulled back further.

Separate...

The Entangled Man saw nothing. Heard nothing. Gone were the rumbles and cries of strife, and the splashes of spilt blood. Gone was the noxious smell of the chemical haze, and the feeling of stitched glass beneath.

He floated in a motionless drift without gravity. Any notion of forward or back, left or right, up or down vanished like a rain drop in an ocean.

The timelines for both worlds became apparent to him at once. He didn't know if it arose out of the nothing, because of the nothing, or if it *was* nothing.

The woven threads entangling the two worlds, all the events and important moments, now seemed simultaneous, with no past, no present, and no future.

Each part of his mind moved along the separate threads.

Without the hindrance of causality, the linearity of time, he could see how they might be separated...

...separated and put back together. He dared not hold it all in mind at once, for down that path lay oblivion.

Each world was pregnant in its possibility, and as the remaining weaves of time pressed into simultaneous points, he could see the lines of possibilities for each world. As before, at one end, there was actual existence infinitely far away. At the other end, a world with exactly zero probability of existence, at another infinity.

The human and dinosauroid worlds' lines of possibility twisted into one. They were entangled, with one at the infinity of existence and the other at the infinity of nonexistence.

With the image held firmly in his mind, he tried bending the line, folding it over itself toward the axis of existence.

But it would not yield. As he had suspected, it required a supreme force to bend the entanglement in such a manner.

He had tried to ignore the threads connecting and entangling the two worlds, and had succeeded in this way in capturing it in his mind.

The truth, however, was that the threads could not be ignored. They had to be accounted for, and for every fibre ripped apart, a new stitch would have to take its place.

He sent two parts of his mind back along the threads, merging with the worlds down to the finest details of differences in grains of sand. He scanned for what connected them, diving so deeply that both worlds grew entwined with his mind, everything entangled and part of everything else.

Of course. Now he could choose. Now he could separate.

He understood that he could make both worlds cease to exist. Part of him wondered if that would be the easiest and the simplest, the most just after all the atrocities committed on both sides.

He could also make both worlds partly real, and partly not. This was the middle ground, the compromise he knew would satisfy neither side.

He could do it, though. He could provide the missing threads. The missing connections that would be absent if the two worlds were partly wrenched asunder. He could see this through to the end.

Existence of both, however, holding both ends of an infinitely long string, made his mind spin just imagining all the fragile quantum tendons he would have to maintain.

For him to do this, he would have to travel to one end of the string, keeping account of every stitch along the way until he reached the end at infinity. If he got there, he would have to remember to turn and hold infinity in his grasp while he made double the journey back. He would have to be much more than an Entangled Man—he would need to be the Infinite Man.

There was no way a single mind could do such a thing.

Then The Entangled Man realized a chilling possibility.

It would come, but only at a cost.

A great and terrible cost.

* * *

The Entangled Man existed in both worlds simultaneously. He floated through each one in a haze. Everything lacked certainty. Everything lacked firmness. He thought it might be getting gradually better, but his thoughts were too fragmented to know for sure.

Separate.

He'd realized that in order to track every fibre along the woven timelines of the two worlds, he'd had to split himself in two. For every stitch he cut to separate them, he'd had to say goodbye to a part of himself, each torn in an opposite direction.

In this manner, once he reached infinity, he hadn't needed to turn back. There was nothing to turn back to.

The pressure had been tremendous, the mental details he sustained utterly overwhelming. Mutually exclusive ideas drove rifts within.

Each world had flooded his thoughts with a demanding rush of distinctions, differences to be upheld. All had to be observed by an external consciousness in order for the quantum wave functions to maintain.

Such demands left room for nothing else.

Each world had poured into him. The Entangled Man had fought to control the flow, but his meagre dams had burst. He'd all but drowned.

Before, he had had a feeling of unity, of wholeness with one mind in two bodies. Now he'd actualized his own mutual exclusion. He would never again feel the same sense of oneness, the satisfaction of accepting the way he was and would be.

He held the threads of each world under the constant strain and uncertainty that they might not endure tomorrow.

He watched each world as its unseen observer.

He hoped as more and more beings chose to see their new reality as real that he could relinquish some of his duties, and that everything could be whole again without his steadying hand.

Despite the pain of separation, the agony of having part of himself infinitely unreachable, The Entangled Man felt a measure of solace. This might very well be his end, but it was an end that carried a measure of justice. Or was it justification? He couldn't be sure. The parts of him that would have known were fractured.

Maybe one day he would be whole again. He might be real again.

For now, he moved through the shadows, in the spaces between, watching the best of both worlds, neither heads, nor tails.

ACKNOWLEDGEMENTS

Mark:

Thanks to my family and friends for support during the time and writing of this novel.

Joseph:

Thank you to our beta-readers for their invaluable feedback, and thank you to my partner and family for their patience and support throughout this work's completion. I can't count the times you've refilled the well when my ink's run dry.

THANK YOU

Thank you for reading *Quantum Worlds and the Entangled Man*. If you enjoyed this book, we'd be grateful if you'd help spread the word by recommending it to friends and family, posting about it on social media, and/or leaving a review on Amazon or Goodreads. Word-of-mouth and reviews remain some of the best ways you can support authors outside of buying their works.

Thank you again!

- Mark & Joseph

ABOUT THE AUTHORS (1/2)

Mark R. A. Shegelski is a Professor Emeritus in physics at the University of Northern British Columbia, having joined UNBC as a founding member in physics in 1994. Through Scroll Press, he has previously published a book of 14 linked science fiction stories, Remembering the Future, available as an eBook on Amazon. He has one hundred physics publications, many of which address the fundamental ideas in this novel. He and Edward Lozowski developed the first theory to account for the motion of curling rocks ("Pivot-Slide" theory published in Can. J. Phys. (2016) and Cold Regions Sci. & Tech. (2018)). He enjoys music (Moody Blues, Jean-Michel Jarre, Kitaro, Marillion and more), reading and sports. He lives with his wife Gail in British Columbia. For more information go to www.markrashegelski.com.

ABOUT THE
AUTHORS (2/2)

Joseph Halden is a wizard in search of magic, an astronaut in need of space, and a hopeless enthusiast of frivolity. He's shot things with giant lasers, worn an astronaut costume for over 100 days to try and get into space, and made his own soap. A graduate of the Odyssey Writing Workshop and a Pushcart Prize finalist, he writes science fiction and fantasy in western Canada. Find more of his work at www.JosephHalden.com.

CPSIA information can be obtained
at www.ICGtesting.com
Printed in the USA
LVHW071118180623
750100LV00001B/93